ZERO OPTION

ZERO OPTION

A NOVEL OF SUSPENSE

P. T. DEUTERMANN

ST. MARTIN'S PRESS 🅜 NEW YORK

ZERO OPTION. Copyright © 1998 by P. T. Deutermann. All rights reserved. Printed in the United States of America. No part of this book may be used or reproduced in any manner whatsoever without written permission except in the case of brief quotations embodied in critical articles or reviews. For information, address St. Martin's Press, 175 Fifth Avenue, New York, N.Y. 10010

Design by Maureen Troy

Library of Congress Cataloging-in-Publication Data

Deutermann, Peter T.
    Zero option : a novel of suspense / by P.T. Deutermann. — 1st ed.
        p. cm.
    ISBN 0-312-19210-X
    I. Title.
    PS3554.E887Z3   1998
    813'.54—dc21   98-21117
                                                                        CIP

First Edition: September 1998
10 9 8 7 6 5 4 3 2 1

This book is dedicated to the proposition that the only real deterrent to the use of chemical weapons against this country is if this country possesses its own chemical weapons arsenal, along with the will to use them in retaliation. Treaties, conventions, and promises to the contrary are nothing more than lethal illusions.

ACKNOWLEDGMENTS

I would like to thank Colley and George of the excellent Blood Mountain Cabins for a perspective on the north Georgia mountains area, Jane from the Georgia DFACS for her insights on state orphanages, Del Ward and Cliff Chandler for their continuing media support of my work, Sandi, Aubrey, and Kathy for their very helpful first readings, and, as always, Carol Edwards for her excellent copyediting. While the names of the military organizations and facilities in this book are real, I have taken some extravagant literary liberties in describing them and their operating procedures in order to enhance the dramatic structure of the story. Any resemblance of the characters in this book to real persons, civilian or military, is unintentional and entirely coincidental.

PTD

1

Wendell Carson sat at his desk in the manager's office wondering if he
should go out to his truck and get his gun. He just knew Lambry was
coming in to shake him down for more money. Should he confront
Lambry, see if he could scare him into backing off? Or just play along
and figure some way out of it later?

He swiveled around in his chair. Bud Lambry was an Alabama hillbilly: a long, lanky, tobacco-chewing, mush-mouthed, mean-eyed sumbitch. He'd been Carson's spotter in the warehouses for eight years, and
Andy White's before that. Let's face it, he thought, Bud Lambry isn't
going to scare so good, so use your damn brains: Play along with whatever he wants, then run some kind of con on him. Lambry can't know
what the cylinder is worth, so keep him in the dark. Agree to more
money—anything—to keep him quiet for just a few more days until the
deal goes through. After that, he didn't care what Lambry might say,
think, or do. Wendell Carson, erstwhile manager of the Atlanta DRMO,
would have a million bucks in his pocket and would be down the road
and gone. That said, he wouldn't mind having his .38 in his middle
drawer just now.

He looked at his watch and then heard someone coming down the
main hallway of the admin building. A moment later, Bud Lambry let
himself in, his suspicious eyes sweeping the office to make sure they
were alone.

"Evening, Bud," Carson said, not getting up. "You said we needed
to talk?"

"Yeah, we do," Lambry said, going over to the window and taking
a quick look through the venetian blinds into the parking lot. Then he

1

turned around and gave Carson a hard look. "That thang, that red thang, how much they gonna give fer it?"

"I don't know yet, Bud," Carson lied. "They're excited about it, but they're a little antsy, too, seeing what it is."

"But they gonna deal?"

"Oh, I think so. If they don't, I'm not sure what the hell we can do with it. But what's the problem now?"

"Problem's money," Bud said, a crafty gleam in his eye. He walked over to the desk and shook his arms out, as if he were preparing to take some kind of physical action. He leaned down, putting both his hands on the desk. Carson could smell him, an amalgam of sweat and tobacco. "That thang's gotta be worth a whole shitpot full a money."

Carson smiled. "And let me guess—you want a bigger cut, seeing this thing's special. And you're the one who found it."

"Damn straight. We ain't never lifted nothin' like this'n before."

Carson nodded, pretending to think about it. Then he nodded again. "I agree, Bud. This thing's going to be worth a small fortune. In fact, it's so big that I'm thinking about just clearing the hell out of here once the deal goes through. First, because the money is going to be major, and second, because the heat is going to be major once the Army finds out it's missing."

"Yeah," Bud said, relaxing a little. "Reckon I might do likewise."

"How's half sound, Bud? After all, you were the one who found it."

Lambry blinked. He had obviously planned to ask for half and settle for whatever he could get. Carson had surprised him. But then Lambry's eyes narrowed in suspicion.

"Okay," he said. "An' I wanna be there, it goes down."

"No problem, Bud. In fact, I need you there. For the money this thing's going to bring, I wouldn't mind some backup, you know what I mean?"

Bud straightened back up. "All right, then," he said. "You lemme know. Them boys give us enny bullshit, I'll fix 'er asses good. I got me some guns."

"They've never stiffed us before. No reason to think they will now."

Lambry looked at him, trying to figure out what Carson's angle was. I've been too agreeable, Carson thought. Should have haggled a little. Lambry looked down at the floor for a second, and then back at Carson, a hard look in his eyes.

"And yew," he said, "don't yew be thinkin' you cin run enny damn tricks, Carson. I want whut's mine."

"I'm going to make the arrangements tomorrow," Carson said as smoothly as he could. Lambry had a violent streak that had gotten him in trouble twice before down in the warehouses. He was known to carry a knife, and he wasn't shy about pulling it.

Carson got up to indicate this little farce was over. He already had an idea of how to dupe Lambry. "I'll catch you on the late shift in demil tomorrow night. Let you know what they decide. But remember now, not a word to anyone."

Lambry snorted. "Ain't never run my mouth, and that's a damn fact." Then he left, slamming the door.

Carson exhaled and sat back down. Fucking Lambry had been getting bolder and bolder lately. He would have to do something, although he wasn't sure what that would be. Wendell Carson was no Andy White. Big Andy would have ambushed Lambry with a two-by-four down in the warehouses one afternoon and beat the shit out of him.

He gave Lambry ten minutes to clear the building, and then he got up and locked his office door. He adjusted the blinds and checked the parking lot, but his truck was the only vehicle left out there. Then he walked over to the wall-length bookcase and reached up behind the three-ring binders on the top shelf. He withdrew the prize: a heavy red plastic tube, four feet long, about four inches in diameter, and covered with stenciled lettering, all U.S. Army alphabet soup. There were four stainless-steel snaps at each end of the tube. Inside was the actual cylinder, itself also stainless steel, and sealed at each end with wide knurled caps. The whole assembly weighed about fifteen pounds.

Carson stared down at it. He had no idea what all the nomenclature meant specifically, but when he'd read it over the phone to Tangent, his client in Washington, and told him where the cylinder had come from, Tangent had reacted as if he'd been hit by a brick. Tangent had gotten back to him in literally five minutes, offering $1 million in cash. Just like that. And now Brother Bud thought he was going to get half.

In your dreams, Cracker, Carson thought. This thing right here is the holy grail. Wendell Carson's main chance. Who'd have thought it? he mused as he put the red tube carefully back up on the bookcase. After all these years of skimming the surplus auctions, he'd hit the jackpot with a cylinder of nerve gas.

2

Senior Investigator David Stafford stood out in the hallway with his boss,
Colonel Parsons, and listened impassively to the sentence of exile.

"Atlanta, Georgia, Dave. There are worse places in this world."

Stafford nodded his head slowly, not looking at Parsons or at any of
the people passing them in the busy hallway.

"And you know I'm doing this to save your ass, don't you? Ray
Sparks is the southeastern regional supervisor. You and he go back. He's
willing to stash you there, no questions, no bullshit. You go down there,
you work this DRMO auction thing, and you keep a low profile. Get
your arm well, get Alice and the divorce off your mind, and then we'll
bring you back once everybody up here calms down."

Stafford nodded again, not really listening. This hallway meeting was
the culmination of the worst eighteen months of his life. He felt like
telling the colonel, Thanks, but why don't I just resign, make it easier
on everybody? Except that, at the moment, he had nowhere to go, a
mortgage and car loans to pay, a résumé with political feces all over it,
a useless right arm, a wrecked marriage, and some serious enemies in
high places right here in River City. It wasn't like he had a lot of options.

The colonel was watching him, waiting for some kind of reply.

"I appreciate it, boss," Stafford said, still staring down at the floor.
"I hate it, of course. I hate every bit of it." Then he looked up at the
colonel. "But I really do appreciate it. Where the hell is Georgia, anyway?"

Parsons grinned. "That's the ticket. You'll be pleasantly surprised.
But remember, no bomb throwing. No making big deals out of a little
deals. This DRMO case has been around for a while, and there's probably less there than meets the eye. So once you get there, take your

time. Your TDY orders are ready down at Travel. Get 'em and get gone, before the Communists find out about it."

The colonel clapped him once, forcefully, on his left shoulder, thank God, and then he was alone in the hallway, conscious of the stares and the muted comments. He took a deep breath and headed down to get his travel orders. The sooner the better, the colonel had said. Well, what the hell, he thought. It might be a nice change to go someplace where his first name wasn't Goddamn.

■■■ FRIDAY, THE DRMO, ATLANTA, 8:30 P.M.

On Friday evening, Carson returned to the DRMO parking lot after getting dinner at a local restaurant. He parked his green Army-issue pickup truck in his reserved spot in front of the building, then lowered his window. He could hear over the soft purr of the truck's engine the demil line running, the sound of rending metal clearly audible behind the admin building. He rolled the window back up and shut the truck down.

Eight-thirty. About thirty minutes more process time on the evening shift. The assembly teams would have left hours ago, after lining up at the feed conveyor belt with stuff to be shredded. Then it would be just the demil operator left to run the line until the conveyor came up empty; after which, he would secure the plant. Carson, as manager, controlled the shift assignments. He had made sure Bud Lambry would be on this evening's shift.

Carson had stopped by a metal shop out on State Road 42 and had a machinist cut a section of pipe about three inches in diameter, shine it up on a lathe, and fit two threaded caps over the ends. The size had been right, but the weight was wrong, so he'd had them fill it with sand. The lathe operator had made a joke of asking Carson if he was making a pipe bomb. Carson played along, told him he was going to blow up the IRS building in Chamblee, just outside of Atlanta. The lathe operator had asked if he wanted some help.

His plan was to take the sand-filled cylinder to his office, switch it with the real one in the red tube, and then carry the thing across to the demil building and explain to Bud that the operation was blown, that they were going to have to destroy the cylinder. The only problem would come if Bud insisted on opening the red packing tube, at which point he would see that the Army warning labels were missing from the substitute cylinder. Carson didn't know whether or not Lambry had ever opened the outer tube, but he was going to have to take that chance. He had tried peeling one of the labels off the actual cylinder and it had immediately torn, probably by design, to indicate tampering. The way to do this was to go fast, to go in there looking all hot and bothered, glancing over his shoulder for cops, and pitch the thing onto the demil line before Lambry had time to think about it. Lambry was a dumb ass; it should work.

He looked again at his watch and then pulled a portable cell phone out of his briefcase and punched in the DRMO number, followed by the extension for the demil control room. The phone rang five times before it was picked up. Lambry's voice came over the line, barely audible over the shattering noise of the machine. "Demil. Lambry."

"It's me. How much longer on the run?"

"Thirty minnits, mebbe. You got sumpthin'?"

"We've got us a big problem. I'm driving in. I'll come over there. Nobody around, is there?"

"Naw. Whut kinda big problem?"

"Tell you when I get there, Bud," Carson replied, then hung up. Five minutes later, he was walking across the tarmac, carrying the red packing tube with the fake cylinder inside. The outside lay-down area was lighted with large rose quartz halogen security lights. He walked confidently across the tarmac, the noise of the demil machine, which the crew all called "the Monster," getting louder as he approached. Then he stopped. There would be no way to talk in there, not with the Monster going full bore. Instead, he went over to the adjacent warehouse, the one from which the Monster was fed, and let himself in through the keypad lock system.

The lights were on in the feed-assembly area. He checked to make sure no one else was in the building. The feed belt was running, and he could see that there were about sixty feet of material left on this shift's demil run. The belt was crawling forward at about two miles per hour, slowly enough to give the machine in the next building time to chew. Even with the rubber noise-barrier strips in the opening between the two buildings, the racket from the Monster was crashingly loud.

He walked over to the steel door connecting the warehouse and the demil building. He looked through the small window in the door, but it revealed only the business end of the Monster, with its gaping maw at the end of the belt, and those seven huge band-saw blades descending voraciously into the materials consigned to destruction. He couldn't go through, for only the demil operator had the keys. Mounted just to the right of the door was a telephone. Looking around again to make sure no one else was in the warehouse, he punched in the control console number.

"Demil. Lambry."

"Leave it running and come next door, Bud," he said, almost shouting. "We've gotta talk. And we don't have much time."

He hung up before Lambry could protest. He stepped away from the connecting door and walked back over to the conveyor line near the screened opening of the interbuilding aperture. A minute later, there was a shadow of movement in the small window in the door, and Bud Lambry stepped through, wearing his hearing protectors and hard hat above his long-nosed face. He saw Carson and paused, as if unsure of what was going on; then he came over, his eyes widening at the sight of the red tube.

Carson hastily explained that the sale was off, that the client had backed out. They were saying the thing was much too hot, too dangerous. "They said we'd better destroy the damn thing before the Army finds out. They suggested we put it through the demil machine. They also told me not to be there when it goes into the Monster."

"Why?" Bud said, an anguished expression on his face. "That thang's gotta be worth some money somewheres!"

Carson shook his head. "They said no way. Too hot. Too dangerous. Said there'd be hell to pay when the Army found out it was missing. That they'd execute someone for losing it, much less for trying to sell it. I had no idea, Bud. I don't think we have any choice. We have to put it on the line here. There's no other place to dispose of it."

Without giving Bud any more time to argue, he dropped the red tube down on the conveyor belt, about ten feet upstream of the aperture between the two buildings. Bud just stood there for a minute as the red tube advanced down the line, his piggish little eyes following. Then, to Carson's dismay, Lambry stepped forward and snatched the tube off the line.

"Now you wait jist a damn minnit," he said. He put it down on the floor. Keeping one eye on Carson, he knelt down and started to undo the snaps on the packing tube.

Carson thought fast. Jesus Christ, now what do I do? He'll know I switched it! He looked around desperately for some kind of weapon, but there was nothing close, and Bud now had the last snap undone. He opened the case, pulled out the fake, and pitched the red tube back onto the belt. He stared at the cylinder for a moment, and then, still in a crouch, whirled on Carson.

"You sumbitch!" he yelled, dropping the fake on the floor. "This ain't it! You done switched it, you sumbitch!" Eyes wild, he straightened up, snatched a folding knife out of his pocket, and, in one practiced motion, opened it, and swiped furiously at Carson's stomach. Carson, already recoiling, felt the blade tip just touch his jacket. There was no mistaking the killing fire in Lambry's eyes. Without really thinking, he kicked out at Lambry, hitting him in the groin. Lambry grabbed himself, shrieking in pain, dropped the knife, and stumbled backward, tripping over the edge of the conveyor belt. He was so tall that he ended up sprawling across the belt, on his backside, his hard hat flying. Almost immediately, the moving belt dragged him up against a support stanchion and turned him parallel. Lambry, flailing wildly, inadvertently stuck his right hand between the belt and one of the rollers. As Carson watched in horror, the belt roller mangled Bud's right hand. Bud screamed anew while he thrashed around on the belt, trying to extract his hand, until he fainted from the excruciating pain.

Carson just stood there, even when he realized that Bud had passed out. But the belt never stopped moving, carrying Lambry's limp form into the steel safety cage enclosure flanking the interbuilding aperture. By the time Carson realized what was going to happen, he could no longer reach Lambry through the screens.

He had to stop the belt.

He ran over to the connecting door, then remembered it was locked. He looked back over at the belt, where Lambry's inert body, the key ring visible on his belt, was pushing aside the rubber sound strips in the aperture.

Jesus Christ, Carson thought, he'll be carried into the Monster! I've got to find the emergency button!

He ran frantically toward the back of the room, trying to remember where the control panel for the belt was, then saw it in the back corner. By the time he reached the console, Lambry was no longer in sight. The sound of the Monster tearing into steel boxes next door was very loud in his ears.

Have to stop the damned belt! He found the emergency button and smashed down on it.

Nothing happened.

Frantically, he did it again. Still nothing.

He snapped his head around to look at the belt, but it was still moving. Then he saw the problem. On the upper right of the console, a red indicator light stared triumphantly back at him: SYSTEM LOCKOUT.

Oh my God, he thought. Because the Monster was running, control of the belt was locked out except at the demil operator's console—in the next building, which he couldn't get into. He stared at the belt as it cranked inexorably forward with its cargo of military components—and Bud Lambry. He did not want to think about what was going to happen, even as his feet propelled him unwillingly back toward the connecting door, where the small window drew his gaze the way a cobra mesmerizes its victim, closer and closer. Don't want to look. You must. Don't want to. Maybe he'll wake up in time. Can't watch this; can't watch this. . . .

He closed his eyes as he reached the window, hoping he would hear something—anything—but heard only the roar of the blades and the shriek of disintegrating metal, which stopped for a moment. When at last he did look, it was about one second too soon. He was just in time to see the seven whipping blades emerge from the top of Bud's skull as it disappeared into the now-bloody waterfall of cooling oil.

He reeled backward from the window, fighting to control a wave of nausea. He closed his eyes again, then looked up into the overhead beams and pipes of the warehouse. One of the ventilation pipes looked exactly like the cylinder. Jesus Christ, what had he done! It was an accident, he told himself. It was self-defense. He pulled a knife, for Chrissakes! But he couldn't get that final image out of his mind.

He staggered out of the assembly room to the tarmac area outside, where he lit a desperately needed cigarette with trembling fingers. He sucked down half of it in one tremendous inhalation. Get a hold of yourself, he thought. You've still got to go through with it, despite what's just happened. You don't need Lambry anymore. Concentrate on the money. Then get out of here.

But first, he realized with a queasy feeling, he had to figure out how to shut down the Monster when it was done with the run. Reluctantly, he went back into the warehouse. He retrieved the fake cylinder. There was only one way: He would have to ride through the aperture on the belt. He swallowed hard.

3

On Monday morning, Carson stood in the baggage-claim area of Atlanta's Hartsfield International Airport. He closed his eyes and commanded his tumbling stomach to be still. This is getting scary, he thought. Really scary. Should have quit when I was ahead. Should have gone and put the real cylinder into the demil machine after Lambry had been . . . Jesus, what was the word for that? Even though Lambry had tried to shake him down. Dumb son of a bitch!

The area was only moderately crowded. Carson was standing between Delta carousels five and six, trying not to attract attention while he waited for the Washington hotshot—correction, the Defense Criminal Investigative Service investigator. Outwardly, he was trying like hell to look calm and collected. Inwardly, his stomach was doing flip-flops. A cold sweat permeated the back of his undershirt, and his eyes felt sandy from lack of sleep.

He was very conscious of all the security people in the airport. He wondered when one of them was going to detect his nervousness and come over to ask him why he was just standing around here. Waiting for someone, Officer. Plane must have been delayed. That happens, right? But he sensed he was exuding fear, the kind of fear that tickles a cop's intuition. He'd just about recovered from the horror of Friday night when the call came through first thing this morning from the Defense Logistics Agency headquarters in Washington. A DCIS investigator was inbound to Atlanta at eleven this morning. "Don't know exactly what it's about, but we want you personally to meet him at Hartsfield," he was told. "He's to be given every cooperation. Call us immediately when you find out why he's there. Oh, and have a great day, Mr. Carson."

Now of all times. And just two days after Lambry had . . . disappeared. He wiped some perspiration off his forehead with the back of his hand. Hot in here, he thought. Was that airport security guy staring at him? He turned away, trying to make the movement casual.

It can't be about the cylinder, he told himself again. It just can't be. There is no way in hell anyone in the DLA could know about that. The fear rose in his throat, a poisonous upwelling of warm bile. Despite his every effort, his heart began to pound again. His face felt flushed. If not the cylinder, then maybe Lambry? Not possible, he thought. Much too soon. He squeezed his eyes shut to make the images go away, but they came anyway, as they had all weekend. Even his wife, Maude, had noticed, and these days, Maude was oblivious to just about everything.

As much as Bud Lambry had pissed him off, he had *never* meant for anything so god-awful to happen. He looked around the claim area again, trying to focus on something, anything, to erase the memory, but it wasn't working. He remembered every bloody detail.

"Are you all right, sir?" someone asked from a few feet away. He nearly jumped out of his skin. A handsome woman with a teenage girl at her side was giving him an anxious look. The girl, he noticed, was giving him an altogether-different look. She had dark eyes, and she was staring at him from behind the woman's arm with an expression of unmistakable horror. As if she had somehow witnessed what he had just remembered.

He found his voice somewhere back there in his constricted throat.

"Yes, I'm . . . fine. I have . . . a really bad headache, that's all."

The woman nodded sympathetically. He looked away, scanning the neon numbers on the flight board above the carousel, and then noticing the crowd of people grabbing for bags. He looked anywhere but at the woman and that girl. He realized with a start that the DCIS guy's flight number was flashing on the board. He glanced around for someone who might be a senior investigator, looking everywhere, desperate to think about something else, to sweep aside the terrible image of Lambry's skull vibrating like the heel of a loaf of bread in an electric slicing machine. An accident, he told himself again, not supposed to happen, not like that, certainly not like that. And all because of the cylinder.

He swallowed hard again and concentrated on spotting the DCIS man, but no one looked the part. There were the obvious businessmen chatting on cell phones while they waited for their bags. There were three beefy young men muscling sunburned forearms into the bobbling train of bags on the carousel, hoisting out golf bags, but there was no one who looked like a Washington guy. They had a look, those Washington people.

He tried to compose himself, but out of the corner of his eye, he saw that damned girl still staring at him. He turned his back on her and tried not to think about Lambry or the cylinder, but the image of it bloomed in his mind anyway: a stainless-steel cylinder bearing all those seals and warning labels. The treasure of treasures that sharp-eyed Bud Lambry had pulled out of the shipment of supposedly empty weapons containers from Utah.

He tried thinking about the money: A million dollars. Cash. He visualized a small mountain of money. He remembered the phone call to Tangent, his contact in Washington. "I've got what looks like the guts of a chemical weapon. Are you interested?" Tangent had asked him to read off the nomenclature printed on the side of the container and then hung up. The offer had come back five minutes later: a million in cash. Delivery instructions to follow. But it was going to have to be soon. Very soon.

And what is Tangent going to do with the cylinder? Not my business, Carson thought quickly. In fact, he fervently did not want to know. But of course he did know. Tangent was going to sell it into the international arms market. An image of what had happened on that Tokyo subway flashed through his mind, all those crumpled red-faced bodies, throngs of dazed commuters desperately clutching their throats, eyes streaming as their carbonized lungs fought to draw breath; dozens of spastic figures on the ground, surrounded by dozens of helpless cops.

There, was that the guy? No. Well, maybe. And then he had another thought: What if this cop guy is here about the other thing? The auction scam? He felt his heart begin to pound again. Not now, he thought. Jesus Christ, not now. He stared hard at the man heading for carousel five. Get a grip, he cautioned himself. The cylinder is your ticket to ride. With that much money, you get a whole new life. This is what you've been waiting for and stealing for all your life.

A man who might be the DCIS investigator was definitely coming toward him now. He was wearing a good suit, had a muscular build, and was carrying a large briefcase in his left hand. His right hand was stuck awkwardly down in the pocket of his coat jacket, as if maybe he had been injured. He had a dead-serious cop face on him.

That's him, Carson thought. Senior Investigator David Stafford, looking right at him, and not necessarily in a very friendly way, either.

Carson glanced around involuntarily, wondering if he was sweating visibly, and half-expecting to see a phalanx of uniforms closing in on him, but there was only the crowd milling around the carousels. And that damned girl. Still watching him.

Look away, he thought.

Can't look away.

He stared back at her, unable to disengage those dark eyes fastened on his like little lasers, and then, suddenly, despite himself, he saw once again the top of Bud Lambry's head disintegrating in a cascade of cooling oil and bright red blood, all to protect the deadly secret of the cylinder, gleaming now in his mind's eye like some alien artifact, suspended in the air between himself and the girl.

He tried to tear his eyes away from hers, to see where that agent was, but then his vision tunneled down until all he could see was the cylinder, and beyond that, the girl's pupils glittering at him, boring into his brain; and then he heard a roaring noise in his ears and found himself immersed in a sudden wet darkness.

Stafford swore out loud, startling the people around him. He had spotted Wendell Carson just as soon as he'd come into the baggage-claim area. The Atlanta DRMO manager's ID picture and a brief bio had been in the case file he had studied on the airplane. Fifty-five-year-old white male, five-eight, receding hairline, roundish face, glasses, paunchier than his file photo. Stafford had been about twenty feet away when he saw Carson lock eyes with a teenage girl standing near the baggage carousel, then saw him collapse like a sack of potatoes onto the floor, all in the space of about two seconds. Some of the people standing near him were backing away while others moved in to help.

Stafford pushed his way through the crowd to see what the hell had happened. By the time he got to Carson, a striking black-haired woman had her arm around Carson's shoulder and was helping him to sit up. The teenager was standing a few feet back from Carson, still staring down at him, an expression of either extreme distaste or fear on her pinched face. Now what the hell is this all about? Stafford wondered as he knelt down on one knee and put his left hand on Carson's right shoulder. Carson's head was up, but he looked dazed as he pushed his glasses back on his face.

"Wendell Carson? I'm David Stafford. Can you hear me? Are you okay?"

"He didn't look well a moment ago," the woman offered, speaking over Carson's head. Stafford had a quick impression of bright green eyes, a milky white complexion, and almost blue-black hair. "He said he had a bad headache."

Stafford started to reply, but Carson was trying to stand up. "Okay," he was mumbling. "I'm okay. Just a little dizzy there. Not sure . . ."

Two black men in suits arrived at that moment and helped Carson to get back up. One was looking Carson over while the other spoke into a small handheld radio. The woman and the teenager began to back away.

"Do you need medical attention, sir?" the first security man asked.

Carson shook his head. "No, I'm okay. Just got dizzy. Hot in here."

Stafford showed the cop his DCIS credentials. "Mr. Carson was here to meet me," he explained. "I'll stay with him. I don't think we'll need paramedics."

The security men backed off, and Stafford helped Carson over to one of the benches near the line of baggage carousels. Carson sat down heavily, then put his head in his hands for a moment. Eventually, he looked back up. "Sorry about that," he said. "I don't know what happened. Had a touch of the flu the past couple of days. Must not be over it. Are you Stafford?"

Stafford nodded. "Right," he replied. "Dave Stafford. DCIS Washington. If you're okay, let me go get my bag. You stay here and rest a minute."

Stafford left his briefcase with Carson before walking back into the crowd by the baggage carousel to look for his suitcase. He kept an eye on Carson, who looked like someone who had just been seasick, all pasty-faced and with shaking hands. The woman and the girl walked by him just then, each pulling a suitcase. The woman gave him a quick look of recognition but kept going. The girl stared straight ahead as she struggled with what appeared to be a very heavy suitcase. There was a sticker on the side of her suitcase that proclaimed GRANITEVILLE, GEORGIA, AN ALL-AMERICAN TOWN. On impulse, Stafford called after the woman. She stopped, a look of mild apprehension on her face. He checked to make sure that Carson couldn't see them talking.

"I'm David Stafford," he said, flashing his credentials. "I'm a federal investigator. Do you know that man who fainted back there?"

"No," she said immediately, looking around for the girl in the crowd. The girl had kept going for a moment, but now she had stopped a few feet away and was looking back in their direction.

"Does your daughter there know him, by chance?"

The woman frowned. She was almost as tall as he was. Her luminous eyes flashed a hint of impatience. "She's not my daughter, and, no, she does not know him. Please, we must go." Her voice was husky and had a hint of a southern accent.

Stafford was almost positive that Carson and the girl had been staring at each other just before Carson fainted. "It's just that—" he began. "Well, look, ma'am, here's my card, in case you think of some reason why that happened back there. Will you call me if you do? It might be important."

She took the card, frowned at it for a moment, and then closed her hand over it. He noticed she wore no rings or jewelry of any sort. Her hands and fingers were long, with the same smooth complexion of her face. She was his age—maybe a year or so either way.

"Thank you," he said before she could come up with a reason to hand back his card. He turned back toward the baggage carousel, watching them out of the corner of his eye as they made their way to the exit doors and stopped to have their claim tags checked. The girl glanced back once in his direction, but the woman took her arm and propelled her out of the baggage claim area. That's an unusual-looking woman, he thought, and there's something very strange about that girl. He thought again about what he had seen just before Carson collapsed, but then he noticed his bag coming around the carousel and, for the moment, put the two of them out of his mind.

Carson had recovered, at least outwardly, by the time he swung the government sedan in alongside the curb outside. He had had a shaky five minutes there on the bench while Stafford went for his bag. It was bad enough to have a Defense Department cop showing up like this on short notice, but to faint dead away in a public place? Jesus, what was happening to him? He shook his head as his heart started to race again. He tried deep breathing to calm himself down. Then he saw Stafford coming toward the car.

Stafford opened the back door with his left hand, struggled to get his bags in, and then climbed in front with Carson.

"You sure you're okay to drive?" Stafford asked. "You want, I can drive, and you can navigate."

"Thanks, but I'm okay. You hurt your arm?"

"Yeah, gunshot," Stafford replied. "Took out some nerves. Most of the time it sort of just hangs there. I'm doing physical therapy, but it's slow going. By the way, who was that girl? Was that someone you knew?"

Carson thought fast. "What girl was that?" he said, making a show of concentrating on traffic.

"I was on the other side of the carousel when you keeled over. I thought you and that girl standing near you were looking at each other."

Carson made a left at the end of the overpass and accelerated into the eastbound lanes of the Atlanta Perimeter. "It was pretty crowded in there," he said. "I don't remember any girl, or anybody else, for that matter. I was just standing there, waiting for you, and then woke up on the floor. Probably forgot to breathe or something. Like I said, I haven't been feeling well the past couple of days."

Stafford nodded absently, seeming to accept Carson's explanation. "Her bag had a sticker on it—something about Graniteville. I thought maybe you knew her."

"Nope." Carson concentrated on his driving, desperately willing Stafford to get off the subject of the girl.

"Where is the Atlanta DRMO?" Stafford asked. "Aren't they usually on a base of some kind?"

"That's right, although Fort Gillem isn't really a base. It's a small Army post. A lot of it is shut down. Kind of a hodgepodge of stuff there now: the local Army bomb squad, several Army transport repair shops, an Army–Air Force Exchange Service distribution center. That kind of stuff. Army's trying to hang on to it. Developers are drooling over the fence while they work out which congressman to bribe."

"That shouldn't be hard," Stafford replied as they crossed over I-75. "How big is the Atlanta DRMO?"

"Forty employees, ten warehouses. We move maybe twenty, thirty million dollars worth of material a year through the reutilization and public auction process. Are you familiar with the DRMO system?"

"Barely," Stafford said.

Carson thought, If Stafford is down here on a DLA matter, surely he has been briefed. Finally, he couldn't stand it anymore. "Isn't there a DCIS office right here in Atlanta?" he asked. He already knew the answer. He'd looked it up in the DOD phone book when the call from Washington had come through.

"Yes, there is," Stafford answered, still looking out the window. Carson took the State Road 42 exit and continued east, driving through wall-to-wall trucking terminals. "Look, I'll give you a full brief once I see your DRMO. That way, you can answer my questions untainted by knowing why I'm down here."

Carson said okay and continued the rest of the drive in silence. Untainted. Right. Bastard knows I'm dying of curiosity. But to be safe, he knew he'd better play it Stafford's way until he had some idea of what this was all about. Please, God, not the cylinder. And *damn* that business at the airport! Graniteville—maybe I need to remember that name.

They drove through the unguarded entrance gates of Fort Gillem, then went about two miles through the post to the edge of what looked like an abandoned airfield, where they turned left into a warehouse complex. The buildings had been there a long time and showed their age. They parked next to a railroad siding, where a dozen rail cars carrying truck trailers were parked. An elderly yard engine sat rumbling by itself on a second siding, gracing the air with dirty diesel exhaust. In front of them was a single-story brick building. A sign above the door proclaimed it the home of the Atlanta Defense Reutilization and Marketing Office. Behind the brick building was a warehouse complex.

Carson took Stafford to his office in the administrative area. The first thing Stafford asked for was a vehicle. Carson told one of the secretaries to requisition a sedan from the base motor pool. Carson offered coffee, but Stafford declined. The investigator stood by the window for a moment, looking out at the rail sidings. Carson confirmed his initial physical impression: medium-big guy, big shoulders, good suit, large, purposeful-looking hands—or one of them was, anyway—short military-style haircut. He wondered if DCIS investigators carried guns.

"Okay," Stafford said, turning around. "I know this is short notice and somewhat mysterious. But here's what I need first: a tour of this place. Conducted by you, if you can spare the time."

As if I have a choice, Carson thought. "Sure," he said.

"Second, I'd prefer that the staff not know who I am, or, more specifically, what I am."

He had dark blue eyes, a faintly ruddy Nordic face, and a prominent chin. He looked right at you. Carson was determined to meet Stafford's eyes. He willed all thoughts of the cylinder—which was hidden, at the moment, all of eight feet away—right out of his mind.

"Once we've done the walkabout," Stafford continued, "I'll need to make a couple of calls, then maybe we can go to lunch somewhere and I'll fill you in. Right now I suggest you tell people I'm from DLA head-

17

quarters, which, in a sense, is true. Maybe say I'm an auditor. And if there's a spare empty office, I'd appreciate being able to camp out there."

Every cooperation, DLA had ordered. Carson nodded, punched the intercom, and told the secretary that he would be taking Mr. Stafford out into the material bays for about an hour. He asked her to set up the assistant manager's office, which was empty, for Mr. Stafford's use. She asked whose name she should put on the sedan requisition, since Carson already had a Fort Gillem motor-pool vehicle. Carson told her that Stafford was an auditor from DLA headquarters. She needed Stafford's grade, and Carson raised his eyebrows at Stafford.

"Fifteen" was the reply. Carson passed that to the secretary. GS-Fifteen, Carson thought. Three grades senior to him. He knew all about grade creep in Washington, but this guy was no midlevel gumshoe. He felt the familiar grab in his stomach, but he suppressed it with a deep breath. There was no way they could know.

"Okay," he said. "Let's walk around a bit."

When they stepped into the cavernous warehouse, Stafford was glad he had kept his coat on; it was almost cold. The injured tendons in his right arm duly protested.

"Okay," Carson began. "DRMO stands for Defense Reutilization and Marketing Office. Basically what we do here is collect all sorts of stuff from a variety of organizations in the Defense Department. Technically, *surplus defense material*, but the word *stuff* really covers it better. The material is anything the Defense Department no longer needs—surplus raw materials, obsolete repair parts, broken equipment components, or even the equipment itself, office furniture, general supplies. Anything that a DOD agency or military service deems surplus to its operations is supposed to end up in a DRMO."

"Where you guys auction it off, right?"

"Well, not initially. Remember the *R* in DRMO. It stands for *reutilization*. The first thing we do after initial classification is to advertise in-house to all the government agencies what we've got here. 'Government' includes both federal and state agencies, by the way. That way, for example, if an agency is looking for some replacement desks, or maybe a window air conditioner, they can come to the DRMO and see if we have one. They can then requisition it, and get it basically at no cost. Saves the agency money, and the stuff gets recycled."

"I had a surplused desk in the Pentagon once," Stafford said. "But as I recall, it was brand-new."

"That happens," Carson replied. "The surplused material doesn't have to be worn-out or even used to come here, although it usually is. It might be a case where an agency buys ten new desks but then loses a fight over office space with another organization, so they can only use eight of them. We'd get two brand-new desks to put out for reutilization. But most of the stuff that comes here of that nature, especially office furniture, is very used and pretty dilapidated, as you're going to see."

Two warehouse workers came by on a forklift, forcing Carson to wait for a moment for the noise to subside. Stafford noticed that they didn't wave to Carson or greet him, which he thought was odd. Workers in a forty-man organization would normally at least acknowledge the boss. On the other hand, Wendell Carson was about as plain vanilla a civil servant as one could find, almost a caricature of a government bean counter.

"The important items, monetarily," Carson was saying, "are the material that comes in designated to go through the demil process. *Demil* is short for *demilitarization.* I guess I need to back up a little. When material first comes in, it has to be classified. Some is going to go directly to the general public auctions: building supplies, pipe, wire, bricks, lumber, cans of roofing tar, barrels of lubricating oil, things like that. But some of it's fully serviceable military equipment. Obsolete maybe, but functional. Things like tank gun sights, machine-gun barrels, radar components, fire-control computers, components that've been replaced by a new weapons system acquisition but which still work or could be made to work."

"Who classifies it?" Stafford asked. His arm was aching and he was ready to start walking.

"The organization that sends it down to us is supposed to classify it. But we are supposed to double-check it. Especially after that helicopter gunship flap in Texas—remember that?"

Stafford did remember. Some guys in Texas had been able to buy enough helicopter parts at a DRMO public auction to reassemble completely a fully operational Army attack helicopter. The press had had a field day with it.

"So anyway, if it comes with a demil tag, or if we determine that it should be demilitarized, we have a separate facility that handles that. We'll see that after we see some more warehouses."

They started walking. The first warehouse was filled with steel racks that went from floor to ceiling. On them was every kind of thing the government bought. Stuff, Stafford thought. *Stuff* was exactly the right word.

"This is one of the public auction areas," Carson said. "This material has been through initial categorization and the reutilization process."

Stafford was amazed at the variety: typewriters, coils of wire, boxes of bolts, ancient computers, adding machines, mattresses, chairs, rolls of printing paper, black-and-white televisions, a box of fluorescent light-bulbs, some of which looked used, new and used airplane tires, and a military vehicle's olive drab fueling hose.

"This is the junk man, flea market end of the spectrum," Carson said as they walked down an aisle between the racks. "It's been available for viewing for five days, and the public auction will be held Tuesday." He looked at his watch. "I guess that's tomorrow. The bigger items are outside in the lay-down area."

"And the high-value military components?"

"That begins in the next warehouse. In a way, the DRMO is set up as an assembly line. Material comes in all the time, sometimes by the freight-car load. Goes into the receiving and general storage area for cataloging and classification. High-value, serviceable, but nondemil material goes into warehouses one and two. Large high-value components that have to be demiled go to warehouse five, which is attached to the demil facility. Intrinsically lethal, or HAZMAT, demil materials go to warehouse four, which is right next to five. The warehouses have different levels of security depending on what's in them. TV cameras, that sort of thing."

" 'Intrinsically lethal'? 'HAZMAT'?"

"Hazardous materials—cannons, denatured ordnance, drums of toxic chemicals or chemical waste, missile front ends, bomb cases, rocket bodies. Weapons, primarily. The military service generating the surplus takes the high explosives out, but then we get the iron."

They walked out of the warehouse and into the bright sunlight of the lay-down area. Carson seized the opportunity to light a cigarette. He offered one to Stafford, who shook his head.

"Thanks. Quit five years ago." Stafford thought he saw Carson's hands shaking. "What on earth can you do with bombs and rockets?" he asked.

"Bomb and rocket *casings*, remember. Not supposed to hold high explosives. They become monster feed."

" 'Monster feed'?"

Carson grinned through a cloud of blue smoke. "Show you in a bit. Basically, we cut them up in the demil facility. Turn 'em into shredded metal and various liquid products, and then auction off the by-products to scrap dealers. This here is the general lay-down area. Mostly just bigger stuff."

Stafford looked, wishing he'd brought his sunglasses. There were long rows of palletized material, containing such things as industrial-size drill presses and lathes, a clutch of old refrigerators, a fire-fighting vehicle from a military airfield, skip boxes of scrap metal, industrial air-conditioning units, several rusty-looking water heaters, and mounds of used truck tires.

"Bigger stuff," Stafford said. He really was interested in the high-value components, but he was satisfied to let Carson to do his thing.

"That's right. This is more of the general auction inventory. That's warehouse two over there; number one's right behind it. They contain the small, high-value items. The hundred-thousand-dollar radar amplifier tubes that happen to be obsolete, by military standards."

"Who buys those?"

"Usually the FAA. They're still using a lot of old, tube-driven radars."

"That's a comforting thought."

Carson nodded as they walked across the lay-down area. Stafford realized they were crossing tarmac and wondered if this area had been part of the abandoned airfield. There were forklifts chugging around the area, moving pallets in and out of the warehouses, which were arranged in two lines on either side. He asked Carson about it.

"This area used to be the main hangar and maintenance facility for an Army helicopter base. It was shut down a long time ago, before I got here. They knocked down most of the actual hangars except for one. That contains the demil facility. That one, over there."

They changed course slightly to avoid a backing forklift and headed toward the ex-hangar building. One warehouse in the line backed right up to the hangar building. Stafford could hear a loud tearing noise from inside. Carson stopped about fifty feet from the doorway.

"Normally, we run demil in the evening, but there's a backlog. Demil is a hazardous industrial area. We'll pick up hearing protection, hard hats, and safety glasses in the vestibule inside that doorway. Then we'll sign in."

"What's the noise?" Stafford asked.

"The Monster," Carson said. "Basically, it's a really big shredding machine. The process starts with seven diamond-tipped saw blades, followed by a bank of chipping hammers, then a grinder. Turns anything that goes in there into fragments. 'Monster feed,' the guys call it. Then there's a bank of electromagnets to separate ferrous material from nonferrous, an acid bath to dissolve electronics insulation, a centrifuge for separating the liquid products, and some further screen separators. At the very end are collection modules for the resulting scrap, and those streams are led to compactors. This is the place where those rocket and bomb casings come, as well as any classified design stuff, like military radar klystrons, antenna arrays, things like that."

"Take a big crew to run it?"

"Nope. Takes three, four guys to set up the run—that whole warehouse back there houses the feed-assembly system. But once the belt starts, it takes one guy to sit in the control room and basically watch. The machine chews up anything—metal, wood, plastic, organic substances. Liquids are separated, filtered, centrifuged, broken down with acids, centrifuged again to separate water from organic liquids, and then pumped to the toxic-waste tanks for settling and further processing. Anything solid and nonmetallic is consumed in the acid wash, and anything that survived *that* is compressed into blocks of scrap metal for sale to the metal merchants, who in turn sell the blocks as feedstock for steel or aluminum reprocessing. When the run's done, another crew empties the compaction modules, usually the next morning. Let's go on in."

Carson pushed a call button by the door, which clicked, allowing them into a vestibule area. Even in the vestibule, the noise level was very high, and Stafford reached gratefully for the ear protectors. They signed the access log, although Stafford noticed that there was no one in the vestibule to supervise access. He assumed the operator's control of the door took care of that.

Carson led the way through the next set of doors and into a large industrial bay where a huge locomotive-sized steel machine hunkered down on the concrete floor. The top of the machine reached almost all the way to the ceiling girders of the hangar, some sixty feet up. The bulk of it measured about eighty feet long and twenty wide. A five-foot-wide conveyor belt emerged from safety-caged double doors on the left side of the bay. It was traveling at about waist height, carrying plastic boxes filled with all sorts of military equipment. The belt approached the maw of the machine from left to right, then folded under itself and returned back into the feed-assembly warehouse. There was a glass-enclosed control booth to one side of the room, where an ear-muffed operator was visible at a console.

Carson led Stafford over toward the opening of the demil machine. There were safety screens and yellow hazard markings on the floor all along the route of the conveyor belt. The business end of the machine was impressive. Several wicked-looking band-saw blades came down vertically across the five-foot square of the machine's mouth. The blades appeared to be about ten inches wide, spaced about an inch apart, and bathed in silky sheets of cooling oil. Anything hitting the blades was immediately engaged and cut into segments in a fiery shower of sparks and smoke from the rending metal. The process produced a hideous tearing sound. A large hood above the entry gobbled up all the smoke and metal vapors. The other components of the maceration process were apparently contained out of sight within the machine. Behind and below was a complex nest of large pipes coiled under and around its foundations, leading to large boxlike components marked MAGNETIC SEPARATION, AIR FILTRATION, PARTICULATE SCRUBBER, and NEUTRALIZING SCRUBBER. Three enclosed conveyor systems led into the next building, where, Stafford assumed, the resulting rubble was compacted or contained for movement to the auction warehouses.

It was clearly impossible to hold a conversation in the presence of such noise, so Stafford indicated he'd seen enough and they went back out into the vestibule. Three men were there looking at clipboards and discussing the current run. This time the workers nodded at Carson, but their greetings appeared to be entirely official. Stafford noticed that Carson returned their greetings in similar fashion. No love lost between the DRMO boss and his employees here, he thought, confirming his earlier impression. They went back outside to the relative quiet of the tarmac. For some reason, Carson looked relieved to be out of the building. He lit up another cigarette. Stafford confirmed that Carson's hands were definitely shaking.

"You can see why they call it 'the Monster,' " Carson said. "It cost eleven million dollars, but it does the job. You get a compacted mixture of very clean metallic dust and bits out the back end, and a variety of fluids. That building over there is devoted to fluid separation, detox, and recovery. We sell the output of that, too. The employees call that 'Monster piss,' naturally. There's a plan to put up a generating system where we'll burn the volatile products and make our own electricity. There's nothing in the fluid-processing area but a control room and a few miles of piping systems, but we can go see it if you'd like."

"That's okay," Stafford said, still assimilating the idea of Monster piss. "Does every DRMO have one of these demil machines?"

"No, which is why we tend to get a lot of the military equipment that's still serviceable."

Stafford nodded. "Right," he said. "What's in the rest of the warehouses?"

"More stuff," Carson replied. "If the trucks stopped coming today, we'd have a six-month workload here."

"Okay, thanks for the tour. Let's go get something to eat, and I'll tell you what this is all about." Sort of, he reminded himself silently.

They took their sandwiches to a table at the back of the officers club's tiny dining room. Carson noticed that Stafford was pretty adept with his one good arm.

"As I said, most of Fort Gillem is in cadre status," he explained. "That's Army speak for being shut down and waiting hopefully for the next war." He was trying hard not to appear anxious. There is no way they could know about the cylinder, he kept telling himself. That just happened. Or about Lambry. No way in hell. Keep cool. Show him that you're interested in why he's here, but that, whatever it is, it does not affect you personally.

Stafford had started in on his sandwich, eating it awkwardly with one hand. Carson waited for a moment and then did the same, although he had still not recovered his appetite after Friday night. The big man across the table was obviously hungry and dedicated to doing something about it. The dining room was almost empty, with only a few other civil servants gossiping about the latest base closings and layoffs in the Defense Department.

Stafford finished his sandwich quickly, keeping his right hand out of sight below the table. "Okay," he said, wiping his mouth with a clutch of paper napkins. "You know the difference between the DIS and the DCIS?"

"Uh—"

Stafford cut him off. "DIS, the Defense Investigative Service, does security clearance background checks on military and civilian employees of the Department of Defense. The DCIS, that's the Defense *Criminal* Investigative Service, investigates cases of fraud against the government. One's admin, one's criminal work. I'm a senior investigator with the DCIS. The Defense Logistics Agency, which owns all the DRMOs, called us with a problem. They think someone has been rigging the auctions."

Shit, Carson thought. It *is* the auction scam. He forced his face into an expression of mild surprise. "Rigging the auctions?" he said. "I'm surprised. You saw that stuff. What's to rig?"

Stafford gave him a cool look. "Actually, I didn't. Not the stuff we're talking about here. I saw the bedpans and pipe-rack stuff. The DLA is talking about the high-priced items. Avionics components. Electronic repair parts. Nondemil but high-value radar and communication equipment. Satellite transponders. The gold foil in magnetron power amplifiers. Not materials that're hazardous, but items that have value in a secondary market. Like those radar components the FAA depends on."

Carson was suddenly paying close attention. Stafford's casual use of the word *nondemil* indicated he might know more about the DRMO business than he had let on. He put the remains of his own sandwich down and wiped his hands, trying not to look at Stafford. He had been wondering when this day would come ever since he had taken over the scam. He would have to be very careful here.

"The auction process is pretty straightforward," Carson said. "I don't know how it could be rigged. I mean, it's a regular call auction. The bids are called right there on the floor. If the auctioneer gave it to someone else, the rest of the bidders would protest."

"DLA thinks this scam has been going on in the sealed-bid system," Stafford said, still looking at him.

"But who would gain from that?" Carson responded, shaking his head. "Maybe way back when, but the way it works now, if there is a sealed bid, the auctioneer starts with that bid amount. If he gets no takers from the floor, then by definition, that's the winning bid."

Stafford nodded patiently. "Way I understand it," he said, "DLA thinks the scam comes after that. They think the so-called winning bid is altered, after the fact, by someone inside the process, so that the winning bidder doesn't pay what he said he would. That way he gets a really good deal. Anyhow, that's the theory. That's what I've come down here for. I want to make a reality check. I want to do an audit on the paper trail of some high-value, nondemil stuff that's been to auction. I want to know what was sold, to whom, and how much the winning bid was supposed to be, and then I want to see proof that that's what the guy paid for it."

Carson nodded slowly, keeping his expression neutral as he asked the all-important question. "Why the Atlanta DRMO, specifically?"

Stafford seemed to have an answer ready for that one. "Because you're one of the bigger ones, with a good-sized monetary volume. And you get a large spectrum of surplus stuff coming from the whole Southeast." Then he smiled disarmingly. "And because I've never been to Atlanta."

Carson managed a laugh at that. To a civil servant, the last reason rang true. He thought about it for a minute. DLA was getting close. There certainly was a scam running, but they were not quite correct about how it worked. But if this was all that Stafford pulled the string on, there were enough cut-outs in place to keep Carson reasonably safe. On the auction scam, anyway. The cylinder was something else. Not to mention the little matter of Lambry's death.

"Not a problem," Carson said. "Although it might be tough to get the proof on how much the winning bidders actually paid, because they don't pay us. They do for the flea-market stuff, but for the high-value items, they pay the local Defense Contracts Administrations Office. You'll have to talk to them and the people who actually bought the stuff." He shook his head. "But given that outside loop, I'm still not sure how anyone could scam the system. Or why. What kicked this off?"

Stafford finished his coffee. "To tell the truth, I'm not sure what it was. They often don't tell the field investigator, because they want us to look at a problem with a clear filter. If I knew what alerted DLA, I might restrict my investigation to just that and miss a bigger picture. You know, go out and try to prove them right. This way, I take a fresh look at the process, and see if all the numbers jibe. If they do, I go home. If they don't, we'll either work it or call in the FBI."

Carson nodded again. The FBI. The last thing he needed right now was that bunch of anals poking around the DRMO. "Okay," he said. "Let's go see if that car's ready. Then we'll find you a hotel. You want to stay out here in the sticks or go downtown?"

At five-thirty that afternoon, Carson closed up his office. After they left the officers club, he'd taken Stafford back to the admin building, where the secretary had his temporary office ready. There'd been the usual hassle about the car, but eventually the motor pool turned loose a General Services Administration Crown Vic. Stafford had elected to stay in downtown Atlanta at the Peachtree Center. Carson had his secretary dump binders of the relevant rules and procedures for DRMO sales on

Stafford's desk, along with the auction reports for the past six months and a personnel roster. Stafford had left at three-thirty to check in at his hotel, and he said he'd be back at eight-thirty the next morning. An hour later, the rest of the staff had left for the day. Demil's backload had been cleared, so there was no evening shift. The Monster was quiet. Digesting, no doubt.

Carson lit up a cigarette and walked through the suite of offices and cubicles to make sure everyone was gone. He checked Stafford's office, but there was nothing there except the reports and binders. He turned off the overhead lights and walked back down the hall. There were two sets of windows in his office, one that looked out at the parking lot by the railroad siding, the other that looked into the flea-market warehouse. He opened the elderly venetian blinds and peered into the semidarkness of the warehouse.

Wendell Carson had grown up poor in New Jersey, the son of a longshoreman with a drinking problem. His mother had been a waitress, and there had been three unhappy children stuffed into one room of a dingy, crowded apartment in beautiful downtown Newark. From his early teenage years on, he had dreamed of escape, and he joined the Army in 1960, on the day after he graduated from high school. He went first into the infantry and then, after bribing the company clerk, engineered a lateral transfer into the Quartermasters Corps. He had been smart enough to advance to buck sergeant by 1966. Sensing that Army duty was about to turn serious, he elected to get out just before Vietnam blew up, but not before learning the ropes about petty larceny from some of the older NCOs. He'd used his veteran's preference to get a civil service job at Fort Belvoir, near Washington, D.C., in the personal property shipping office. After mastering his own job, which took about two weeks, he had begun sniffing around the household goods warehouses, looking for what he knew had to be there—namely, a ring of thieves who pilfered the shipments bound for Army posts all over the world.

Carson was no street thug. He had neither the physique nor the stomach for the physical side of crime. He had always been a paper-pusher, and it was at Belvoir that he first established his strategy for life: Don't steal anything yourself. The trick was to make the guys who did the actual stealing pay him for top cover, such as protection from the inspectors, adjustments to shipping invoices, prompt payment for the claims that inevitably came back from the military people at the new destination, judicious assignment of work crews to particular shipments, all in return for a piece of the action. It had never been big money, but it had been steady.

Over the years, he had parlayed his sideline into increasingly larger-scale situations as he moved around from job to job within the organization that eventually became the Defense Logistics Agency, until finally he landed in the central office that administered the sale of surplus defense materials throughout the country. Surplus sales was the mother lode of opportunity for a paper-pusher with the inclination to jigger the system to his own benefit, and Carson had burrowed deep into the system. In 1983, the entire surplus sales auction system was decentralized, forcing him to evaluate which of the several DRMOs around the country might offer the best situation. He had come to Atlanta in 1983, then moved up to the head job eight years later. Tangent had contacted him in 1994, and he had been a reliable buyer. Carson now had almost thirty years in the civil service. He had been spending a lot of time lately figuring out how and when he was going to retire, and then the cylinder had fallen into his lap.

One million dollars. A life-changer.

He reset the blinds, locked his office door just to be sure, and then went over to his desk to sit down. He stretched his hands out and confirmed that they were still trembling. He thought about Lambry. Was he now a murderer? He kept coming back to it: Bud had attacked him, after all, not the other way around. So really, it had been self-defense. Yeah, self-defense necessitated by the fact that the both of you stole something: a million-dollar something. And then there was the dream.

He had begun having the dream Friday night. Something about being swept along in a river at night, together with many other people. Somehow he knew they were all dead. The river was black and cold, and he was having trouble staying afloat because he was carrying the cylinder. They moved downstream in total silence until the rolling thunder of an enormous waterfall became audible. The dream ended with him sailing over the edge, with all those dead faces staring at him as they plunged down into oblivion.

He opened his eyes and took a deep breath. Friday night, Saturday night, Sunday night, the same dream. Tonight he was going to take a damn pill.

He got up and walked over to the steel bookcase. He removed two fat binders from the top shelf. He reached through the space to grasp the cylinder with both hands. There was no red plastic tube now, just the heavy stainless-steel cylinder, covered with decals and seals bearing dire warnings. He held it in his hands for a moment, caressing it. A million-dollar stainless-steel log. The metal was cold. He put it back.

He'd been in a state as to where to hide it after Bud had brought it to him. At first, he'd thought somewhere out in one of the warehouses, where he, as manager, had unrestricted access. But so did everyone who worked out there, and one of them might find it. He'd then thought about the demil facility, but other than the self-contained Monster, there were no hiding places in that building, no nooks, crannies, or hidey-holes. He'd been afraid to break his ironclad rule about never taking anything physically out of the DRMO complex. He looked up at the gleaming cylinder, noting its steely perfection while trying to put its deadly contents out of his mind. It was as safe here as anywhere in the facility, unless he received an indication that the Army had learned it was missing.

He pulled the binders together and returned to his desk chair. The building was silent except for the sounds of the big vent fans running out in the warehouse. He thought again about that girl in the airport, and the strange way she had looked at him. What had Stafford said? Graniteville, that was it. He pulled a state map out of his desk and looked that name up in the grid index. B-9. North Georgia mountains. That figured: The girl had that pinch-faced, hillbilly look to her. Everyone knew that a lot of those people up there were dumber than stumps, so why did Wendell Carson faint in the middle of Baggage Claim, out of a clear blue sky, *not* having had the flu, as he'd told Stafford? He could not forget her eyes, locked onto his, or how he had been unable to tear his own eyes away.

He fingered the coordinates on the map, and found it. Graniteville. A tiny dot at the edge of the federal wilderness areas up along the northern border. It had to be one of those depressing little side-of-the-mountain towns, where the children occasionally came with six fingers per hand and not too many branches in their family tree. It wouldn't be hard to find a girl like that in a small town, but was she even a threat? How could she be? He sat there for a moment, drawing the name Graniteville on his desk blotter and circling it idly with a ballpoint.

He put the map back in the drawer. No, he thought. Wendell Carson's only problem is this policeman—investigator—whatever he was. Forget about the girl, he told himself. All you have to do is keep Stafford in the dark. Long enough to work out the delivery arrangements, and how you'll get your money without getting bumped off in the process. Wendell Carson wasn't a criminal, really, not in the case-hardened, street-tough sense of the word, but he knew that for a million in cash, his normally casual relationship with Tangent might change. And there was the obvious time bind: All of this had to happen before the Army found out the cylinder was gone, assuming they would. Tangent seemed to think they would, and Tangent was a Washington guy.

The scam had evolved to a specific system. He dealt with only one buyer, Tangent, who had a standing wish list consisting of general military material but who occasionally requested specific items. Carson maintained the wish list, instructing his "eyes" down in the warehouses, Bud Lambry, to be on the lookout for the required items, especially in the high-value area. When something on the wish list showed up, Lambry would notify Carson, who would call the client and confirm his interest. Then Lambry would ensure that the items of interest were put in selected lots for auction. Carson, as manager of the DRMO, would ensure the items did *not* appear on the reutilization lists. Then Carson would rig the sealed-bid process so that his client "won" the auction, except that he would hold the winning bid until after the auction, reduce it, and then submit it to the contracts people. The client would pay the new "winning" bid. Carson's fee was a small percentage of the value of the item, based on how much he had saved the client. From the kickback, Carson paid Lambry, in cash.

The key was to do it infrequently, never actually touch anything himself, and keep the money within reasonable bounds. Most of the fraud cases he read about arose because the perpetrators got too greedy. It had been a very nice, quiet, and unobtrusively profitable scam, one that he had planned to work until his retirement—about twenty thousand a year, in cash. He had it stashed in safe-deposit boxes in banks all around Atlanta. If Maude ever discovered it, he would say that he had been dabbling in the stock market and doing pretty well. Once a year, he would tell her that he had a government trip somewhere, to a conference, say, and then take a week's leave and go to Vegas for some high living.

By limiting the scale and dealing only in cash and with only one buyer, he'd managed to keep the whole thing off the DLA auditors' radar screens. He smiled as he thought about it. It was just about a perfect little scam.

Only very rarely had he taken operational military equipment from the demil list, because that had to be done practically on the conveyor belt in front of the Monster. From time to time, he had done this though, because he had been able to arrange for Bud Lambry to be the demil operator anytime there was a requirement for an evening shift in the demil facility. The beauty of that was that once something had been certified by the demil assembly crew as having been destroyed, it was virtually untraceable. The only vulnerability he had ever had was with Bud Lambry, ace spotter, and now that vulnerability was dissolving in the nontoxic hydrocarbon holding tank. Carson quickly banished that image.

Lambry's supervisor had reported him absent this morning, which was not entirely unusual for a Monday. He would have to explain Lambry's continued absence somehow. With Lambry gone, the problem now was to keep Inspector Stafford in the mushroom mode while Wendell Carson executed the cylinder deal. Either way, he thought, he needed to tell Tangent about Stafford. He pulled out his phone list and looked up the 800 number and dialed it. He got the machine and left the callback message. He gave a time of one hour from now, which would allow him time to get home. Tangent wouldn't be happy about the DCIS development, but Carson was pretty sure they could still pull it off. Stafford wasn't here about the cylinder, and that's all that counted right now.

■■■ THE PEACHTREE CENTER HOTEL AND CONVENTION CENTER, ATLANTA, 4:25 P.M.

In his hotel room, Stafford put his clothes away, raided the minibar for a beer, and took a look out the window. The room cost more than his whole day's per diem allowance, but at this moment, he didn't give a damn. The skyline of Atlanta gleamed indifferently back at him. He was surprised at all the high-rise buildings. The place had grown a lot in the ten years since he'd last been here. Careful, he thought. You told Carson this was your first time in the city.

Dave Stafford was forty-three. Born in Norfolk, Virginia, he had lived on the outskirts of the city, near the sprawling Naval Operating Base, where his father worked as a security guard and his mother as a telephone operator. Growing up around the Navy and the base, he had gravitated naturally to the Navy upon graduation from high school, especially since there was no money for college. He left the Navy after one hitch and joined the Norfolk Police Department, advancing from rookie cop to the detective bureau in five short years. But the cop's life wore him down, and he began thinking about college. Then one week-end, he attended a government job fair and learned that the Naval Investigative Service was hiring. He took a job at the NIS, and transferred to the Defense Investigative Service, later the DCIS, in 1988. He'd met Alice that same year, and they had married after a four-month courtship.

Savvy, sexy, ambitious Alice. She had been almost his own age and had never married. She had money in the bank, a good government job as an office manager in the Defense Intelligence Agency, and was as determined as he was to get ahead. For the first two years, he couldn't believe she was his wife. Now she wasn't.

He sat down heavily in one of the overstuffed chairs, his right arm hanging straight down, pointing at the floor until he remembered to drape it on the armrest. He had regained almost all of the feeling in his hand and fingers, which the docs said was a good sign, but the big motor muscles were a long way from home. The orthopedist at Walter Reed had said that with proper rehab exercise he should get his arm back to about 50, 60 percent, but so far, it was at about 2 percent. Maybe the docs were just wrong, or maybe they wanted to let him down easy. Either way, the virtual paralysis of his right arm was just the topping on the cake of disasters he'd been through in the past two years.

You *knew*, he thought. You *knew* what happens to whistle-blowers. What *always* happens to whistle-blowers in Washington. You're just a damn fool, that's all, Mr. Straight Arrow—by the book, full speed ahead and damn the consequences—David Stafford, ace investigator. Yeah, right. He'd spent about a year investigating a senior DCIS bureaucrat named Bernstein, who had been selling inside information to a major Defense contractor whom the DCIS had been investigating for contract fraud. When the DCIS upper management dragged its heels on prose-cuting Bernstein, Stafford had talked to a reporter, after which life had become interesting. To his utter surprise, the eighteen months following his disclosures about Bernstein had been absolute hell, proving beyond a shadow of a doubt the extent of his naïveté. Instead of giving him a commendation for rooting out evil, a wounded bureaucracy had reacted angrily to the exposure of one of its more senior officials. As everyone told him in the corridor, "Sure, Bernstein needed exposing, but, man, did you have to do it quite so publicly?" And did he understand that he was going to pay for it professionally? In fact, his entire division in DCIS had suffered as senior management retaliated under the cover of budget cuts and interference in case assignments. Worse, an FBI agent implicated by Bernstein had been shit-canned, so now the Bureau was after his ass, too. He acquired a new first name when people began saying "Goddamn Stafford"—a lot.

His marital problems predated the Bernstein incident. He and Alice had been living the comfortable, if somewhat frenetic, lifestyle typical of career Washington bureaucrats with joint incomes. They had their individual schedules of commuting and working, and if one included their separate car pools, both of them spent more close time with other people on a day-by-day basis than they did with each other.

Their respective jobs took them away on travel routinely, but with the conceit of husbandly trust, Stafford had assumed she wasn't playing around just because he never did. But a year before the Bernstein flap erupted, he had begun to suspect that she might be having an affair. With her boss, no less, an Air Force colonel with whom she often traveled on business. It wouldn't have been that hard to find out, one way or another: He was an investigator, after all. Later, much later, he had realized that he must not really have wanted to know. When she finally announced that she had found someone else, he had been hurt but not totally surprised.

The arm came last, like some sick cosmic joke. His career was on the skids, Alice had kicked him out, and one night, as he waited for change at a gas station, a couple of kids tried a holdup and then panicked. They pulled out automatics and started blasting everything in sight. The attendant had been killed and Stafford had been shot in the arm.

He sighed and looked at his watch. Now that he was finished feeling sorry for himself, maybe he should get back to business. DCIS procedures required that he check in with Ray Sparks, the DCIS supervisor for the southeastern region, upon arrival. Well, arrival had been this morning.

He went over to the desk phone and disconnected the line. He set up the portable PC on the desk, then hooked the phone line into the PC's X jack. He worked on the beer while the PC booted up. Using the encrypted telephony program, he placed a call to the Atlanta DCIS office out in Smyrna, a suburb north of Atlanta. He appreciated modern technology, but it still felt weird to be talking to a computer. The office manager got Sparks on the line.

"Ray, this is Dave Stafford. Go secure. I'm encrypted on my portable."

There was a noise over the line. "I'm secure, Dave. Welcome to Atlanta. I think."

"Yeah, I suppose I'm persona not so freaking grata just now, huh?"

"Yeah, something like that. We were told you were coming. How's the broken wing?"

"Still broken." He and Ray Sparks had been partners on a case some years ago and had become pretty good friends. Sparks was also probably the only regional supervisor who would accept him at the moment. There was a moment of silence on the line.

"So what do you plan to do down here?" Sparks asked. "Not your normal 'throw in a grenade and see what evidence comes back at you' routine, I hope?"

"Nope. I've decided to leave the eternal search for truth and justice to Batman and Robin. Right now I plan to just roll with the punches, keep my head down, try to get my arm back, do this job, whatever it is, and try not to cause you or anyone else any problems. After these past eighteen months, I'm a born-again believer."

"Bernstein had it coming," Sparks said. "He was an officious prick, as everyone in the whole DCIS would be happy to admit. From the safety of the sidelines, of course."

"Well I know, compadre. Those sidelines got pretty far away there for a while. My first name has been changed to Goddamn, especially after that FBI guy got reprimanded. But, yes, I promised the colonel no grenades."

"That's the smart way, Dave. The colonel knows how to work the web. He'll get you rehabilitated if anyone can."

"Isn't it fascinating that I need rehabilitation after exposing corruption?"

"It's your career that needs rehabilitation, Dave. You embarrassed DCIS."

"I would have thought it was Bernstein's corrupt behavior that embarrassed DCIS, but never mind. I know what you're saying."

There was a fractional pause. "Well, good, Dave," Sparks said. "That's great. Barb said to invite you out, once you're settled in. Maybe we'll burn some beef."

Stafford could hear the effort in Sparks's voice, and wondered if that mythical barbecue would ever really happen. They both knew damned well that a DCIS supervisor socialized with a DCIS pariah at his professional peril. But it was nice of him to make the offer.

"I appreciate that, Ray, as well as the friendly reception. But look, you feel you have to shut the door on me to keep your own ass warm and dry, you just do it, okay? I'm told that I smell a lot like ozone these days. I don't want to take anyone down with me."

"Screw that noise," Sparks protested. "Besides, we're too far from Washington for anyone to care. So what's with this DRMO thing?"

Stafford gave him a summary of the case file. Another investigator had been working the DRMO auction fraud case for two years, but it had deteriorated into one of those seemingly hopeless muddles. It had begun when a Lebanese arms broker in New York had been caught exporting some surplused Air Force missile-guidance radars. The components had been purchased at auction from a New Jersey DRMO. The Defense Logistics Agency headquarters had called in the DCIS, who promptly asked for the audit records on that particular DRMO. It turned out that serious audits were conducted only every five years, and, naturally, it had been four years since the last one. So of course the DCIS effort was stopped while DLA conducted an audit.

The DCIS investigation had revealed what looked like a perfectly legitimate auction, but there were aspects that smelled wrong. The first was in fact clearly wrong: Those components should all have gone through the demil process. The consigning agency had marked them improperly, or the receiving DRMO had screwed up, or someone deliberately knew what he was after and had removed the demil paperwork.

The second was what the indomitable Colonel Parsons called "a pattern problem." Parsons maintained that fraud perpetrated by smart bad guys *inside* the system often manifested itself in patterns as opposed to single, discernible incidents. The supposedly obsolete missile components had been shipped to the DRMO in five different shipment lots, but they had been auctioned off as a single block of components, almost as if someone had arranged that whoever won the bid on that block got all the guidance assemblies. That was where the trail had ended. There was no evidence tying any identifiable persons definitively to the New Jersey DRMO's auction process. The guy who had caught the New Jersey case reported back to his boss that he'd come up empty. Colonel Parsons had been less than sympathetic, and he had told the guy that if he couldn't break the specific case, then he should examine the whole system for that specific pattern.

After three months of ploughing through mind-numbing DLA back records of DRMO auctions and audits, they had uncovered another sale manifesting the same pattern as the one in New Jersey, which is when they'd realized that the auction had been a sealed-bid auction, controlled from Washington—within the DLA headquarters. Checking back on the New Jersey case, they'd found it was a sealed-bid auction as well. They'd been looking at the wrong target: Whatever was being scammed was being orchestrated in Washington by someone involved in the sealed-bid process. Another three months of going back into prior years had turned up intermittent evidence of the same pattern, going back several years, but in each case, it was impossible to determine precisely how the thing was being done in Washington.

Stafford pointed out to Sparks that the investigation had stalled right about the time the Bernstein corruption flap reached a crescendo, which was why Colonel Parsons, realizing that Stafford was probably not going to survive the political heat, had seized on the DRMO problem as a pretext for getting him out of town. So here he was.

He gave Sparks a debrief of the day's events, including Carson's fainting spell at the airport. Sparks was silent for a moment. "That's medium weird," he said finally. "Do you suppose Carson and that woman are involved with each other? And maybe the girl resents it or something? Some deal like that?"

"Don't know. Probably can't know, at this stage. Carson claims he didn't even remember seeing them. Said he was feeling woozy, just getting over the flu. Like I said, I don't know. The girl's suitcase had a sticker that said GRANITEVILLE on it. Otherwise, I wouldn't even know where to start to find them, assuming I ever had to. I did give the woman my card."

"Which she'll probably shit-can. You say Graniteville? I think that's a small burg up in the mountains of north Georgia. Black hats, long beards, moonshine country. Not friendly to federal anything. Although now it's all marijuana: There's no money in 'shine anymore. And you say they were talking?"

"Not exactly. More like looking at each other. Carson and the girl, not the woman. The girl was looking at Carson like she'd seen a snake, and then he fell down."

"Is there any reason for Carson to suspect you're after him?"

"Don't think so. I inherited this case very much on the fly."

"Maybe just plain old nerves: A senior DCIS guy coming in unannounced would make anybody nervous. What'd you tell him about us local hicks?"

"He did ask, now that you mention it. Gave him some BS about this being a headquarters pattern-of-fraud probe. Told him I didn't want to stir up the locals. That kind of stuff. He seemed to buy it."

"Okay. If he pulls the string, we'll be appropriately ignorant. Our normal posture anyway."

Stafford laughed. "Okay, Ray, I'll keep you posted, and I'll try not to rock any boats."

"That's the ticket," Sparks said. "Call us if you need anything."

They both hung up, and Stafford unhooked the computer and restored the hotel's phone line. He picked up his beer and went back to the window. What he wanted right now was to go down to one of the fancy bars he had seen in the lobby and get reacquainted with Mr. Tanqueray's oblivion potion, but he'd done enough of that after Alice bailed out and the reality of his disability penetrated. Colonel Parsons, a whipcord, buzz-cut retired Army officer ten years his senior, had cured of him of incipient alcoholism as only he could. He'd invited Stafford to join him for lunch one badly hungover day at the colonel's downtown athletic club. The dining room had turned out to be a boxing ring, where the colonel proceeded to beat the hangover out of him with sixteen-ounce gloves. The colonel had kept it fair by tying his own right hand behind his back. He still had beaten the shit out of Stafford. Parsons then informed him he could start drinking again just as soon as he could defend himself at the skill level of a Girl Scout. From his supine vantage point on the canvas floor, Stafford had decided that, arm or no arm, agreeing with the six or so colonels swimming in his bloody vision was probably the best course of action. Since then, he had become a workout convert, having discovered that intense physical exercise was an excellent stress-eater, not to mention his only chance to regain a normal set of wings.

He finished his beer and pitched the can left-handed at the trash can. And missed, as usual. For $169 a night, he thought, they ought to have bigger trash cans.

4

SP4c Latonya Mayfield pushed the calculator to one side of her cluttered desk and rubbed her eyes. It was almost lunchtime, and she had been running these numbers for the entire morning. The dreaded destruction inventory match audit. It had to be done on every shipment that went out to the Army's large-scale destruction facility at Tooele, Utah. It was dreaded because it was a three-way line-by-line audit: The entire shipping manifest was compared with the receiving manifest report from Tooele, and then those numbers were compared with the inventory of the surplused storage containers.

My own damn fault I got tagged with this, she thought wearily. I just had to bring up the fact that the platoon's Human Relations Council hadn't met in over two months. The sergeant reacted with a bland smile, and then this lovely little assignment, a task normally done by a Spec-3. Not that she could make a legitimate gripe: She was, after all, a chemical warfare weapons accountability specialist, wasn't she?

After three and a half hours, all those rows and columns produced by the high-speed line printer were beginning to run together, and if she didn't have a number mismatch, she would have filed the whole thing with a "no discrepancies" report. She'd never heard of there ever being a discrepancy in the two years she's been assigned to the control office. Movement control and security procedures for chemical weapons materials were just about as tight as they were for nuclear weapons materials.

She rubbed her eyes again, and thought about coffee, and then thought about lunch. The other clerks in the office were already shuffling around as they prepared to break for the chow hall, but she knew there was no way she'd be able to stay awake doing this shit after lunch. And,

38

Houston, baby, we do appear to have us a problem here. She pulled the printouts back to the center of her desk, shuffling back through them to find page one of fifty-seven. The mismatch was one number. Just a single error, and she couldn't find it. The grand totals did not add up, but each of the three various reports did add up. Something had not been shipped, or had been shipped and not received, or there was one more storage container—lovingly called "coffins" in the CW business—than there were chemical cylinders involved. The thought crossed her mind that the last possibility had better be the answer, or the mother of all flaps was going to erupt right here in Toxic Town.

Hell with it, she decided. I'm going to lunch, and then I'm going to look for the discrepancy one more time, and then I'm going to do what I should have done an hour ago—take it to the staff sergeant. So there.

■ TUESDAY, FORT GILLEM DRMO, ATLANTA, 9:20 A.M.

On Tuesday morning, Carson checked in with Stafford to make sure he had everything he needed. Stafford was sitting at the desk, surrounded by open binders, and making notes on a legal pad.

"Coffee mess is two doors down the hall," he said. "Feel free to help yourself."

"Thanks. I did," Stafford replied. "You feeling better today? No more fainting spells?"

"Much. Still don't know what the hell that was yesterday."

Stafford nodded, gave him a thin smile, and went back to his paperwork. But then, as Carson was turning away, Stafford asked another question. "Do you have any significant personnel problems here? Anybody who's a known trouble maker? Anyone who quit on you with no notice recently?"

Carson stopped in the doorway. First the questions about that weird girl. Now what was *this*? Lambry, maybe? "Not really," he said, thinking fast. "There are personnel problems from time to time, of course. But they're mostly my Monday-morning alcoholics, or people fooling around with time sheets or sick leave, or workmen's comp stuff. But do I have any real bad actors? I'd have to say no. Why?"

Stafford shrugged. "Standard procedure when we're chasing possible fraud. Sudden departures sometimes indicate a bad guy who got antsy. Or if there've been calls made to the DOD fraud hot line—malcontents sometimes do that just to cause trouble. We check that out as a matter of routine. Oh, I have the personnel roster. Can I have access to your actual personnel files, please?"

"Sure. See Mrs. Johnson in Human Resources. I'll tell her to get you anything you need. Anything else?"

"Nope. That ought to do it." Stafford smiled again. "For now."

For now, Carson thought as he went back to his office. He wondered if Stafford had learned of Lambry's disappearance. He'd put the word out Monday that Lambry had quit Friday night after getting mad about something. He'd planned to construct the covering paperwork this week, but after Stafford's question, he'd have to get something down in writing, and quickly. But then he stopped: Based on what he'd just said, Stafford would probably want to follow that up. Oh, shit, maybe he'd even go out to Lambry's house, snoop around. Who knew what that idiot might have left in his house? He hurried to his office, placed a quick phone call to personnel, and asked for some termination forms. Fifteen minutes later, Mrs. Johnson, a large black lady, brought the forms and last week's time sheets into Carson's office.

"You get Mr. Stafford what he needed?" he asked without preamble. He did not like Mrs. Johnson, and she did not like him.

"Yes, I did," she said. "Who is that man, anyway? Nobody can figure him out."

"He's an auditor from DLA," Carson said. "It's nothing special to do with us. DLA's looking for a pattern on some old fraud cases, apparently. Which files did he want, exactly?"

"He wanted all the personnel files. Well, not actually—he wanted *access* to all the files. Including yours, by the way."

Carson kept his expression neutral. "That's fine. There's nothing here that DLA doesn't already have on file in Washington. Give him whatever he needs. And bring me Mr. Lambry's file. He apparently was serious about quitting, so we need to start the termination paperwork on him." He looked back down at his own paperwork as she started to leave. Then she stopped in the doorway. "Oh," she said. "He wanted a map of Georgia. Ella Mae had one in her car."

Carson looked up again, perplexed. "He say what for?"

"Nope. That man don't exactly talk it up, you know what I'm sayin'?"

"Okay. Close that door on your way out, please."

After she left, Carson swiveled around in his chair. He thought about the Georgia map in his own desk. She hadn't said city map. She'd said state map. Hadn't she? He picked up the phone and called her back.

"Did Mr. Stafford want an Atlanta map or a state map?" he asked.

"State of Georgia. Said he had an Atlanta map. I believe the motor pool provides a city map in all their cars." Mrs. Johnson sounded a little huffy.

He hung up without replying. So it *was* a state map. Now why in the hell would Stafford want a state map? And what was that bit about the fraud hot line? The more he thought about it, the more uncertain he was about what Stafford was doing here.

The buyer hadn't been thrilled, either. Tangent had called him from home, using the usual code, but Maude had been across the street visiting a sick neighbor, so Carson didn't have to go find a pay phone. He'd told Tangent why Stafford was there, and expressed the opinion that he wouldn't be there very long. Tangent had requested Stafford's full name, civil service grade, and home organization.

"Why?" Carson had asked after giving Tangent the information.

"We'll check him out. See if he's telling the truth about why he's there."

"You can do that?"

"In our business, Carson, we *always* do that. Lots of people say they're one thing, turn out to be quite another. It doesn't take long, which is good, because we don't have all that much time."

Carson was alarmed by that last. "Has something happened? Is the Army—"

"No, nothing yet," Tangent interrupted. "But we have to operate on the assumption that they'll discover it's missing. If they don't, great. If they do, a sale might become very tough to pull off. You do understand that, right?"

Carson had said that he did, and Tangent said he'd call in the next day or so with a reading on Stafford.

Now Carson thought about his million-dollar prize. This damned Stafford was definitely not a complication he needed right now, especially if he pulled the string on Bud Lambry's sudden disappearance. Carson knew he should be doing something about that, but he wasn't at all sure what to do.

Stafford closed the oversized three-ring binder and plopped it back onto the desk. He'd been skimming through the DRMO reference binders for the past hour and a half, doodling on the blotter pad as he thought about the case. Most of the people who had been caught fiddling the surplus-material system had been tripped up by their own runaway greed: GS-11s and GS-12s who suddenly sported Cadillacs or second homes on a mid-five-figure salary. Coworkers would always notice, always. Eventually, someone would call into the Defense Department fraud hot line. The usual pattern was a small scam that got bigger and bigger, until the scammer attracted attention by overreaching.

But headquarters knew that there had to be guys out there who were smart bad guys. Tap the honey pot, but do it infrequently, with lots of cutouts between you and the actual stuff, and make your money after the fact through kickbacks from the people who were getting an unfair bidding advantage, not from stealing or selling stuff directly.

He'd been telling the truth when he told Carson that he'd picked the Atlanta DRMO partly because of its size. But now that he was here, he wasn't sure about what to do next. Carson was a potentially interesting guy, but that alone didn't make him a suspect. He shuffled through the personnel folders to find Carson's file. He went immediately to the DD-398 form, the security personal-history questionnaire and read it. If there was an auction scam in place here, Carson would just about have to know about it. If Carson was running something, Stafford's request for access to the personnel files and that throw-away mention of the DOD fraud hot line should have seemed like opening shots. He thought he'd seen the man's face tighten up when he'd asked those questions, although it was hard to tell. Carson had perfected one of those civil-servant masks of workday insouciance, an expression of blandness of which dirt would be proud.

He decided to get some early lunch, then spend the rest of the day walking around by himself through the DRMO industrial areas to see what he could learn by getting people to talk to him. Maybe stir up the employees a little bit, see if there were some grudges out there. It wouldn't be long before that action got back to Carson, and maybe that would shake something loose. He couldn't think of anything else to do.

He started his walking tour an hour and a half later, beginning in the outside lay-down area. Talking to the employees wasn't as easy as he had thought it would be, since most of them were driving forklifts in and around the warehouse complex. He did notice that no one seemed interested in challenging him when he went into areas clearly marked with RESTRICTED ACCESS signs. He finally came upon the employee lunch room in warehouse two and went in for a cup of coffee, but his efforts at conversation with the half a dozen or so people in there were politely rebuffed. He left after a half hour of getting nowhere, then remembered his cover story: He was a DLA auditor. Auditors brought only trouble, so of course the employees weren't going to invite him to their coffee breaks. They might even be afraid of him.

He wandered through some more of the warehouses, which by this time had all begun to look alike. He ended up in the warehouse immediately adjacent to the demil machine. The Monster apparently was not running. The feed-assembly area contained both the feed and back loop of the demil machine's conveyor system, which snaked around this warehouse's floor, surrounded by a pair of waist-level safety railings that paralleled the course of the belt. The belt-loading area was in the back of the warehouse, where three heavy steel doors admitted forklifts from other warehouses. The belt, carrying the material to be destroyed, exited this warehouse through the connecting wall, entering the demil building through a screen-shielded aperture that was draped with stiff strips of rubber in front of two steel flap doors. There was a normal walk-through door with a small window in it just to the right of the interbuilding aperture.

A crew of four men was loading the conveyor belt with material as it was brought in by roaring, smoky forklifts. Three of them were black; the fourth, a stupid-looking man of indeterminate age, was white. They would pile the components into plastic cartons on the belt, and then one of them would advance the belt a few feet to make room for the next pile. Stafford walked to the back of the room and watched for a few minutes. The crew ignored him except for the white man. Finally the last forklift backed out and the warehouse was silent. The three black men walked toward the back, where there was a small coffeepot on a table. The white man ambled over to Stafford.

"Yew the auder fella?"

Auder? "Auditor," Stafford replied.

"S'what I jist said. You him?" The man was eyeing Stafford with visible suspicion.

"Yup. But I won't bite."

His attempt at humor was apparently lost, as the man appeared to consider his chances of being bitten. Finally he nodded as if he'd come to a momentous decision. "Heard about you. Folks here get stirred up, auder's come aroun'. What you want here?"

Stafford thought about that question, and how to play it. He could turn on his cop face and bust this guy's balls a little, or he could play it down. The guy was obviously some kind of serious hick. "Routine checks," he said. "We go around to the DRMOs to make sure everything's being done by the book and nobody's stealing anything. That kind of stuff." He must be about six feet tall, Stafford thought, but skinny as a rail. It was wonderful what a childhood diet of Twinkies and soda pop could do. "What's your name?" he asked.

The tall man peered down his long, bony nose and thought about that for a moment. "Corey," he replied finally. "Corey Dillard. What's yours?"

"I'm David Stafford. How long have you worked here, Mr. Dillard?"

"Fifteen years and some."

"And what do you do here?"

Dillard appeared to be puzzled by the question, as if no one had ever asked him that before. He bent down a little to talk directly into Stafford's face, exuding an aroma of tobacco and decaying teeth. Stafford blinked, forcing himself not to step back.

"Ah do what Boss Hisley tells me to," Dillard answered. "Mostly, Ah feed the Monstuh. Load up'n this here belt, then we feed that thing. Looka heunh, you ain't a cop? I seen auders, and you don't look like no auder. Boss Hisley, he's sayin' you's a govmint cop."

Stafford grinned at him. "Boss Hisley worried about cops, is he? Should I go talk to him, you think?"

Dillard straightened up, a look of alarm flashing across his face. "I ain't sayin' nothin' about Boss Hisley."

"Okay. I won't tell him that you did. So what do you want to talk about?"

Dillard looked over his shoulder at the three men standing by the table in the corner of the building. They were well out of earshot, but they were definitely watching him.

"Looka heunh," he said, bending forward again, "if'n somebody had somethin' to tell you, he gonna git hisself in trouble, he tellin' it?"

Well, well, well, Stafford thought. "I'm not sure what you mean, Mr. Dillard," he replied, wanting to see where this was going.

"I seen it on the TV. Man had somethin' to say, them cops done give him 'munity."

Better and better, Stafford thought. "Absolutely, Mr. Dillard. Although I'm not a cop, you understand. But I do know that cops offer immunity all the time. For the right kind of information. Long as it's done right."

"Done right? How's that?" Dillard asked, his eyes narrowing. He had put his hands in the pockets of his overalls. He was standing in front of Stafford, looking like a nervous stork.

"Two things. First, the man wanting immunity has to tell what he knows *before* the cops find it out for themselves."

Dillard blinked, then nodded his understanding.

"The second is that if more than one man knows something, the first man to do the telling gets the immunity. Everybody else takes their chances. Like that."

Dillard absorbed that and nodded again, and once more he looked over his shoulder before replying. The largest of the men at the coffee table was staring openly at them. That would be Boss Hisley, Stafford thought.

"How long you gonna be heunh?" Dillard asked.

"Don't know, Mr. Dillard. A little while, probably. Like I said, though, I'm an auditor, not a cop. Is there something you want to talk about?"

Dillard started to say something, but then he shook his head after glancing back over at the big black man. "Reckon not," he replied. "Later, mebbe." With that he started to shuffle back over toward the conveyor belt just as another forklift came bursting through the double doors at the back of the warehouse. Dillard stopped, and, turning his head, said something that Stafford couldn't hear over the forklift's engine noise.

"What?" Stafford called, cupping his left ear.

"Lambry," Dillard shouted, keeping his back to the others. "Y'all need to find Bud Lambry."

Stafford watched as the loading team went back to work, then he tried the walk-through door connecting the feed-assembly room to the demil building. It was locked, so he went outside. So much for his cover story about being an auditor, he thought. The collective blue-collar antenna had sensed already that something was up and there was a Washington cop of some kind here. Still, now he had something to do: Find some guy named Bud Lambry.

He went into the demil building after finding that door unlocked. There was nobody in the control booth when he entered the demil chamber. The empty conveyor belt led straight to the now-silent shredding bank. There were steel screens up on either side of the injection point, as well as plastic spray shields. With all the piping and other ancillary machinery coiled on either side of the shredding bank, the huge machine looked like a crouching steel dinosaur. The vertical band-saw blades glinted dangerously in the fluorescent light. He jumped when the conveyor belt started and then stopped, but then he realized the men next door had advanced it to fit the next load.

So maybe there's something going on here after all, he mused as he stood looking at the Monster. The working stiffs knew he wasn't a DLA auditor. The one man who had been willing to get anywhere near him, Dillard, had started talking about immunity. Saw that 'munity stuff on the TV. I love it. But immunity for what? He couldn't imagine that rocket scientist being capable of knowing anything really significant. So what was the next step? Ask Carson about this Bud Lambry? Or maybe get back to Dillard, in the cop mode this time, and ask Dillard about Carson? Maybe that's why everybody here seemed to have a hate-on for the manager. Maybe they knew he was running a scam of some kind. And—what? Not sharing? Probably.

He decided he would casually drop Lambry's name the next time he talked to Carson. Say somebody he'd met out in the industrial area had mentioned the man's name. See if Carson had any particular reaction. Then he would put a call into the local DCIS office and ask them to run a NCIC check on Lambry. Careful, he reminded himself as he walked across the tarmac to see some more warehouses. You're not supposed to go stirring things up. Heaven forbid you go do your job and uncover some actual crime here. He rubbed his aching right bicep as he walked back.

■ TUESDAY, ANNISTON ARMY WEAPONS DEPOT, ANNISTON, ALABAMA, 3:45 P.M.

Sergeant McCallister was not pleased. "Forty five minutes before we secure the area for the day, and you're bringing me *this* shit? I do not need this, Mayfield. I do *not* need this."

Latonya Mayfield stared down at the pile of reports she had put on the sergeant's desk, but she said nothing. The sergeant was not one of her favorite people on this planet, and he was also not one of the world's great listeners.

"Well?" he said. "Are you completely sure of these numbers? You've run 'em more than once? You've checked them?"

"Yes, Sergeant," she said patiently. "Even had Spec Three Luper run them." Luper was the clerk who was supposed to do this audit. "There's a discrepancy."

McCallister stared down at the report as his face got red. "Where's a discrepancy, for Chrissakes? This is the destruction inventory match audit, goddamn it. There can *not* be a discrepancy in the destruction

46

inventory match audit. You know that. I know that. The whole fucking Army knows that. This thing has to match up. If there's a discrepancy, it has to be in your paperwork, not in this report."

"Yes, Sergeant," she said in a "if you say so" tone of voice.

"Damn right, yes, Sergeant," he said. "All right. Tell Henderson I want to see him. Don't tell him why."

"Yes, Sergeant," Mayfield replied, and went out to find Spec-5 Henderson. It took her a few minutes because Henderson, getting a little jump on four-thirty secure, had been in the men's locker room changing into civvies.

"It's sixteen-ten, Mayfield. What is this shit, anyway?"

"Man said for me to tell you to go see him," she said. "Said he'd tell you when you got there."

"Aw, man! Shit!" He looked at his watch. "All right. I gotta get back in the bag first." He went back into the locker room.

Mayfield went back to her cubicle, wondering what to do next. Henderson was a weapons safety specialist, not a clerk. He would be seriously pissed when he found out that he had to do the destruction inventory match audit. She had to decide in the next five minutes whether to hit the road, Jack, or stay to help him. She thought about it. Henderson was an okay guy for a white man, but he'd hate her forever if he thought he was having to pick up after her. On the other hand, she had discovered the discrepancy; for a clean audit, he would have to do it by himself to catch her mistake.

Fifteen minutes later, Henderson solved it for her. He came by her desk with the report in his hands and gave her a black look. "Thanks a fucking heap, Mayfield."

"I'll stay and help you with it, you want," she offered.

He shook his head. "Man said I had to do it by myself. Said you'd fucked it up. Shit, I've never done a goddamn audit. This'll take fucking hours."

"I didn't mess it up," she said. "I found a discrepancy. That's why he's pissed. I'll show you how it's done. Maybe you can find it."

"You serious? There really is a discrepancy?"

"I think there is. Spec Three Luper says there is, but he couldn't find it, either."

Henderson's anger evaporated. He looked back across the room, but McCallister's door was closed "Okay," he said. "But don't let old Shit for Brains see us."

Carson sat as his desk and considered the word that had reached him thirty minutes earlier. That the Washington guy had been seen talking to people out in the warehouse. That the DRMO's pet rock, Corey Dillard, had said something to Stafford about Bud Lambry. What, or in what context, had not been overheard. Or the blue-collar guys weren't willing to say.

Great, he thought. Just fucking great. Dillard had been Bud Lambry's helper from time to time, but Bud had assured Carson that Dillard knew nothing about the scam. But what might genius Lambry have told genius Dillard about the magical cylinder and all the money that might be coming Bud's way? He got up and looked out into the flea-market warehouse. The auction had been today, and the bidders had been carting out the spoils to the loading dock all day.

He turned away from the window and walked slowly around his office, feeling uneasy as he relived what had happened to Lambry. He repeated to himself his new mantra: It was an accident. Wendell Carson is not a murderer. But there was no getting around the enormity of what he had gotten himself into: stealing the cylinder in the first place, and now the death of Bud Lambry. He went over to the bookcase and put his hands between the binders. He felt with his fingers the smooth steel, cold and deadly to the touch.

Before Stafford had begun nosing around, it would have been sufficient for him simply to announce that Lambry had quit and disappeared. Now he might have to think of something more elaborate. And then a scary thought occurred to him: If Stafford really started looking into Lambry's disappearance, what loose ends had Lambry left?

Spec-5 Henderson threw his pencil across the darkened office. Mayfield, sitting in a chair at another desk, watched him with a small smile of satisfaction on her face. She had gone into the women's locker room at 4:30, until one of the other girls told her that McCallister had left for the day. Then she'd rejoined Henderson and helped him crunch the numbers. He'd gotten the hang of it during the first hour and then run the report audit himself.

"I give up," he said. "I get the same thing you did. One number off. One fucking number."

She nodded. "Now what?" she asked.

"We tell McCallister, that's what. He's the sergeant."

"He gonna go hermantile."

He looked over at her. "Lemme get this straight: This discrepancy means one of three things, right? More shit went out of here than got there, or more shit got there than went out of here, or something's missing, right?"

"That's it."

He shuffled back through the fifty-seven page destruction report and frowned.

She really wanted to go home, although this might get interesting very soon. "What?" she asked.

"I'm looking to see what was shipped."

"Buncha alfa-bravo-charlie gobbledygook," she said.

Henderson didn't say anything while he studied the report. He'd been focusing on numbers. Now he was looking at the alpha-numeric ammunition designator codes down the left side of the printouts. He rubbed his eyes. Then he stopped.

"Whoa," he said softly.

"What?"

"At first I couldn't recognize this designator code. But now I remember what this shipment was. This is fucking Wet Eye."

"Wet Eye. Now that sounds like some lovely shit."

He looked back over at her, and something in his eyes made her straighten up.

"We need to call McCallister," he said. "Like right fucking now."

After a half hour of trying unsuccessfully to find Sergeant McCallister, and then Lieutenant Biers, McCallister's boss, Henderson had taken it upon himself to call the depot's command duty officer. He explained that he had a problem and couldn't find either the sergeant or the platoon's lieutenant, then asked if the CDO could come over to the control office. The CDO, a first lieutenant who was an instructor at the Chemical Warfare School, wanted to know why Spec-5 Henderson wouldn't come over to the duty office. Lieutenants did not go to see E-5s.

"Sir, it's complicated. And it may turn into a really, really big deal. That's all I can say over an unsecure phone, sir."

"We need MPs here, Henderson? This isn't some sexual harassment shit, is it?"

"No, sir. Nothing like that. You just need to come over here. Please?"

Although he was just a first lieutenant, the CDO had been in the Army long enough to recognize what that "please" meant: An enlisted man thought he was looking at some serious trouble and now wanted an officer folded into it before whatever it was got worse.

"Okay, I'm on my way, Henderson. Tell me again where that office is."

Ten minutes later, a green Ford sedan pulled up in front of the control office. Specialist Mayfield escorted the CDO in. She was pleased to see that he was black and a Chemical Corps officer. Once they were in the office, Henderson explained what he'd been doing, with Mayfield's assistance. At first the CDO did not understand what the problem was. Henderson laid out the bottom line for him.

"A cylinder of Wet Eye may be unaccounted for."

The CDO stared at him. "No shit? You sure of this, you two?"

Henderson shook his head. "The destruction inventory audit doesn't add up," he said. "Mayfield here worked it all day, then another guy did it, and then Mayfield here told the sergeant, who had me do it again. We've been here since sixteen-thirty. It still doesn't add up." He paused. "It could be a fuckup at the other end, at Tooele," he said hopefully.

"Let's hope and pray it is. When was the shipment?"

"It left here by train not quite a month ago," Mayfield said. "This report came in last Thursday."

The lieutenant stared down at the report for a long moment. "Okay," he said. "You two come with me. I'm going to call the CO."

"How about our chain of command?" Henderson asked. "Sergeant McCallister is gonna kick our asses, we jump the chain and go right to the CO."

"You didn't jump it. I did. And I'm the *command* duty officer. This looks like a possible shit storm to me, so I'm calling the CO. He's always telling us, when in doubt, call him. So I'm gonna call his ass, if it's all the same to you, Specialist."

Carson eased his government pickup truck down the street on which Bud Lambry lived. Used to live, he reminded himself. The dilapidated neighborhood was an enclave of old houses cornered by the airport rail lines on one side, a phalanx of trucking terminals on another, and Interstate 285. At this hour, the street was dark and empty.

Lambry's house lay at the dead end of the last street, nestled under a fifty-foot-high embankment carrying the rail line. It wasn't much more than a one-story shack, with sagging front and back porches, a few dying trees on either side, a rusty propane tank, and a dirt front yard containing three junked cars. There were some small outbuildings in various states of collapse out back at the base of the railroad embankment. The house across the street appeared to be abandoned; the house next door looked possibly occupied, but darkened for the night. There was a mound of trash at the dead end of the badly potholed street, and one rusting car nosed into the embankment like some burrowing animal.

Carson rolled to a quiet stop in front of Lambry's house and switched off the engine. He took a final drag on his cigarette and then mashed it out. It had taken him a few hours and a visit to the officers club's bar to muster up the courage to come out here, and another hour to find the house. But if Stafford was going to start poking around into Bud Lambry's sudden disappearance, then Wendell Carson had better take a look inside Lambry's house to see if he had stashed any sort of incriminating evidence. He wasn't quite sure what he was going to do here. Given Lambry's Alabama hillbilly antecedents, he could just imagine what it was like in there.

After waiting fifteen minutes to see if anything was stirring, he stepped out of the truck. He paused again to make sure there were no dogs. A quick scan of the street revealed nothing moving but a single gray cat skulking through the cone of light produced by the one remaining streetlight, which was about a hundred feet away. He walked as casually as he could to the side of the house, trying not to act like some kind of burglar.

A lot of things had changed since Friday night. He had the advantage of knowing that the owner would be out forever, so there should be no surprises here, unless Lambry had a wife or someone else in the house. That thought stopped him as he approached the trash-littered back porch. No, no wife. Lambry had no dependents listed in his personnel file. But then again, Lambry, ever the secretive hillbilly, might not have bothered to tell anyone.

He took a deep breath and stepped up onto the back porch. The porch boards felt soft and spongy. He tried the back door, which was not locked. It appeared to be warped. He let himself into a kitchen area, where his nose told him instantly that this place was going to be every bit as bad as he'd expected. All the windows appeared to be closed, and the air was warm and fetid. He stood there for a moment in the dark kitchen, almost afraid to go farther into the house. It didn't feel like there was anyone in the house, but he would have to make sure. He realized he hadn't even brought a flashlight; some burglar he'd make. Okay, he would have to depend on the dim streetlight filtering through dirty windows.

The rest of the house was as cluttered and smelly as the kitchen area, but there was no one there. After a quick survey, he realized that he would never find anything that Lambry had purposefully hidden. More important, Lambry's house definitely did *not* look like he'd left the area, but, rather, like he had just gone to work one day and not come back.

That was a problem. If Stafford or the cops came out here, they'd conclude at once that something had happened to Lambry. With a sinking feeling, Carson also understood there was no way he could make this place look like the owner had made a planned, orderly departure. Not in less than three days, anyway.

He looked around in despair. Then he had an idea. What if I could start a fire? Burn the damn thing down and then there'd be nothing to search. But how, without triggering an arson investigation? He walked back out into the kitchen area and saw the flickering blue light under the hot-water heater in what looked like a laundry room. Gas. Propane gas—he'd seen the tank outside, now that he thought about it. He went over and checked the stove. Also gas. Well, hell, there it was. Leave a burner cracked on the stove, make sure all the windows were closed, and then let the pilot light of that water heater ignite the pooled propane. He could be miles away when it happened.

He turned a stove burner on full blast to see if it had an automatic pilot, but it was an old stove that required matches. He reduced the gas to low, then went out the back door. And right back in, to wipe his fingerprints off the burner switch. Jesus, he thought. You make a pretty shitty criminal. Then he stepped back outside, wiped off the door handle on both sides, and went back to his truck. He stood by the truck for a moment, shook his head, and went back. He crossed the creaking porch carefully and reentered the kitchen, where he shut off the stove burner. The stink of propane was already strong in the kitchen, so he cracked open a window.

He sat down at the kitchen table, careful not to touch anything. He wasn't thinking too clearly here, he realized. Maybe too much of Mr. Beam's liquid courage. Any decent arson investigator would catch the stove burner trick and ask why the house hadn't gone up four days ago, if Friday was when its owner presumably last used the stove? *Shit!* It couldn't be so blatant as leaving a burner on. He thought he heard a noise out front and rose to peer out a window, afraid that he might see a cop car out there by his truck. But there was still nothing stirring. He commanded his heart to slow down.

A fire was the obvious answer, but how to ignite it and not arouse suspicion? He got up and started going through kitchen drawers, looking for a flashlight. He finally found one in a drawer with some hand tools. He crouched down at the back of the stove and examined the gas line's connection. It seemed to be a threaded coupling of some kind. He went back to the tool drawer and got out a pair of pliers. He was about to grab the coupling when he realized the tube and the coupling were copper. Soft metal. Which would show tool marks. He got back up and found a greasy dish towel, which he wrapped around the coupling. Then he unscrewed it until he heard and smelled propane. He removed the rag and saw no tool marks. Good. This would do it. A leaky coupling— that might take a few days for propane to accumulate.

He sat back on his haunches. Destroying the house wouldn't change the fact that Lambry had just disappeared. But it would remove evidence that he might not have disappeared of his own volition. It would leave a mystery surrounding Lambry, but unless there was a woman or some other relative who cared a lot, it should be a mystery without interest to the cops. The guy was gone, his house burned up, but no one at his place of employment would be looking for him. Except Stafford, maybe, but so what? And if Stafford did uncover the auction scam, the missing Lambry might become *the* suspect. Perfect.

He cleaned up after himself, wiping down anything he might have touched in the house, closed the kitchen window, and took a sniff. He wasn't sure he could smell the gas, but he knew propane was heavier than air and would gather along the floor before filling the room. He let himself out the kitchen door and pulled it as shut as it would go, wiping the door handle with the dishrag. He turned to leave and plunged right through the rotten floorboards, pitching forward onto his stomach, his knees bent awkwardly. His head hit something hard and he saw stars for a moment.

He tried to right himself, but his right foot was stuck, jammed by something under the porch. He tried to get his left foot back onto the porch for leverage, but the boards continued to disintegrate, leaving him nothing to grab. His right knee hurt like hell every time he tried to move. He swore and pulled again on his right foot, but it was jammed tight; it felt like maybe his foot was stuck in a cinder block.

This is fucking ridiculous, he thought as he began to perspire. He tried turning around in the hole, balancing on his hands, but it didn't quite work. The distance from the porch to the ground underneath was about six inches more than he could effectively reach. He was stuck, and everything he tried to use for leverage crumbled under his hands. And then he smelled the propane.

Oh, shit, he thought. The propane. A faint whiff was coming through the partially closed door. He imagined he could hear the opened coupling hissing in the kitchen. How fast would that stuff leak out? How long before it got to the pilot light in the alcove? He struggled hard then, but all he did was to break off more rotten wood and get his foot jammed even tighter. There was a broom parked next to the kitchen door. He grabbed that, tried to pry his foot out, but succeeded only in pinching the hell out of it. He laid the broom down across the opening and tried to lever himself bodily up out of the hole. That almost worked, until the broom handle cracked and then broke under his weight. He was stuck, and there was definitely propane in the air.

He tried the opposite tack, beating at the edges of the hole, breaking off rotten wood to enlarge it. Finally he had it big enough that he could bend down partially and feel around by his stuck foot. His hand encountered a thick, sticky spiderweb, conjuring up visions of black widows about to bite his fingers, which he pulled the hell out of there. But he had felt the cinder block, and his right foot was jammed hard into one of the holes. It felt like there was space under the cinder block, but it was cemented into some kind of structure under there. He looked around the yard to see if anyone was coming, but there were only shadowy piles of junk looking back. Somewhere nearby a dog had begun to bark.

The propane, he kept thinking. It won't happen right away, but I have *got* to get out of here. Then he had an idea. Instead of pulling, he tried pushing, jamming his foot as hard as he could downward, forcing it through the hole. After a minute or so of grunting effort, he felt his foot go all the way through, the edge of the block skinning his shin.

Now there was no way around it: He had to put his hands back down there. He reached down, hit the webs again and shook them off, and then got his fingers under the block and onto his shoe, which he pried off his foot. With that, he was able to extract his foot, stand on the cinder block, and lever himself out of the hole in the porch. He sprawled on his belly and crawled to the steps, where he was able to roll over, get up, and hop down to the solid ground of the backyard.

He glanced back at the warped back door, behind which the kitchen was filling with explosive gas. He thought about retrieving his shoe, said to hell with it, and hopped across the yard to his truck, hoping and praying he still had time to get out of there before the house went up. Once in the truck, he was careful to make no noise when he pulled the driver's door shut. How much time? he wondered. And will it burn or explode? Probably explode in the kitchen, and then the rest of the place will go up. How much time—minutes? Seconds? He tried to think if there was anything else he should have done. Had he left anything behind? He was more frightened now than he had been going in.

Finally, he started up the truck and made a creeping U-turn at the end of the street, keeping the engine as quiet as he could so as to not wake anyone up. He then drove back by the house, afraid to look right at it in case it blew up. He concentrated on just getting up the deserted street and away from there. He saw no signs of life in any of the darkened houses as he made his way out of the neighborhood.

When he reached the state road, almost a mile from Lambry's house, he pulled over onto the parking apron of a closed gas station. He backed the truck up against the building to make it look as if it was just parked there for the night. He watched the dark horizon in the direction of Lambry's house and waited. He wondered if the thing would let go before gas filled the whole house, with that pilot light right there in the kitchen. Jesus, he'd get a lot more than just a house fire if the whole thing filled up with gas first. Then he worried that it might not work at all. Shit! Had he closed that window? He couldn't remember. He could remember only the feel of those spiderwebs.

When a car came past, he slumped down in the seat to avoid being seen. After another half hour or so, he was starting to panic. Suppose it didn't work? Suppose the cops went there, found the hole, found his shoe? Christ! He looked at his watch; it was now two-fifteen in the morning. He began to wonder if he should go back. But how could he do that, when he knew there was propane accumulating in there? And then there was a sudden orange glare through the distant trees, followed by a powerful thump. A very powerful thump, considering he was at least a mile away. Damn, just how big had that explosion been?

He started up the truck and pulled back out on the state road, pointing toward Atlanta, driving awkwardly with just a sock on his right foot. He could see a red glare in his rearview mirror. That had to be a big fire. He hoped like hell that none of the surrounding houses had been damaged. The good news was that if the explosion had been big enough, the arson squad would have nothing to work with. But then he worried again. What had he missed? And what kind of monster was he turning into?

■ TUESDAY, ANNISTON ARMY WEAPONS DEPOT, ANNISTON, ALABAMA, 11:30 P.M.

Col. Tom Franklin, commanding officer of the Anniston Army Weapons Depot, smelled of scotch when he arrived at the headquarters building. He had been driven over by his wife. The Franklins had been hosting a dinner party at their quarters, but it had ended when the call from the CDO came in at eleven P.M. The colonel was still in his civilian clothes when he arrived, circumspectly carrying a mug of coffee with him. He went directly to his own office, accompanied by the CDO. The two enlisted people from the control office were told to wait in the duty office while the colonel listened patiently to the CDO's report. The colonel had been mildly disturbed at being called out in the middle of his party, and he was a bit embarrassed to show up with whiskey on his breath, but he was not drunk, and after he heard the lieutenant's report, he was very damned glad he'd been called.

"Good job, calling me," he said. "It was absolutely the right thing to do. Are we sure beyond any doubt that these troops have done the audit correctly?"

"Sir, I don't know that. But three different people have done the audit, and from the sounds of it, more than once. They were concerned enough to be looking for their chain of command at night. When I heard Wet Eye, well . . ."

"Right. Wet Eye. I'm having that same sinking feeling. Okay, get the G-Three in here right now. And get me the number for the Army Command Center in Washington. I'm going to make a voice report on the secure phone, and that's going to provoke a million questions."

The CDO was writing fast in his notebook.

"Tell the G-Three that I want Tooele's duty office notified right away, and tell him that I want commanding officer Tooele to call me ASAP. Then I want everyone between me and the clerk who found this standing tall in my office in one hour. I'm going home to change as soon as I've made this call. Got it?"

"Yes, sir. Right away, sir," the CDO said.

■ WEDNESDAY, THE U.S. ARMY COMMAND CENTER, THE PENTAGON, WASHINGTON, D.C., 1:15 A.M.

Brig. Gen. Lee Carrothers, deputy commander of the Army Chemical Corps, waited for the satellite conference call to be patched through. He had been awakened in his home in Mount Vernon, Virginia, by the duty officer at the Army Command Center and asked to come down to the Pentagon right away, with subject to be revealed upon arrival. Now the Command Center was setting up a conference call with Maj. Gen. Myer Waddell, commander of the U.S. Army Chemical Corps, who was presently in Stuttgart, Germany, on official travel. It would be 7:15 in Germany.

The third party in the conference call was going to be the Army deputy chief of staff for Operations, Plans, and Policy, Lt. Gen. Peter Roman. The three-star was currently airborne in an Army Learjet over the Pacific between San Francisco and Hawaii. Brigadier General Carrothers had a headache, which he knew was going to get worse before it got better.

"All stations, this is the Command Center. I am confirming a secure satellite link with three stations. I will go off-line when the third principal confirms. General Carrothers, sir?"

"Present."

"General Waddell, sir?"

"Present."

"And General Roman, sir?"

"I'm here. What's this all about, Myer?"

"Yes, sir, General," Waddell said. "We have a potentially major flap in the making. I'm going to let my deputy, Lee Carrothers, brief you, but basically, we may have some chemical weapons material missing."

"Sweet Jesus!"

Carrothers jumped in at that juncture and told the three-star what they knew so far, that they were not positive the material was missing but that the audit system had detected a possible problem and that the Tooele destruction facility was checking their end of it.

"So we don't actually *know* that some stuff is missing? Is that what you're telling me?"

"Yes, sir," Carrothers replied. "We're trying to be proactive here, General."

"When will we know?"

"Tooele will have to reinventory its receipt assets at the large-scale destruction facility. That will take at least twenty-four hours, because it will require a sight inventory of every cylinder, by serial number. And since the cylinders are no longer in their coffins, it will all have to be done MOPPed up. Full suits."

" 'Coffins'?"

General Waddell broke in. "That's Chemical Corps slang for the environmental containment systems. These cylinders aren't warheads. They're the containers used to fill warheads. And unlike our modern warheads, they're not binary-safe."

"Refresh me, Myer. CW is something I try to forget about."

"Yes, sir. American chemical weapons are designed to be safe. We use a binary design—that is, the warheads do not contain chemical weapons. They contain the two main ingredients for the weapon in question in two physically separated containers within the warhead. The warhead has to be fired, or subjected to the forces of being launched, or detonated, to rupture the internal containers. Once the projectile is spinning in flight, the two ingredients mix. From that mixing action comes the chemical weapon itself. That's what *binary-safe* means."

"And what you're telling me is that these cylinders are *not* binary-safe?"

"That's correct, sir. There was one weapon, which we retired a long time ago precisely because it was not safe, which used a high-speed aerosol-dispenser system slung under the belly of a jet aircraft. These cylinders were inserted in the dispenser pod, and then the dispersal mechanism was armed in flight. They contained the real stuff, not just constituents."

"And what hellish brew is in these missing cylinders?"

"Only one cylinder, General," Carrothers reminded him. "It's a substance called Wet Eye."

"With a name like that, I think that's all I want to know, General Carrothers," Roman said. "Okay, I assume the Chemical Corps is going balls-to-the-wall to find out if there really is a problem. I will inform the chief of staff. You two make sure that you get a lid clamped down hard at both Anniston and Tooele until Army headquarters can get a spin package put together. First indication that this stuff really *is* missing, you need to get back to Fort Fumble, Myer. You're going to be on the hook to brief the SecDef and maybe even the White House. I say again, that's *if* indeed a cylinder of this Wet Eye is really missing. And we all better hope and pray that it isn't. Keep me advised on developments. Roman off net."

There was long silence on the net, which Carrothers did not interrupt. General Waddell liked time to think before he made decisions.

"Lee, there's one more call I want you to make," Waddell said finally.

"Yes, sir?"

"First, let's make sure we really do have a problem. Those rail shipments are long and involved logistical processes, and it's entirely possible we'll all get to stand down shortly when they find a clerical error. But I want you to touch base with Fort Dietrick. Just to be safe. I just wish it wasn't Wet Eye. Anything but damned Wet Eye."

"Fort Dietrick, General? USAMRIID?"

"That's right. You're looking for a Col. Ambrose Fuller. He's an Army veterinarian, of all things, but he's my guy at Dietrick. He's smart and he's very discreet. Tell him what's happened, or what may have happened. He's not to *do* anything, and above all, he's not to *say* anything to anybody. I just want him aware of the problem."

"Got it, General."

"Okay, and remember, this little bombshell stays in-house, Chemical Corps eyes only, until we've figured out how to handle it. A mistake like this could finish the Chemical Corps forever. Make sure Anniston rolls up everyone who's been involved to date. Enlisted restricted to barracks. Officers restricted to quarters. No one running his yap. Understand, Lee? That's important."

"Yes, sir. Got it."

"Okay. Keep me advised by secure means. Waddell off net."

Carrothers pressed a key to alert the link operator they were finished, then hung up the handset. He looked at his watch. One twenty-five in the morning. No point in getting this Fuller guy up at this hour just to put his thinking cap on. He'd call him first thing tomorrow. Today, he realized. He called the Command Center duty officer and asked him for the number of the U.S. Army Medical Research Institute for Infectious Diseases, Fort Dietrick, Maryland. As he waited, he wondered why in the hell General Waddell would want a USAMRIID guy notified. Those people dealt in biologic toxins, not chemicals.

59

5

Stafford saw it on the morning news as he was getting dressed in his hotel room: a presumed propane gas explosion in southeast Atlanta. There were some long-range TV news shots of a smoldering crater and small knots of curious people milling around behind fluttering yellow police tape. Blackened debris littered the street and the sides of what looked like a railroad embankment at the end of the street. A couple of junked cars near the crater were still smoking. Spindly trees next to the house had been snapped off at midtrunk. The camera panned to the house next door, which had also been flattened. An ambulance was backed up to that house. A lime green fire truck was parked across the street, and two firemen were playing a desultory stream on the grass of the railroad embankment.

Stafford hadn't been paying a great deal of attention to it all until the announcer identified the house as belonging to a B. Lambry, reportedly a government worker at nearby Fort Gillem. It was not known if Lambry or anyone else had been in the house; the police and the county Arson Unit were still investigating. According to police, the blast had occurred just after two in the morning. An elderly man in the house next door had been severely injured when the wall facing Lambry's house had caved in.

Stafford paused in the delicate task of knotting his tie one-handed and stared at the television set. Well, now, he thought. B. Lambry. Wasn't that the guy that Weird Harold in search of 'munity had told him to find yesterday? Hey, maybe we have developments here. He finished dressing and placed an unsecure call to the DCIS office in Smyrna. Mr. Sparks wasn't in yet, he was told. He asked the secretary to have Sparks call him on a secure line at the administrative offices at Fort Gillem in one hour.

Sparks called right on time. Stafford closed the door to his office, although with its large glass window, the privacy afforded was minimal. They switched to secure.

"You called, Dave?"

"Yeah. Did you see the morning news? Item about a propane explosion in southeast Atlanta last night."

"Yeah, I think I did. Should I care?"

"You might," Stafford said. He saw Carson's secretary walk by, gawking at him as he talked into his computer. "The house belonged to a guy who worked here, a guy named Lambry." He told Sparks about his conversation with Dillard.

"Jesus, Dave, don't tell me you've got something going already."

"If I do, it's all feeling and no facts," Stafford said. "It's mostly the way people are acting at this place. I'm pretty sure the employees have figured out I'm no auditor, and also that they are not surprised that a cop is here. This hillbilly guy, Dillard, was dancing all around something."

"Any idea of what?"

"Not a clue. But I spoke to Carson when I got in this morning— he's the manager down here, remember? And he told me Lambry had quit unexpectedly a few days ago."

"Interesting. Was he in the house when it blew up?"

"Apparently not. House next door had one victim. But that's why I called: I need you to introduce me to whatever cops are working that scene. I'd like to talk to them."

"Okay, I'll make some calls. You want to go to the scene, or just talk to the people doing the investigation?"

"Either one. Their call."

There was a pause on the line. "Dave?"

"Yeah, Ray?" Stafford thought he knew what was coming next.

"You be careful now. Remember what you're really down here for. Don't go getting involved in a local crime, or stirring up the locals with conspiracy theories. You uncover something hinky at that DRMO, we give it to the Feebies, right?"

"Oh, absolutely," Stafford said. "It was just the coincidence, okay? Guy talks to me about Lambry, and then Lambry's house goes into orbit."

Sparks, not sounding entirely convinced, said he'd get back to him, and they hung up. Stafford went down the hall to get some coffee, then decided to walk across the tarmac to the feed-assembly warehouse. You find out something's going on at the DRMO, we give it to the Bureau. Don't make any damn waves, Stafford. You bet, Ray.

He walked through the steel doors to the demil feed-assembly room, where he found the same crew as yesterday, minus Corey Dillard, unloading forklifts. He had to wait until the two forklifts in the warehouse had backed out before anyone could hear anything. He approached the large black man Lambry had called Boss Hisley yesterday.

"I'm David Stafford from DLA," he said. "You Boss Hisley?"

"That's me," Hisley said. The other two men walked away toward the table with the coffeepot. "He'p you with somethin'?"

Carson had to tilt his head back to look Hisley in the eye. "Yeah. I understand from Mr. Carson that a guy named Lambry quit recently. Can you tell me about that?"

"Mr. Carson say he quit?"

"Yeah."

Hisley considered this for a moment. "Mr. Carson say he quit, then that's what he done."

"But you didn't know anything about it?"

Hisley shook his head. "He didn't quit on me, that what you askin'."

"Did you know that Lambry's house blew up last night?" Stafford said.

"Yeah, seen that," Hisley replied. Stafford could read absolutely nothing in Hisley's broad, impassive face.

"If something had happened to Lambry, would Mr. Carson maybe know about it?"

Hisley's eyes flashed briefly with some hidden knowledge. "Shit happens here in the DRMO, Carson's the man, know what I'm sayin'? Nice talkin' to you."

He wanted to ask Hisley if he knew where Lambry was now. But he knew if he pursued the matter with any further questions about the explosion, he would absolutely blow his cover as a DLA auditor. And he still didn't know if Lambry had even been in that house last night. He thanked Hisley and walked away, trying to decipher Hisley's cryptic comment about Carson.

Sparks got back to him thirty minutes later with a name and the number of the Arson Unit investigating the explosion at Lambry's house. He also reported that NCIC database had come up dry on Lambry.

62

Stafford contacted the team leader, a woman detective named Mary Haller, and she agreed to talk to him.

"I guess my first question is, Was this arson?"

"Too soon to tell," she said. "It was definitely a propane gas explosion, and it did what propane usually does—leveled the place."

"A leak? Pilot light in a stove or something like that?"

"Like I said, Mr. Stafford, this was propane. Propane pools on the floor until two things happen: It achieves between a nine and eleven percent mixture with air, and it finds a point of ignition. The vapor then ignites and blows everything up and out. Whatever's left burns with a very hot fire. We have a bunch of blackened concrete-block pilings surrounding a hole at the scene, and a neighborhood full of Kibbles 'N Bits. We're still rounding up all the identifiable pieces."

"No human remains?"

"Doesn't smell like it."

"Wow."

"Yeah, well, that's how we usually tell. There was a geezer next door who was blasted out of his bed when the east wall of his house went west. He's in the hospital with a concussion. We're waiting to interview him, but he's not conscious yet."

Stafford wondered what age she considered old. She sounded as if she was in her twenties, tops.

"Now, one for you," she said. "Is whatever you're working likely to surface a reason for someone to blow up this house deliberately?"

"No, or at least not yet. Look, I appreciate the courtesy of your talking to me, but I don't really even have anything going here yet. I talked to one Corey Dillard, here at the DRMO yesterday. He was sort of speaking in tongues, and I'm damned if I know what it was all about. My cover is that I'm supposed to be an auditor for the DLA. Anyway, he mentioned Lambry's name, said I ought to find Lambry. That's all I've got, which is to say, nothing. If there's a connection between my case and any of that, it's not visible yet."

"Well, if you make a connection, we'd appreciate knowing. We're going to have to go out there to Fort Gillem eventually to do some interviews."

"Fine. I'll generate some notes. Just remember, I'm supposed to be an auditor with the Defense Logistics Agency, not a DCIS guy. Only the manager here, a guy named Carson, knows I'm with DCIS."

"That's okay with us. We'll give you any further info if and when we have it, Mr. Stafford."

He thanked her and they hung up. Stafford wondered what to do next. He had told the arson investigator the truth: He didn't really have anything of substance going here at this DRMO, other than the small mystery of what Dillard had really wanted to tell him, and then the bizarre coincidence of what had happened to Lambry's house. But he couldn't just go around here making a big deal about Lambry; everyone in the DRMO would wonder what the hell he was doing, including Carson. And right now, Carson was becoming more interesting than Lambry.

■ WEDNESDAY, THE PENTAGON, WASHINGTON, D.C., 8:10 A.M.

Brig. Gen. Lee Carrothers hung up the secure phone gingerly, as if afraid it would explode in his hand. He had just spoken with Colonel Fuller at Fort Dietrick, and now his headache was back with a vengeance. Surprisingly, Colonel Fuller had not had much to say about the specific substances in the missing weapon, but he had been very clear about one thing: "If you guys've lost a can of Wet Eye, that's worth a Soviet-style 'lock up all the participants in a mental asylum for life, stonewall until the end of time' cover-up, General. Tell Myer Waddell I said that."

"That's really peachy, Colonel. Please remember that all the general wanted you to do was think about it, okay?"

"Trust me, General Carrothers: I'll be thinking of nothing else. Please call me later and tell me this is an exercise. Soon, okay?"

Carrothers rubbed his eyes and buzzed for more coffee. Colonels didn't normally talk like that to generals, but, what the hell, this guy was an Army vet. And he'd used General Waddell's first name. Carrothers had placed a call to General Waddell in Germany after talking to Fuller, and he was waiting for a call back. In the meantime, he called the commanding officer of the Tooele Army Depot in Utah to see how the sight inventory was coming. The CO told him they were conducting a destruction inventory match audit.

Carrothers exploded. That's what Anniston had done. What the situation needed now was a sight inventory, not another damned paper drill. "We know the paperwork is screwed up. What we need to know now is what you did actually receive in that shipment. Anniston doesn't have the shit anymore; *you* do. So go do the fucking sight inventory right fucking now. And I don't care if your people have to suit up in the

64

fucking noonday sun. Do it, and do it now!" The CO, properly chastened, would order a sight inventory immediately. Carrothers slammed down the phone. His clerk buzzed him on the intercom. General Waddell was on the secure line. This day gets better and better, he thought miserably as he reached for the phone.

■ WEDNESDAY, FORT GILLEM DRMO, ATLANTA, 8:15 A.M.

Carson watched through the venetian blinds as the forklifts brought some more flea-market stuff into the warehouse. He had gotten home at nearly four in the morning, but his wife, her face draped in a sleep mask over some kind of cold cream, had not even budged. What sleep he did get was fitful, and he was pretty sure he'd been visited by the dream again. He shivered.

He was surprised that he felt absolutely nothing about what he had done the night before. Not guilt, not concern for the old man next door, not fear of being caught, nothing at all. It was as if he had stepped over some psychological threshold back there when Lambry went into the demil machine. His fear in the airport, his apprehension about actually making this sale and getting his money—both were all gone. He didn't feel invincible exactly—that damn dream was kind of scary—but he felt stronger than he had felt before last night. Doing Lambry's house had been smart: The blast had reduced any traces of Lambry's previous life to flinders. He saw his reflection in the glass: Wendell Carson, master criminal. Well, if that's what it took to grab a million bucks, that's what it took.

Stafford could still be a problem, of course, but with Lambry truly out of the picture now, Stafford would be on a very cold trail. All Wendell Carson had to do now was tie off the loose ends of Lambry's quitting: a final paycheck, closing the personnel folder, and rearranging the work assignments. There would be local cops sniffing around, no doubt, after that explosion, but, surprisingly, Carson found he just wasn't worried about any of that. He needed to focus now on the physical turnover of the cylinder for the money, and on how to make sure he got the money with his skin intact.

He thought about the cylinder, sitting right here in his office. Maybe he needed a better place for it. He lived southwest of Atlanta, on five acres in a semirural area. Take it out there? If someone suspected him and came looking, either the Army or, for that matter, Tangent, they

would certainly search his office and his home. So it really should be better hidden, maybe somewhere out there in the DRMO warehouse complex. He almost wished he had one of those environmental containers—what did the army guys call them? Coffins? But they had all gone through demil.

He checked his door and then pushed the books apart to make sure the cylinder was still there. It looked even more lethal now without its protective plastic container. He sat back down and thought about where else to hide it. What was the old rule? When you really want to hide something, the best place is often right out in the open. One of the warehouses, he decided. He sat back down at his desk and doodled idly on his desk blotter. He saw the name Graniteville circled on the blotter. Another loose end there? Despite all his newfound confidence, the memory of that little episode in the airport was still able to tickle his hackles. Why had that girl looked at him that way? And why in the *hell* had he fainted?

He looked at his watch. A good time to take a walk through the warehouses, see what struck his fancy as a better hiding place. He took a deep breath. He was safer than he had been twenty-four hours ago. What had happened to Bud had really been an accident; hadn't he had tried every way to stop the belt? But what was done was done.

A million dollars. No more shitty little civil service job. No more sullen employees. No more skulking around for chump change with the auction scam. No more coming home to a crazy old woman whose nighttime mud packs would stroke out a vampire.

A new life. Very soon. With that kind of money, Wendell Carson could go anywhere, do anything. After everything that had happened, he had no other options: He had to complete the deal.

Stafford was about to go to lunch when Ray Sparks called him. "Got a message from the Washington office," Sparks reported. "Apparently some woman from Georgia called your number up there; said she needed to talk to you. Got a writing stick?"

Stafford wrote down the message and hung up. He studied the message on the pad: "Gwinette Warren. Calling from Graniteville, Georgia. Wanted to talk to Mr. Stafford. Please call this number."

Graniteville, he thought. Then he remembered. The woman in the airport. Carson and the girl. He reached for the phone but then thought better of it. This one might be better done from a phone outside of the

DRMO phone system. It wasn't that he suspected anyone of eavesdropping, but this call probably involved Mr. Wendell Carson of the shaky hands. Better to do this at his hotel.

Stafford made it to his room at five after one. He planned to talk to this lady, see what she wanted, and then go out to see Ray Sparks and the DCIS crew in Smyrna. He needed to make his courtesy call, and also to get his hands on a car phone. He called the woman's number, but she was not there. He left a message that he could be reached at his hotel number. She called back fifteen minutes later.

"This is Gwen Warren," she said. "Thank you for returning my call."

"No problem, Ms. Warren. I'm just glad you kept the card. Is this about the incident at the airport the other day? And I can put this call on my nickel if you'd like."

There was a moment of hesitation. "Can you possibly come see me, Mr. Stafford? Up here in Graniteville? This isn't something I want to discuss over the phone."

"I suppose I can, Ms. Warren. Can you give me a hint?"

Another hesitation. "It involves the girl who was with me in the airport. You said you were a federal investigator, is that correct?"

"Yes, ma'am, with the Defense Criminal Investigative Service."

"What is that, exactly?"

"A Department of Defense agency. That's the Pentagon, in media parlance. We investigate cases of possible fraud against the government."

"And why are you there in Atlanta?"

Whoa, wait a minute, he thought. That's my business. "Ms. Warren, maybe you're right. I think I should drive up to Graniteville, as you suggested. How about tomorrow? How much of a drive is it from Atlanta?"

"It's two and a half to three hours, depending on how fast you drive and road conditions in the mountains."

"Okay, that's doable. I'll probably wait until after morning rush hour. How's about noontime? Is there a motel there?"

"Yes, there is one motel. It's called the Mountain View. I'll make you a reservation. They can give you directions to the Willow Grove Home. I'll expect you around noon?"

"Okay, I'll be there," he said, writing the information down in his notebook. "And Ms. Warren, you sound somewhat anxious. Please don't be. If this involves a minor, let me assure you we can be very discreet and very careful."

"I'm glad to hear that, Mr. Stafford. You'll need to be both. Until tomorrow then. Good-bye."

He hung up the phone and sat back in his chair. Dave Stafford, master of discretion and care—now, there was a joke. Except this didn't sound like a joke. He thought back to what had happened at the airport. He had thought all along that there had been some interaction between that girl and Carson, and now this Gwen Warren had just confirmed that hunch. But what could it be? Obviously nothing to do with the DRMO. Some man-woman issue between this Warren woman and Carson? Looking at them, he would not have made that connection. She was a woman who appeared to be way beyond the likes of Wendell Carson—and David Stafford, more than likely. He shook his head and looked at his watch. It was time to take his chances with the Atlanta metro traffic and head out to beautiful downtown Smyrna, Georgia.

■■ WEDNESDAY, THE PENTAGON, WASHINGTON, D.C., 3:30 P.M.

Brigadier General Carrothers returned from the Pentagon Officers Athletic Club feeling somewhat better. His one hour workout had left his cheeks bright red when he walked back into his office. Nothing like a small war with the weights to burn off stress, he thought, and he had had plenty to burn off. Lee Carrothers was six four and extremely fit, having never lost the habits of physical training that had helped maintain the desired lean and mean Army officer image. He was a West Point graduate who had steered himself along the conventional career path from second lieutenant to brigadier in twenty-four fast years. He had a narrow hatchet-shaped face, white-blond, buzz-cut hair, a ruddy complexion, a prominently hooked nose, and bright blue eyes under almost white eyebrows. He'd been fortunate enough to marry a general's daughter, and thereafter he had alternated between specialty tours in the Chemical Corps and front-office aide and executive assistant jobs. Jealous colleagues who groused about Carrothers's early promotion said he'd done it all on his hawklike good looks and his wife's connections, but more than a few of them had discovered, often to their discomfiture, that Lee Carrothers was a great deal smarter than the average bear. His image as a lean and mean ambition machine was just icing on the cake.

It was assumed among his contemporaries in the Chemical Corps that he would be the next CG of the Chemical Corps.

The clerk in the front office handed him a message as he walked through the door. General Waddell was returning early from Europe. He would arrive at Andrews Air Force Base at 2300 tonight.

Incoming! Carrothers shouted mentally as he went into his office. The commanding general of the U.S. Army Chemical Corps had been predictably furious when he found out that precious hours had been wasted out in Utah doing another inventory audit. 'What part of sight inventory didn't those idiots understand?' he had roared over the satellite link. Good fornicating question, Carrothers thought. Waddell had asked about Fort Dietrick's reaction to the news, but Carrothers, unsure of what operators might be listening to the satellite call, had sidestepped that question. He's thinking about it, General, just like you told him to. Waddell caught on immediately and did not press the issue. Carrothers would brief Waddell on the colonel's advice about clamping the mother of all lids on this little mess when the general was in a better frame of mind. Yeah, like at 2300, after a seven-hour flight back from Germany. Shee-it.

He called Tooele for a status on the sight inventory. Twenty-five percent complete. Estimated time of completion, twenty-four hours. As the general was aware, these things were not all stored in one pile. Several underground bunkers had to be opened and safety-tested. Since the cylinders were no longer in coffins, they had to be individually un-stacked, serial numbers verified, end caps safety-checked, et cetera, et cetera. The general, Carrothers had replied, understood results, and he hoped that was abundantly clear to every swinging dick out there who wanted to keep his present rank and commissary privileges.

He called the commanding officer at Anniston. "Is everybody involved sequestered?" he asked. Everybody was, from the base ops officer down to all the clerks involved. "Anything stirring on the troops' grape-vine?"

"Not yet."

"Keep it that way. If in doubt, clamp harder. And do that audit again."

"Already doing it."

Anniston was conducting a sight inventory of their own, looking to see if there was an extra coffin lying around. "Good move," he said.

He hung up and reflected on the difference between the two commanding officers. Colonel Franklin at Anniston was obviously trying to think ahead of the problem; the CO at Tooele was behind the power curve. He rubbed his eyes. What should *you* be doing besides waiting for word, oh proactive one? he thought. You should be anticipating Waddell's questions, that's what. The general would be sitting on that airplane thinking up a hundred questions that would come rapid-fire as soon as he stepped off the transport. Carrothers called his clerk and asked him to hit the microfilm archives on Wet Eye. It wasn't what he wanted to do. He wanted to go out there to Tooele and kick ass to make things go faster, but he knew from experience that when the general wants it bad, he usually gets it bad. The good news was that they had managed to clamp a lid on this little fiasco until they could find out what had really happened. Wet Eye. His headache was coming back.

■ WEDNESDAY, FORT GILLEM DRMO, ATLANTA, 3:45 P.M.

Carson returned to his office and flopped down in his chair. He had found an almost-perfect hiding place for the cylinder—in the demil room, of all places. He had wandered all over the DRMO, ostensibly on a manager's walk-through, aware, as usual, that the walkie-talkies would be in action the moment he was between warehouses, alerting the next crew. He knew they sneeringly called him "Gwendell" behind his back. That was okay with him; his little walks had an effect analogous to that of the empty cop car parked behind a sign on the freeway. And, as he was fond of reminding them, they filled out time sheets. He could sign them or he could hold them, in which case no checks would be forthcoming, so it was Gwendell, sir, if you don't mind.

He had gone looking for a hiding place that was, first of all, safe. He couldn't put it in some of the gear waiting to be auctioned, because Murphy's Law would guarantee that it would be auctioned, and then he'd have some Bubba opening the thing at a flea market and depopulating Atlanta. He couldn't hide it out there among the dozens of dark nooks and crannies in the warehouses, because that was where a professional search team would start looking. If the Army found out the cylinder was missing, the DRMO would be one of the first places they would look, because this was where the coffins had ended up. The coffins, of course, had all been demiled. Could he prove that? With records, yes. One thousand environmental weapons containers received from the Anniston Army Weapons Depot in Alabama, after they had been returned to Anniston from the Army chemical weapons destruction facility

70

in Tooele, Utah. All marked for demil, no reutilization, no public access. Straight up Monster feed.

In fact, he had realized, the Army might be happy to hear that. With any luck, they might assume that if the cylinder had gone missing, it had probably been demiled with its coffin. Whatever the hell was in it would have been sucked into the Monster, unless it was an explosive gas of some kind. Then who knows what might have happened? In a twisted sense, Lambry's find may have prevented a real tragedy right here at the DRMO. Yeah, right. Nice try.

But if they discovered it was missing they would surely come looking, and depending on what was in that cylinder, they would come with some pretty sophisticated chemical weapons detection equipment. Now, obviously that cylinder wasn't leaking, or everyone around would have been flopping and twitching by now, but he knew enough about the packaging of special weapons to know that the Army might have put some kind of tracking device on or in that cylinder.

He had been drawn to the demil room more by a dread desire to revisit the scene of Lambry's demolition than from any expectation of finding a hiding place. He was still faintly amazed at himself, that he could be so calm and collected about that. He must have been more afraid of Bud than he had realized. Once in the demil room, which was inactive as the conveyors were being loaded next door, he had stared at the Monster for several minutes. Was there a way to hide the cylinder inside the Monster? Probably not. Behind the band-saw blades were several other lethal phases of destruction, all of which involved several meaningful moving parts. Beyond that were the chemical treatment phases, so that wouldn't work. But then he saw the steel rollers of the conveyor belt that fed the Monster. Steel cylinders, about four inches in diameter, spaced every three feet or so. They were partially obscured by the rubber of the belt and the expanded metal screens surrounding the Monster's maw.

Making sure no one was watching through the small window in the door between demil and feed assembly, he had walked over to the belt where it entered the safety screens and bent down to take a look. Just as he did so, the belt jumped into motion, startling him. He'd forgotten they were loading the belt in the next building. He bent down again. Inside the safety screens, where the belt turned down toward the floor and then back toward the other building, the rollers were spaced much closer, about eight inches apart. As he stared at the assembly, the belt stopped moving. He thought it might just be possible, if he could get the end cap off of one of those rollers. He'd have to take a better look tonight, when the run was finished and the place was empty, but the roller would make a very good hiding place.

The next physical problem would be the actual handover of the cylinder. He hadn't heard back from Tangent yet, but he knew that this was going to be a far different transaction from all the previous ones. Before, the "winning" bidder had simply come into the DRMO and picked up the stuff he'd bought at an ostensibly legal auction. That had been one of the advantages of the scam: Wendell Carson had never physically touched any of the things he had diverted to his client.

But this time might be different. He could visualize one of those drug deals in a dark parking lot where everybody had one hand on his gun and the other on either the money or the merchandise. Unlike the drug kingpins, Wendell Carson would not be accompanied by a phalanx of beefy guys with wraparound sunglasses and ponytails who sported MAC-10s, whereas Tangent might. So he was going to have to figure something out, something that gave *him* some advantages, like doing the transaction right here at the DRMO, where he knew the ground.

■■ WEDNESDAY, FORT GILLEM DRMO, ATLANTA, 11:15 P.M.

Carson knelt down by the safety screens encasing the conveyor belt and removed all the nuts holding the side screen onto its frame. He got the screen off, put it to one side, and sat back on his haunches. Tonight's demil shift had ended at eight-thirty, and he had waited for almost three hours before making his move. The first stage was to take a toolbox over to demil and get the screen off, and then see if he could get the end cap off one of the rollers.

It took him twenty minutes of huffing and puffing before he managed to pry the bearing assembly off of the third roller back from the feed aperture. He then measured the inside diameter of the roller: four inches. The cylinder, feeling warm in his sweaty palms, was about three inches in diameter, and not as long as the roller. This would work. He left everything in pieces and walked back over to his office. He was safe from video-camera surveillance, since all the security cameras except two were inside the warehouses. He had let himself into the security control room and turned the tarmac cameras off. There was never anything of high value stored out on the tarmac, just the flea-market stuff that was too big to sit on the shelves inside, but he didn't want any tapes showing him going into demil at this hour. The only thing he had to watch out for would be an MP car making its rounds. There were no windows in the demil building, so there would be no lights observable from the outside.

By midnight, he had the cylinder inside the roller and the entire assembly buttoned back up. He stood up, satisfied with his work. The only way anyone would ever find that thing would be if it came open, in which case he definitely would not want to be around for the happy occasion. It was time to go home. The next move was Tangent's. He looked at the silent maw of the demil machine for signs of what had happened to Lambry, but the blade bank gleamed back at him indifferently. As he walked out, he remembered to go back to Security and reenergize those two cameras. He also wondered, Was it just my hands, or was that cylinder getting warm?

■■■ WEDNESDAY, ANDREWS AIR FORCE BASE, WASHINGTON, D.C., 11:45 P.M.

The commanding general of the U.S. Army Chemical Corps dropped into the backseat of the sedan with a grunt and a sigh. He was very definitely not in conformance with the required physical image of the modern Army, and a week in Germany had not helped his weight problem. Carrothers got in on the left side, in deference to General Waddell's seniority. The official sedan drove off the terminal apron and headed for the main gate.

"Jesus, these cars keep getting smaller," Waddell complained. "Okay, Lee, where are we with that um, situation, at Anniston?"

Carrothers, eyeing the civilian driver, debriefed Waddell in oblique language. "The western unit is conducting a sight inventory. Should be done late tomorrow if there are no discrepancies, day after tomorrow if there is a discrepancy. The southern piece of it redid their paperwork, a sight inventory of the empty tombs, and came up with the same results."

"Let me get this straight: Isn't the audit done by the sending agency an audit of what the receiving agency end reports it received?"

It was late, and Carrothers had to think about that for a second. "Yes, sir. That's how they check on each other."

"And a sight inventory, on the other hand, physically checks to determine what's there that wasn't there before the last shipment."

"Yes, sir. And if that number does not equal what the southern people came up with, then we probably habeas a corpus."

"Wonderful," Waddell grunted. He was silent for a few minutes as the sedan merged onto the Beltway and headed for Alexandria, Virginia, where Waddell had a town house. "And everyone involved has been, um . . ."

"Yes, sir. Everyone."

"Good. That needs to be airtight. If either CO thinks he needs to make it more airtight, he has my permission. Whatever it takes."

"Yes, sir."

"And I want to see Ambrose Fuller tomorrow first thing. What's the buzz from the E-ring?"

"General Roman briefed the chief of staff. If the CSA went up his tape, I haven't heard about it. I've got his EA primed to give me a heads-up."

"Good. I suspect the CSA has *not* told our civilian masters yet."

The general was silent for the rest of the ride, until the sedan delivered him to his house. While the driver waited in the car, Carrothers got out and walked up to the front door with General Waddell, where he told him what Colonel Fuller had actually said. Waddell's face sagged.

"I knew it. Damn!" Waddell said. "Okay. We have to be proactive here, Lee. I want people to start thinking about where this thing may have wandered off to. I want a task force set up in my office. Like right now. I want Chemical Corps, intel guys, COMSEC guys, the works. But Army eyes only for now, okay? No outsiders. No JCS staffers. No goddamned civilians. If we have to tent this thing, I want people I can trust to keep their mouths shut. I couldn't say it in the car, but I got a call from the chief of staff."

"Yes, sir?"

"And he reminded me that all things chemical are in ill repute these days. The whole world wants chemical weapons just to go away, and, by association, the experts who feed and care for chemical weapons. That's us. The only hook we have to hang our professional hats on now is in the area of defense *against* chemical weapons. We're the pros. We know how. But if we lose one, we're not the pros; we're the assholes du jour. The Army Chemical Corps as we know and love it will be history."

"Yes, sir, I understand that," Carrothers said. He hesitated. "But what if we have indeed lost one?"

Waddell pursed his lips and looked out onto the car-cluttered street with its faux gas lamps fluttering historically in the night air. Then he looked back into Carrothers's eyes with all the force of his thirty-five years in the Army and said, "Lose a can of Wet Eye? That just cannot happen, General." Then he went inside.

74

6

If the motel was in Graniteville, Stafford concluded, it would necessarily have a mountain view. The entire town, what there was of it, had nothing but a mountain view, nestled as it was in a deep valley between three green-clad granite peaks. The town itself was small, consisting of one main drag that led the state road north into and around the courthouse square. All the side streets appeared to go for only a few blocks before running into one of the mountains.

He drove the white government Crown Vic carefully along the main street, which was lined with stores typical of small-town America: clothes, hardware, stationery and office supply, most complete with second-story false fronts. The traffic sign at the square directed drivers to circle the square to the right, yield to anyone coming from the left, and to continue all the way around to get to the granite quarry. From the square, there appeared to be three options: one north, one east, and a third, which led up to what looked like a quarry on one of the western slopes. The courthouse itself was a traditional Georgia landmark, red brick with lots of gingerbread, complete with a white clock tower and slant-in parking on three sides. The obligatory white marble soldier monument to the heroic Confederate dead, its back turned pointedly toward the perfidious North, leaned precariously on the eastern lawn of the courthouse.

Stafford drove all the way around the square twice, dodging pickup trucks and looking for signs for the motel. He finally took a chance on the road leading north up and out of town between the two highest hills. As he left the square, he picked up a cop car in his rearview mirror. He passed a large Baptist church, a closed-up diner called Huddle House, a dilapidated feed store, three vacant lots, and a lumberyard as he left the town square. As he crossed a deep ravine through which a mountain stream cascaded down towards the town, the motel appeared on his right hand side. The cop car stayed with him.

He pulled into the motel parking lot and shut the car down. There was a small Waffle House diner surrounded by pickup trucks in front of the motel. The motel itself was a single line of ten rooms that stretched back toward a creek, with the office on the end nearest the diner. The motel appeared to be at least fifty years old, but the place was clean, at least on the outside. A small red neon light in the office window proclaimed that there were indeed vacancies.

He got out and stretched. It had taken a little longer than he had expected to get to Graniteville, but a brilliantly sunny day and the north Georgia mountain scenery had been worth the drive. The air was fresh and cool after the hazy heat of Atlanta. He had called Carson's secretary and told her that he would be out for the day, but he had not told her where he was going. The cop car, something of an antique Ford Fairlane, complete with a bubblegum dome on top and a huge chromed spotlight on the driver's side, pulled into the diner parking row. The lettering on the side of the car proclaimed LONGSTREET COUNTY SHERIFF'S DEPARTMENT.

Stafford got out, put his suit jacket on, and reached back into his car for his briefcase and an overnight bag. Because of his arm, he had to pull them out one at a time. When he straightened back up, a large uniformed man was approaching him. He wore a dove gray Stetson hat and had huge black eyebrows over down-sloping dark, almost black eyes, whitish gray sideburns, and a large black handlebar mustache that reminded Stafford of pictures of Wyatt Earp. He wore a tan uniform shirt and trousers, brown boots, and a large chrome-plated pistol on his right hip. The expression on his face seemed generally friendly, for which Stafford was suddenly glad.

"Good day, Mr. Stafford. I'm Sheriff John Lee Warren. Welcome to Graniteville, suh."

Stafford returned the greeting, offering his left hand, which caused an awkward moment, but then the sheriff took it in his own right hand.

He wondered how the sheriff knew his name. The sheriff anticipated his question. "Mrs. Warren told me you'd be comin' up from the city. Asked if I might show you out to Willow Grove."

"I'd appreciate that, Sheriff. Should I call Mrs. Warren first?"

"Oh, I don't think so, Mr. Stafford," the sheriff replied. He had a deep, authoritative voice. "But you might want to grab a bite; the food here isn't bad. If you'd care to join me?"

"My pleasure, Sheriff," Stafford said. He put his bags back in his car, locked the doors, and followed the sheriff over to the diner. Propriety required he tell the sheriff why he was here. He hadn't exactly been sneaking into town, not with the big white government sedan. But he knew about the power Georgia county sheriffs exerted within their rural fiefdoms, and he guessed that up here in the mountains, that power was not trivial. He also wondered about the name Warren.

"What happened to the arm?" the sheriff asked as they entered the diner.

"Zigged when I should have zagged," Stafford said. "Caught a nine through the humerus. I'm working on getting it back again."

The Waffle House was full of locals, but the sheriff walked confidently to a back corner table, which was evidently his for the lunch hour. A waitress followed them back. He invited Stafford to order and told the waitress he'd have his usual. When she left, he gave Stafford an expansive look and asked what might be bringing a federal officer to Graniteville. He had a southern accent, but it was not very pronounced.

"Not quite sure myself, Sheriff," Stafford replied. "I got a call from a Ms. Gwen Warren that she would like to talk to me, so here I am."

"And how might that lady know you, suh?" The sheriff's expression remained amiable, but those dark eyes never wavered. Stafford was aware that people in the diner, mostly men, were giving the two of them covert glances.

Stafford explained a little bit about the DCIS, then briefly described the incident at the airport. "I'm following up on an ongoing investigation involving possible fraud at one of the Atlanta military bases. I gave her my card that day in the airport. Her call came as a surprise, frankly, but she didn't want to discuss it over the phone, so here I am. Oh, and here are my credentials."

The sheriff examined his ID and then handed it back. "Thank you, suh. I knew about the FBI, the CIA, the ATF, and the DEA. I must admit that DCIS is a new one to me. And I apologize for all the questions, but sometimes we have federal officers who come through and, uh . . ."

"I understand, Sheriff. It's my agency's policy to keep local law-enforcement officials informed anytime we operate off the federal reservation. I would have checked in with you in any event, except that I still don't know what this is about."

The sheriff nodded as the waitress brought Stafford his hamburger. The sheriff had a platter of scrambled eggs, bacon, grits, biscuits, and hash browns. The sheriff fell to his late breakfast without further conversation, so Stafford did the same. The diner was noisy, with waitresses calling in raucous orders in the code peculiar to Waffle House restaurants throughout the South, acknowledged by ribald comments from the cook amid the clash and clatter of crockery from behind the counter. When they had finished, the waitress brought them both a cup of hot black coffee without their asking, then cleared the plates away.

"So, Mr. Stafford," the sheriff began. "You think mebbe Mrs. Warren knew this man—what was his name, Carson?"

"I don't know, Sheriff," Stafford replied. "Well, actually, when Carson went down, he appeared to be engaged in a staring match with a young girl who was with Mrs. Warren."

The sheriff paused with his coffee mug in the air and gave Stafford a searching look. "Can you describe the girl, suh?"

Stafford did, and the sheriff began to nod his head slowly. "That there would be Jessamine," he said. "She's one of the children at Willow Grove."

"Jessamine? And Willow Grove is what, an orphanage?"

The sheriff nodded again. "They're not called that in Georgia anymore, of course. *Orphanage* is no longer politically correct. Now they're group homes. State-licensed, inspected, and, to a degree, funded. Mrs. Warren is the director."

"Jessamine," Stafford said. "Interesting name."

The sheriff gave him a speculative look. "A jessamine is an Appalachian flower," he said. "And, yes, she is an interesting child. A very interesting child. And I suspect that's what Mrs. Warren wants to talk to you about, but I think we should let her do that. When you're finished, I'll show you the way up there. The motel will keep you a room."

They left the diner after paying at the register, and Stafford followed the sheriff in his own car. They drove back into the town center, went around the square, and headed out the eastern road. They crossed what appeared to be that same deep creek that ran by the motel, then began to climb through a narrow canyon, flanked on either side by sloping slabs of dynamited rock. After a few minutes, a small plateau opened up on the left, revealing a large two-story farmhouse set back about two hundred feet from the road. The house was an old Victorian with screened porches surrounding all four sides on both floors and had a dark green copper roof. A landscaped driveway led up from the road to a graveled circle at the front of the house. On the left was a large pond surrounded by a dense stand of willow trees; on the right was an orderly grove of old pecan trees. There was a sloping open field with protruding rock ledges to its right. The pond dam, which overlooked the road, was partially obscured by the willows at the lower-left side of the property. A small creek flowed under the road from a deep pool at its base. There was a rambling white picket fence running from the corner of the pond across the front of the property, with drooping double wooden gates at the driveway. There appeared to be horse paddocks and outbuildings behind the main house, although Stafford did not see any horses in the fields. A tree-covered mountain slope on the opposite side of the road loomed close above the road, and the fields behind the house were shaded by an even larger hill. The pastures behind the house occupied what little flat land there was on the property.

The sheriff turned in at the drive, drove straight up to the house, and parked. Stafford followed, parking off to one side. The sheriff went up onto the front porch and rang a bell. Stafford waited on the steps until the door opened, and the woman from the airport greeted them. She was wearing a gray dress and had a light sweater draped over her shoulders. She appeared to be perfectly composed, except that Stafford noticed that she was gripping the edges of the sweater with the fingers of her right hand.

"Gwen, this is Mr. Stafford from Washington," the sheriff said. "We had lunch down at the Waffle House. Had us a little chat." He paused for a second, as if suddenly lost for words. Stafford noticed that some of the sheriff's authority seemed to have deserted him. "Well, I guess I'll leave y'all to your business, then," he finished.

"Thank you, John Lee," the woman murmured, dismissing him with a brief smile as she opened the screen door for Stafford to enter. She did not offer to shake hands, sparing Stafford the embarrassment of the left-handed dance. The sheriff nodded once at Stafford and went back to his car. She looked after John Lee Warren for a moment, long enough to give him a parting wave, which gave Stafford a moment to examine her. She was indeed tall, almost exactly his own height, but he was fascinated by her face. In profile, she reminded him of a Roman cameo: upswept hair, pronounced high cheekbones framing extraordinary green eyes, full, slightly parted lips. Her expression was serene, almost regal, enhanced by the composure of a woman who knows she is attractive. She appeared to be in her early forties, and she had an attractive figure, which her workaday clothes did little to flatter. When he finally realized she was looking back at him, her eyes held the barest hint of a smile. He felt himself blushing a little.

"Shall we go inside, Mr. Stafford?"

■ THURSDAY, FORT GILLEM DRMO, ATLANTA, 12:15 P.M.

At the agreed time, Carson placed a call to Tangent at the 800 number.

"This is Tangent."

"Carson."

"Right. We are ready to proceed."

Carson stopped to think out what he was going to say. An 800 number from a pay phone would be hard to tap and trace, but not impossible. They both understood that it was prudent to speak somewhat in code.

"All right," Carson replied. "Do you have a proposed date?"

"We do. This coming Sunday. Time at your convenience."

"That'll work. How about here at the DRMO? Say after nine P.M.?"

This time it was Tangent who hesitated. "I don't know if that will work. We were thinking somewhere off federal property."

Dammit, Carson thought. "But here in Atlanta?"

"Oh, yes. Our pickup team is prepared to go anywhere you want in Atlanta. Within reason, of course."

Pickup team. An image of the drug deal in a parking lot flashed through his mind again. "All right," he said. "But I was proposing here at the DRMO so that the item doesn't have to be moved. For obvious reasons, I should think."

Another hesitation. "Yes. We understand. Let me speak to my principals. How do you want the payment?"

"In cash."

"That's available. But you might want to think about other forms of value. That amount in cash is a lot of paper. Don't mistake me—we can and will do that. But there are other possible modalities."

"Such as?"

"Such as diamonds. Purchased by us from a jeweler of your choice. He authenticates their value for you and holds them as trusted agent. We get the item; it's what you say it is, you go get the diamonds. Just as good as cash, if not better. And much easier to conceal. We're talking twenty top-quality stones."

Carson knew absolutely nothing about diamonds. "Let me think about that," he said. "I'm . . . I'm nervous about all this. This is a lot of money."

"I understand."

"I mean, everything up to now has been some cash in an envelope. Money by mail. But this—"

"I understand. For a million, you're afraid we might stiff you. But consider this: We stiff you, you can always go public. Yes, you'd be in trouble, but if it got out that there was a cylinder of this stuff loose in the arms market, we'd be unable to sell it. It would become a useless, dangerous liability. Surely you understand that we're going to make more than we're paying you for this thing. I'll be honest with you: What you're getting is the ultimate client's deposit money, okay? But it's not our money, so we have no motive to mess around with this deal. More importantly, the whole thing has to remain secret. Optimally, the Army won't even know it's missing, and no one else can know it's moving through clandestine commercial channels. That's also your protection."

"Yes, I suppose," Carson said, not wanting even to mention the obvious: They could take the cylinder and kill him, and maintain their precious secrecy. Tangent seemed to read his thoughts.

"And you could always preposition something that could be released to the public in the event something happened to you. We're assuming you will have done that. Look, Carson, we've been doing business for a long time. Good business. Smart business. Low-level, intermittent, nothing to attract auditors. Yes, this is a lot of money. But it's potentially a hell of score for us, too. And we know this is a onetime deal. Hell, we could both retire, you know? So we have no motivation to screw around here. You know you can't move it by yourself. You can't even destroy it. Where would you dispose of something like that?"

"That's true." Actually, that isn't true, he thought. There's always the Monster. The real question is, Why would I ever *want* to destroy it?

"So think about those payment terms, and get back to me in, say, twenty-four hours. We'll evaluate the DRMO as the place to do the deed. Okay?"

"Okay."

"Now, second item—Stafford. Our sources tell us he is who he says he is, but the real reason he's down there has very little to do with any auction scams or even with DRMOs."

"That sounds like good news."

"It is. He's been shit-canned. Thrown out of Washington. He's a damned whistle-blower. Got some Senior Executive Service guy in the DCIS up on charges, and then got a senior FBI guy in the shit, too. Now he's a pariah in the DCIS. He may make it sound like he's on some big-deal case, but he isn't. We'll need to be circumspect, of course, but our information is that he's not a player."

"That is good news."

"Yes, we think so. This is a guy whose world is imploding. His wife left him when all the shit started over the whistle-blowing. Divorced his sorry ass and ran off with some Air Force colonel. And in the middle of that, he was getting gas one night in some minimart. Unbeknownst to him, two of Washington's upstanding citizens were doing a smash-and-grab. He took a stray round in the arm."

"Yeah, that's him; he's basically one-armed. Keeps his right hand in his suit pocket all the time."

"Right, that's the guy, then. He supposedly started drinking big-time, but our source wasn't sure if he was still on the sauce. Hell, after all that, I'd be drinking like a fish. Anyway, be polite, bury him in cooperation and bureaucratic bullshit, but let's proceed. I've gotta go. Let's talk same time tomorrow, okay? Think about how we're going to do this thing."

"Okay," Carson said, feeling much better already.

"Here's the new eight hundred number," Tangent said.

Carson wrote it down, hung up, and walked back to his car. Everything Tangent had said made sense, and it confirmed his own judgment about Stafford. He could forget Investigator Stafford. Truth was, it wasn't Stafford he was worried about; it was Tangent and that royal "we" he used all the time. He realized now that he knew absolutely nothing about Tangent other than a constantly changing 800 number and his voice. And several years of reliable cash, he reminded himself.

But this deal was for a million dollars, which upped the stakes considerably. So now he had to think in detail about how to do it. As he left the pay phone, he felt a return of that fluttery feeling, a sense that what he was up to was perhaps getting away from him. By the time he got back to his office, his secretary had returned from lunch. He asked her where Mr. Stafford was. She said he had left a message that he would be out for the day. Back tomorrow afternoon. He thought about that. Now what was that guy up to? On the other hand, he thought, why should I give a shit?

General Waddell shut the door behind them as he escorted Colonel Fuller into his private office. They had just come from the first meeting of the newly formed Security Working Group. Carrothers had come up with the name, saying they needed something that would point directly away from the real focus of the task force. Colonel Fuller, an old friend of General Waddell, had been appointed chairman of the task force.

"Well, Myer," Fuller said. "This is a real mess."

"Tell me something I don't know, Ambrose."

Fuller eyed the general for a moment. "Okay, I will," he said. "Being probably the only ex–biological weaponeer still on active duty, I'll tell you something no one else knows. Not those smart young officers out there, nor anyone at Fort Dietrick, either."

Waddell just stared at him. The reports in from Tooele and Anniston were pointing more and more toward the distinct probability that a cylinder of Wet Eye was missing. None of the bright young men at the meeting had had the first idea of what to do next, including his deputy.

"Wet Eye is not entirely a *chemical* weapon," Fuller said. "To be succinct, it's a hybrid."

Waddell leaned forward, putting his elbows on his desk and resting his head in his hands. He peered over the tips of his fingers at Fuller. "I don't think I want to hear this, Ambrose."

"Somebody has to hear it, Myer. Might as well be you, seeing as you're the proud owner of this developing shit cyclone."

"Okay, lay it on me."

"Wet Eye is a hybrid weapon. The only one developed under this great nation's *biological,* not chemical, weapons program, before Tricky Dicky shut the BW program down back in 1968. It is a chemical weapon, but it has a biological constituent, a very special pathogen that prospers in a toxic chemical soup. It's a one-two punch: The chemical constituent disables the victim; the pathogen then does some serious physiological damage."

"Specifically?"

"It eats the eye. It literally propagates a bacterial chain reaction that consumes the human eyeball. The chemical creates the disabling pathology that gives this stuff its name, a wet-looking, bleary, teary, swollen eyeball that can no longer focus—hence, Wet Eye. The pathogen then consumes the eyeball tissue all the way back to the optic nerve root."

"Great Christ," Waddell muttered.

"Yes. Strategically, it was a hell of a weapon—instead of killing, it blinds. The enemy is presented not with corpses, which they can ignore in the heat of battle, but with mega casualties that overwhelm their medical facilities, not to mention gutting their capacity to fight."

"Great Christ," Waddell said again.

"Indeed. But there's more. I went back into the BW archives to see when this stuff was developed and tested. Found out something interesting. We didn't develop this stuff. The Russians did."

"Somehow that makes me feel better," Waddell said.

"Hold that thought, General," Fuller replied with an ironic smile. "Apparently the CIA acquired this substance when a defector came over from the other side. He brought with him a film clip. I've had it copied into video format. I have to warn you—this is pretty gory stuff. The Russians used humans for the test."

"Humans?"

Fuller nodded. "Probably residents of the Gulag. This film goes back to the late fifties. But I wasn't sure this should be seen by those men out there in the working group."

"Okay, Ambrose," Waddell said with a grimace. "Roll that pogue."

Fuller put the videocassette into the VCR and adjusted the controls. A grainy black-and-white film without sound came on the screen. The scene showed what looked like a dirt prison yard, complete with guard towers and high barbed-wire fences, the bottom half of which were clearly studded with electrical insulators made of black glass. Beyond the prison yard, there was only a dense, dark forest. The film had obviously been shot from one of the guard towers, and the barrel of a machine gun protruded into the frame, somewhat out of focus. In the center of the yard, thirty disheveled prisoners sat on the ground with their hands in their laps. Most were staring down at the ground, with only a few looking up at the camera. They were dressed in ragged shirts and pants, and their heads were shaved clean. They were not quite close enough for their expressions to be visible.

At first, nothing happened. Then there was movement on the other guard towers, and the guards could be seen stepping back inside the huts and closing their doors. The machine-gun barrel moved a couple of times, pointing down into the compound. There was an awkward jump cut to a close-up. Suddenly, the prisoners began grabbing at their faces. Some rolled down onto the ground, others got up, and still others began writhing in place. All of them were grabbing at their faces, and then at their eyes. The shot jumped again, showing individual faces; the prisoners were screaming soundlessly and rolling around in the dirt, some holding their eyes, others clawing at theirs. The scene finally focused on one man who had stood up, backing blindly toward the fence. He kept clasping his hands to his face and then bringing them forward, as if to see what was on them. Watching a close-up of the man's face, Waddell gasped. The man's eyes were gone. In their place were two empty sockets, blood streaming down the man's face even as he smeared it all over himself while attempting to feel his eyes. He kept backing up until he hit the wires, which blasted him back out into the yard with an arc and a puff of white smoke. He fell headlong to the ground and did not move, a pool of fluids spreading out around his face in the mud.

The victims were usually moving too much for individual faces to be discernible. When certain faces did come into focus, they were all the same, however. There were two gaping black holes where their eyes had been, from which blood and fluids covered their faces like some deadly aboriginal war paint. Fuller shut off the video.

"There's more," he said. "But you get the picture, I think."

"Jesus H. Christ!" Waddell said. "Reagan was right. The Russians *were* the evil empire."

"Were?" Fuller said. "What makes you think they've gotten rid of this stuff?"

Waddell sighed and rubbed his eyes, then realized what he was doing and got up and walked over to the window. "Put what we've just seen in technical context, Ambrose. How dangerous is a single cylinder of Wet Eye?"

Fuller dropped the VCR remote onto the table. "The truthful answer is that I don't know," he replied. "It's not a particularly stable brew. It's temperature-sensitive. It has to be stored in special environmental containers. There are indications—not proof, mind you, but indications—that the pathogen is capable of mutating if not maintained under those specified conditions. Now unfortunately, these were statistical projections, as opposed to facts based on lab evidence."

"We didn't test it?"

"We never tested it. Not after seeing that film. In fact, a few years after we synthesized it, the program was terminated, because we could never be sure of what might going on in the cylinders. That's one of the reasons the BW division didn't make much of this stuff."

"One of the reasons?"

"The other reason, of course, was that it wasn't binary-safe."

"Ah, right. So it was undiluted demon spawn right there in the can. But I thought we destroyed all that biologic shit when the program folded."

"I love the way the Chemical Corps denigrates biological weapons," Fuller said with a wary smile. "As if chemical weapons were somehow a more wholesome proposition."

"Cut the shit, Ambrose. We're in trouble here." Waddell's tone was more that of a major general than friend.

"Yes, sir, we are. Sorry, I guess I've been in this business too damn long. To answer your question, yes, *almost* all of the biologics were destroyed. But the biological weapons destruction facility was originally at Pine Bluff, in Arkansas. Wet Eye was stored at Anniston, Alabama. Nothing happened for a few years, but then when the Army got around to the Wet Eye arsenal, it had to get permission to move it. You know, the Environmental Protection Agency, the Centers for Disease Control and Prevention, the Department of Transportation, like that. When they got a look at what it was, they all said no, naturally. Since the Army couldn't get permission to move it, one thousand cylinders of Wet Eye just sat there in the tombs at Anniston until this year, when this country finally ratified the Chemical Weapons Treaty."

"I don't remember going after permission to move this stuff," Waddell said.

"I asked the Army international-law types about that. It seems your JCS reps to the CW Convention put language in about five years ago, stating that unannounced movement of chemical munitions for the purposes of *destruction* was authorized. Since that language is now in a treaty, and since treaties supersede national laws, your people did not have to ask permission. They just shipped it."

"Wow. And when we finally shipped them, we lost one."

"So it would appear. But I guess my point is that we have even more reason to find it quickly, because if it isn't in its coffin, it might be changing into something a lot worse than Wet Eye."

"Is that possible? Jesus. This is awful."

"Well, I'm going to have the group do some discreet checking. The cylinders purportedly were taken out of their coffins and put into tombs awaiting destruction at the contained furnace facility at Tooele. If it had been my call, the cylinders would never have been separated from their coffins."

"Why in hell were they?"

"You're going to love it. Federal regulations, this time covering surplus, reusable Defense Department material. Remember all that 'Fleecing of America' TV coverage last year on the Defense Logistics Agency's huge spare-parts inventory? Well, now the Defense Department is required by Congress to offer *any* reusable thing it declares surplus to the DRMO system. The rules go so far as to state that any nontoxic or nonhazardous material associated even with the chemical weapons program has to be destroyed in the DRMO demil process."

"That's crazy. The coffins could have been destroyed right there at Tooele!"

"Left hand, regulate the right hand. Yes, sir, they certainly could have. I suspect this rule probably had more to do with sustaining work for the DRMOs than with the CW program. Anyway, the empty coffins were then all shipped from Tooele back to Anniston, which, in turn, consigned them to the nearest DRMO, which is in Georgia, we think. Being CW-related material, they would have been earmarked to go directly to demil, of course. I'm not sure how the demil process works, but if you approve, the Security Working Group is going to trace them."

"If I approve?"

"As soon as Headquarters U.S. Army starts asking questions about a shipment of CW containers, wouldn't you expect a buzz? I didn't want to do anything until we've thought through the risk of public disclosure. Was I right?"

Waddell rubbed his face with his hands and nodded. "Yes, of course you were. Especially considering this business about the biological component." Waddell returned to his desk before continuing. "This aspect, I think, we should keep to ourselves for the time being."

"Really, General?"

"Yes. The group doesn't need to know about the biologic angle in order to find it."

"And General Carrothers?"

"Same argument. This is a need-to-know issue right now."

Fuller just looked at him for a moment, but Waddell wouldn't look at him. Then Fuller had an idea. "I think I need to turn some of my people on to a simulation drill," he said. "See if we can determine or predict what might be happening in a cylinder of Wet Eye living outside of its coffin."

"Okay," Waddell replied distractedly. "But surely if someone at a

DRMO found something in a CW container, wouldn't we have been notified?"

"You're assuming that anyone at a DRMO would open a CW environmental container. I know I wouldn't. Look, if we're real, real lucky, Myer, and the demil process is a totally contained process, we can maybe make the case here that the cylinder must have been destroyed. If it was lost, it was in one of those coffins. All the coffins have probably been destroyed by now. Shit on us for letting one get loose, but everyone can relax now, because it most likely went through a contained demil process."

Waddell sat back in his chair. This was the first ray of hope he had seen since this crisis had begun. It would depend on the DRMO, of course, but Fuller was right: If they could certify that a batch of *containers* had been shipped from Utah, the same number as had been shipped originally from Anniston, and assuming that no one at the DRMO had opened them, just sent them directly to a closed destruction process, then the logical assumption was that anything in the containers would also have been destroyed, assuming it was a contained process, as Fuller had pointed out. Lots of assumptions there, he thought. He blotted out a quick vision of a dozen civilian workers streaming out of a building somewhere with bleeding sockets where their eyes had been. He looked over at Fuller, who was watching him work it out.

"Which DRMO in Georgia, exactly?" Waddell asked.

■■ THURSDAY, WILLOW GROVE HOME, GRANITEVILLE, GEORGIA, 1:15 P.M.

Gwinette Warren led Stafford across the large screened porch and through a formal entryway. The ceilings inside were at least fourteen feet high, and the interior was cool, somewhat dark, and smelled of crayons. The front doorway opened into a main hallway, with a large airy parlor room on the left that had been converted into a classroom for small children. The double doors to what should have been its twin on the right were closed. A staircase rose up the left side of the hall to the second floor. Stafford wondered where the children were, but Mrs. Warren walked straight back into an expansive well-lighted kitchen area, and then she turned right into an office, where she invited Stafford to sit down.

The office was long and somewhat narrow, reflecting its antecedent as the kitchen pantry. There was a desk near the single window and high bookshelves down one of the long sides. The opposite wall had several framed academic certificates, as well as what looked like a collection of family pictures. A large white PC sat to one side of the desk, and behind and to the left of the desk, there was an alcove crowded with other office equipment. In front of the desk were two upholstered chairs, and behind them a small conference table. She sat across from him in one of the upholstered chairs and crossed her slim legs.

Stafford found himself distracted by this woman. He secretly wanted another moment to examine her face, but he forced himself to get back to business. "Well, Mrs. Warren, I believe you called me."

"Yes, I did," she said. Her voice was husky, as he had noticed before, and her diction was unusually precise, with only the barest trace of a Georgia accent. "Before we begin, I'd appreciate it if you would explain what you are, Mr. Stafford. I'm not familiar with your organization." Her gaze was direct, but if she was aware of his interest in her as a woman, she gave no sign of it.

Stafford proffered his credentials, which she dutifully examined. He briefly explained the mission of the DCIS, and why he was in Atlanta. "I'm assuming your call has something to do with what happened in the airport that day?"

She gave him a long, level look before replying. In the subdued lighting of her office, her enormous green eyes were the color of jade.

"Yes, Mr. Stafford, it does," she said. "I'm not sure where to begin with this. Perhaps I ought to tell you about Willow Grove School first."

"This is a school? I thought the sheriff said it was a home."

"It's both, but he's right. It's first and foremost a group home, what used to be called an 'orphanage.' This house has been in my father's family for a long time. My father was a doctor, and my mother was a schoolteacher here in Graniteville. This place was called Willow Grove Farm back when I was born here. I came back to it permanently almost ten years ago, when I was divorced. It was my father's idea, originally, to start an orphanage."

"How many kids do you have here, Mrs. Warren?"

"Now only six. We're licensed for eight. That's fairly typical of group homes in Georgia. Few of them are very large. We have five youngsters and Jessamine, who is a teenager."

"That's a most unusual name, Mrs. Warren," Stafford said. "The sheriff seemed to know her."

"We call her Jess."

"And Warren? That's also the sheriff's name."

"Yes, Mr. Stafford." She was giving him that faintly challenging look again. "John Lee and I were married, after I came back to Graniteville from the university. We're divorced now, but it's—what's the word? Amicable? It's difficult to be anything else in a town and county as small as this."

"Especially if he's the sheriff," Stafford said, trying to lighten it up a little.

She regarded him thoughtfully for a moment, as if still trying to decide whether or not to trust him with something. He heard noises from upstairs.

"Yes," she said. "I suppose that's true."

"And where do these kids come from?" he asked.

"The north Georgia mountains, primarily. The process begins when the state has taken custody. These are basically normal kids who've been abused or neglected or even abandoned by their parents. The situations are usually bad enough that they're never going back home."

"So you don't work with autistics, or things like that?"

Her expression changed to dismay. " 'Things'? Autistics aren't 'things,' Mr. Stafford."

"Sorry, I didn't mean the kids were things. I meant conditions such as autism, Down's syndrome, problems like that." He concluded that she must be pretty nervous to have snapped at him like that.

"No. We're not equipped to deal with the special cases. And the school part of it is a supplementary schooling. We mainstream our kids as quickly as possible once we can determine a grade age for them. But most of them need a great deal of remedial work, both academic and emotional, as you might imagine."

There were definitely noises coming from upstairs. "Naptime is over," she said, glancing up at the ceiling. "Mrs. Benning will be bringing them down soon. The littles have their lessons in the morning, then lunch, then naptime. In the afternoon we usually do a group project with the farm animals out in the barn."

"And Jessamine?"

"She's in public school." She rose. "Why don't I give you a tour?"

"Sure. But Mrs. Warren? Then you'll tell me what this is all about?"

She eyed him warily. "If I think I can trust you, yes, I will." She paused at the doorway, standing in a way that revealed the fullness of her figure. "That's perhaps unfair," she said. "Let me rephrase: If I think you can handle something that requires extreme sensitivity and discre-

90

tion, and not act like some government cowboy closing in on Ruby Ridge, yes. I know that's perhaps impolite, but I don't know you, and you do come from Washington."

Stafford, taken aback by her vehemence, managed a game smile. "And neither of those things much recommends me, I take it."

She did not return the smile. "That's correct, Mr. Stafford. You're in the north Georgia mountains now. People here have a low regard for Washington and all its works."

Stafford nodded. "In my experience, Mrs. Warren, that's a sentiment shared by more than a few people, but I am a federal officer. My job is to ferret out fraud against the government, fraud committed by government employees, for the most part. In my small way, I serve the taxpayers. None of us in federal law enforcement, however, ever expects to mitigate the larger frauds perpetrated by the government."

She detected the exasperation in his voice. "I apologize if I've hurt your feelings, Mr. Stafford. But this matter involves a young girl who's been through some very difficult times. I suppose what I'm saying is, I need to take your measure before I proceed with this. Please be patient with me, and I think you'll understand."

He felt like telling her to knock herself out; he had nothing else to do with his afternoon. And yet her concern seemed genuine. She hadn't asked him up here just to rail against the federal government and all its minions. Besides, she was interesting. He wanted to know more about her, the home, and what she was doing here. "As you wish, Mrs. Warren," he said. "How about that tour?"

She took him through the lower floor of the house, showing him the classroom and the dining area, which was really just one big table rigged for small children in the kitchen area. There were play areas out on the left-hand porch, and a small playground outside, which he had not noticed when he arrived.

"What's in there?" he asked, pointing to the closed double doors to the right of the main hall.

"That's where I live, Mr. Stafford. I have a small suite of rooms on the ground floor, and that side of the porch has been blocked off."

He nodded without comment. She moved with unusual grace, and he found himself staring at the back of her neck as she turned away, the glimpse of smooth white skin beneath all that luxurious black hair stirring him. At that moment a chattering group of children came flying down the main staircase, followed by an older woman who was telling them to walk, not run. They skidded to a stop, piling on top of one another on the last step when they saw Stafford. There were three boys and two girls, all somewhere between four and seven years old. Mrs. Warren made introductions.

"Kids, this is Mr. Stafford. He's a federal investigator from Washington, D.C. Mr. Stafford, these are the kids. We use family nicknames here."

She pointed in turn to each of the three boys. "That's Crash, that's Hollywood, and that's No-No." She then turned to the two girls, both of whom were trying to hide behind the boy known as Crash. "That is Too, on the left, and, last but not least, is Annie. And supposedly in strict control of this crew is Mrs. Benning, one of our teachers."

Stafford nodded at them while putting a smile on his face. They all stared back at him as if he were from Mars. Mrs. Benning took charge and herded them all out the front door, where the noise level resumed at full volume. Mrs. Warren indicated they should follow.

"We have three elderly horses, six Nubian goats, chickens, some guard geese, and undoubtedly some other assorted creatures back in the barn," she said. "The kids do projects out there in the afternoon. Mr. Jackson is the barn and grounds caretaker. He takes care of the animals and teaches the kids something about animal husbandry. We've found that caring for animals improves their chances for dealing successfully with people."

He caught a faint scent of perfume as she walked in front of him. "And why do you suppose that is?"

"Because animals have personalities, needs, fears, and urges. They communicate these things, just not in English. By teaching the kids to be conscious of how the animals do communicate, they learn to pay attention to another being, to look for those manifestations I spoke about. If you catch them young enough, and they have the basic intelligence, they'll eventually apply those same skills to humans, and if they do that, they're more likely to succeed than people who don't."

"Which is most of us."

"Well, you say you're an investigator. I would imagine you pay attention, don't you?" She said this with a hint of a smile, which softened her face. First the Iron Lady. Now a hint of the coquette? Was she flirting with him? He was confused, but he certainly was paying attention.

They walked around the side of the house and out toward the barns. The pond on the left was rippled by a small breeze stirring through the bright green limbs of the surrounding willows. "How many employees do you have here?" Stafford asked.

"We have four: Mrs. Benning is one of two full-time teachers; Mrs. Correy is the other. They alternate days, taking the kids through lunch, nap, and the afternoon activities. Mr. Jackson is only here in the early morning and afternoons. Mrs. Hadley is our cook, but she's only here at mealtimes. They all have families down in Graniteville. We have a doctor and an LPN whom we can call. I live here except when I'm traveling on research trips."

"Do you teach?"

"Yes. I take care of individual learning problems and run the home. It's funded by the state, which pays a per diem allowance for each child under care. There's a lot of paperwork."

"I'm in the government, Mrs. Warren. You don't have to tell me about paperwork. You mentioned travel."

"Yes, I'm a doctoral candidate at the University of Georgia in Athens. I'm studying indigenous American sign languages. And sometimes there are other trips."

"Like the one where we met in Atlanta?"

She stopped by the gate to the barnyard area and looked across the field to the base of the mountain that rose behind the farm. "Yes. With Jessamine."

She did not elaborate, so Stafford kept his silence while they watched the kids groom two of the horses under the direction of an elderly black man. She'd tell him when she was ready, or not tell him at all. He sensed there was no point in his asking any direct questions about the elusive Jessamine. The warm breeze molded her dress to her body, and he was a little embarrassed at how hard it was to keep his eyes off her. He imagined for a moment that there was a sexual tension growing between them, but then he immediately dismissed it as the product of an overactive imagination amplified by prolonged abstinence. It had been ridiculous for him to think she'd been flirting with him. And yet . . .

They had been standing there for a few minutes when a noisy yellow school bus ground its way up the hill out front and stopped in front of the driveway. A lone passenger got out, and the school bus roared away in a cloud of diesel exhaust, wearily pursued by a stream of frustrated cars and pickup trucks. Stafford watched as the girl came up the driveway, carrying her book bag like a baby across her chest. She was dressed in baggy jeans, a blouse, and a sweater. Stafford was unable to get a clear look at her features because of the distance. The girl waved tentatively at Mrs. Warren with the fingers of her right hand, then went directly into the house.

"That's Jess," she said.

"She doesn't join the horse activities?" he asked.

"When the kids are done, she'll come out to ride. She's a teenager, Mr. Stafford. She doesn't play with the little kids. Do you have children?"

"Nope. I was married for several years, but we recently divorced. We never made time for kids."

She nodded but, to Stafford's great relief, didn't say anything.

"What's back there, Mrs. Warren?" he asked, pointing to a gap in the willows where a well-defined path paralleling the creek led back toward the mountain's slope.

"Please, call me Gwen," she said. "Back there is Howell Mountain and the national wilderness area. Fancy a walk?"

"Sure, and please call me Dave."

The path took them through the tail end of the willow grove along the banks of the creek, with the pasture fence to their right. After fifteen minutes they entered a small gorge. The green bulk of Howell Mountain loomed up on both sides. He wondered if either one of them was properly dressed for a hike in the mountains, but it quickly became apparent that this was a regular exercise path for Gwen Warren. She led the way at a fairly brisk pace, without speaking. Stafford was suddenly glad he had been exercising, although he was having to control his breathing to keep from puffing out loud. He also had some trouble balancing himself with one arm stuck in his pocket.

After twenty minutes they reached a clearing next to a pool formed by a small waterfall. The view back down the gorge was spectacular. The air was cool and clean, scented with the aroma of leaf mold, wet stone, and falling water. The path continued on up the gorge, although it looked to be much steeper. She paused and asked how he was doing.

"Fine," he said, still trying to mask his heavy breathing. It hadn't looked it, but they had climbed nearly two hundred feet. Only the top of the house was visible through the trees. "How far does the path go?"

"Up to the top of the gorge. There's a bigger waterfall up there. After that, the federal wilderness area begins. Want to continue? I always ask, because some people are unused to climbing."

He explained about his balance problem, and she walked over to the edge of the path and found him a stick. She asked him what had happened to his arm.

"I was at the wrong place at the wrong time," he said. "Couple of hopheads hit a convenience store and started shooting. I caught a ricochet in the arm. Sitting in my car, if you can believe it."

"Did you shoot back?"

"No, this one came through the window. We're not normally armed, Gwen. I'm not a street cop. Most of what I do involves unarmed paperwork."

She smiled. "Will you get it back?"

He took his hand out of his pocket and extended his arm slowly and very carefully. His right hand was somewhat pale in comparison with his left. He was barely able to make a fist, and his fingers trembled visibly.

"They tell me yes," he said, trying not to show the strain he was feeling. "I do a series of rehab exercises, and I guess there is some minimal progress."

He was surprised when she took his right hand in both of hers. Her hands were surprisingly warm. "Keep trying," she said. "At our age, minimal progress constitutes victory." Then she smiled at him again, released his hand gently, and turned to continue up the trail.

He took off his suit jacket, loosened his tie, and put his hand back in his pants pocket while he followed her up the mountainside. It was harder going, with more rocks and ruts than before, but with the stick, he made better progress and was mostly able to keep up with her. He was content to enjoy the mountain scenery as well as the occasional glimpse of her beautiful legs ahead of him. Forty minutes later they reached the second waterfall, which was indeed much larger. The spray from the water chilled the air, causing him put his coat back on, even while he thought how nice it would be to plunge into the deep pool at the bottom of the falls. She must have read his thoughts.

"I sometimes come up here to swim," she said. "Although that's a lot colder than it looks. We're nearly to the top of the pass; let's finish the climb and then we can rest."

He followed her again, this time on a path that snaked diagonally across the side of the mountain, whose top appeared to be nearly a thousand feet above them, until they reached another notch in the mountain. The path up this defile was steep and narrow, and he had to concentrate on keeping his footing. A couple of times he nearly went down on all fours to maintain his balance. Gwen, he noticed, was simply picking her footing more carefully than he was. After fifteen minutes, they reached the top, where she sat down on a flat benchlike rock. He stood by the rock for a moment to recover his breath. He noticed that she did not seem to be particularly winded, although the direct sunlight had brought out a sheen of perspiration on her brow. She hiked the dress back up over her knees, and extended her feet to stretch her legs. He looked away, not wanting to be caught staring at her again.

The view from the notch was well worth the climb. Willow Grove was clearly visible in the narrow valley below, bounded by intermittent patches of white concrete where the state road climbed the lower flanks of Howell Mountain. A church steeple and the clock tower of the county courthouse in Graniteville were visible across an expanse of trees, and the scarred, rocky shoulder of the gravel quarry rose up into the mountain air on the other side of town. The view through the notch behind them was even more magnificent, extending for miles to the north, east, and northwest, presenting a veritable sea of rolling tree-covered hills and rocky crags, all draped in a smoky blue haze. There were even larger blue-green shapes crouching on the distant horizon. A warm wind blew through the notch.

"That's the tailbone of the Appalachian Mountains directly to the north," she said. "That's Tennessee to the left, North Carolina to the right. The area directly in front of us is part of the Chatahoochee National Forest. It's all federally protected wilderness area, which begins right about here. The Willow Grove property comes to the top of this notch."

"Wow. This is some prime real estate. I take it that your family has been here awhile."

"Yes, awhile," she said, looking out over the panorama in front of them. A solitary hawk soared soundlessly in lazy circles above them. The breeze stirred the mass of black hair on her head, revealing the smooth line of her neck. She patted her hair back into place. He felt a sudden strong desire to touch her, an urge he quickly banished. Get a hold of yourself, he thought. She is not coming on to you.

"Anyone live out there?" he asked, pointing north.

"Officially, no. That is all a federal wilderness area. Nothing can be taken in or out of there, not even firewood. You can walk through it, but don't get hurt, because any rescue will have to be done on foot. No helicopters, ATVs, or any sort of motorized vehicles can go back in there."

"So no one would be allowed to live out there."

"Not officially, no. When the wilderness area was created, the government moved everyone out. But some of the families had been there for two, three hundred years, Mr. Stafford. It wouldn't surprise us if some of them hadn't slipped back to the old ways and the old places."

He nodded, picking up on her use of the word *us*. In other words, we locals know some things that you, an outsider, will never be permitted to know. What had Ray said? Black hats, long black beards, and moonshine? Then he noticed something else that made him ask another question. "And would some of the children who end up here in Willow Grove possibly come from out there?"

She turned to look at him, her eyes widening in surprise. "What prompted that question?"

"The fact that the path keeps going," he replied, pointing to the far side of the notch. The path indeed kept going, showing up again halfway down the opposite slope before disappearing into a stand of hardwoods halfway down the mountain.

She looked down the path for a long moment but did not reply. Then she got up and brushed past him, saying, "We should get back." He again decided not to push it. He had to assume she was still making up her mind about him. The less he said, the better chance he had that she would come out with it.

As they came out into the clearing near the lower falls, he heard the sounds of hoofbeats coming up the path. Moments later, Jessamine appeared, mounted on a black horse. She saw them at once, reined in gently, and waited for them to approach. She was very slim, but surprisingly full-breasted for a teenager. She was wearing short boots, jeans, and a sleeveless white shirt. Her arms were tanned, and she had much darker eyes than Gwen had. Her face had the pinched look of someone struggling with a chronic illness. As Gwen drew near, the girl began to sign excitedly with her hands. Dave, not used to being around horses, remained a few steps back.

"She was getting worried when we didn't come back," Gwen said. "Normally, I don't take visitors beyond the lower falls." The girl was looking over at Stafford, clearly expecting an explanation. Gwen introduced them. "This is Mr. Stafford from Washington, Jess," she said. "We saw him in the Atlanta airport, remember? When that man fainted?"

At the mention of the man fainting, the girl's face froze for a moment. Gwen immediately reassured her. "No, Jess, it's all right. Mr. Stafford is a policeman. I told you I was going to invite him up here, remember?"

The girl gave him another frightened look, and then she began to shake her head slowly. She was clearly agitated now, and the horse was picking up on it and starting to dance around. With one hand on the reins, she managed another few seconds of signing, then pulled the horse around and trotted off, not giving Gwen a chance to reply.

"I assume that she's not happy to see me?" Stafford said as horse and rider disappeared into the first of the willow trees below them.

"She's scared," Gwen said with a sigh. "Oh, this is so complicated. I don't really know what to do."

Stafford thought about that for a moment. "Is there someplace you and I can have dinner around here?" he asked. "Besides the Waffle House?"

"No, not really," she replied, starting back down the path. "There's a tourist lodge over in Calloway, but that's a thirty-mile drive through the mountains—one way. Not good at night." She paused. "Why don't you stay here for dinner?" she said. "Mrs. Hadley is a competent cook, and what we have to talk about is going to take some time."

"I'd like that very much," he said. "Let me get checked into the motel, and then I can come back, say, what, six-thirty, seven?"

"That's fine. The house and kids should be settled down by then." She looked in the direction the girl had gone. "Most of them, anyway."

■■■ THURSDAY, FORT GILLEM DRMO, ATLANTA, 4:20 P.M.

Carson received the first call from the Pentagon at four-twenty in the afternoon. A Major Mason from something called the Security Working Group at Army headquarters was on the line, wanting to speak to the DRMO manager. His secretary patched the call to his office and then left for the day.

"This is Wendell Carson speaking."

"This is Major Mason, Mr. Carson. I'm with the Security Working Group, HQDA. We're a long-range study group trying to scope out better ways to apportion funds to secure logistical assets. I won't bore you with our full terms of reference, but we came up with a question you might be able to help us with."

"Sure, Major. Fire away."

"Do you have a demilitarization facility at your DRMO?"

"Yes. We're the only one with a full-scale demil facility in the South-east."

"And can that facility contain toxic by-products of the demil process?"

"Yes."

"How toxic? And how completely are they contained?"

Carson explained the thoroughness of the Monster's digestive system. Mason was silent for a moment as he made notes. "Okay," he said. "Then if something went through your demil system, say a container with a CW residue, there would be no release of any by-products of that process?"

Oh shit, Carson thought immediately. They're here.

"No. The system is completely contained. If something was radioactive, the residue would still be radioactive, but chemicals? No, chemicals are neutralized. Why? Do you think some CW has gotten into the DRMO system?"

"Oh, no, nothing like that," Mason replied quickly. "Better not be anything like that going on, right? No, I was just using that as an example of an extremely toxic substance."

Carson thought he detected a whiff of anxiety in the major's almost-too-quick reply, but he played along. "Damned right there had better not be anything like that getting into the DRMO pipeline. But the system is pretty safe. We have the EPA in three times a year to ensure we're right and tight, and the by-product dealers, especially the bulk chemical feedstock companies, run tests on everything they buy from the demil process."

"Okay, great. Thanks for your input, Mr. Carson."

Carson thought fast. "If you have any further questions, Major, feel free to call. Oh, and may I have your number, please?"

"Sure," Mason replied, and gave him a phone number.

Carson recognized the Virginia area code. He hung up and studied the number, which looked to him like a Pentagon exchange. HQDA, Mason had said. Headquarters, Department of the Army. Asking about the demil process and containers for chemical weapons. A tendril of apprehension coiled in his belly. If the Army had discovered that a cylinder of CW was missing, how would they go about tracking it down?

Carson knew his Army. They'd be extremely surreptitious about it. The Security Working Group. That could mean anything, or nothing. Then another thought whacked him between the eyes: Was this perhaps the real reason Stafford had shown up on his doorstep, apropos of absolutely nothing? Without warning from DLA, other than that single "look out, here he comes" phone call? With some fanciful cover story about his being shit-canned out of headquarters? Jesus H. *Christ*! Did they suspect him already?

He pushed aside his stack of paperwork and sat there in his office, mulling over the possibilities for almost an hour before finally picking up the phone and calling back the number Mason had given him. No one answered. He studied the number, then called it again, subtracting one from the final number to see if it had been an extension. The phone rang, but still no one answered. It was five-thirty, so most of the Pentagon inmates would have escaped for the day. Then he had an idea. He got out his Department of Defense phone book and looked up the number of the Pentagon information operator. He gave her the number and told her it didn't appear to be a working number. She tried it, and came up with a ring but no answer. He asked if he might have transposed a digit. She did some checking and then came back on the line.

"That number is a working number. It's an extension in the office of the commanding general of the Army Chemical Corps," she said. "Do you want to try the base number in the general's office?"

"No," he said. "I just wanted to make sure I had the number right. I'll try them again in the morning."

He hung up the phone gingerly, as if not wanting to provoke a return call. Son of a bitch, he thought. The Army Chemical Corps. Mason had been lying.

So they knew the cylinder was missing.

And they knew where to start looking. They were tracking the shipment of environmental containers.

He got up and paced around his office. The bad news was that they had found out the thing had gone missing. The good news was that the only other person who had *known* that the cylinder was here had been "processed" out of the picture. Which left two loose ends: whatever investigation was going on about Bud's house fire, and, possibly, but only possibly, Investigator Stafford, who was out of town for the day.

He went down the darkened hall to Stafford's temporary office, which was unlocked. He switched on a light. All the DRMO reference binders were still piled on the desk. The blotter was covered with doodles and scribblings, a couple of phone numbers Carson didn't recognize, and the names Lambry and Graniteville.

Graniteville? Why did that name ring a bell. He studied the blotter. Then he remembered. The weird girl in the airport. Had Stafford gone to Graniteville? Was that why he had wanted a state map? He sat down in Stafford's chair, thinking hard. If the Army knows, the Army is going to come here, sure as shit. I've got to warn Tangent. The deal has to go on hold for the moment. The thought of maybe losing his shot at a million dollars almost made him physically sick. But, he thought, this still might work out. If I can convince the Army that all the containers went straight through to demil, then they might take the easy way out—claim that the cylinder was destroyed, declare victory, and go home. That would leave the cylinder even easier to sell. Then the only loose end would be Stafford and whatever the hell he was doing up in Graniteville, and with whom. He went back to his office to retrieve the current 800 number for Tangent.

■ THURSDAY, WILLOW GROVE HOME, GRANITEVILLE GEORGIA, 8:30 P.M.

Mrs. Hadley had proved to be more than a competent cook, and Stafford was comfortably replete as he sat down in one of the rocking chairs out on Gwen's private porch. There was a three-quarter moon rising over Howell Mountain, and he thought he could still see the spring colors in the willows and fields around the house. Gwen brought out a tray of coffee and sat down in the other rocker. She had changed clothes for dinner, wearing now a much more flattering dress. The kids had been fed early and sent upstairs. She had been more animated during their own quiet dinner in the kitchen, telling him more about Willow Grove, how the state programs for orphaned children worked, and of the constant battle for funding. He told her about his own work with kids in the Boys Club program up in Washington, and how funding had become pretty difficult for that operation, too.

After dinner, she told him about the children and their origins. Crash, a four-year-old fast neutron who never quite seemed to make it around corners and fixed objects without a collision, had been orphaned by a trailer fire. Hollywood was the oldest boy; his nickname arose from his fascination with video movies. His father had killed his mother in a drunken argument, packed his three children into the pickup truck, and then had driven it into a mountain river at fifty miles an hour. Hollywood, the only swimmer, got out and made it to the shore, where he was found curled up on a tree stump two days later by a deputy sheriff. No-No came from less violent circumstances: He had been found hiding in a Dumpster up along the Tennessee border as a two-year-old—

parents or relatives entirely unknown. For the first six months at Willow Grove, the only word he spoke was *no-no*.

Of the little girls, Too had been handed to the Department of Family and Children Services by her mother when her heroin addiction had closed in and she sensed she was dying. The child had been on the brink of death by starvation by the time the state intervened. Her nickname also arose from something she said, which was most often heard at mealtimes, where she would hold out her hand and say, "Too," meaning, they finally realized, "Me, too," whenever food was handed out. It had taken her a year to understand that she wasn't going to be starved anymore. Last, and saddest, was Annie. Annie was a crack baby, a bright, energetic, loud child who could learn anything—for two minutes. Then it was as if she had never even seen the person who had just taught her to tie her shoelaces. Annie was bound for special placement as soon as she was five, or as soon as there was an opening, whichever came first. Courtesy of her mother's crack habit, Annie would never be able to learn and retain anything, although she would probably live as a ward of the state well into old age.

Stafford had wondered aloud if the children would make it into normal, mainstream life in America.

"That's our job here," she replied. "I should say, That's our objective. We have to bring them up from some deep negative number, get past zero, and into a positive mental and physical environment where they finally believe that what happened to them wasn't their fault. Then we can proceed. Success after that is based a lot on their native talent."

"And the care they get here."

"That, too. But the truth is, if their parents were dullards, and *their* parents were dullards, genius is not likely to manifest itself. There is no escaping one's mental heredity."

"Are they classified as emotionally disturbed?"

"Sometimes. I must confess to applying that label, although at the mildest classification. The per diem for the home is increased if there are emotional disturbances. We barely break even as it is. But we make do, and we do our best."

"You make it sound so matter-of-fact, so, I don't know, professional. I don't think I could handle some of the emotional embers you must touch from time to time."

"Ah, yes, those," she said, looking away for a moment. "Like when Hollywood goes sleepwalking, calling out for his mama in a voice very much like Bambi in the Disney movie. Especially when he says, 'Mama,' followed by 'Sh-h-h-h, Poppa's comin.' That'll do it." There was a special shine to her eyes when she told him this.

"Yes, I guess that would." He was about to ask her about Jessamine, but then he decided to keep waiting. He asked Gwen instead about her coming back to Graniteville.

"It's my home," she said. "When you're a southern woman and you're no longer married, you either go far away or you go home. I was actually born and raised here."

"But you said you were a doctoral candidate at the university? At one time you've lived elsewhere."

She nodded in the shadows. "Yes. Technically, my field of study is child psychology. I've discovered that there are different dialects of sign language practiced in the hill country, especially among children from some of the more dysfunctional families. Jessamine is an example. That's not ASL she's using; it's her own."

"Inbreeding is still a problem up here in the mountains?"

"That's an indelicate phraseology, but the phone book is pretty revealing," she said wearily.

"And you were married? To John Lee Warren?"

"Yes," she said softly. "For a while. We had grown up together through high school. He stayed behind here in Graniteville to work for the Sheriff's Department when I went off to college. We got married when I came back home."

"Was that always in the cards? That you would come back here?"

"My father insisted that I go away to college, but in my heart, I never left this town. Especially after Mom died while I was in college. Graniteville isn't such a special place, but this farm is, and so are these hills, although at times they seem lonely, too, with all the people gone."

She had shifted the conversation away from her marriage, so Stafford went with it. "As I said earlier," he noted, "I'm not so sure these hills are all that empty. Of people, I mean."

She looked past him again but did not directly answer his question. She has that mountain secretiveness about her, he thought. He was utterly intrigued by this woman, by her physical grace and intelligence, all cloaked in a dignity that he had not seen in his world of Washington and government. He found himself wishing she were plain and uninteresting, because now it really was time to get back to business.

"So, Gwen," he said. "The business at the airport. Jessamine."

"Yes," she said with a small sigh. "The airport. First, I have to tell you why we were at the airport. We were returning from Charlotte. I'd taken Jess to the Braden Institute there."

"Which is?"

"A hospital specializing in young adult brain tumors."

"Oh my."

"Yes. She went to be tested. The good news is that all the scans were negative."

"That's wonderful," he said. "What on earth could be the bad news with a report like that?"

She turned to face him directly. "This is the part I need you to promise to keep to yourself," she said. "I mean, you can know it, but I need to know that you won't make it part of your official world."

"I'm not following, Gwen," he replied, equivocating a little.

"I know. But will you promise? It's for the child's protection, not mine. I think you'll understand when I tell you. But I guess what I'm saying is that even though you can know about it, you won't be able to act on it. I simply can't permit that."

"Well," he said, "I can promise to be discreet. And since you're her guardian, if you won't permit her further involvement, that pretty much settles it, doesn't it?" But even as he said it, he knew that wasn't true, either.

She thought about his answer for a moment, then nodded her head. "All right. As I said, it's complicated. Jessamine—Jess—is, we think, a psychic."

What did this have to do with the price of rice? "Oh" was all he could manage.

"Yes, 'oh.' Emphasis on the 'we think,' of course, because it isn't all that cut-and-dried. And then there is the problem of her speech, or the lack of it. But I, for one, think it's true. The question is, To what degree? And what to do about it. She appears to have the ability of presence telepathy."

" 'Presence telepathy,' " Stafford repeated. He stood up, suddenly needing to stretch his injured arm. All he knew about psychics was that a certain government agency had gotten its bureaucratic mammary glands in the media wringer recently over a program called Stargate. There had been quite a flap, with the press preaching indignantly about millions spent on questionable research, joined eagerly by a horde of self-righteous congresspersons. He remembered all the talk of so-called mind readers communicating with clandestine agents and seeing through walls in far-off places. Right.

"Do you know anything about the subject of psychic research?" she asked.

"No. I was just thinking about Stargate and the fiasco that caused."

She nodded. "Yes, that was unfortunate, because there's more to it than palm readers by the roadside. Believe it or not, there is a growing body of professional research literature on the subject, such as the Macklin study done at Princeton."

Stafford struggled to be polite. "I suppose there is," he said. "And a lot of charlatans in the field, as well."

"Oh, yes," she said, sounding a bit defensive. "Except I've personally seen manifestations of it in this child."

Stafford sat back down. "Look, Gwen, I'm basically a cop. I've been trained to see the evidence in front of me. I kind of have a problem with the whole concept of psychic powers, or whatever you want to call them. I'm not saying they don't exist, mind you, just that I've never seen anything remotely resembling convincing proof of it."

"How about those people who help the police? And aren't most of them women?"

He couldn't answer that one. He had read about enough of those cases to make him wonder, but he remained skeptical.

"So what can she do?" he asked. "Bend spoons, things like that?"

She froze in the act of lifting her coffee cup. Dammit, he thought, that was a dumb thing to say. "Forget I said that," he said. "It's just—"

She put down her coffee cup, her face a pale mask of annoyance, and for a moment he thought the evening was over, but then she surprised him.

"I understand, Mr. Stafford," she said patiently. "I should have anticipated that. It's not an . . . unreasonable reaction to this whole subject."

So now it was back to Mr. Stafford. He tried again. "Look, Gwen, you asked earlier what I was doing down here in Georgia. Well, officially, I'm pursuing a long-standing fraud investigation that involves the auctioning of surplus government material. Unofficially, I've been sent—or maybe *exiled* is a better word for it—to Georgia for committing some political indiscretions within my agency. Add to that the fact that my wife left me for another man a year ago, and add to that the loss of my right arm. I'm probably not the most focused government investigator you'll ever meet. That said, I must tell you that I haven't exactly uncovered the crime of the century down at the DRMO in Atlanta, either."

"What's a DRMO?" she asked. He explained the term, concluding with the fact that Carson, the man who'd fainted at the airport, was the manager. "If there is something going on there, I would have to look hard at the manager, Carson, because it would be tough to run the kind of scam we're looking for without his knowledge or even participation. But so far, there is no real evidence of that. Right now, the only odd thing about him is what happened at that airport."

She thought about that for almost a minute. Finally, she spoke.

"You asked what Jessamine 'does.' Well, what she does is a form of what most of us would call 'mental telepathy.' "

"You're saying she can read minds?"

"Not exactly. I hate that term—*read minds*—because it provokes an image of science fiction."

Or science fantasy, he thought.

"But the best way I can describe it is to say that she can apparently form a mental image—a picture, if you will—of what another person is thinking, provided that person is in an agitated mental state. If they're very angry, for example, or very afraid."

That made him stop and think back to the airport. Carson had been staring at the girl when he passed out. Stafford was positive of that. Had Carson been in an agitated mental state? He hadn't seemed so, at least not after the incident. And yet, Stafford had not been there *before* the man had fainted. Had Carson been scared witless there in the terminal because the DCIS was paying him a no-notice visit? And if so, for what reason? Had the girl perhaps detected the reason?

"So you think maybe Jess 'saw' something," he said. "Or received this mental image of some evildoing on Carson's part just before he fainted? Why do you think that?"

"Because he fainted," she said softly. "That's what happens when she sees something. It's happened here in the home. Twice. On the first occasion, one of the other kids, a child who is no longer here, accused her of taking one of his books. He was not very stable, emotionally, and he got really ugly with her, got right in her face with lots of shouting and name-calling, and then suddenly he just fainted. Jess looked around for a moment, then signed to me that the thing he was looking for was not a book, but a magazine, and that it was hidden behind his own bureau. I went and looked, accompanied by Mrs. Benning, by the way, who also saw this. The magazine was right where she said it was, taped to the back of the bureau. It was one of those porn things."

"She could have already known that it was there," he pointed out.

"Then why did the boy faint when he got into it with Jess?"

"Hyperventilated, maybe? Got so mad, he held his breath?"

She looked at him patiently.

"Okay, and the second time?"

"The second time involved a teenage boy who worked afternoons for Mr. Jackson in the barn. Jess was down there one day, getting ready to ride, when the boy came into the stall aisle. She looked at him, dropped the reins, picked up a broom, and went after him. This time, she was the one who was extremely agitated. The kid just backed away, but she kept after him. She can't speak, remember, so the only way she can express serious anger is by doing something."

"Like beating him up with a broom?"

"Yes. Fortunately, Mr. Jackson was there, but as he ran to break it up, the boy suddenly fainted. Mr. Jackson had to restrain her physically from doing some real damage."

"What had he done?"

She refilled their coffee cups. "This was a little more difficult to get out of her," she said, "but apparently, when the school bus was late, Jess had been going directly to the barn and changing clothes in one of the stalls. The stall was next to the feed room, and the boy had a peephole and had been spying on her when she got undressed. He was very likely thinking some seriously impure thoughts when this episode erupted. He was fifteen, raging male hormones and all that, and she is, as you've seen, developed. We found the peephole, and there was evidence that it had been used frequently."

"Damn," he said. "And what did the kid do when he woke up?"

"He was disoriented and embarrassed, in about equal proportions."

Just like Carson, he thought. "Did you have any tests done in Charlotte in this area?"

"Not beyond a brain scan. She'd been complaining of headaches, and I suppose I thought . . ." She didn't finish the sentence.

He remembered her comment about good news. "And the bad news was that you were hoping they'd find a physiological explanation for the two incidents you described?"

"Yes. I believe the thing at the airport makes three."

Stafford finished his coffee. "As I recall the press reports on the

Stargate program, they were trying to find people who could establish a telephathic relationship over long distances."

"Well, you know more about that than I do. But if that was the case, Jess couldn't have helped them. This phenomenon apparently happens only when she's right in front of the other person, *and* that person is mentally agitated."

"Or *she* is. Have you talked to her about it? I don't mean the incidents, but the phenomenon itself?"

"Tried. We have the basic problem of having to use sign language, and my having to explain new terms to her. Plus, she went through a pretty horrific experience as a very young child. Talking about this phenomenon is very tricky, because any teenager, and especially Jess, is hypersensitive to any implication that there's something different, or wrong, with them. I told you, Dave, this is complicated."

It certainly is, he thought, although he wanted to know more about why Gwen was being so protective of the girl. On the other hand, that was, after all, her job. But assuming the phenomenon was real, what had the girl seen in Carson's mind?

"Would you consider letting me talk to her?" he asked. "With you present, of course; I can't read sign language, so you'd have to translate. But I guess I need to know what she saw in the airport."

Gwen had to think about that, and he gave her time. He could not imagine what the hell Carson could have going at the DRMO that might trigger one of the girl's psychic episodes.

"That depends," she replied finally. "On what you're investigating at that place, and what would happen to her if you catch this Carson person because of something Jess saw."

"As I said, at the moment I don't have any evidence that Carson is doing *anything* wrong. I don't much like the guy, nor do his employees, but that's neither here nor there. But if I had to wrap up and report to my boss right now, I'd say there's very little going on at that DRMO."

"Well, what I'm getting at is that I won't expose Jess to some media circus over a case of stolen airplane parts. Maybe we should just drop this."

He nodded thoughtfully. For his part, he could just see himself bringing in a report to Ray Sparks based on a fourteen-year-old's—what, visions?

"I could go along with that, Gwen. Unless she 'saw' a murder or something equally serious, that might be the best course of action."

She looked at him for a moment. "You still don't believe it, do you?"

He sighed. "There are a lot of things in this world I don't understand. Understanding is different from believing. But like I said, I'm supposed to see what's in front of me. I can't see mental telepathy."

She nodded. "Neither can I. But let me get something for you."

She got up and went through a screen door. A light went on in her office and he could hear her looking for something. He got up and stood by the porch railing. Her side of the house faced away from the pond, overlooking the grove of sprawling, moonlit pecan trees. The scent of swelling greenery perfumed the darkness, and he could hear the first peeps of the nocturnal tree frog chorus. Gwen came back out onto the porch and handed him a piece of paper.

"What's this?" he asked. It appeared to be a crude but detailed pencil drawing of a cylinder. In the background were several dozen small x's, scattered randomly across the paper. No, not x's. Crosses.

"I asked her to draw what she had seen when she encountered Mr. Carson in the airport. This is what she produced."

He studied the drawing. A cylinder. So what? "And these marks? Crosses?"

"She told me that the cylinder was filled with dead people. Thousands of them. Millions of them."

"Terrific. What in the hell does that mean? I wonder."

"I don't know. She doesn't want to talk about it anymore. She said the man was bad, but that this thing, whatever it is, was worse. Much worse."

He studied the drawing again. The cylinder had knurled caps at each end, a detail he had missed the first time. "Can I keep this?" he asked.

"I'll make you a copy." He gave it to her and she went back into the office. He picked up the empty coffee cups and followed her.

"I still feel like I should interview Jess," he said. "Although actually, I don't know what I would ask."

She smiled at him over her shoulder, and his breath caught in his throat for a second. "Your first instincts were probably correct. Here's a copy. Perhaps it will make sense later."

He took the drawing and folded it into his coat pocket. He looked at his watch and said he should probably go. He didn't want to, but he couldn't think of an excuse to prolong his stay. She smiled again and walked him to the door. He thanked her for dinner and said he would let her know if anything came of the drawing. She took his hand for a moment. Her fingers were warm and soft.

"Mostly, keep it away from us, will you?" she said. "Whatever it is?

This is a pretty fragile group of kids, despite appearances. Your world would not bring us anything good."

"My world?"

"You're a federal policeman, Dave. What's in your world that's good for kids?"

Absolutely nothing, he thought. He thanked her again, reluctantly letting go of her hand, and walked out to his car.

As he drove out onto the state road, he looked back at the big house framed by all those trees, but all the outside lights were already out. He went down the hill toward town, driving slowly on the unfamiliar road, thinking about Gwen Warren. There was so much he wanted to know about her. After the wreckage of his own marriage, the upheaval of the whistle-blowing incident, and his arm's uncertain prognosis, he had pretty much put women out of his mind. Every attractive single or divorced woman he met in the Washington milieu looked or sounded like his ex-wife, so putting them out of his mind had been easier to do than he had expected. But Gwen was not like them at all.

As he drove into the town of Graniteville and turned right up the hill toward the motel, he became aware of headlights behind him. The car followed him, some distance back, almost all the way to the motel, until he turned up the driveway by the Waffle House. As he pulled into the parking lot, he saw the car slow and then turn around. It was a police car. Now that's interesting, he thought. He wondered if that might be Sheriff John Lee, minding the store.

7

Carson saw the two county arson investigators out the front door of the admin offices and went back to his own office. The Haller woman had wanted some background on Bud Lambry, what his job had been here at the DRMO, and why he might have quit. Carson was pretty sure he'd deflected any further inquiries. He'd told them Lambry had just gotten mad and quit. Man even took the demil control console's keys with him. Damned inconvenient. The personnel records indicated the address in southeast Atlanta, no further family data, no prior criminal convictions or serious disciplinary problems, and certainly no motives for arson. He had asked Haller if it had been arson, but she hadn't really answered the question, giving him instead some "We're still investigating" BS. Fair enough. He'd seen the television news report. They'd need an aircraft accident investigating team down there to prove anything other than that a propane leak touched off an explosion. Well, no shit, Sherlock. Hardly a surprise event in those dilapidated old houses down there.

He sat down at his desk and thought about his latest conversation with Tangent, who had been less than thrilled at the news that the Army might know the cylinder was missing. Carson had switched immediately to the offensive: They would come and check the place out; he was sure of it. Once the Army saw the demil machine, however, they would assume the missing cylinder had been destroyed in its environmental container, and then Tangent would be buying an object that didn't exist. Tangent hadn't been so sure the Army would make that assumption, but Carson had pointed out that the Army would also be looking desperately for a reason, any reason at all, to cover up their screwup. He had suggested that they shelve the deal for a few more days. Tangent reluctantly agreed, but he wanted to be informed the instant the Army backed out.

Carson tapped a pencil on his desk. Now he just had to wait. He had not been blowing smoke; he was sure in his bones that the Green Machine would be here, and probably very soon. Maybe even today. He wanted to go get the records of the Tooele shipment, although he dared not. Anything he did now connected with the containers would raise suspicions. The shipment had come in and the containers had become Monster feed. That's all. And nothing could escape the end processes of the Monster. Not metal cylinders, not toxic substances, not the mortal remains of Bud Lambry. And this had happened some time ago. He listened with some satisfaction to the muted shrieking of rendering metal floating across the tarmac from the demil building.

One million in cash. All he had to do was wait. And keep his cool. The only wild card now was Stafford, but there was no way he could know anything. And the cylinder was hidden well. He could and would worry about it, but his sense of the matter told him his secret was safe.

■ FRIDAY, THE DCIS REGIONAL OFFICE, SMYRNA, GEORGIA, 11:20 A.M.

At Stafford's request, Ray Sparks agreed to go to lunch with him. Stafford had not wanted to discuss what he had learned at Willow Grove right there in the office. They went to a local chain restaurant, where he reviewed what had happened to date. Sparks was politely skeptical.

"Let me get this straight," he said. "You have no direct evidence of any crimes at the DRMO. All you've got is a strange occurrence at the airport involving this guy, Carson, and a teenage girl from an orphanage, whose director claims the girl is some kind of psychic. The girl can't physically speak, and all this woman can produce is the girl's drawing of a cylinder and her impression that the cylinder is a bad thing. Right?"

"Not your basic winning grand jury package, is it?"

"Well, there you have it, Dave. I mean, I know you've barely scratched the surface at the DRMO. You've been there—what, two business days altogether? I think you ought to forget all this extraneous stuff and see if you can find out some way the guys at the DRMO could fix the auction process and make some damn money."

Stafford was silent for a moment as Sparks finished his sandwich. "Trouble is," Stafford said, "I'm beginning to think there's something else going on. I know, I know, all I've got is a gut feel. And it's not what I'm supposed to be looking for, but something else, out there at the edges."

112

"Your trademark, as I recall," Sparks reminded him.

Stafford grinned. "Yeah, but tally it up: that weird guy coming up to me and talking about immunity, and then telling me to find Bud Lambry. Next day, Lambry's house has been blown up. The employees down there seem to have a hate-on for the manager, and they knew from the git-go that I was a cop and not some auditor down from DLA. The incident at the airport? Well, who knows what that means? Except I've got a responsible citizen telling me that it's happened before around this girl, accompanied by evidence that she was able to visualize what someone else was thinking."

" 'Evidence'?" Sparks said, looking at Stafford over the tops of his glasses. Stafford had trouble meeting Sparks's eyes.

"Okay, I'll bite," Sparks said. "What's your 'evidence' tell you is going on?"

Stafford threw up his hands. "Beats the shit out of me. Maybe this is just a case of my trying to make this assignment into something, when we both know that it's mostly a put-up job."

Sparks tactfully did not reply to that, concentrating instead on stirring his sweet tea. Stafford was beginning to feel like a fool for even bringing up the psychic angle. "Okay," he said. "I'll go back to the DRMO auction angle."

Sparks grinned at him. "Was she good-looking? This Warren woman?"

"Up thine, as the Quakers say," Stafford replied.

■ FRIDAY, THE PENTAGON, THE SECURITY WORKING GROUP, 3:30 P.M.

Colonel Fuller was chairing the afternoon meeting when Brigadier General Carrothers came in and sat down. The Security Working Group space had been set up as a mini command center, with secure communications, status boards, a conferencing facility, and several PCs. Fuller gave Carrothers a quick recap.

"General, it's now fifteen-thirty. The reaction team should arrive at Fort Gillem in about an hour and a half," he said. "Two semis, one with the troops and their gear, the other with the sensor pack and comms suite."

"Plain vanilla trailers, right?" Carrothers asked. "No visual markings?"

"Yes, sir, that's correct," one of the majors said. His name tag indicated his last name was Mason. "Anniston is treating this as an exercise of their Civil Chemical Emergency Response Team. There will be one officer on the team who knows what this is really about. Everyone else on the team will think it's a routine exercise. We arrive about seventeen hundred to minimize contact with employees."

"Good. What's the procedure?"

"The trucks will go in as unobtrusively as possible, park, and take initial readings while the main team itself remains in containment. If there are no immediate sensor hits, the team leaders will determine where the Tooele containers are and then proceed to secure that area for individual inspection."

"And if they've already been destroyed?"

"Then they'll check the demil facility itself, and whatever by-product assembly areas are connected to demil."

"We expect the sensors to find nothing," Colonel Fuller interjected. "The cylinder is, of course, hermetically sealed. If the containers are still there, and if it's in one of the containers, they'll retrieve it and get out of there. If the containers have already been destroyed, they'll have to run some tests on the demil output streams to see if there's any residual evidence that the cylinder itself was processed."

"If it went through demil and contaminated that facility, what do we do then?"

"That's not likely," Fuller said. "This is Wet Eye we're talking about. If that had happened, we would have already known about it. The whole world would have already known about it."

Carrothers thought about that and then nodded. He was about to ask another question, then stopped short. He gave Fuller a sign that he wanted to talk to him privately, and he left the room. Fuller came out a minute later, joining Carrothers in the empty hallway outside the room. Fuller was General Waddell's friend, but he did not really know Carrothers. He kept it formal. "Yes, sir?"

"See if I have this right: The best outcome is that the environmental containers are all still there, we find the cylinder, get it out of there without anyone knowing it was there, and declare the 'exercise' successful, right?"

"Yes, sir."

"And the worst outcome is that all the containers have been destroyed, and we find no evidence of the cylinder, chemical or otherwise?"

"Not necessarily, sir."

"Huh? Ambiguity is not in order here, Colonel."

"It might be, General," Fuller said, pausing while a staff officer walked by them. He walked Carrothers through the container demil scenario, being careful to highlight the assumptions. "Yes, we're pretty sure we lost one. No, it did not get loose. The screwup is an internal matter, which we deal with internally. Shoot some guilty bastards and close the records."

"That's the mother of all cover-ups you were talking about."

"Yes, sir, sort of. But what purpose would be served by admitting we lost one, if no harm was done?"

"Colonel, what worries me is that there's always the possibility some-one found the cylinder and kept it."

"To do what?"

"To sell it, of course."

Fuller looked both ways up and down the hallway before answering. "We feel that's a highly unlikely possibility, General."

" 'We'?"

"General Waddell and I," Fuller replied smoothly.

Carrothers gave him a long look. He started to object, but the sig-nificance of that "We" was beginning to penetrate. A "right answer" was developing here.

"Okay," he said. "Have the team leader report the moment they find something, or when he has concluded it's *not* there."

"Yes, sir. Of course, sir."

■ **FRIDAY, FORT GILLEM DRMO, ATLANTA, 4:45 P.M.**

Carson's secretary knocked once on his door, opened it, and announced that a Mr. White and a Mr. Jones were there to see him on urgent business. The fact that she hadn't used the intercom, and that both Mr. White and Mr. Jones were standing right behind her, told Carson everything he needed to know. The Army Chemical Corps had ar-rived. First, he needed to downplay their arrival so as not to alarm his secretary.

"Oh, yes, fine. Come in, gentlemen. That's all, Mrs. Vonner. I'll see you Monday."

His secretary gave him an odd look, but she withdrew, shutting the door behind her. Carson indicated to the two officers that they should sit down, but they remained standing. They were dressed in civilian suits, but their physical bearing and haircuts gave them away at once. They flipped out their wallets and presented military identification cards. The younger-looking one spoke first.

"Sir, I'm Captain White from the Anniston Army Weapons Depot in Alabama. This is Captain Jones. We're here to conduct a no-notice exercise of the Army's Civil Chemical Emergency Response Team. We understand that a shipment of chemical weapons environmental containers was shipped here recently, originally from Tooele, Utah?"

Carson pretended to think. White and Jones. Right. "I'd have to check our records, Captain," he said. "We move a lot of things through this facility. Tooele, Utah, did you say?"

"Yes, sir. One thousand containers for chemical ammunition. Aluminum and composite construction, with external umbilicals for total environmental containment. They're not large—maybe four feet long, four point five inches in diameter. Originated in Tooele, transshipped through the Anniston Depot."

"Interesting. Unfortunately, you've come just after quitting time. Let me go down to our Records Department. Feel free to wait right here. This won't take long. Have some coffee."

He left them standing there and went down the hallway, where the last of the admin office employees were leaving for the day. He went into the Records Department and sat down at one of the PCs. Ordinarily, this would have taken some time to make a database search, but in this case, he knew precisely where the records of the Tooele shipment were. In a minute, he had them printing out in his secretary's office. He walked back and collected the readout.

"These are the records of the container shipment," he said, handing them over to Captain White. "As you can see, they went directly to demil. Head of the line, so to speak. Nobody wanted to fool with those things."

"Very good, Mr. Carson," White said. "What we want to do is to run the team and its gear through a survey of the demil building and surrounding areas."

"Sure. You'll want to survey the assembly areas and the end-product warehouse, won't you?"

"Yes, sir, those, too, if you don't mind. And can we see a system diagram, please?"

"Mind, Captain? Hell, I don't mind. What I'll mind is if your guys find something."

"Not likely, Mr. Carson," Jones said.

"Why's that, Captain?"

"If there's anything to find, you'd all be dead, sir."

Carson smiled back at him. "Well, then, chances are that this is going to be a dull exercise, right?"

"Only kind there is, sir," White said. "Exercise, that is."

"We're not running a demil shift this evening," Carson said. "If you're going to need my people—"

"No, sir. The team is totally self-contained. The exercise calls for us to gain access and conduct the sweeps. We prefer it when there's no one around. Keeps rumors under control. We do have a Public Affairs officer with us; she'll deal with anyone who happens to show up and ask questions."

"Okay, let me show you a process diagram, and then I'll show you the demil area."

Dave Stafford drove up to the DRMO a little after five-thirty P.M. He had gone back to the office with Sparks for two hours after lunch to update his case file on the DCIS computer system. He had then headed back toward the DRMO, only to get mired down in the world's worst traffic jam out on the Atlanta Perimeter road. It was like being back in Washington. The admin office windows were all dark when he arrived, and he realized he did not have a key. Now what? he thought. Maybe there was a late shift and someone could let him in. He had been hoping to find Carson still there, especially since Carson's government pickup truck was still parked out front by the rail siding. He decided to walk around through the truck park to see if he could get into the lay-down area.

He walked around the corner of the admin building and then down a dark alley between the first warehouse and the facility's chain-link fence. He passed three commercial semitrailers parked on their jack stands. As he came around the last trailer, a spaceman stepped out in front of him, startling the hell out of him, especially since the spaceman was holding an M16 rifle at port arms. The hooded figure was saying something to him through a large respirator mask. It was then he noticed the cordon of ropes strung between sawhorses across the entry drive into the lay-down area, and the U.S. Army logo on the spaceman's suit. The spaceman was asking for his identification.

Still getting over his surprise, Stafford pulled his credentials with his

117

left hand and handed them over to the soldier, who began talking into a radio mike that appeared to be inside his headgear. Beyond, out on the tarmac, Stafford saw two large unmarked tractor-trailer trucks parked by the demil complex. There were several other spacemen moving around purposefully in the dusk, under the glare of halogen lights. He thought he caught a glimpse of Carson talking to two civilians up by the cab of one of the semis. The lights looked ominous in the early-evening light.

"So what's going on?" he asked the guard.

"Lieutenant Roberts is on her way out, sir," the soldier replied. "She's PAO. You're requested to wait here, sir."

The guard had made it clear he was not going to be allowed back into the DRMO working area until he had talked to the PAO.

Lieutenant Roberts came over a minute later. She was a tall, good-looking blonde wearing Army dress greens, and she was carrying a notebook and a small tape recorder. She looked very much out of place among all the other personnel wearing chemical protection suits, but the purposeful expression on her face indicated a professional press liaison officer.

"Mr. Stafford, is it?" she asked, offering her hand. He took her hand in his left hand. "I'm Lieutenant Roberts, Army Public Affairs? How can we help the DCIS tonight?"

"Pleased to meet you, Lieutenant. You can start by telling me what's going on here."

"This is an Army exercise, Mr. Stafford. What you see here is the Anniston Depot's Civil Chemical Emergency Response Team. The Anniston Army Weapons Depot is a CW ammunition depot."

"Good Lord! Has something happened?"

"No, sir. This is an exercise. We deploy the team from time to time as if there had been an accident involving CW. We like to do it on Army facilities, usually after hours. We picked this DRMO because there was a shipment of CW environmental containers sent here from Utah recently. We practice securing an area, surveying it for toxic substances, and then doing containment and cleanup. It usually takes about six hours; then they pack up and go."

"And do they usually bring a press officer?"

"Absolutely. Sometimes people see what's going on, and we need to assure them that it's just an exercise. Or sometimes people just drop in," she added pointedly.

"Yeah, well, I've been working here this week, quasi-undercover as a DLA auditor, but I'm actually investigating a long-term case involving the DRMO auction system. The manager, Mr. Carson, can vouch for me."

"Quasi-undercover?"

"That means I've been announced as a DLA auditor, although I'm afraid the workforce here has figured it out that I'm a cop."

"Can't imagine why," she said, giving him an amused once-over.

He ignored her comment. "May I speak to Mr. Carson?"

"I'll ask him, but I'm afraid we can't let anyone into the containment area, though. Is there somewhere you can wait?"

"That's what I need Carson for. I failed to obtain an after-hours key to my office. Or to the building, for that matter."

"I'll go talk to him. If you'll wait right here . . . ?"

He watched her walk back toward the trucks, enjoying the view. He then observed the operation out on the tarmac for a few minutes under the watchful eye of the guard. He felt like commenting on the lieutenant's fine walk, or commiserating with the guard about being suited up, but the guard appeared to be concentrating on his job. Carson came over a few minutes later, his identification tags hanging from his coat pocket.

"They give you any warning of this?" Stafford asked him.

"Nope. But apparently they don't let people know they're coming."

"But what the hell's a CW outfit doing here?"

"They're drilling some kind of emergency response team. There was a shipment of CW containers that came through here a short while back for demil."

"Yeah, she mentioned that. But chemical weapons? Here?"

"No, no, not the weapons, just the environmental containers. They call 'em 'coffins.' The weapons went to Tooele, Utah, from Anniston, Alabama, for destruction. Then they sent the empty containers here. I'm assuming it's because we have the Monster. They said they'd be done in five or six hours."

"Damn. Scary visitors in the night. But what I need right now is a key; I forgot to get one."

"Oh, sure. Come with me. We'll have to go around."

As they walked back to the admin office's front door, Carson asked casually how Stafford's day trip had gone. Stafford demurred, saying something vague about the local DCIS in Smyrna and some internal liaison work. Carson didn't pursue it. He got them into the admin office, found Stafford a spare key, and gave him a keypad combination card in case he came in after hours when no one was there. Stafford went to his office, and Carson went out through the back door to watch some more of the exercise.

Stafford waited ten minutes, then went down to the back door. He cracked it slightly to see what he could see. The two big trucks were still out on the tarmac, but most of the people had disappeared. He saw that the doors to the demil feed-assembly warehouse and the demil building itself were open, and that there were lights on in both buildings. He could see into the end of one of the trailers, which appeared to be a mobile operations center. What the hell, he thought, everybody looks pretty busy.

He stepped quietly out onto the tarmac. The sound of portable generators assaulted the evening quiet from atop the trailers. He hung his credentials from the pen pocket in his suit coat like Carson, then walked casually over to the open trailer. He stood on the tarmac outside the operations trailer for a few minutes, watching what was going on inside. Just beyond the ramp, there were five soldiers suited up in CW gear sitting at consoles of some kind, surrounded by status boards and bright lights. Another soldier stood behind them, filling out a form on a clipboard. If they were communicating with the people inside the warehouses, Stafford could not hear them over the noise of the generators. There was no sign of Carson or the pretty PAO lieutenant, or the two civilians.

As he was about to give it up, the soldiers at the consoles got up from their seats, grabbed gear bags of some kind, and came down the ramp, accompanied by the supervisor. They paid no attention to him as they went around the truck and into the demil building. Stafford was tempted just to walk up the ramp and look around, but he thought that might be pushing it a little. The PAO had told him to stay out of the area. A moment later, he was glad he'd hesitated, because an extremely fit-looking young man with a military haircut came around the corner and stopped short when he saw Stafford.

"Stafford, DCIS," Stafford announced immediately, turning his badge so the officer could see it. "I'm observing with Mr. Carson."

The officer shot him and his credentials a quick look, nodded, and then went on up the ramp and into the trailer. Stafford stepped away, pretending to stare out into the tarmac area, but then he eased back to the ramp so he could see inside the trailer. The officer was sitting at the end console, nearest the ramp, and speaking urgently into a microphone headset. Stafford still couldn't hear anything over the generator noise, but there was a lot of head shaking and gesticulating going on as the officer's hand flew over the console's control buttons. When he saw what came up on the monitor, Stafford stopped breathing momentarily.

There, in living color, rotating slowly in three-dimensional motion, was a stainless-steel cylinder with a knurled cap at each end. It was almost identical to the drawing Gwen Warren had given him in Graniteville, except for the decals with bright red lettering running the length of the cylinder. There were warning banners down both sides of the screen, but all Dave could make out were the words *Top Secret* at the top.

A little voice in his head told him to beat feet out of there, and for once in his life, he listened.

■ SATURDAY, FORT GILLEM DRMO, ATLANTA 12:45 A.M.

From the edge of the tarmac, Carson watched the two semis grind their way out of the DRMO parking lot. It had gone perfectly; in fact, almost amusingly, as the Army team tried to pretend this was just some scripted exercise. But he knew better. They had examined the feed and product streams for the Monster in clinical detail, but apparently they'd found nothing. How could they? The cylinder was still sealed. The fact that it had been hidden right in front of them added to his sense of victory. Now Wendell Carson was safe, although he knew he was making some assumptions about what the Army would do next. From his own days in the Quartermaster Corps, he was pretty sure he knew what that would be. Give the Army an opportunity to cover something up and all those eager-beaver, forward-leaning, team-playing general staff officers would positively sprint with it.

He went back into the demil complex and shut off all the lights and reset the door locks. It was too late to call Tangent. But first thing in the morning, he'd give him the good news, then agree on a date to transfer the cylinder. Sunday was still good: There'd be nobody here, and now that the Army had come looking for it, he had a better argument than ever for not moving the cylinder off the DRMO premises. He let himself in the back door of the admin office and walked down the hall to his own office—where he found Stafford sitting in his chair. He had to work hard to catch his breath.

"That wasn't an exercise, was it, Carson?" Stafford said, folding his hands under his chin and looking up at him very much like a cop.

"What?" Carson barely managed to keep his voice from squeaking as he pushed the office door shut.

"That team being here tonight. That wasn't an exercise, was it? They were looking for something. Something I think maybe you've got."

"What the hell are you talking about? What are you doing sitting at my desk?"

"Waiting for you. I've had a sense about you since I came here, but I couldn't put my finger on it. DRMO auctions. That's small potatoes. Maybe steady beer money, or Vegas money, but nothing to shout about. But CW? That's different. Wa-a-a-y different, Carson."

"What the *fuck* are you saying?" Carson shouted. He was trying not to sound scared, but he sensed he wasn't succeeding. "You accusing me of something, you come right out and say it. Then I'll go get a lawyer and you can say it to him, and then we'll sue your ass and your agency for harassment. You think you can just waltz in here like—"

Stafford put his hand up for silence. He got up and started walking around the room. "So tell me: What really happened to Bud Lambry?" he asked.

Jesus, where the hell did that come from? Carson wondered. His knees felt buttery, so he went around his desk and sat down. "Lambry?" he said. "What's Lambry got to do with anything? He quit. I told you that. Good riddance. Guy was a pain in the ass."

"Must have been. One of your guys talks about Lambry, and then his house blows up. Did he know something he shouldn't have? Like about the cylinder?"

For an instant, Carson thought he felt his heart stop. What had Stafford just said? The *cylinder*?

Stafford had stopped pacing and was looking at him. "That's right, the cylinder. Let's see: stainless-steel, a few feet long, maybe—what, three, four inches in diameter? Sound about right? Containing some grotesque CW shit?"

"I don't know what you're talking about," Carson squeaked. Even to himself, he sounded scared. There was just no fucking way . . .

"Oh, I think you do. I think you and Mr. Lambry found something in that shipment of containers the Army press lady out there was talking about. I think that's the real reason the Army is suddenly down here conducting some kind of bullshit exercise. Something's missing."

"You're whacked out, Stafford," Carson said, shaking his head. He needed to stop this, stop this right now. He decided to attack. "Totally whacked-out. This the kind of shit you were doing up in D.C., got you thrown out of town?"

He saw that it was Stafford's turn to be surprised. He stood up behind his desk. "Yeah, that's right. I checked up on you, Pal," he said. "I know some people who know some shit up there in D.C. So before you go making any more wild-ass accusations, you better think about why you're here in the first place. The way I hear it, you make any impolite noises, the DCIS isn't exactly going to jump right on it. Now just get the hell out of my office."

Stafford gave a crooked smile and walked over to the office door. "Nice try, Carson," he said. "But I don't have to convince my people back in Washington. All I've got to do is convince the *Army*. Tell them I think it's here and that you've got it. I'll bet they've got some seriously mean bastards who might want to come talk to you. Think about that, smart guy. Because I think you've made a huge mistake. I can't prove it—yet—but if I tell them, maybe I won't have to. Happy Trails, Carson."

Stafford hurried to his car, anxious to get out of there in case Carson had a gun stashed somewhere. The DRMO manager had been white with either fury or fear when he'd slammed the door on him back there, and there was no telling what he might do. As he drove away from the DRMO, he thought about Carson's reaction: That had been a direct hit if he'd ever seen one. The man had all but pissed himself when he'd said the word *cylinder*. Son of a bitch stole it, and I'll bet he's going to try to sell it. Damn, he thought: Could it be the girl was for real?

He tried to think of what to do next. And how the hell had Carson found out about his problems in D.C.? Whom had he been talking to? Sparks? Had Ray been playing him along all this time? He didn't want to believe that. He really didn't want to believe that. He hit the state road and sped down through the wasteland of trucking terminals. He'd been bluffing about calling the Army, of course, and about telling anyone else: How could he, when his only "evidence" was a supposedly psychic child's drawing? He could always claim that Dillard had told him, but of course he hadn't, and Dillard was hardly reliable witness material. But if he was right about the cylinder, Lambry might not have just quit. It might yet be determined that Lambry's remains had been dragged off into the bushes by the rail-yard dogs after that explosion.

And maybe he was all wrong about the Army's little exercise at the DRMO. Except you weren't wrong about what you saw in living three-dimensional color on that monitor, he thought. That thing was a perfect match to the girl's drawing.

Maybe the thing to do is to go to that team's home base. Where is it—Anniston? Go to the Army installation at Anniston and see if anything is stirring. Surely if they had lost something like a chemical weapon, there'd be things happening, some visible undercurrents of a crisis. He was a fed; he could get onto a military base.

And do what?

The interchange with the Atlanta Perimeter was visible up ahead. There was an all-night gas station on the right, and he swung the Crown Vic into the parking lot next to a fuel pump. The sign on the pump informed him he had to prepay at the money window.

He pulled out the government bag phone and called Ray Sparks's home number. Sparks answered, and Stafford was relieved to hear the sound of a television in the background, which meant Sparks was still awake.

"Ray, this is Dave Stafford."

"Why did I know that, Dave?" Sparks said in a weary voice.

"Ray, look, I'm nonsecure on a car phone. I think I've found out what's going on at that DRMO. We need to talk."

"Okay."

"I mean we need to meet and talk. No phones."

"Jesus, Dave. Now?"

"Yeah, now. It's much bigger than simple fraud against the government. I'm in southeast Atlanta, near the Perimeter. Can we meet somewhere?"

Sparks sighed. The television sounds were not audible anymore.

"Okay," Sparks said. "But this better be good, Dave. And within the bounds of your current assignment, right?"

"Not even close, Ray. But definitely worth your time." The store attendant was watching him through the bulletproof money window.

" 'Not even close.' Why did I know that, too? All right. You don't know your way around Atlanta, so I'll come down to your hotel. What are you driving?"

"It's a white Crown Vic, government plates."

"Okay. Park out front of the hotel. You'll be reasonably safe downtown in a government car. I'll be there in forty-five minutes. And, Dave, no shit, you'd—"

"I haven't done anything, Ray. Not yet. I'm bringing it to you first, all right? Just like I'm supposed to. Just get downtown, buddy."

He hung up before Sparks could protest further. He got out and walked over to the window.

"I need ten bucks' worth of regular and a map of Alabama," he said to the black man behind the glass.

SATURDAY, FORT GILLEM DRMO, ATLANTA, 1:10 A.M.

Carson sat in his office clenching and unclenching his fists. That *goddamned* Stafford! How in the hell had he figured it out? How in the hell could he know what the cylinder even looked like?

Lambry. Fucking Lambry must have said something to that idiot Dillard before his little accident. Boss Hisley had mentioned that Dillard had been seen talking to Stafford. *Shit!*

The Army had come and gone. He still owed Tangent a call, but Stafford had thrown some serious shit in the game. Should he tell Tangent that Stafford knew? That could well and truly queer the deal. But if he didn't, and Stafford did go to the Army, the deal might be queered anyway. They'd either come back and tear the DRMO to pieces, or— what?

He thought furiously. It all depended on how the Army was handling this thing internally. They'd be in an uproar if they thought some of their precious CW was missing, but they'd be just as terrified about their screwup becoming public knowledge. They might just tell Stafford to take a hike. What Wendell Carson needed now was some leverage, some serious Washington leverage.

Well, hey, how about Mr. Tangent?

Tangent claimed to be well connected. He'd tell him exactly what had happened and let *him* neutralize Stafford, especially since Stafford was already in bureaucratic disgrace. The original source of Stafford's information, however indirectly, had to have been Lambry, but Lambry was Monster piss and his house was a blackened memory. If Lambry was indeed the source, Stafford was shit out of luck. And evidence.

A feeling of calm certainty settled over him. Only Wendell Carson now knew where the cylinder was. Lambry was dead, so Stafford had to be bluffing. The Army had not found it, and they were probably even now breathing a sigh of relief in the fervent hope that it had gone into the demil process with the shipment of coffins.

So tell Tangent, he thought. Tell Tangent and ask him to poison the well there in D.C. Absolutely. Discredit Stafford badly enough and no one would listen to him, least of all the Army, who had every incentive not to want to hear it. Yes, they might have to put off the transfer for a day or so, but once Stafford was out of the picture, they'd be in the clear. Then all he had to worry about was getting his money without losing his skin in the process.

He picked up the phone and called the 800 number.

■■■ SATURDAY, THE PENTAGON, SECURITY WORKING GROUP, 2:00 A.M.

Colonel Fuller rubbed the sides of his face with his hands as Major Mason concluded the briefing. "So, basically, nothing?" he asked. "No trace elements detected, the containers have all been cut into scrap metal, and the DRMO is clean?"

"Yes, sir. They gave the demil area and the compaction modules a very thorough sweep. The demil machine is, of course, designed to destroy toxic organics using multiple acid interactions. It's a totally closed system, so even if the cylinder went into the machine inside one of the coffins, any release would have been contained anyway, and then neutralized."

"Well," Fuller said, stretching, "I guess that's it. I'm going to recommend to the general that we take our packs off here. Obviously, one of these things was overlooked during the unloading process at Tooele, then shipped back out with the containers to the DRMO. We'll have to have a warm body or two swinging for that little screwup, but other than that, I think we're done. You did say the manager at the DRMO confirmed that nobody inspected any containers?"

"Yes, sir. The CERT leader confirms that. The containers went right to demil just as soon as Receiving read the shipping manifest. The manager said they put them at the head of the line that very day."

"That's certainly what I would do with CW containers," Fuller said, looking around the table for any signs of disagreement. Six eager staff officers were nodding back at him in total agreement.

"Right. So our official conclusion is that the cylinder was very probably destroyed in the demil process, and destroyed without a trace. Agreed?"

More nods. No dissent. The general had picked his team wisely, Fuller thought. Probably why he was the general.

He got up and told them to disband the working group and resume their normal duties, warning them once more that silence was literally golden, careerwise. He didn't have to say that twice. He walked down to the executive assistant's desk, which was empty at this time of night, and, per General Waddell's instructions, placed a call to his home. He gave his report and the official conclusions.

"Nobody disagreed?"

"No, sir. Unanimous. Basically, that demil machine saved our asses."

"The guy who runs that DRMO—did he catch on to what the 'exercise' was really all about?"

"We don't think so, General. They took along a good-looking blonde from the headquarters Public Affairs Office with the team, with instructions to keep the manager's mind off things chemical."

"And nobody but the manager knows about the 'exercise'?"

"There was a DCIS agent there when the team came in. He's apparently working with the manager on some internal investigation having to do with auctions of surplus equipment."

"Is that a problem?"

"No, sir, we don't think so. He apparently observed for a little while, then left. We have his name, and I've got one of the Security Working Group staffies running it down within DCIS channels, just to make sure."

"Then we can declare victory and go home, you think?"

"Yes, sir. I assume you'll hang some guilty bastards for letting it get loose, but otherwise, yes, I think we're done. You might, um, want to have a word with General Carrothers. I'm not totally convinced he'll be in agreement with our conclusions."

"Not a problem. Lee Carrothers wants to be my replacement. Good night, Ambrose. And thank you."

"Yes, sir," Fuller said, and hung up. As he went out into the hallway, he thought about the Wet Eye biologic simulation his people were running back at Dietrick. Should he shut that off? He stopped in the hallway and thought about it. No, let them proceed. It might be interesting to see what they came up with, even if the immediate problem was over.

8

A flare of headlights in the mirror announced the arrival of Ray Sparks. Stafford unlocked his doors and Ray slid into the passenger seat. Two hotel security officers who had been giving Stafford's government car the eye went off to do other things. One government car bore watching; two government cars meant problems, and the security guys wanted nothing to do with government problems.

"Okay, hotshot, lay it on me. From the beginning."

Stafford walked him through the events of the past week again: his unfocused suspicions about Carson; the reportedly sudden exit of Bud Lambry, followed by the mysterious propane blast; his own visit to Graniteville. He trod carefully through the details of that visit, then reviewed its antecedents in the airport.

"Okay, right." Sparks said. "And that the woman thinks the girl is a psychic."

"That's right. There have been two other witnessed incidents like that."

Sparks was silent for a minute. Outside, the Peachtree Center plaza was empty except for a few passing pedestrians hurrying through the roseate light.

"Okay," Sparks, said, "Let's stipulate the girl's a psychic and that she saw that cylinder thing in the drawing you told me about. What's happened to get me out here at two in the morning?"

"Because two Army semis from Anniston, Alabama, showed up at the DRMO tonight," Dave said. "Ostensibly to conduct a no-notice exercise of some kind of chemical response team."

"And?"

"And there's apparently a chemical weapons ammunition dump at Anniston. And during the course of this so-called exercise, I happened to see the thing in the girl's drawing revolving in three dimensions on a monitor in one of the Army semis while an officer appeared to be explaining something about it."

Sparks opened his mouth to say something but then shut it.

Stafford went on to describe what the press officer had told him about it being just an exercise. "I don't think that was an exercise, Ray. I think those guys were looking for something under the cover of an exercise. My guess is that the cylinder contains some kind of chemical agent: nerve gas, or something lovely like that. I think maybe one of those environmental containers shipped in from Utah wasn't empty, and Carson, probably with Lambry's help, found it and concealed it. Carson was thinking about it in the airport when I showed up on an unannounced visit from the DCIS in Washington."

"And you're saying he had the misfortune to think about it in front of a passing psychic? A teenage girl who can't speak?"

"She can communicate. And she can draw. She says—"

"She *says*?"

"She can communicate, damn it! She uses sign language. And what she saw has been giving her bad dreams since they came home from the airport."

"Why were they at the airport?"

"They were coming home from Charlotte. Gwen had taken the girl there for some medical tests."

"What kind of medical tests?"

Uh-oh, Stafford thought. "The kid has chronic headaches. Gwen wanted to make sure the girl did not have a brain tumor."

"Uh-huh," Sparks said. "And Gwen is—"

"Gwen Warren is the woman who runs the school. Ray, she wanted no part of me or the DCIS, but she still felt compelled to call. Isn't it obvious? Carson stole that cylinder. We've got to tell the Army before he sells the fucking thing."

But Sparks was shaking his head. "No way, Dave. No way in hell. Look, the Army treats its chemical weapons the way the rest of the military treats nuclear weapons. They simply don't lose that shit. And if they had, there'd be a full court press involving every federal law-enforcement agency to find it."

"Would there? This is the Army we're talking about. The Green Machine. I think they'd cover it up like hell while they tried to recover it in-house. Like that little 'exercise' down at the DRMO, which just *happened* to have been the destination for the supposedly empty containers."

"Yeah, but c'mon, Dave: a psychic, for Chrissakes? I didn't say anything at lunch because it didn't seem to make a shit, but this . . . Look, picture yourself telling DCIS headquarters this story. Picture my telling the colonel that you were coming in with this story. Based on the visions of a teenage girl living in one of those state homes for the sexually abused or otherwise mentally fucked up."

"They're not mentally fucked up, Ray. They're just kids. They're orphans, basically. This Willow Grove isn't a loony bin for disturbed children. It's a group home for wards of the state. They're just kids from the north Georgia mountains." But even as he said this, Stafford remembered Gwen's words about augmenting the state funding by including mild emotional disturbances in her charter.

Sparks was shaking his head even more emphatically. "No, Dave," he said. "Putting aside the physic bullshit, this is all supposition. I can't have you roaring off into the night raising hell about a problem that doesn't officially exist. Don't you understand that this is the sort of shit that got you sent down here in the first place?"

Stafford sat back in the seat and took a deep breath. Sparks grabbed Dave's right forearm and then let go when he remembered. "Look at me, Dave. Listen to me. Besides the colonel, I'm probably the only friend in the business you've got right now. This assignment down here is your last chance, okay? The colonel made that very clear, at least to me. And to you, I think. You come yelling out of the fucking woods with your hair on fire about something like this and they're gonna terminate your ass. It's not like you have legions of defenders up there in D.C., right? An office full of people ready to go to the mat for you? Do you? *Do you?*"

Stafford said nothing but shook his head slowly. Sparks nodded. "You know I'm fucking right. Now tell me something: Do you have any admissible *evidence* that this guy Carson is running some kind of theft scam at the DRMO?"

"Nothing but the pattern we detected in D.C."

"But that was at another DRMO, right? Not this one?"

Stafford nodded, staring straight out the window. Disaster, he was thinking. Again.

"Then I suggest you put your head down and see if you can develop some admissible evidence, Dave. Not from psychics, not from peeping into the back of Army trucks doing some kind of Weird Harold exercise, and not about an emergency that does not exist. Work your brief, and nothing but your brief, because if you don't, you're going to be an unemployed civilian. Hey, you didn't go bracing Carson up on this by any chance, did you?"

Stafford said nothing, but his silence spoke volumes. Unmitigated disaster. I should have known.

"Aw *shit*, Dave. Goddamn it." Sparks sighed and slumped in his seat. "Okay, I'm not sure I can help you anymore. If Carson goes crying to his bosses in DLA, and they go to DCIS, this may be out of my hands. I think you better come up to Smyrna in the morning. Do *not* go back to that DRMO. You understand me? I want you in my office in the morning *before* the shit hits the fan."

"And you will not even try to believe me?"

Sparks gave him what appeared to be a pitying look. "On the word of a mute psychic teenager, Dave? Can't we go for at least a mutant Ninja Turtle?"

"And on the word of a trained child psychologist who's run that school for many years? Who does not want that kid involved in this?"

"I don't know that and you don't know that. For all I know, she wants to be a star on *America's Most Wanted.* Is she a psychic, too, Dave? Look, I think you're just overwrought. Go get some sleep. Then come into the office in the morning. Maybe if we can piss on this fire early enough, we can put it out, okay? Lemme make some calls, head this thing off. I'll tell 'em you were whacked-out on your meds or something."

Sparks slipped out of the car but held the door open. "Remember who your friends are, Dave," he said.

"Yeah, right," Dave said. "Both of them."

"Bingo. So get some sleep. Forget about goddamn psychics. That's an order."

■ SATURDAY, MOUNT VERNON, VIRGINIA, 10:00 A.M.

Brig. Gen. Lee Carrothers rejoined his wife, Sue, out on their patio, where she was having coffee and reading the *Washington Post.* It was a glorious spring day along the Potomac, with the cherry blossoms and dogwoods competing with one another to set the woods ablaze in pink and white. Only the constant muted thunder of jets from National Airport marred the otherwise-pristine air along the river. He was decked out in shorts and a sweatshirt, having just mown their backyard.

"So what did Himself want?" she asked. "You don't have to go in, do you?"

He sat down in a deck chair next to hers and took her hand. "You know that flap I've been dealing with all week? What I called the 'Anniston problem'?"

"Yes?"

"Let me run something by you." He then proceeded to tell her the story of the missing cylinder, ending with what the team had reported to the Security Working Group and what the group had concluded in its report to General Waddell. She was silent for a minute when he was finished.

"So," she said finally, "they're going to assume that thing was destroyed when the containers went into the—what'd you call it? The demil process?"

"Right."

"And what if it didn't? What if somebody heisted it?"

He nodded silently, looking out over the freshly mowed grass. They could hear the susurrations of Saturday-morning traffic out on the G. W. Parkway behind their backyard fence. His dear wife, Sue, was absolute hell on getting right to the heart of the matter, which was why he often consulted her, security or no security. Besides, she could keep her mouth shut.

"I asked that very question, early on, when we decided to send in a monitoring team to the DRMO at Fort Gillem, disguised as an exercise. Got a 'Who farted in church?' reaction. Himself sort of made it clear that the right answer was going to be found there, at Fort Gillem, one way or the other. Either they'd find the containers, and the cylinder in one of them, or the containers would have been demiled, and we'd have to assume the missing cylinder was destroyed right along with them."

"In other words, there were no other thinkable alternatives."

"Right. Losing a cylinder of this stuff was simply 'not possible.' Himself was calling to reiterate that sentiment this morning."

"Why? Did you object to the group's findings?"

"Just to Fuller, that biological weapons guy from Dietrick. I think maybe he had a word with Waddell. That maybe I needed my loyalty calibrated."

She put the paper down. "Biological weapons guy? I thought we were talking CW here."

"Oh, we are. As if that's not bad enough. Ambrose Fuller's an old pal of Waddell and keeps him apprised of what's going on out at USAMRIID. He used to work the BW program before 1968. He's a veterinarian. They used vets back then, and now, for all I know, to work the infectious disease vaccine programs there."

"So why was Fuller pulled into this problem?"

Carrothers had been thinking about that. Good question. "Because Waddell wanted him to chair the Security Working Group."

"Lee?"

"Yeah, right. Why a biological guy? Shit."

"What exactly was the good Herr General conveying this morning?" she asked. "That maybe your future as crown prince of the Chemical Corps was dependent on manifestations of right attitudes? Like he wants to see Chairman Hillary's little red book prominently displayed in your breast pocket?"

Carrothers laughed out loud. Sue knew how things worked. "Nothing quite so subtle," he said. "This is Myer Waddell we're talking about. He said to go along with the report, and to keep any doubts I might have until such time as I was head of the Chemical Corps, at which time I would be free to open fire on either one or both of my feet as I saw fit."

"Uh-huh. And meanwhile?"

"Meanwhile? Well, hell, they might be right. The Working Group, that is. It is logical that the missing cylinder was left in a container. It's also logical that all the containers went unopened into the demil process. Who the hell would go opening up a CW container?"

"Lee."

"Lee's not here. Lee's away on TDY somewhere."

"Lee!"

"Hush, Sue. I'm going to have to think about this one."

<hr>

■ SATURDAY, FORT GILLEM DRMO, ATLANTA, 9:15 A.M.

Carson had come into his office, even though it was a Saturday morning. The DRMO, of course, was empty, and his pickup was the only truck out in the lot. He had told his wife that he needed to catch up on some paperwork, but the real reason was that he needed time to think. His latest conversation with Tangent had been nip and tuck.

In retrospect, he had probably done things backward. First he had told Tangent that the Army had come and gone—satisfied, he was pretty sure, that the cylinder had been destroyed in the demil machine. Then he had told him that the DCIS guy, Stafford, had tumbled somehow to why the Army was there, evidently because of something Dillard had told him. Tangent had been worried about this sudden Army "exercise," but he'd gone positively hermantile over Stafford's accusations.

"He knows? He described the item?"

"Pretty close, he did. But look, he has no evidence. Lambry is gone, and I'll guarantee you Lambry did not know where the cylinder is hidden. Only what it looked like when he brought it to me."

"I don't know, Carson. We may have to dump this thing. What if Lambry's in hiding somewhere, just waiting to testify? What if *they* have his ass?"

"Who? The Army? The DCIS? Is that likely? Stafford wouldn't be running his mouth in my office if they had anything at all. They'd be all over this place waving warrants, and my ass would be in the slammer. They have nothing. Stafford was just trying to spook me, that's all."

Tangent thought that one over. "So where the hell is Lambry?"

"Who the hell knows? I think he got scared when Stafford showed up. He's a hillbilly from Alabama somewhere. We're not talking math major here, okay? Probably got scared and hightailed it back into the piney woods. Left the gas on in his house in southeast Atlanta and burned the thing down."

"I didn't know that."

"Well, he did. Day after he failed to show up for work." It had, of course, been more than one day, but Tangent didn't need to know that. "The arson cops came around, but they didn't think it was arson. No bodies or anything. No insurance policy. He just cleared out. Unfortunately, he must have leaked something to Dillard, and Dillard was seen talking to Stafford."

"That's what I'm worried about. Where's Stafford now?"

"Don't know. But you said you had some influence up there. You found out his political situation. Why don't we act on that? The Army's come and gone; they're not going to want to hear any noise about any missing CW cylinder. If you can neutralize Stafford quickly, after all that trouble he got in up there in Washington, then we'll be home free."

"And how are we supposed to do that?"

"I'm thinking of complaining up my chain of command that Stafford is making wild-ass accusations. I'll start it with a side bar to the local DCIS office in Atlanta. Make it sound like Stafford's lost it—you know, become some kind of nutcase. You say you can make things happen up there. You get DCIS headquarters to pull him back to D.C. Get Stafford out of the picture. The Army's already out of the picture. Like I said, we're home free. Better yet, we'll be dealing with an object that isn't missing."

"That's probably going to be harder than it sounds," Tangent said. "My people have no direct leverage on the DCIS."

"Well, get some, goddamn it," Carson said. "Stafford's the only thing between us and some serious money, right? You said he was on a shit list up there. Pull the string with the people he burned. Didn't you say he took down a Bureau guy?"

"Yeah, that's right. The Bureau. There is an angle we can work with the Bureau."

"Well, all right, then. I guess you have to wait until Monday."

"No, I don't. But you let us worry about that. From what I've heard about this guy, all it's going to take is a few words that he's running wild again, and somebody'll step on his neck."

"But it's Saturday: Nobody—"

"Every department in government law enforcement has a duty officer, Carson. Which is even better: When the duty officer calls, the bosses react first, and then pulse their staffs on Monday."

"What do you want me to do?"

"Nothing. Sit tight. Don't call DLA. You're right. This is the way to go. We'll have this Stafford prick off the boards by Monday."

"Okay, but then what? Should we sit on things for a week, let the dust settle?"

"I don't think so. Stafford can be neutralized, but short of somebody shooting him, he can't be silenced. No, if anything, I think we have to move up the transfer. Our clients are anxious, and we don't want them to get wind of any shit brewing in DCIS circles. I want you to call me at six P.M. tomorrow, that's Sunday." He gave Carson another 800 number and hung up.

Carson thought about all that. So now it was hurry up and wait, while the Washington ballerinas did the monster mash on Stafford. Short of shooting him, Tangent had said. Well, if he gets between me and my money, I may have a go at that option.

He decided to go over to the demil building and make damned sure that no one had messed around with the roller casing. But first he would take a little stroll, make sure that bastard Stafford wasn't skulking around the warehouses somewhere. He patted his windbreaker pocket as he left his office. His snub-nosed Colt felt reassuringly solid.

▬ SATURDAY, ANNISTON, ALABAMA, 10:45 A.M.

Stafford had taken a motel room at the Holiday Inn out on I-20 after having a late breakfast at one of the ubiquitous Waffle Houses. After his meeting with Sparks, he had gone up to his room in the hotel long

135

enough to pack his stuff, get five hours of sleep, and then hit the inter-state west out of Atlanta. It had taken him an hour and a half to get to Oxford, which was the turnoff for Anniston to the north of the interstate. The motel room would provide a base of operations with a land-line telephone and a local directory, and he would probably be staying over-night, depending on what shook out from his inquiries at the Army base. As long as he kept his government-issue cell phone off the air, Sparks could not know where he was, which should give him forty-eight hours of breathing room. Until Monday, that is, at which time Ray Sparks would expect him in the DCIS office in Smyrna. He smiled ruefully. What Sparks had actually said was that he expected Stafford in his office *this* morning, but Stafford had decided to misunderstand.

Forty-eight hours. On a weekend. Not much time.

He made a call to the local newspaper and talked to a harried-sounding female reporter who was about to go out to cover a local char-ity golf tournament. He identified himself as a freelance writer, gave a false name, and said he was looking for local interest stories in small-town Alabama. He said he'd heard a rumor that there was something big going on at the Army base, something to do with chemical weapons. She laughed and told him that there were always rumors about the CW depot, but the only news came when they made a shipment out west somewhere and the local environmental protestors did their bit along the railroad right-of-way. Because a lot of people in this town were dependent on the base, though, the protests never amounted to much. Otherwise, there was nothing shaking that she knew about, and she said she really had to get a move on. He thanked her and hung up.

He tried the same probe at the local radio stations in Oxford and Anniston, but everyone was out doing something called "remotes" at shopping centers or car dealerships. Nobody had heard about anything out of the ordinary going down at the Army base.

He sat back on the bed. This was going to be much harder than it had seemed last night. Somehow he had to find out whether or not the Army had lost a chemical weapon. If they had, what would they do? They'd initiate an internal investigation, both at this base and probably at the shipment destination point. He thought about the Army Criminal Investigation Command, what used to be called the CID. They were the investigatory branch of the Army military-police organization. If there were a big-deal investigation going on behind closed doors, the local CIC people would have heard about it, even if they weren't involved. As a DCIS investigator, he could go into any

CIC office in the country, ask for help in his current DRMO investigation, and, from there, make a casual inquiry about what was shaking at Anniston.

Unless, of course, Ray Sparks had already begun some damage-control efforts by alerting the duty office at DCIS Washington that Dave Stafford had, once again, wandered off the reservation. And if he'd done that, DCIS Washington might in turn be alerting their counterparts in the military services to be on the lookout for a Stafford, David, unit of issue one each, even as we speak. Shit.

It all depended on how fast Ray moved, and whether or not he would wait until Monday. Civil servants, even the police variety, almost never worked weekends, but there were duty officers at every level of the chain of command whose job it was to cover weekend contingencies. Hell with it, he thought. I'm going to go over to that base and talk to the Army CIC people. If I run into a white-eyed stone wall, that in itself will tell me something.

The map provided by the motel showed Fort McClellan on the north side of the town of Anniston. He wondered where the hell they kept all the evil shit. He was very surprised when he turned in at the first gate he came to and found it unguarded. Fort McClellan was an open post? He drove down the road until he found a headquarters office, where he obtained a map of the post.

He finally found the provost marshal's office, which was located in a headquarters area three blocks from the sprawling Chemical Warfare School. He parked the government car and went in, where he found the Army version of a police station desk area. There was a waiting room in the front, facing a railing with a gate in the middle that spanned the room. A young black man, who appeared to be a civilian, was sitting in the waiting room. To the left was a door marked CIC. Bingo.

He walked up to the railing and waited for the female sergeant to get off the phone. He presented his credentials and asked if the CIC people were in.

"No, sir," she said. "It's Saturday. I have a beeper number I can try. Except—"

"Except?"

"Well, this weekend is the annual campground cleanup. Everybody's going to be working up in north post. It's a volunteer thing every spring. I don't think he's gonna be close to a phone. He's already had one call this morning, and he hasn't answered. Can I maybe help you with something?"

137

Stafford had to think fast. He had planned to ease into this question. "I'm running an investigation in Atlanta, at a DRMO," he said. "That's one of those surplus sales offices. Yesterday a team from here went in and ran a CW exercise, and I wanted to talk to the CIC agent here to see if that exercise was possibly connected to my investigation."

"A CW exercise? From Fort McClellan?"

"Well, they said they were from Anniston. I assumed Fort McClellan."

"They say they were from the Chemical Warfare School?"

"No. It was some kind of emergency response team. They were all suited up, except for the officers who were in charge. Two big-ass trucks. About twenty people."

The clerk thought for a moment, then shook her head. "There's nothing like that here at Fort McClellan."

"Is there anything going on here on the base that might initiate an exercise like that all the way up in Atlanta? Some big exercise? War games?"

She shook her head again. "No, sir, not that I know of. Not here. But maybe the team came from the depot."

"The depot?"

"Yes, sir. The Anniston Army Weapons Depot. That's not here. It's a special weapons storage area, about ten miles west of here. They might have a CW response team like that. Fort McClellan doesn't."

"I see," he said. Now what? he thought. Wrong Army base? "Well, I guess I need to go over there, then. So there's nothing going on here that might have emergency response teams running around Atlanta?"

"No, sir, it's just a normal Saturday, far as I know. Fort McClellan doesn't store weapons, sir. We're mostly about schools here."

"Okay. Let me leave a name and number for your CIC duty officer, in case he calls in for his messages. I'm staying down at the Holiday Inn, on the interstate in Oxford. Room number 405." He repeated his name, then let her see the credentials again. She wrote it all down and promised to try the beeper a couple of times. He got directions from her to the Anniston Depot, thanked her, and left.

Her directions took him back into the center of Anniston, where he stopped into a Burger King for a caffeine fix. He then drove west out of town on Highway 202, which was a two-lane road that took him through open farmland and wooded hills, interspersed with clusters of trashy-looking trailers crouching by the road. He kept looking for signs to the depot, but there was nothing marked. After ten miles, he stopped and asked for directions at a gas station minimart, and the lady pointed him to the next intersection. Sure enough, there was an inconspicuous sign up on a hillside announcing the presence of the Anniston Army Weapons Depot.

He turned right and headed down an extra-wide road. There was nothing on either side but pine woods. He had sort of expected razor wire, guard towers, and electric fences, but then, a CW storage area was probably not a favorite place for local deer hunters. After about a mile, the road crossed over what looked like a mainline railway, and then made a sweeping right turn down into an area resembling the assembly area in front of a ferry landing. There were several semis parked diagonally in waiting lanes, and ahead was a large reinforced steel gate that was closed. Beyond the gate, several large industrial buildings were visible. The buildings were constructed entirely of windowless concrete. There was an expansive railroad-siding area, with rail spurs running under closed steel doors into the concrete buildings. No humans were visible on the other side of the gate area.

He drove down the hill. An armed civilian guard came out of the gatehouse. Dave stopped and showed his credentials, hoping that his ID and the government car would get him in.

"This is a closed post," the guard declared, holding on to Stafford's credentials while studying them. "Unless you have a point of contact who's there now and whom we can call on the phone, we can't let you in."

"No," Dave said. "I don't. I was hoping there was a CIC office here at the Depot."

"Nope," the guard said, still looking at the credentials. "CIC's over at Fort McClellan."

"Okay," Dave said. "Is there a CERT of some sort based here? A team that might go out to do its thing in two big Army semis?"

The guard's expression revealed absolutely nothing. "Don't know anything about any teams, sir," he replied, handing back Stafford's credentials. "This here is a special weapons storage area. Can't let you in. You can back up and turn around right over there."

Stafford thanked him and turned the car around. As he drove off, he could see the guard through the open door of the gatehouse; he was writing something down at his desk. Probably has to record the name of anyone coming, going, or refused entrance, Stafford thought. He wondered if that procedure might come back to haunt him.

He drove back to Anniston with the afternoon Alabama sun blazing in his mirror. Now what? he wondered.

"Lee, it's the Pentagon duty officer," Sue Carrothers said, handing her husband the portable phone.

"General Carrothers," he said, frowning. Saturday-afternoon calls were never good news.

"Sir, this is Major Mason, Chemical Corps duty officer. We've had a call from Fort McClellan. From the post operations officer. Can we go secure, sir?"

Carrothers handed the portable back to his wife and went into the study, where he initiated the secure link on his desk phone. The phone emitted a tone, and then the digital window indicated the line was secure. "Go ahead," he said.

"Sir, this is in reference to the Security Working Group. A Defense Criminal Investigative Service agent by the name of David Stafford went to the McClellan provost marshal's office this morning, asking to speak to the CIC rep. The clerk took his name and number and offered to beep the CIC rep, but apparently they're all out in the woods doing some kind of base cleanup, so they don't think the CIC guy ever called him back."

"And why precisely do I care?" Carrothers asked.

"Because he was also asking about the CERT that went to Fort Gillem yesterday."

"Oh shit."

"Yes, sir. There's more. She, the clerk, is an E-Five MP. She had never heard of any CERT, so she sent him over to the depot."

"Oh shit squared."

"Yes, sir. We've checked with the security people there, and he did in fact show up. He apparently tried, although not very hard, to get into the depot, and then he asked the guard about the response team. The guard blew him off, of course, but he wrote it all down, including Stafford's badge info, and he called it in to the depot duty officer as an unusual gate event. The duty officer called the CO of the depot, and since they had dispatched the reaction team to Gillem in response to our orders, he called me."

The chain of command, Carrothers marveled. Sometimes it actually works.

"Who is this guy again?"

"A GS-Fifteen investigator named David Stafford, on assignment to Atlanta from DCIS Washington. We've checked him out with the DCIS duty officer, and he's legit—sort of."

"Sort of, Major?"

"Well, sir, it seems he was a whistle-blower. Bit of an odd duck. Senior investigator, good, if somewhat unorthodox, professional reputation in DCIS until he dropped a dime on some SES-Two named Bernstein, as well as another senior guy at the FBI."

"What was going on?"

"Standard Washington dance card, General. The guy I talked to said this Bernstein apparently was selling information to a congressional staffer—something about a sensitive DCIS case involving a big Defense Department contractor. The staffer would then have lunch with the contractor's lobbyist, who in turn would feed the inside dope to the company, giving their corporate legal team a leg up. The company kept it sweet by making a campaign contribution sent in through the lobbyist to the staffer, who took a piece and also cut Bernstein in for a piece of the contribution as a 'consultant.' "

"Lovely. How did Stafford pick up that scheme?"

"Stafford pulled the string on Bernstein's lifestyle. The word in the DCIS was that Bernstein had jumped in Stafford's shit over some unorthodox gumshoe work, and Stafford was just getting back. But then this Bernstein apparently panicked and reached out to a buddy who was a senior guy in the FBI with a request to hassle Stafford. Once that shit started, Stafford got pissed and pulled in the IRS. Net result was the discovery of a whole grunch of undeclared income, and then the whole thing unraveled."

"Bernstein go to jail?"

"No, sir. He was a political appointee. He flipped to the IRS side against the Defense contractor and the FBI official, in return for a nolo contendere and the opportunity to write the IRS a big check and let bygones be bygones. The administration sent him overseas somewhere to a new assignment. The FBI guy got reprimanded but that was all."

"That's usually enough in the Bureau, which means Stafford's on at least two shit lists. So what's he doing in Atlanta?"

"Technically, an investigation on possible fraud within the DRMO system, but the DCIS duty officer said he'd heard Stafford had been unofficially shit-canned. He had one other interesting piece of information: Apparently, the DCIS regional supervisor in Smyrna called in looking for Stafford within the past twenty-four hours. Stafford was supposed to have reported to the Smyrna office this morning, but he didn't show."

"Because he was snooping around in Anniston. Why did they want him?"

"The duty officer didn't know, General. Only that if we knew where he was, the local DCIS office sure as hell wanted to know, too."

Carrothers was silent for a minute while he thought. Something was way off the tracks here, and, of course, it would have to be on a damned Saturday. "Okay," he said. "I'm really glad you had the duty, Major. Good work all around. I'd better call General Waddell. I'll get back to you."

Carrothers called Waddell's home in Alexandria, but the general was not in. He left a message requesting the general to call him, then hung up. His wife was polishing some silver in the kitchen when he walked in.

"Fire somewhere?" she asked.

"In a manner of speaking. This is that matter we talked about this morning. I have this bad feeling it's not going to stay buried."

"Should it, Lee? Stay buried, that is?"

He sighed and looked out the window for a moment. "My gut instinct is to climb into my dress canvas and get my young ass into the building."

"Well, you're always saying you should trust your instincts."

"Yeah. I'm always saying that."

"Just make sure you trust *all* your instincts, Lee. Our second star isn't worth being a part of something that can't stand the smell test."

He stood there, his hands in his pockets. "Waddell as much as told me that my accession to the CG job depended on how well I handled this little tar baby," he said. "This was my chance to demonstrate that I really knew how to play the game when the stakes got high."

She put down the polishing rag. "And now?"

"And now I don't know. *I* think some bastard has stolen a chemical weapon."

"Wow. And the bigs don't want to hear that."

"Too right."

She leaned over and put her hand on his cheek and kissed him. Her fingers smelled of silver polish. "I still have my Realtor's license," she said. "You go do the right thing, Lone Ranger."

"I hear you, Mrs. Carrothers," he said, shaking his head. "Sometimes I think we never learn a damned thing in the Army."

"Your Monday uniform is rigged and ready in the closet."

He was upstairs changing when General Waddell called back. They went secure on the phones and Carrothers told him what Mason had reported and that he, Carrothers, was on his way in to the Pentagon.

"DCIS, huh?" the general said. "Ambrose Fuller told me there was a DCIS guy at the DRMO when the team went in. Mason think this Stafford knows about the cylinder?"

"It sounds like he at least suspects something. First he was there at Fort Gillem when the team went in. And now he's knocking on doors at McClellan and the Anniston Depot."

"We don't need this shit. The McClellan people know where he's staying there in Anniston?"

"Actually, yes, sir, I think they do."

Waddell was silent for a moment. "Okay," he said. "The MP school is there, right? That means there are at least five hundred MPs at Fort McClellan. Pick him up. Have them find him, pick him up, and hold him. Now. And notify the DCIS once we have him."

"Pick up a federal agent, General?"

"That's right. His supervisor's looking for him, right? He tried an intrusion at a special weapons facility. We can always say we were not convinced of his identity. Then when DCIS admits he's theirs, we'll hand him over, *after* they agree to pull him out and keep him out of our official hair."

Carrothers tried to keep any hint of doubt out of his voice. "Yes, sir. I'll get right on it," he said, but the general had already hung up.

■■■ SATURDAY, OXFORD, ALABAMA, 5:30 P.M.

It was going on sundown when Stafford got back to the motel. He had stopped for a late lunch in Anniston, then spent a long time crawling through the Saturday-afternoon traffic getting down to Oxford. He parked the government sedan reasonably near his room in the fourth building and was unlocking the door when a voice behind him said his name. He whirled around and found a black man there.

"Yes?" he said, trying to keep the surprise out of his voice. It was times like this that he really missed the use of his arm.

"I'm Kevin Durand. I was in the provost marshal's office this mornin.' Heard you askin' if there was somethin' goin' on 'bout chemical weapons and shit. Heard you say you were a federal agent and that you were stayin' down here."

"Is there something going on, Mr. Durand?"

"Yeah, I think there is." He looked up and down the line of doors, as if uncomfortable talking about it out in the open. Stafford decided to take a chance.

"Come on in then," he said. "Tell me about it."

Durand went in with him and sat down in the chair by the television. He told Stafford a story about his girlfriend, Specialist Latonya Mayfield, who was reportedly being held in the disciplinary barracks, which is why he had been at the provost marshal's office that morning. The word Durand was getting through the grapevine was that she and some other enlisted were being held incommunicado because of some flap having to do with some missing materials over at the depot. He hadn't succeeded in getting any answers.

When Durand had finished, Stafford asked him what Specialist Mayfield's assignment was. When Durand told him, Stafford nodded thoughtfully. Durand's story had essentially confirmed one element of the puzzle: It really did sound as if the Army had lost something, and it was probably Durand's girlfriend who had discovered it in the first place.

"Are you able to talk to her?"

"No, sir. I've tried to call, and I even went to the depot to see if I could get in. All's I've had is one message from some clerk, who says she's okay and for me not to worry about her. Says she's on some special detail. But that's not what I'm hearin'."

"But you are worried about her, right?"

"Yes, sir," he said. "There's definitely some kinda shit goin' down over there."

Stafford thought about what to say next. He wasn't sure he wanted to share what he knew—correction, what he *suspected*—with a civilian. Even though the civilian had had the grace to share what he knew with him, his conscience reminded him.

"Mr. Durand," Stafford said, "I happen to think you're right. I suspect they're holding Specialist Mayfield until they get their problem sorted out, whatever it is. And somehow, this all ties in with something I'm working on back in Atlanta. Tell me, you have somewhere to go?'

Durand stared at him. "Say what? You mean like get out of town?"

"Yeah. That's exactly what I mean. Lower your profile. Take a short trip."

"What about Latonya?"

"If what I suspect is happening is indeed happening, they've got much bigger problems than Latonya."

"And you think I oughta just *split*?"

"Yes. Can you do that without too much trouble?"

Durand smiled. "Can a black man disappear in Alabama? You kiddin'?"

"Okay. Then I'd get out of sight if I were you."

Durand shook his head. "But what've I done?"

"Nothing, Mr. Durand. It's what the Army thinks you might *know* that could get you in trouble."

"But I'm a civilian!"

"Would you call this an Army town, Mr. Durand?"

Durand pursed his lips and thought about that. He nodded. "Oh yeah. No doubt 'bout that."

"Well, then."

Durand thanked him and then left. Stafford looked up the number for Ray Sparks's office. He should be at home, he thought. It's a Saturday, and it's almost six o'clock, but I better check the office, just in case.

The phone was answered on the first ring. "DCIS, Sparks. We're nonsecure."

"Ray."

"Dave! Where the hell are you? You were supposed to come in here this morning." Stafford thought he could hear someone else in the office, but then Sparks apparently hit the mute button on his handset.

"Thought you meant Monday, Ray," Stafford said, trying to keep it light. "Never knew you to work Saturdays."

"I said *this* morning. So where the hell are you?" Definitely key-set mode, Stafford thought. Sparks was having to press a key to talk, which meant he wanted to keep any background conversations in the office off the line.

"Anniston, Alabama."

"Dave, Dave, Dave: I told you to leave that Army thing alone."

"I know, but let me tell you what I've found out." He went on to describe the essence of what Kevin Durand had told him, naming Durand only as a confidential informant. "They've lost a weapon, Ray. I just know they have. And I'm willing to bet that slippery bastard Carson has it. We can't just sit on something like that."

There was a pause. Stafford wondered if Sparks was talking to someone else. "Where exactly are you in Anniston, Dave?" Sparks asked.

Stafford felt a chill. "Exactly? In a motel, Ray. Why?"

"Which motel, Dave? Got a number so I can call you back? A room number?"

"You sound like I'm a fugitive from justice, Ray. You getting some help with this matter?"

"Dave, don't be cute. Where are you? Which fucking motel?"

Stafford slowly hung up the phone and then stared down at it. What the hell is this? He thought for a moment. What had he told the clerk at the PM office that morning? Enough, apparently. Durand had found him easily enough. Sparks wouldn't be far behind.

He packed up as fast as he could with one hand, strapped his briefcase to his bag, and then got the hell out of there. He stopped at the door to the parking lot and scanned the area, but nothing out of the ordinary appeared to be going on. He walked as casually as he could to the Crown Vic and put his bags in. He looked around the parking area one more time, and then he got in and drove out of the lot. Diagonally across the four-lane highway was a Best Western motel. He drove down an access road to a stoplight, went across the road, and then drove back one block to the Best Western parking lot, turning so he could face the car toward the Holiday Inn, which was now diagonally across the state highway from him. He parked but kept the engine running.

Damn, damn, *damn*, he thought. What in the *hell* is going on here? He could understand Sparks's earlier reluctance to believe his theory about a missing weapon, but when he called in with corroborating evidence, Sparks had acted as if he was setting up an arrest. My arrest, he realized. He recalled what Carson had threatened to do. Maybe Carson hadn't waited until Monday.

Twenty minutes later, he saw what he had been waiting for: Three Army MP cars with flashing blue and red lights emerged from under the interstate overpass to his left and pulled into the access road across the way. They sped into the Holiday Inn parking lot, and a dozen MPs in uniform spilled out and headed for the motel building. An Army sedan drove in behind them.

Dave didn't hesitate. He backed up the Crown Vic, then drove it down the access road on his side to the intersection containing the ramps leading to the interstate. But then he had a thought. If Sparks is part of this, the MPs have to know what I'm driving, and they will expect me to be hauling ashes somewhere out on I-20. So don't do that. What I have to do is get rid of this very conspicuous car.

He thought fast, waiting for the light to change. Where's the last place they'll look for me? Back on the base. Back at Fort McClellan, where there's a base motor pool, and where maybe I can fake a problem with this car and get another one while the military police are out scouring the highways. He made up his mind as the light changed and he pulled out, turning left and heading north on the state road back into Oxford. He watched the red and blue police lights fluttering behind him in his mirror until the interstate overpass blocked them from view.

Thirty minutes later, in near darkness, he pulled into the base motor pool at Fort McClellan, thanking his household gods that the post gates were unguarded. He parked the Crown Vic in the lane nearest to the motor pool's office. There appeared to be one person on duty in the small office. There were three lanes' worth of trucks and sedans parked around him, probably because it was a Saturday night. He shut the car down and reached under the dash to find the fuse box. He discovered that the car had circuit breakers instead of fuses. Cracking the door, he scrunched down under the dash to read the labels by the light near the edge of the door. He found the breaker marked HEADLIGHTS and pulled the wires out of the breaker. Just to make sure, he used a pocketknife to cut them off where they disappeared into the fire wall.

He walked into the office and identified himself to the duty sergeant as a DCIS agent. He told him a story about his Fort Gillem car's lights crapping out on him and said that he needed a replacement car right away. The sergeant insisted on checking out the problem with the lights, saying that he wasn't sure if he could issue a replacement car, since this was Fort McClellan and the Crown Vic belonged to Fort Gillem. Dave blustered his way through all the bureaucratic objections. Fifteen minutes later, he was headed back out the southernmost gate in a very used black two-door Chrysler sedan.

He turned south on the state road and headed back through Anniston toward Oxford, watching for MP vehicles. Seeing signs for I-20, he turned off the main drag onto Highway 78, which led him east toward another interchange. He did not fancy being in an Army car down near the Holiday Inn interchange, assuming they were still down there beating the bushes.

Once he got to the interstate, he headed east, back toward Atlanta, not exceeding the speed limit. He figured that this Army car would suffice for about one night. His plan was to go to the airport, park the sedan way out in economy parking, and then go into the terminal and rent a civilian car. He looked at his watch. It was an hour and a half to Atlanta, so he should be able to get to the rental car desks before they closed for the night.

After that, he had no idea of what he was going to do. At the very least, he had to warn Gwen Warren. Two people knew he had been to

Graniteville. Sparks was one, and he knew why Stafford had been there. Carson was the other, although he shouldn't know about the girl, unless he remembered the airport incident and put two and two together.

He dreaded calling Gwen Warren after all his promises to keep the government away from the kids at Willow Grove, but he'd told Sparks about the girl, and now it looked like Sparks was working *with* the Army. Would he tell them about the girl's psychic vision of the cylinder? He swore as he thought about that. Gwen Warren would kick his ass for that. The Army had to be going apeshit over the cylinder; the appearance of military police at a civilian motel was proof of just how desperate they were. Have to get rid of this car. He pushed it up to eighty, and watched for cops.

▆ SATURDAY, THE PENTAGON, WASHINGTON, D.C., 10:15 P.M.

Brigadier General Carrothers sat in the Chemical Corps operations module of the Army Command Center, sipping his second cup of their notoriously noxious coffee. The Army Command Center, unlike those of the other services, had been constructed down in the basement of the Pentagon, presumably to protect it from enemy bombers. Despite heavy-duty air conditioning, the place smelled of mildew. The entire Pentagon building had been built on pilings in a tidal swamp; the state of the tide in the Potomac could be determined by how far up the wall the concrete was sweating. Legions of bored watch officers over the years had marked the range of various tides on the wall in black Magic Marker.

Major Mason was on the phone, having a discussion with the duty officer at the Anniston Army Weapons Depot, when the module intercom sounded off.

"CW module, you have a call from Fort McClellan on line thirty-six, secure."

Carrothers signified he would get it and picked up the STU-III handset. The caller was the provost marshal, asking for Major Mason.

"No, this is General Carrothers. Did you pick that guy up?"

"Good evening, sir. No, sir, we did not. He wasn't at the motel, and the local police report no sign of the Fort Gillem sedan in either Oxford or Anniston. We have the Highway Patrol looking. The sedan is distinctive: it's a white GSA Crown Vic. If he's out on the interstate, they should find him."

"Is there any indication that he knows people want to find him?"

"Well, General, we called the DCIS regional office and spoke to his supervisor, a Mr. Sparks. He says he talked to Stafford this evening, but Stafford wouldn't tell him where he was exactly. Only said he was in Anniston."

"Did this Sparks have any idea why one of his people was nosing around the Anniston Depot?"

"Sir, he got kind of coy when I asked that question. I got the sense that he wanted to get his hands on Stafford just as much as we do, so there's a chance he does know what the guy's up to. But if he does, he wasn't going to tell me. I think we've got a pretty good chance. That vehicle is pretty distinctive."

"If he's still in it," Carrothers said. "Where's the last place you would look for that vehicle?"

The provost marshal thought for a moment. "Here, on post."

"Yeah. And the local cops won't look there, either. Get your post MPs out and take a look around. This guy may be smarter than we thought."

Twenty minutes later, an embarrassed provost marshal was back on the phone, announcing the Crown Vic's discovery in the motor pool's parking lot. Stafford was now driving a black Chrysler sedan.

"And when did he engineer this little swap, Colonel?"

"This evening, General. While we were downtown rousting the Holiday Inn. If he's running to Atlanta, he's there and then some by now."

Carrothers hung up on him without reply. He had successfully suppressed the urge to yell, but he figured telephone rudeness would convey his displeasure. He back-briefed Major Mason.

"He's a cool one, this guy," Mason observed. "Assuming he figured out the MPs were on the way, that took some balls to drive back to the post and swap cars."

"I've got this bad feeling that somehow this guy has figured out why that team showed up at the DRMO in Atlanta," Carrothers said. "His boss is obviously pissed off at him, and yet he apparently went all cute when the provost tried to find out why DCIS wants him back."

Mason nodded. "Well, sir, the bad news is that we may have an intergovernment coordination problem; the good news is that the missing cylinder was destroyed with its container."

Carrothers stared across the module at the major. Their faces were gray in the artificial red-tinged lighting. "You absolutely, positively sure of that, Major?"

"Oh, yes, sir, General," Mason said, putting a stiffly sincere expression on his face. "General Waddell said that's what happened, so that's what happened. General, Sir."

Carrothers treated Mason to a stony glare, but then he looked away. The screens on the Command Center communications consoles stared back him. Waddell had made things very clear to him. The Army Chemical Corps could not have lost a weapon. It was simply not possible. And senior officers in the Chemical Corps who persisted in turning over rocks related to this unfortunate matter would do so at their professional peril.

But what had Sue said? Trust your instincts? All of them?

"Mason, here's what I want," Carrothers said, getting to his feet. "I want that Anniston sweep team reconstituted and reinforced. Four trucks instead of two. I want them sent back into that DRMO at Fort Gillem. Tonight, like between zero one hundred and zero five hundred. I want them out of there before first light. Out of Atlanta before sunrise. This time, I want them to search that whole place, not just the demil area. I don't want anyone to know about this at the DRMO. I want an MP detachment from Anniston to go along to set up a discreet cordon around the DRMO so nobody intrudes while this is going on. If anybody does intrude, I want that person apprehended."

"Yes, sir," Mason said, reaching for the secure phone. "I'll get right on it. And General Waddell, sir?"

"I'll handle General Waddell, Major," Carrothers replied. "He's got a social function tonight, and he's leaving for a PACCOM tour on Monday. One more thing: I want that DCIS supervisor, Sparks, on the horn after you get the reaction team in motion. Move out, Major."

"Yes, sir. Moving out, sir."

Carrothers walked through the main operations center and out the glass doors into the basement segment of the F-ring. He walked along the semidarkened corridor, which was lined with forklifts and stacked pallets. The ceiling was cluttered with steam pipes and electrical cables serving the enormous building above. He walked along the silent corridor until he came to the escalator up to the ground level. It being a weekend evening, the escalator was turned off, so he sprinted up the seventy feet of steel steps to the A-ring. Then he did what he usually did when he needed to think about a problem: He walked around the five-sided A-ring at a brisk stride, his leather heels echoing in the empty corridors.

He was already way out in front of his friendly front lines with the orders he had just issued. The higher echelons of the Army obviously wanted this matter buried. There would be some swift and meaningful retribution handed out at the lower levels in Anniston, or, more likely, at Tooele, for letting the thing get away, but if Waddell found out he was having the team go back into the DRMO, Carrothers knew he might join the various guilty bastards up on the scaffold. His chances for a second star and command of the Chemical Corps would vanish.

Luckily, General Waddell was going on travel again, which is why he wanted them in and out tonight, on a weekend, when there should be nobody there. He personally would call the commanding officer at Fort Gillem and tell him that the last exercise had turned into a Lebanese goat-grab and that he was rousting the team out to do it again, until they got it right. Just one more exercise, if you don't mind, Colonel. No big deal.

But the crucial question remained: Had the weapon been destroyed, as everyone was hoping and praying? Or had it been found and stolen by someone at that DRMO? And if it had been stolen, what would the guy who found it do with it? Try to sell it? Or maybe blackmail the Army for money? Pay me off or I'll tell the world you lost one? He didn't even want to think about the other possibilities that a missing can of Wet Eye presented.

He couldn't escape the conclusion that this DCIS agent, Stafford, had stumbled onto something relating to the missing cylinder; that Stafford had somehow discovered that the Anniston team's first visit had *not* been an exercise. But there was no way he could know that—unless that was what he was doing down there in the first place.

He shook his head. No way. He was thinking in circles here. Just as he was walking in circles around the five sides of old Fort Fumble by the Sea. A propane-powered tractor rattled past him, pulling a wagon train of Xerox paper down the otherwise-empty corridor. He headed back toward the basement escalator.

Two issues to resolve, he thought. First, Fort Gillem: Revisit that DRMO, make damn sure there is no trace of a Wet Eye cylinder there. And, second, talk to the DCIS supervisor in Smyrna, find out what the hell his Washington agent was really doing at that DRMO in the first place, and why he had gone off on his own to Anniston. He'd have to think of a pretext for the call. Well, for starters, the guy had shown up at the Anniston Army Weapons Depot, where he had no business to be.

We fervently hope, he thought as he trotted down the escalator.

Wendell Carson sat in the dark on his screened back porch, nursing a beer and considering the problem of Senior Investigator David Stafford. It was unseasonably warm this evening. The trees in the backyard stirred uneasily in the humid night air, and heat lightning flared over Alabama on the distant southwest horizon. His wife was inside watching television in the bedroom while she painted on her nightly fright mask. He could hear the awkward drone of the weekend fill-in concluding the local eleven o'clock news.

Stafford knew.

He knew why the Army team had really been there, and he knew what the cylinder looked like.

And he had said he was going to tell the Army.

Carson no longer cared how Stafford had found out. Bud Lambry had obviously confided in Dillard after all. Maybe to protect himself, he'd told Dillard more than he had let on, and then that dumb ass had gone running his mouth to Stafford. Had to be.

Unless . . .

A calf bawled in the darkness of the farmer's field behind Carson's property, and its mother lowed back reassuringly. Farther away, someone's chained-up dog was barking neurotically in the distance, its persistent yapping noise annoying the stillness. The beer bottle was sweating in all the humidity, trickling cold rivulets across the back of his right hand. He felt himself zoning out, his perception collapsing to a cube of space right in front of his eyes, which were closed, almost against his will.

He had been having the recurring bad dream ever since the thing at the airport, the one where he was trapped in a river and headed for a waterfall. Now the waterfall image reappeared. Once again, he felt the deadly wet grip of that surging current, and then the stomach-levitating sensation of going over. And he was not alone. There were other people in the river with him, dead, every one of them, and yet looking at *him*, ten thousand distorted faces frozen in soundless screams. Superimposed on this frightening image was the face of that damned girl, scanning the back of his braincase with those obsidian eyes. The girl from Graniteville.

Graniteville.

He opened his eyes with a start. Stafford had gone to Graniteville.

152

Damn! Was there some kind of connection there?

He realized he was gripping the beer bottle hard enough to hurt his hand. He forced his fingers to relax. Stafford had gone to Graniteville and then had come back talking about a cylinder. Which he could never have seen himself, because it had been either in Carson's possession or stuffed into that roller. Even the Army team, with all its sensors and experts, hadn't been able to find it, hidden right in front of them.

Graniteville.

He had a sudden intuition that he should go to the DRMO. His entire future was that cylinder, and suddenly he was desperate to lay his hands on it, to make sure it was still there. But first he would need an excuse to get out of the house.

He finished his beer and pitched the bottle in the trash as he went through the kitchen. He went quietly out the front door to his Army pickup truck, where he retrieved his government-issue bag phone. He carried it into the living room of the house and turned it on. Once he had a signal, he called his home number on a roamer circuit and then laid the handset down. He stepped quickly over to the house phone and caught it on the first ring.

"I've got it," he called down the hall, then pretended to have a brief conversation. He hung up and walked back to the bedroom.

"MPs have a problem down at the DRMO," he said. "Somebody tried to break in. Kids, most likely. I'll be right back."

His wife, intent now on a *M*A*S*H* rerun, nodded absently. He looked for a moment at that fat face covered in what looked like zinc oxide, then realized once again how important the cylinder and the money from its sale were going to be. He got a jacket in case it turned cooler later, picked up his bag phone, and went back out to the truck. At this hour, it would take only about forty minutes to get to Fort Gillem.

He had to see it again, to make sure it was still there. Then he would worry about any possible loose ends in Graniteville. If he was going to pull this deal off for really big bucks, nobody could know the cylinder even existed. The Army had to believe it had been destroyed, which left Stafford, and, just possibly, that girl in Graniteville. The image of Bud Lambry disappearing into the Monster in a shower of blood and oil bloomed in his mind. He shifted one small mental gear, and Lambry's face was replaced by Stafford's. He took a deep breath as he pulled out on the county road and turned toward town. In for a penny, he mused, in for a pound. For a million bucks, he would do whatever it took.

9

"General Carrothers, sir, call on line thirty-five, nonsecure. A Mr. Ray Sparks, DCIS, Smyrna."

"Thank you," Carrothers said. He picked up the phone and asked Sparks to go secure. He nodded across the room at Major Mason, who picked up a muted handset to listen in. A moment later Sparks was back up on secure.

"Mr. Sparks, I'm sorry to roust you out at this time of the morning, but we have a little problem with one of your people."

"That would be Dave Stafford?"

"That's right, Mr. Sparks. We're trying to figure out why a Washington-based DCIS agent is knocking on the front door of the Anniston Army Weapons Depot, asking for the CIC office, which is not located there, which is something we have reason to believe he already knew. Any thoughts, Mr. Sparks?"

There was a perceptible pause. "Well, General, we're not quite sure ourselves what he was doing there," Sparks said. "He's supposed to be on assignment to the DRMO at Fort Gillem on a fraud case. All I can think is that he was present when your chemical team arrived the other night and he wanted to find out what that was all about."

Carrothers caught the unspoken question. "What that was about was a no-notice tactical exercise of a Chemical Emergency Response Team, Mr. Sparks. Now that we're in the business of shipping chemical weapons to the national destruction site out in Utah, we keep one of these teams in readiness at each of the Army's special weapons depots. We exercise them frequently. We send them to military installations, usually at night, to keep the civilian population from getting unduly alarmed. I guess my question is, Why would your guy care?"

"He's not *my* guy, General. He's on assignment from your fair city,

154

in fact. But let me ask you something else: Is there any chance that your team went to Fort Gillem for something other than an exercise?"

Mason's eyes widened as he looked over his handset at Carrothers. "Not that I know of, Mr. Sparks," Carrothers said quickly. "We have a number of sites we send the teams out to. The ops center here randomly picks one and gives the go order. What prompted that question?"

"Something Mr. Stafford alluded to the other day, General," Sparks replied. "But I probably misinterpreted it."

"I'd sure like to know what he had in mind," Carrothers said. "Any chance we can talk to Stafford?"

"Well, there's a small problem with that, General. We can't seem to find Mr. Stafford. Last contact we had was by phone from Anniston, Alabama. Oxford, actually. See, the weird thing is, I talked to the Alabama state cops. You know, I thought maybe he had had an accident out on the interstate or something. Driving in Alabama can be something of a blood sport sometimes. But anyway, they said funny I should ask, because there was a stop-and-hold warrant out on Stafford's car, and it was the Fort McClellan military police who had put the want out."

Carrothers shook his head slowly as Sparks's unstated question once again hung in the air. Mason was now busy writing notes and avoiding eye contact with the general.

"Once again, I'm cold, Mr. Sparks," Carrothers replied. "Unless the base CO at Anniston thought maybe Stafford had been running some kind of perimeter security–penetration drill. I guess I'd better pulse our circuits, see what the hell is going on down there. How about this? You hear from Stafford, get him to explain what the hell he was doing, and why. Then call me back, if you would. In the meantime, I'll get onto my field people and find out why they put out a stop-and-hold on a DCIS agent."

"Yeah, I'd be interested in the answer to that, General. We're all on the same team here, I thought. You know? DCIS? DOD?"

Carrothers understood the implied threat: DCIS worked directly for the Department of Defense, which was senior to the Department of the Army.

"I quite agree, Mr. Sparks," Carrothers said, anxious now to terminate this conversation. "Team play is very important." As in, Why don't you know where your guy is and what he's doing, smart-ass?

Sparks ignored the gibe. "We'll get back to you as soon as we hear from Stafford, General."

"Thank you, Mr. Sparks. And I suppose it goes without saying that if there *is* something going on, we'd all profit from keeping it in-house until we can get our arms around it, don't you think?"

"I understand perfectly, General. DCIS operates on that very same principle to the greatest extent possible. Good morning to you, sir."

Carrothers hung up the phone a bit more forcefully than he intended. Mason raised his eyebrows at him.

"Damn," Carrothers growled. "This thing is getting away from us. I can just feel it. You heard that question?"

"Yes, sir. And that last bit, about keeping things in-house. 'To the greatest extent possible.'"

"Right. In other words, Sure, we'll keep it quiet, unless we catch the Army at something really egregious, and then we're gonna yell."

"Yes, sir. But how in the hell could this Stafford guy know what the team was doing there?"

Carrothers got up and began to pace. "How indeed? More important, where is Stafford now? I hope to Christ he's not skulking around that DRMO, not with another inbound response team."

Mason nodded. "Well, if he is, maybe we'll get him this time. I think we'd be in a better bargaining position with DCIS if we had their guy in, um, protective custody. He burned senior management in DCIS. There has to be an angle there we can work. Go over this Sparks guy's head, maybe. Talk to the DCIS here in the building."

"We might have to do just that. I need to think, Major. We've *got* to get this thing back in the bottle."

SUNDAY, FORT GILLEM DRMO, ATLANTA, 12:30 A.M.

Stafford opened his car window and poured the dregs of his coffee out onto the gravel of the truck park. He had backed his rental in between two large deuce and halfs in a line of transport vehicles parked across the railroad tracks from the DRMO, which positioned him to watch the entrance.

The run to Atlanta from Anniston had been uneventful. He had passed some state troopers lurking in the median strip, but they'd seemed more interested in watching for real Hotlanta-bound speeders than in his nondescript Army sedan. He wondered when the Army would figure out what he had done with the Fort Gillem Crown Vic, but that was their problem. It would put them on notice that he was aware of their interest, though. Perhaps he should have done something a little less in-their-face. A pang of conscience had prompted him to mail back the keys to the Fort McClellan motor pool, along with the parking stub. That officious sergeant would probably get his ass handed to him.

So what's the plan, Stan? He wasn't entirely sure why he had come back to the DRMO, except that Sparks might be having his hotel in Atlanta watched, and he couldn't just show up in Graniteville at four in the morning. He was convinced more than ever that the Army had some-how managed to lose a cylinder of some seriously bad shit. The visit of the CERT, the military police showing up at his motel, and Ray Sparks's entire demeanor were signs of real trouble. He wished he had not told Sparks what he suspected, because if Sparks and the rest of the DCIS went into the cover-up mode, he'd be out in the cold. Again.

He had also promised Gwen Warren not to drag the girl into this mess, but by telling Sparks about the girl, he'd blown that, too. That, he really regretted.

A Fort Gillem MP car on night patrol came down the main street in front of the truck park and turned across the tracks into the DRMO complex. After a minute, he could see the car's headlights reflecting off the back buildings of the complex, and then the car emerged at the far end, crossed back across the tracks, and resumed its patrol. Stafford was pretty sure his car was just about invisible in the pocket of shadow between the two large trucks.

And then there was the problem of Carson. Stafford was equally convinced that Carson either had the cylinder or knew where it was. He had told Sparks he suspected Carson. The question was, Had Sparks told the Army, and what would the Army do about that? If they couldn't even admit they'd lost the cylinder, would they be likely to move against Carson? After seeing those military police at the Holiday Inn, he thought they might just be looking to pick his ass up and take him to the back-woods of the Anniston Depot. On the other hand, he wondered if today's politically correct Army really had it in them to squeeze someone. He doubted it. So all Carson really had to do was sit tight and not say anything, and he could do whatever he wanted to with the cylinder in due course, assuming the Army didn't find it.

He rubbed his eyes with his left hand, around and around. So what *was* the plan? It was Sunday morning, so there shouldn't be anyone coming to the DRMO until Monday. Maybe go in and take a look around himself? He yawned as the caffeine wore off. Not much point in that, he concluded. All those warehouses filled with stuff—it could

157

be anywhere, or not even here at all. What he needed now was some sleep, and then he would head for Graniteville at daylight. This time, he would talk directly to that girl, Jessamine. What a fascinating name. Then he fell asleep.

At twelve-fifty in the morning, Wendell Carson drove through the gates of Fort Gillem. He drove by the empty guard shack, up the deserted main drag, and then turned across the railroad tracks toward the DRMO parking lot. The lot was empty, as was the rail siding. The nearest vehicles were a few dozen Army troop transports spotted across the tracks. He parked in his usual place and shut down to wait and watch for a few minutes. He wanted to be damned sure no one was watching the place, and he would prefer not to be unlocking the front door just as the night patrol came past, necessitating explanations he'd rather not give.

After fifteen minutes, the night patrol did come by. Carson slumped down in his seat, but they did not appear to notice the Army pickup truck that had not been there the last time. When the MP car went back across the tracks, Carson got out and let himself into the admin office. He left the lights off and went straight through to the back door that led into the auction warehouse. He stopped at the back door of the warehouse to examine the lay-down area through the window in the door. The tarmac was well lighted by rose-colored security lights mounted on all the warehouses, but all he could see out there were the darkened lines of palletized materiel. There were four flatbed trailers parked over by the demil building, but no trucks or other vehicles were visible anywhere in the area. He noted the time. The MPs came around about every thirty, forty minutes, but they wouldn't stop and check a building unless something seemed wrong from the outside or one of the alarmed warehouses had signaled a problem.

He let himself out the back door and walked confidently across the lay-down tarmac. If someone was watching, he did not want to appear as if he was anything but the manager checking the place out. He went straight to the feed-assembly building and let himself through the cipher-locked door. Inside, the warehouse was dark except for two security lights. The stacked shelves were empty, as was the conveyor system leading next door to the Monster. He did a walk-through of the entire warehouse anyway, just to make damned sure. If someone wanted to watch the demil building, this would be a good place from which to do it, but the place was empty, with only the forklift battery-charging station displaying any signs of energy.

He went back outside, after once again surveying the lay-down area through the door window for a few minutes. Then he let himself into the demil building itself, carefully closing the door to make sure the cipher lock had reset. He walked through the darkened anteroom and into the control area. Here there were small security lights set high up on the wall, illuminating the great bulk of the demil machine, the open area in front of the Monster, and the conveyor belt coming through the wall from the feed building next door. The control booth was shut down and devoid of lights.

He walked over to the conveyor belt, took one last look around, and then put his hand down on the last roller before the feed aperture of the demil machine. I should have brought a flashlight, he thought as he counted back to the third roller from the aperture and squatted down to examine the bearing assembly and end cap in the dim light. It looked no different from the ones on either side.

He put his hand on the highly polished steel surface of the roller by the edge of the conveyor belt and was surprised to find that it was warm. He took his hand away and tried again, then compared the sensation by touching the rollers on either side. They were cold. The third one was definitely warm. He remembered thinking the cylinder had been warm the last time he touched it, too.

He removed his hand and thought about that. Why in the hell would it be warm? Some chemical reaction going on inside that cylinder? Could the thing be unstable?

He touched the roller again. No doubt about it. In marked contrast, he felt a cold tendril of fear stirring in him as he straightened up. Would it be safe to open the roller assembly to retrieve this thing? Suppose it was building up pressure, or worse, about to burst or start leaking? He almost didn't hear the rumble of several large trucks outside, until one of them locked his air brakes, causing Carson nearly to jump out of his skin.

He ran to the anteroom of the demil building, but unlike the one next door, this front door had no window. He listened. Trucks, several of them. Large doors opening, the sounds of several people out there. A radio. A car door, maybe two. The clump of heavy boots and the scrape of equipment being moved.

He tried the door leading into the assembly warehouse, but it was locked. He swore out loud, realizing that he needed the operator's key ring to open it. After Bud's demise, they had had to generate some spare keys, but they were now all in the security control room. He couldn't go out the front door, and there was no fire door in the rear. He was trapped in the demil room.

If they came in here, how in the world would he explain what he was doing? And there was sure as hell no place to hide.

He looked around frantically as the noise level outside grew. There were definitely several people out there, making vaguely familiar noises. Then he focused on the bat-wing doors through which material came from the feed-assembly building into this building. He remembered the night Lambry had gone through those doors, how he had been unable to pull them open from the other side. But that was because they opened only one way, into this side. From here he could open them!

He moved quickly to the conveyor belt and climbed up onto it. Hunkering down on all fours, he went into the safety cage and reached the two flap doors. There was a full inch of space between them, enough to get his fingers through. He pulled and they moved, but just barely. The hinges were obviously spring-loaded, but something else was holding them. He felt around in the darkness to see if there was a release of some kind, but there was only a line of small metal tabs on the edge of the conveyor belt. Then he understood: The tabs on the moving belt probably hit a detent button in the door assembly, which would allow them to open. He tried to move the belt, but that was impossible.

He had to get out of here. Whoever that was out there, they could find him in any building except this one.

He crawled back out onto the floor and ran to the control console. He hit the master power button, then found the controls for the belt. He couldn't start up the Monster; that would make much too much noise. But he could energize the belt. He hesitated for an instant, then pushed the button to activate the belt. The belt began to move with a distant hum of large electric motors back in the feed-assembly building. Hurry, he told himself, they'll hear that in a minute. He ran back over to the belt and climbed on, crawling in the opposite direction of the belt's travel. Behind him the feed aperture of the Monster, motionless steel teeth poised, waited in silence.

He crawled to the doors, and, sure enough, they were partially ajar. They would probably open fully when the first article hit them from the other side. He reached for the doors and pulled them open; he was about to go through when he remembered the console would still be energized. He swore, then slipped his belt off and tied one of the doors back against the safety cage. He turned around to crawl back out, but his pants began to fall down. He let go of the cage long enough to grab his pants, but not before the right cuff caught underneath the belt on something. He swore again and pulled, but the damn thing was stuck hard, and not only stuck; each succeeding roller was tightening the pants against his ankle. And he was moving.

He looked up, aghast. He was caught on the belt and being taken straight into the feed aperture of the Monster. The demil machine wasn't running, of course, but those steel band-saw blades were right there, waiting to strain him into baby food. He fought hard not to panic, feeling each succeeding roller bumping his knees as he pulled against the fabric of his trousers. The grip around his ankle was getting very tight, and he was losing all sensation of feeling in his right foot.

Wait, he told himself. Just wait. The cuff will be released when it gets to the last roller. There were only five more rollers, then four, then three. He twisted his body around to jump off the belt at the last instant, then pulled as hard as he could when his foot bumped over the last roller, just one foot in front of the row of band-saw blades. But instead of coming loose, his foot was twisted savagely *under* the belt as it descended beneath the rollers and headed back toward the flap doors. His body tumbled off the belt and he hung momentarily upside down, his right leg trapped up in the roller assemblies, his left leg frantically scrabbling for traction on the polished linoleum floor. For a terrifying instant, he thought he was going to be pulled back into the rollers, but then suddenly he was free, sprawling out onto the floor with a grunt.

He stood up, windmilling his arms because of the pain in his ankle. The noises from outside were getting louder. He had to shut off the belt and get the hell out of there. Pulling up his trousers, he limped awkwardly across the floor to the console and quickly shut it down. Then he hopped back across the floor, crawled up on the now-stilled conveyor belt, and, banging his knees across every one of the rollers, reached the flap doors. He pushed his body through into the next building, then reached back through the opening to retrieve his belt. But then he stopped. Would the damned doors slam shut and trap his hand? He let go of the belt and pulled himself through the safety cage into the feed-assembly warehouse and got down off the belt. He looked around and saw a stack of the plastic material trays in which small demil items were placed before being put on the belt. He grabbed one and climbed back into the safety cage, wedged the tray where the doors ought to meet when they closed, and released his belt. Sure as hell, the steel doors snapped shut, nearly trapping his hand as they squashed the flimsy tray. He pulled hard on the edge of the bowed tray and it popped out, propelled by the edges of the doors.

He scuttled back out of the safety cage, his heart pounding, and limped like a wounded crab to the front door of the feed assembly warehouse, discarding the bent tray in a trash bin. He took a look out onto the tarmac area. It was the Army again, only there were four big trucks this time, and a lot more people. A hell of a lot more people. Two of the trucks had big generators going, and there were some portable light stands blazing out on the tarmac.

Gotta get out of here, he thought, but not this way. The good news was that this warehouse had a back entrance. He got his clothes back in order as he lurched toward the back of the warehouse. The even better news was that he was safely out of the demil building. He tried not to think about being trapped on that conveyor belt, pinned like a bug by that wholly uncaring web of industrial machinery. Almost like Lambry, only conscious, he reminded himself.

He got to the back door and stopped. There was an alleyway behind this row of warehouses, big enough for forklifts but not for trucks, and then a high chain-link fence beyond that. Once into that alley, he could go either way around the back of the whole complex and get back to his truck. He checked the door. It was a fire door, with a horizontal handle allowing someone to get out but not back in. He checked to see that it was not alarmed, then pushed the handle, opened the door, and entered the dark alley.

Once outside, he could hear all the noise from the other side of the building, which was good because it had probably masked the sound of the conveyor belt starting up. He went right, limping a little as he hugged the back wall of the warehouse. When he got to the end of the building, he peeked around the edge, toward the tarmac. Two huge figures dressed out in what looked like space suits were looking right back at him from about six feet away. One of them crooked his gloved hand at Carson.

Dave Stafford banged his left elbow on the steering wheel when he was startled awake by something. He rubbed his elbow on his thigh, then rubbed his eyes as he tried to figure out what had awakened him. He looked at his watch, realizing as he did so that there were some very bright lights on behind the admin building, in what had to be the tarmac area. He looked at his watch again: two-thirty in the morning. He could hear the sound of portable generators running, and there were also lights on in the admin building, across the tracks from where he was parked. As he stared into the lighted windows, he saw two figures in full chemical warfare protection gear come out of one office and enter another.

What the hell is this? he wondered, sitting up in his seat. And then he quickly ducked down as an MP patrol car came by, this time very definitely going slowly enough to take a look at everything going on at the DRMO. The first car was followed by a second one, and then a third. Stafford waited until he was pretty sure all three cars had passed before peering over the edge of the door window.

From the sounds of it, that chemical response team was back, this time in larger force, at two-thirty A.M. on a Sunday, with the apparent full cooperation of the Fort Gillem military police. One more point. He took another look at the admin building and confirmed that the people moving around inside were in full protective suits. They've lost something all right, and it isn't a jar of Grandma's applesauce. Then he saw Carson's truck.

Whoa, what's this? That truck hadn't been there when he fell asleep. So the Army was back, and they'd called the DRMO manager in to do— what, gain access to the warehouses? Should he just get out of the car and go over there, ask for the guy in charge, and tell him what he knew? He shook his head. He could just see himself trying to convince some soldier in a space suit that, according to his very own psychic adviser, there *was* a cylinder of something bad hidden in the DRMO and that Brother Carson there knew where it was. Right. Plus, even if the Army did believe him, they might not necessarily be nice to the messenger.

He ducked down as another vehicle came around the corner from the tarmac area. Looking just over the rim of the dashboard, he could see that it was a large olive drab Suburban with police lights mounted on top. As it passed in front of the lighted admin office, he caught a glimpse of two military policemen in the front seat, and one individual in the backseat. He sat up straighter: The guy in the backseat looked as if he was wearing a motorcycle helmet. Weird. Then there was sudden flare of brake lights on the Suburban, and all the doors were opening. Here they came, right toward his car.

His heart sank. Goggles. The guy in the backseat had been wearing night-vision goggles. Bastards had seen him on infrared. He unlocked the door and got out of the car.

Carrothers was dozing in his chair when the Operations Center duty officer called in with a secure phone call from the Chemical Emergency Response Team's leader at Fort Gillem.

"This is General Carrothers."

"Sir, this is Captain McLean, CERT-Six. Reporting negative results, General. No hits on any of the surveillance monitoring equipment, and no visible sign of the missing cylinder."

"You're satisfied you gave the place a good search, Captain?"

"A good search, General? No, sir, not possible, not in three hours. No way, General. There must be thousands of items stacked on shelves and in bins or on pallets, as well as several tractor-trailer loads of stuff parked and waiting to be unloaded. We did a complete chemical-trace survey, at molecular sensitivity settings, inside each of the warehouses. We've got that new mark-seven nose. We followed that up by a sight survey of as much as we could cover in the buildings in three hours. You want to really take this place apart, we'd need a battalion and a couple of months to do it."

Carrothers was silent for a moment. Damn. "Okay. Get the team out of there and close the place back up. And make sure the local MPs keep their mouths shut. You used the exercise cover story again?"

"Yes, sir. The Fort Gillem ops officer was here; he's handling the Gillem MPs. I told them the first drill was screwed up and that we'd decided to do it again. Nothing they haven't heard before. There was one other thing, General: We did pick up that DCIS guy who'd been snooping around the Anniston Depot. One David Stafford."

Oh shit, Carrothers thought. "What the hell was he doing there?"

"He declined to say, General. He was apparently already here when we got here. The Anniston MPs caught him on a night scope, watching us from a car across the way from the DRMO. We also encountered the manager of the DRMO, one Wendell Carson. He, too, was apparently here before we got here. Two of our monitors caught him making tracks down a back alley."

Carrothers sat up straight. "The manager was there? In the early hours of a Sunday morning? And he was running away?"

"The MPs said he was trucking down a back alley behind one of the warehouses. Looked to them like he was trying to get out of there without being seen."

"What did *he* have to say for himself?"

"He said they'd been having some problems with someone stealing stuff on the weekends. He thinks it might be some of his employees. He says he decided just to come down in the middle of the night, see what he could see."

"The Fort Gillem MPs know anything about that?"

"Haven't checked, General. We've been real busy here. I asked him why he ran, and he said he wasn't running. Said he wasn't sure what was going on and that he was only trying to get back to his office, on the other side of the tarmac."

"Did he know that Stafford was there, too?"

"I don't think so, sir. I went ahead and gave Mr. Carson the cover story, and he said he would just stay out of our way. To my knowledge, he just went home."

"Okay. And what did you do with Stafford?"

"I decided to have our MPs take him back to Anniston, General. Our briefing was that any unauthorized personnel who intruded on this operation were to be held until we received further orders. It looked to me like the manager had every right to be here. Stafford didn't, so I held him."

"Exactly the right decision, Captain. I don't want Stafford talking to *anyone* until we get someone from Washington down to Anniston. He is a federal officer, so treat him in a civil manner, no stockade cells or anything like that, but keep him isolated until you hear from me."

"Yes, sir, General. I'll relay that to the depot operations center ASAP. They'll hold him until further orders from you."

"Right. One more question: Any chance Stafford and Carson were there together?"

"Don't think so, General. I would think Stafford would have said something when he realized we were going to hold him."

"Okay, that computes. Now get your collective asses the hell out of there."

Carrothers hung up the phone. Major Mason had been listening on the muted extension and copying down the salient points of the conversation.

"Who's going to go down there, General?" Mason asked expectantly.

"Three guesses, Major. And you're going with me. Get us a jet out

165

of Andrews—Priority One. I want to leave by ten hundred, and I don't care if it is Sunday. File direct to the strip at the Anniston Depot via Atlanta. And get in touch with the FBI operations center here in Washington. See if they can lend us a polygraph operator from their Atlanta office. Get yourself relieved here as duty officer now, then go home and get packed. Have a car pick us both up."

"Yes, sir. How long in Anniston, sir?"

"One day, max. If we can't find out what we need to know by then, we'll have bigger problems up here than down there."

■ SUNDAY, ANNISTON ARMY WEAPONS DEPOT, ANNISTON, ALABAMA, 2:00 P.M.

Dave Stafford sat in a state of cold fury in a windowless room somewhere at the Anniston Depot. They had arrived at the depot in company with the truck convoy just after sunrise. The response team's trucks and the MP vehicles had gone right through the main gate, past the parking lot still filled with a dozen or so semis, and then through the industrial area of windowless concrete buildings. The trucks had peeled off the base's main road after a half mile or so, but the MP cars kept going until they reached what appeared to be the depot's administrative area. There was a small grassy square, surrounded by very old office buildings and some typical amenities of a military base, such as a post exchange, a medical clinic, and a small theater. Three of the MP vehicles had pulled into what looked like a motor-pool area, while the fourth, containing Stafford and two large MPs, continued on down yet another tree-lined road farther into the depot's interior.

The salient feature of the depot was the seemingly unending number of trees. Thick stands of pines lined every road, making it look as if the depot were a collection of small outposts scattered about in a large pine forest. It was only after looking at it for a while that Stafford realized the trees were probably a screen for the real business of the depot, which had to be several thousand acres of ammunition bunkers lurking back in there somewhere. And yet there were no fences visible or even signs indicating a security area.

His vehicle had taken him down a series of two-lane roads bordered by dense woods, until they arrived finally at what looked like an operations center of some kind. A large windowless building dominated several smaller workshops and truck parks. There were several complex antennas mounted on top of the big building, and what appeared to be a nest of air-filtration machinery mounted on one side. The vehicle Stafford was in descended a ramp on one side of the building. At the end of the ramp were steel doors, which opened as they approached. The vehicle drove directly through the doors and into a parking bay inside the building. Two more MPs were waiting when the doors closed behind them.

"This way, Mr. Stafford," the shorter of them said when Stafford was let out of the backseat. Short was a relative term; they were all over six feet in height.

He had tried blustering, demanding to know why he had been brought there, demanding to see the commanding officer, and so forth. The MPs had ignored him as they fell in beside him, with the shorter MP leading the way and another guard right behind him. They marched through some more steel doorways and into the interior of the building. Stafford noticed that the steel doors all had heavy rubber hermetic seals. They had taken him down one long hallway, up a set of concrete stairs, and into another hallway before taking him into this room, which was about twelve feet square. It contained a metal table, four metal chairs, and a water fountain in one corner. A door on the back wall was partially open, revealing a washroom. The walls were painted pea green. There they had left him.

He initial anger had been with himself, for letting them catch him that way. He certainly should have thought about infrared sweeps. His warm upper torso contrasted with the otherwise-cold interior of the rental car would have shown right up as a heat source. They had taken him back into the DRMO complex, holding him by the side of the entrance to the tarmac area. No one had spoken to him, probably because the noise of the portable generators made conversation nearly impossible. He had observed that one of the trucks was a mobile operations center of some kind, just like the last time, but this time there was no pretty girl to make public explanations. He had seen one officer, not suited up, but dressed in what looked like Desert Storm fatigues, going in and out of the mobile command trailer.

At one point he had simply tried to walk away, which is when his two guards had put him none too delicately into the backseat of the Suburban parked between two buildings and locked him in. He hadn't even tried to struggle. With just one arm, he was definitely out of the physical heroics business for a while. There had been no door handles in the back, and there was a metal screen between the front seat and the back, which told him all he needed to know about his real status. An hour or so later, the team had packed up. When his Suburban joined the convoy back to Anniston, he realized he might be in serious trouble.

He wondered then if Sparks had made some calls. Was this a follow-up on the little operation at the Holiday Inn in Oxford? This reinforced team had not seemed to be making even a pretext of doing an exercise this time. These people had been looking for something, and he had literally squirmed in the backseat of that Suburban thinking about what he could tell them. But after another hour of just sitting there, he had begun to take stock. Okay, so they knew who he was and they wanted to talk to him. Thank you, Ray Sparks. He also knew that one thing he had going for him was the fact that they had not admitted, and would probably never admit, that a weapon was missing. In a way it was check-mate: As long as they couldn't admit they had a weapon missing, and as long as he kept his mouth shut about what he suspected, he should be safe. All of which assumed they were going to question him in a civilized manner and not take him out to a deserted rifle range somewhere for a meaningful physical experience. The downside was that if he kept his mouth shut, he couldn't tell them what he suspected about Carson, either, for more reasons than one.

If his reasoning was correct, taking him back to the Anniston Depot might be something of a bluff on the Army's part, which further rein-forced his sense that he should play the role of the aggrieved civil servant, admit nothing, and try to put them on the defensive as fast as he could. The anger he was generating now was consciously contrived. He wanted to work himself up into a state of righteous indignation. He was positive that this was the right way to play it.

Provided that someone was actually going to come in there and talk to him. He was hungry and thirsty. He got up and tried the water fountain. Nothing but air came out.

■ SUNDAY, FORT GILLEM DRMO, ATLANTA, 8:00 P.M.

Wendell Carson sat in his pickup truck outside a phone booth, waiting for Tangent to return his call. Carson had never called his contact on a Sunday, but the developments of the early-morning hours couldn't wait. Those Army bastards had come back, and this time with twice the people and twice the equipment. And they'd nearly caught him inside the demil building. He'd been lucky the officer in charge of the Army team had been a young captain and not some hard-boiled lieutenant colonel.

There was no getting around it: They had come back. Which confirmed they knew the thing was missing, and that it had ended up at the DRMO. This had to be Stafford's work. He'd said he was going to tell them.

The phone rang. He got out of the truck and picked it up. "Yes?"

"It's me. What's the problem now?" Tangent sounded impatient.

Carson recapped the events of the night before. He finished with his conclusion that Stafford had to be behind the Army's revisit. Tangent was silent for a moment.

"How could Stafford *know* that the cylinder is there?" he asked.

"He can't, and that's what's bugging the shit out of me. The only guy who knew what this was all about was Lambry, and Stafford never talked to Lambry."

"Do you *know* that? Do you *know* where Lambry went? Is there a possibility that he's still in the area and that maybe Stafford found him?"

"No, I don't *know* it," Carson said. He couldn't let Tangent know the truth about Lambry. Stealing the cylinder was one thing; Lambry's demolition was quite another. "Remember I told you Lambry had a helper," Carson replied. "Guy named Dillard. But as far as I know, Dillard never actually saw the cylinder. He may have known Lambry swiped something, but not exactly what. And definitely not what it looked like. I'm stumped."

Tangent disagreed. "You can't know that, either. If Lambry caught on to what this thing might be worth, he could have told his buddy everything, or enough to cover his ass if you tried to stiff him. It was Dillard who talked to Stafford?"

"Yes."

"Well, hell, there it is, then. You pulled the string with Dillard?"

"No. I figured let sleeping dogs lie. If I talk to Dillard, he'll know something's up. This way, everything just subsides. Nobody who works here has seen the Army teams."

"You're probably right; you know the guy and I don't, although I'm getting a little more concerned about this Lambry's unexplained disappearance. You sure he didn't go to Baby Jesus when his house blew up?"

Carson gripped the phone harder. He had forgotten telling Tangent about that.

"I guess that's possible," he replied carefully. "Except the arson peo-

169

ple said no one was in the house when it went." Eager to get off this line of conversation, he asked Tangent what he was doing about Stafford.

"We're working that. Why, you got something new?"

"I've been thinking," Carson said. "We need to get all this heat off the DRMO, at least long enough to do the deal, you know what I mean? This shit is beginning to spook me. I just want to do the deal, turn this damned thing over, get my money."

"My client doesn't know squat. Yet. So I'm all ears, you got some ideas."

"Yeah, well, is there some way you can make the Army think Stafford's got this thing? Which is why he's running off his chain?"

There was a moment of silence on the line. "That's fucking brilliant," Tangent said. "It doesn't even have to hold up for very long."

"Yeah, that's what I'm thinking. By the time the Army convinces itself he doesn't have it, or even know where it is, we can be down the road and gone."

"I like that. And, yes, I know just how to do that. The Army's working this thing way off-line. They have to be in a fucking panic. This fits in with what we were going to do anyway, only this is much better. Look, you go back to your daily routine. Everything normal. No more night visits to the DRMO. Be thinking of how we'll do the swap. How you want your money. Keep it simple. Think next forty-eight hours, max, okay?"

"I hear you."

The line went silent as Tangent hung up. Carson put the phone back and looked around the exchange parking lot to see if anyone had been watching him, but he saw nothing out of the ordinary. Stafford with the cylinder, he mused. He smiled then. "Beautiful," he announced to the air as he got in his truck. "Fucking beautiful."

The Army Learjet touched down with two bruising puffs of blue smoke from its tires at almost exactly six P.M. On board were Brigadier General Carrothers, Major Mason, and an FBI polygraph operator named W. Layon Smith. The plane had been delayed getting out of Andrews due to a movement of the presidential 747; Carrothers's single star had not been enough to get them a ramp time before the field was locked up while *Air Force One* landed after a maintenance stint in California. Then they had been stacked up over Atlanta by the Sunday-afternoon business travelers' rush hour, followed by more delays in getting Smith's gear through airport security. None of this had improved Carrothers's attitude.

The jet pulled up to the ops building and shut down. Carrothers emerged first, where he was met by the depot's commanding officer and his operations officer. They went directly to an Army staff car. Major Mason and Smith followed in a Suburban. The commanding officer, a full colonel, looked tired and drawn. Carrothers afforded him little sympathy. The investigation had narrowed the cause for this fiasco down to two possibilities: Either Tooele had screwed up the arrival transfer of the special weapons shipment in Utah or Anniston had screwed up the outgoing shipment here in Alabama. Until one or the other was proved, both commanding officers were good prospects for a general court-martial. The staff cars proceeded to the commanding officer's office. Once there, Carrothers held a quick conference.

"You have this man Stafford in isolation?"

"Yes, sir, General," the colonel replied. "Since this morning." The operations officer nodded eagerly in confirmation.

"Okay, I have a one-hour-stay time here. We're going to stage a little drama out in the tombs. Here's what I want to do."

They came for Stafford at 6:30. There were three of them, fully dressed out in Army chemical warfare protective gear: camouflaged full body suits, sealed gloves and black rubber boots, hoods and respirators. They did not speak, just motioned for him to follow them. They were not armed, but they were big enough for that not to matter very much.

It was dark when they took him outside, through a different door this time, to a waiting Humvee transport. They motioned for him to get in, one actually helping him; then two of them got in back with him, one on either side. The third got in on the driver's side, and they rumbled off into the evening. They went down a long, straight two-lane road for about ten minutes before turning off onto another road, which had a rail line running down the middle of it. Stafford could see fairly well out the windows, but there wasn't much to see other than the endless pine forest.

They finally arrived at a gate complex, which consisted of two gate towers flanking a fifty-foot-wide sliding double-gate assembly set into a thirty-foot-high double chain-link fence with razor wire at the base and on the top; there was a dog run in between the fences. Insulators on the wire strands indicated that the fence was electrified. There were sodium-vapor light fixtures mounted beneath the guard towers and every fifty feet along the fence, turning the dark green of the trees an ominous black where the fences curved into the forest. The rail line went under the gate and then turned to the right behind one of the guard towers. Stafford thought he could see what looked like a machine-gun barrel protruding from each guard tower.

The Humvee stopped at the gate and the driver communicated with someone in one of the towers. His voice sounded strangely clipped from inside the hood. Stafford could not hear a reply, but the outside gate rolled back, allowing the Humvee into the space between the fences. Then the outer gate closed behind them, and the inner gate opened. The Humvee drove over a vehicle-trap mechanism buried in the roadway, then turned carefully through four enormous concrete tetrahedrons planted in the road as crash barriers. The road continued straight through some more trees, with the rail line running right alongside.

They went about a half mile before turning off onto a cinder road. A spur from the rail line turned with them. They passed through about a hundred more yards of trees before coming upon the first of the bunkers. Stafford sat up when he saw them; this didn't look like a place where interviews would be held. Not polite ones, anyway. All his imaginative plans for righteous defiance looked less and less like a medium for success here.

The Humvee drove down between two lanes of bunkers, which were much bigger than he had expected. They were nearly a hundred feet long and about thirty feet in width. They looked like concrete Quonset huts that had been partially submerged in the red Alabama clay. There were sodium-vapor lights mounted at each end of the bunkers, illuminating concrete ramps descending to steel doors. Branches from the rail spur went down the ramps to the steel doors of each bunker. He looked out both sides of the vehicle. The bunkers stretched in endless rows and lanes, looking like some kind of industrial mausoleum. This depot must be enormous, he thought.

They finally stopped in front of one of the bunkers, and his escorts got out. There were more suited figures waiting by a second Humvee under the lights by the entrance, and Stafford could now see that this bunker's steel doors were open, although he could not see inside the bunker because of the painfully bright lights. His escorts invited him to step out, and he did, cautiously, wondering why he was the only one out

172

here not dressed out in protective gear. He was taken down the long concrete ramp to the front of the bunker, where one of the guards motioned for him to wait. Two of the hooded figures were taking readings from an electronic monitoring panel mounted beside the external doors.

They waited. There was no sound other than the raspy inhalations and exhalations from the soldiers' respirators, and the occasional squawk from one of the Humvee radios. He tried to see into the bunker, but saw that there was a second set of steel doors, which were still closed. They appeared to be hydraulically operated, as there were four large hydraulic cylinder arms reaching from concrete pylons to the middle of the doors. Everyone waited some more, and Stafford remembered the old Army adage about hurry up and wait.

Carrothers finished suiting up, leaving only his hood and gloves off before getting into the mobile ammunition carrier. He thought about what he was about to do. He had studied Stafford's bio sheet on the plane ride down. David W. Stafford, senior investigator for the Defense Criminal Investigative Service. Forty-three years old. Formerly with the Naval Investigative Service and, before that, seven years as a private investigator for a law firm after having been a police detective with the Norfolk, Virginia, metropolitan police. Four-year enlisted hitch in the Navy before that. Solid citizen, and a professional investigator. There was nothing in the bio about any whistle-blowing incident. He thought about the little maneuver with the Crown Vic. Heads-up ball, that.

The question was, What did he know? General Waddell would be all for locking Stafford up at the depot until they found the cylinder. Carrothers was not so sure about that option. The elephants, as the three-and the four-stars in the Pentagon were known, were starting to panic, which meant that lesser beings like brigadier generals now ought to be reviewing their own political escape routes. Waddell had made it clear that Carrothers's second star was riding on getting this ball of snakes back into its box. And yet . . . If someone had stolen a cylinder of Wet Eye, that constituted a genuine national emergency. Maybe Waddell was right: Whatever it takes, do it. But find it. Get it back. Which was why he was trying this little stunt.

"Okay," he said. "let's go."

■　　■　　■

After about fifteen minutes of just standing there, Stafford heard something coming. He thought it might be another Humvee, but he saw instead an enclosed vehicle of some kind coming down the rail spur, powered by nearly silent electric motors. The vehicle had a passenger compartment forward, and what looked like twenty-foot-long dual enclosed cargo bays behind the passenger compartment. The interior of the passenger compartment was red-lighted, giving the vehicle a menacing buglike appearance, an image reinforced by two whip antennas mounted above the cab. The vehicle clicked along the rail spur, slowed, and then turned left and descended into the bunker alley in front of the steel doors, where it stopped with a squeal of hydraulic brakes. Stafford saw that everyone around him was now standing at attention, as best they could manage in their suits. The doors of the cab opened upward like gull-wing flaps, and a tall figure, also dressed out in a chemical warfare protective suit, got out of the right side of the cab and walked over to where Stafford, who was trying not to reveal his apprehension, stood.

"Open the inner doors," the tall figure ordered, his strong, commanding voice overcoming the acoustic masking effect of his respirator. Two men went to separate control panels mounted on either side of the inner doors. They each put a key into a lock, put their hands on two separate switches, looked at each other, nodded their hoods once, turned the keys, and depressed the switches simultaneously. There was a loud hiss as the partial vacuum inside the bunker was broken, and then the hydraulic arms began to retract, pulling the steel doors open on steel tracks embedded in the concrete. Lights came on inside the bunker, and the tall figure motioned with one outstretched hand for Stafford to precede him inside the bunker.

Feeling almost naked among all the suited figures, Stafford willed his feet to start walking while he stared into the bunker. Inside were stacks of bombs. The bombs were massive, painted olive-drab, and about six feet long and three feet in diameter. They were girdled with two steel reinforcing rings around their circumference. The tail-fin assemblies were missing, and there were shiny fuze ports blanked off at each end. Each bomb was resting in a wooden cradle, the wood smashed down under the crushing weight. There was white stenciling on each bomb case, indicating a hang weight of two thousand pounds. There was a bright yellow band painted around the midsection of each bomb's nose, and some more letters, which were unintelligible to Stafford.

The tall figure motioned for him to go farther into the bunker. Stafford noticed that none of the others followed them in. He had to be careful of his footing, because the rail line came all the way into the bunker. There was an ammunition-handling crane positioned all the way at the back of the bunker, and a gantry track running along the arched concrete ceiling. The figure stopped when they had reached the ammunition crane. Dave turned to face him.

"Mr. Stafford, do you know why you're here?" the figure asked. His voice had a hiss to it, but there was still no mistaking the authority in it. Stafford could not make out a face behind the goggles above the respirator mask, only piercing eyes. He had to struggle to find his own voice; the atmosphere in the bunker was very dry and filled with the peculiar smell of very old metal.

"No, I don't. Who are you? And why am I being held this way? What is this place?"

"This is the Anniston Army Weapons Depot, Mr. Stafford, as you well know. It is a depository for special weapons—chemical weapons. This is a CW storage bunker, sometimes known as 'a CW tomb.' These are two-thousand-pound gravity bombs. They contain substance VX, which is a nerve gas. These bombs are almost fifty years old. In theory they are not leaking. Our monitoring instruments tell us they are not leaking."

"Well, I'm glad to hear that," Stafford said, trying to put some sarcasm in his voice. "Seeing as I'm the only one not in protective clothing. Why have I been brought here?"

The figure stared at him, as if waiting for Stafford to realize something. Then he leaned forward. "Mr. Stafford, we want you to understand something, and understand it very clearly. The substance in these bombs is one of the most lethal compounds ever devised by man. One cubic centimeter volatizing can paralyze simultaneously the central nervous systems of a thousand human beings. One of these bombs exploded upwind of a medium-sized city would extinguish very nearly the entire human and animal population in a matter of a very few minutes."

Stafford just looked at him. The figure leaned even closer, to the point where Stafford could smell the rubber of his suit. "Mr. Stafford, you should understand that while these bombs are extremely toxic, they do not contain the most toxic substances in the arsenal. There are some substances which do far more horrible things than VX does. There are substances that cause human blood to boil. There are substances that

175

cause the arteries in human lungs to swell and rupture. There are sub-stances that consume human skin. There are substances for which we have no names, only numbers."

Stafford swallowed hard. "Why are you telling *me* this?" he asked in a strained voice. The smell in the bunker seemed to be getting stronger. The tall figure stepped back away and looked around, as if listening for something. Then he turned back to Stafford. "These are the most lethal man-made substances on the face of the earth, Mr. Stafford. We are experts in containing and handling them, and we are *terrified* of them. Nevertheless, we feel very strongly that we do not need your help or anyone else's help with any aspect of these weapons. Any aspect at all." He paused for a moment. "Unless, of course, you know something we do not, Mr. Stafford. Unlikely as that seems to me, we felt it only ap-propriate to ask. Once."

The figure stared down at him. "Well?" it said.

Stafford was tongue-tied. Do it, his brain screamed at him. Tell them what you know. But he couldn't do it. He was afraid. This was a part of the Army he had never seen, and there was a ruthless edge to the tall figure's voice. He did not want to end up being held incommunicado out here, and his instincts were to keep his mouth shut. First get free. Then regroup, find some way to warn them. From a distance.

"Just so, Mr. Stafford. The Army appreciates your cooperation in coming here tonight. We have one last detail to attend to with you, but for right now, you may return to your vehicle."

The figure pointed Stafford toward the entrance to the bunker. Dave had to resist the impulse, a very, very strong impulse, to bolt. He had not missed the sarcasm about his cooperation. As if he had had any choice in the matter, which was, of course, the point the man was mak-ing. Mustering as much dignity as he could, his useless arm stuck in a pocket, he picked his way among the huge bombs, nearly twisting an ankle and losing his balance when he stepped into the indentation of the rail line running down the center of the bunker. When he reached the inner doors, the guards motioned for him to proceed to the Humvee. He got back in, as did his escorts, and the vehicle doors were closed. They drove back out to the service road between the line of bunkers. The last image he had of the bunker was a small crowd of suited figures silhouetted in the lighted entranceway of the bunker, all looking his way as the Humvee pulled away.

■   ■   ■

176

General Carrothers pulled off his hood and mask once he was back inside the ammunition transport carrier. Beside him, Major Mason did the same. The car operator, isolated in the control cab of the car, remained suited up as they proceeded back toward the main gates, following the route taken by the Humvee containing Stafford.

"Did it work, General?" Mason asked.

"I'm not entirely sure. He should have been scared shitless in there. Instead, I think he was processing. He was a little scared, of course, but I had the impression he knows more than he's telling. He even tried to bluster a little bit. He may be too cool a customer for what I have in mind. Don't forget that little caper with the car from the motor pool."

"Do you think he's in a suitable mental state to be fluttered?"

"I don't know. The FBI guy is supposedly set up and waiting for him right now."

"Suppose he refuses to take a lie-detector test, General?"

Carrothers's face hardened. "Then I'll let him spend a couple of nights underground in one of the bunkers. One of the really old mustard gas bunkers."

Mason shivered involuntarily. "Christ," he said, glancing over at the control cab. "I'd go out of my mind, and I know these weapons are safe. But a lie-detector test wouldn't be worth much after an experience like that, sir."

"I don't really give a shit about the results of the test, Major. I've given Smith the two questions I really want answered, and he's salted them into a laundry list of CW-related questions. The only truth I'm after is how sensitive he is to those two questions. That will tell me what I want to know."

Mason glanced again at the back of the driver's head as the transport approached the security gates and was switched out onto the main rail line. "And if he does know? Do we just let him go?"

"Actually, yes. We have no legal justification to hold him, although we don't have to let Stafford know that. If we get an indication that he knows something, turning him loose might be to our advantage: My guess is he'll try to find the cylinder. If in fact someone's taken it, an individual investigator like Stafford might be more effective than we are."

"Sir?"

"Because we can't admit we're looking, Major, that's why."

177

"Yes, sir, I understand that. But if he's loose, he can talk. Complain to his superiors. Maybe go public."

"General Waddell talked about that possibility when we first found out about DCIS snooping around that DRMO. The general has been talking to the head of DCIS. This Stafford apparently has made some significant enemies up in D.C. General Waddell said DCIS can be neutralized if necessary, although I'm not sure how that would be managed."

Mason was perplexed, and Carrothers caught the expression on his face. "See, Major?" he said. "Even brigadier generals don't know everything."

Mason snorted. "Only second lieutenants know everything, General," he said.

Carrothers laughed. "You'll go far, Mason."

"You want me to what?" Stafford exclaimed. "No fucking way!"

The stumpy lieutenant colonel standing in front of him nodded patiently. They were back in the windowless room again, accompanied by two more oversized MPs. This time everyone was back in regulation working fatigues. The lieutenant colonel had identified himself as the Anniston Depot's provost marshal. He had just asked Stafford if he would submit to a polygraph test. The provost marshal had made it sound as if he was asking him to have a cup of coffee.

Stafford was getting tired of all the games. He knew instinctively that the little séance in the bunker had been intended to intimidate him, although to what exact end, he wasn't entirely clear, and he really wanted to know who that tall guy in the chem suit had been, especially after watching everybody come to attention when he'd first arrived. But even more importantly, these people had no legal authority to hold him in the first place, much less to ask him to take a lie-detector test.

"What's your name again, Colonel?" Stafford asked.

"What's that got to do with anything?" the lieutenant colonel said, even though his name was spelled out in black letters right there on his shirt. Stafford pressed on.

"Because my business is law enforcement, Colonel," Stafford said, his voice rising. "Federal law enforcement. Right now I am planning to file charges of kidnapping, illegal search and seizure, attempted intimidation of a federal law-enforcement officer, and obstruction of justice against every officer in the chain of command at this post between you and the CO, you included. I work for the *Defense* Criminal Investigative

Service—Defense, as in *Department* of Defense—which organization is senior to the Department of the fucking Army, in case you've forgotten. Now I want a vehicle to take me back to Atlanta and I want it now. And then you and your cohorts here need to go find a good lawyer."

The lieutenant colonel looked at him impassively. "And if we don't?" he asked.

"Don't what?"

"Don't get you that vehicle. Don't let you out of here. Don't tell a fucking soul that you're here. On a restricted special weapons reservation. Where nobody comes unless we let them. What then, Mr. Big-Deal Federal Agent with One Arm?"

"Then my boss will find out I'm missing, and he'll tell every cop in Atlanta that another cop's gone missing. They'll end up here at your front gates eventually."

"That boss being one Mr. Sparks?"

Stafford tried to keep the sinking feeling from showing in his face. "He's the local supervisor," he said. "He's not the one who sent me down here in the first place."

The lieutenant colonel pulled a notebook from his pocket. The two MPs looked on with interest, admiring their boss at work. "That would be Colonel Parsons, AUS, retired, am I right? Selected for one star, elected to take early retirement for the DCIS job? That Colonel Parsons? *Troy* Parsons?"

Stafford just looked at him. The message was pretty clear. Parsons may be DCIS now, but he was one of us long before he was one of you. The lieutenant colonel closed his book.

"Look, Agent Stafford," he said. "Here's how we think things shake out: You're off your reservation. You were not assigned to stick your nose in here or anywhere other than into a fraud case at the DRMO in Atlanta. Your local supervisor is apparently eager to have a little chat with you about that, by the way. *We*, on the other hand, are interested only in the national-security aspects of your attempted intrusion into the depot here and a restricted Army exercise in Atlanta. The polygraph operator is a civilian from the Atlanta office of the FBI. You take the test, we'll give you back your ID card, get you that car, and you're free to go anywhere you want."

"And if I don't?"

"C'mon, Stafford, that was my line, remember? You don't have that option and you know it. We're not afraid of all your threats. Put it another way: Where chemical weapons are concerned, my generals can

179

beat up your colonel. Or better yet, we can make a deal to keep a shit storm from happening, you being such a popular guy up there and all." He put his notebook back in his pocket. "Hell, you're a big agent now," he said, clearly mocking him. "Haven't you ever secretly wanted to see if you could spoof a flutter?"

Thirty minutes later, Stafford sat rigidly in a straight-backed chair at a small table in yet another windowless room. The polygraph operator, who had introduced himself as a Mr. Smith from the FBI, looked like every Bureau technician Stafford had ever encountered: quietly competent. The operator was sitting behind him at a second table with his equipment.

"Remember," he said. "Only yes or no answers. One word, each question. Yes or no. Ready? Say yes or no."

"I guess so," Dave said deliberately.

Smith sighed. "Yes or no, Mr. Stafford. You can do it. I know you can. Here we go. First question: Is your name David Stafford?"

"Yes." Dave was very conscious of his breathing and his heart rate. Even so, he imagined that the instruments, wires, and cuffs attached to his skin were somehow hardwired to his lungs and heart. And his nerves.

"Are you an agent of the DCIS?"

"Yes."

"Are you a GS-Fifteen grade in the civil service?"

"Yes."

"Is your height five feet ten inches?"

"Yes." The man was obviously reading data from his credentials. Stafford knew enough about polygraphs to recognize the calibration procedures.

"Are you of Chinese descent?"

"No."

"Are you Caucasian?"

"Yes."

"Are you presently located at the Army Anniston Weapons Depot?"

"Yes."

"Do you know what CS is?"

"No." But I have an idea, he thought.

"Do you know what VX is?"

"No. Yes." The bombs in the bunker. The tall man had told him VX was nerve gas. There was a scratching on the paper behind him.

"Do you know what VX is?" the operator repeated.

"Yes."

"Do you know what cryptosporidium is?"

"No."

"Do you know what anthrax is?"

"Yes." Cow disease. Cryptosporidium? Anthrax? These weren't chemical weapons. Those sounded like biologics.

"Do you know what Wet Eye is?"

"No."

"Do you know what botulinum toxin is?"

"No."

"Have you seen it?"

Dave felt his heart jump and mentally cursed. Seen what—the cylinder? Damn it! That needle must be going all over the place. But he had not seen it. *She* had.

"No."

There was a pause, some more rustling of paper. Then the list of questions started all over again.

"Is your name David Stafford?"

"Yes."

The man went through the same initial questions. This time, when he got to the one asking if he'd seen it, Stafford had himself under much better control. The man kept right on going this time, without the ominous pause of earlier.

"Do you know the kill density per cubic centimeter of substance G?"

"No."

"Do you know the visible signs of a mustard gas attack?"

"No."

"Do you know the chemical constituents of phosgene gas?"

"No."

"Can you name the four agents known as 'blood boilers?' "

"No."

"Do you have it?"

Another surprise. But he was almost ready for it. "No."

The operator then shifted gears and asked him fifteen more questions about chemical weapons, each one increasingly more graphically specific as to its effects on the human body. Stafford answered no to every one of them.

"Okay," the man said. "From the top. Is your name David Stafford?"

They went through all the same questions again, including the two Stafford figured had to do with the missing weapon. Then the man did

181

something that caused his trace machine to begin what sounded like a print session while he stood up and began to remove the sensors from Stafford's body.

"That's it, Mr. Stafford. I'll go get the provost: I think you're all done here." The way he said the word *done* made Dave wonder if it was meant innocuously, but Smith's face revealed absolutely nothing.

"Did I pass?" Stafford asked, struggling to get his right arm into his shirt. Smith had gathered up a long roll of trace paper and was at the door.

"Pass, Mr. Stafford?" The technician stopped in the doorway. "There's no pass-fail in a polygraph test. Just questions and answers, truth tellers and liars. Simple, really. Like saying yes or no."

Stafford did not reply as the man closed the door. Twenty minutes later, he was in the backseat of an Army staff car, speeding through the Alabama countryside, headed back to Atlanta. He was in the dark, literally and figuratively.

Carrothers sat in his chair in the executive cabin of the Learjet, listening to Smith debrief the polygraph session. The flight crew was making final checks for departure, and one engine was already running. Major Mason stood beside him, taking notes. Carrothers pursed his lips when Smith had finished.

"So, in your opinion, he does know something about the item in question?" he asked.

"His answer indicated a lie, especially on the 'Have you seen it?' question. He was able to damp down the reactions on the repeat runs, but the anomalies were still there. Since I don't know what 'it' is, I couldn't branch down the questions."

Carrothers nodded. "Yes, I understand. In this case, Mr. Smith, ignorance is truly bliss. We thank you very much for your help. We'll be launching for Atlanta directly."

The FBI technician nodded and withdrew to the middle cabin. Mason remained behind.

Carrothers rubbed his eyes and then fastened his seat belt. "I love working with the FBI," he said. "Nobody knows when to shut his trap like an FBI man. Okay. First thing tomorrow, I'm going to reconstitute the Security Working Group, only this time it will consist of you, me, and Colonel Fuller. Second, we need to take this Stafford fella off the board. I'll need General Waddell's help with that. Third, I need to know that our fluttermeister in there is going to keep his mouth shut about this little excursion."

"I think he will, General. I briefed the whole thing to him as an internal Army CIC effort to trap a dirty DCIS agent. I told him that Stafford was a whistle-blower who burned some people in Washington, including a Bureau man, but now we think all that was done to cover up his own game."

"In other words, payback. The Bureau guys are into payback. He buy it?"

"The Bureau does not love whistle-blowers. He sincerely wished us luck. Said he was glad to help."

"But he'll have to report it, right?"

"Oh, yes, sir. I told him to contact us if his bosses had any further questions. Full cooperation. We owe them one, that sort of thing. I'm hoping the SAC Atlanta will just put it away in his favor bank."

"Okay, let's rock and roll. And Major?"

"Yes, sir?"

"As far as General Waddell is concerned, this thing has been destroyed, just like you said. So all we're doing now is making sure there are no loose ends. Like Stafford."

The hatch closed with a bump and a hiss. Mason frowned, looking worried. Well he should be, Carrothers thought as he watched Mason's face. He was proposing to go behind the commanding general's back, with the major's connivance. It would be interesting to see if Mason remained loyal to him or to the CG.

"With respect, General," Mason replied, "is there a new 'right answer' to what's happened to that thing?"

Carrothers rolled his eyes as the aircraft began to taxi. "Go get your seat belt on, Major. Tray tables and seat backs in the upright position, and all that."

SUNDAY, PEACHTREE CENTER HOTEL, ATLANTA, 9:30 P.M.

Dave parked the rental car on the street a block from his hotel and walked in through the front plaza area, looking for signs of surveillance or unmarked government cars. Then he realized they might just park in the underground garage and wait inside. Like in his room. He went up to the front desk and asked for the night manager. A prosperous-looking young man came out of a back office, wiping his chin with a handkerchief as if he'd been interrupted at dinner. Dave identified himself as a federal agent, presented his DCIS credentials, and asked if a Mr. Sparks from the DCIS had gained access to one of the hotel's rooms that afternoon. The manager blinked and said that yes, he had. Dave thanked him and walked away before the manager could ask any questions. He headed for the mezzanine lounge bar.

He took a table, ordered a Tanqueray martini, and then asked for a table phone. He called his room number and let it ring. After ten rings, the phone was picked up. "Ray," Stafford said. "I'm in the mezzanine bar. Lemme buy you a drink."

There was a brief sigh, and then the phone was hung up. A few minutes later, Sparks walked into the lounge, with two of the local DCIS agents behind him. Sparks motioned for them to take a nearby table, and then he sat down across from Stafford. When he saw the backup men, Stafford slipped his left hand beneath the table, doing it in such a way that they would see him do it. His useless right arm remained on the table.

"Haven't lost your touch, Dave," Sparks said. Stafford managed to lift the index finger of his right hand and point to his own drink while raising an eyebrow, but Sparks shook his head. He gave Stafford a searching look before asking the burning question. "What the hell have you got yourself into now?"

Stafford kept his left hand under the table and stirred the ice in his drink with a finger. He tried to keep it casual, but his right hand still trembled when he lifted it. He smiled. "You guys here to pick me up, Ray?"

"You bet your ass we are. Washington is suddenly very interested in what you are doing and why, and, oh by the way, you're to knock it off, as of yesterday, if not sooner."

Stafford leaned forward, the smile gone. "I've been shanghaied once today, or rather, last night. I'm not going to be taken anywhere by anybody for a while, not tonight, not anytime soon."

"Really," Sparks said as he returned Stafford's stare and casually unbuttoned his suit jacket, allowing the butt of a government-issue 9mm a little breathing room. Stafford saw the other two follow suit as they moved their chairs to face in his direction.

"Yeah, really," Stafford said. "What, you proposing to have a gunfight in the lounge of one of Atlanta's most expensive hotels?"

"Takes guns on both sides to have a gunfight, Dave," Sparks said. "I don't recall issuing you a weapon. You're not armed."

"That something you *know,* Ray? This is Georgia: They sell guns at the church socials down here."

"You're bluffing, goddamn it. Now give this shit up. We don't want to get civilians into a deal here."

"Your call, Ray. Or you could relax for a few minutes, go into the receive mode, maybe learn something you need to know. Don't you think as regional supervisor you ought to know where I've been lately? Hell, Ray, don't you even *want* to know? Just a little? You used to be an investigator, remember?"

Sparks flushed, his lips tightening. But then he sat back and rebuttoned his jacket. He gave a little shake of his head, and the backup men relaxed, although they did not change the position of their chairs.

"Okay, so talk." Sparks said.

Stafford took him back through it, right from day one at the airport and all the subsequent events relating to the cylinder. Sparks listened patiently, having heard a lot of this before, until Stafford got to the part about the MP sweep on his motel in Oxford.

"They did what?"

"Hell, Ray, I figured you'd sent them. You were sure as hell interested in knowing precisely where I was, as I recall."

"Fucking-A, I was. But that was for my information." He paused, seeing the look on Stafford's face. "Okay," he admitted. "I was gonna come get you, but not because of the fucking Army."

"It gets better," Stafford said, and then described the events of early Sunday morning.

"They picked you up? Arrested you? The *Army?* Did you show them ID?"

"Hell yes, but they knew who I was and they obviously had orders in place to pick me up. Now let me tell you where they took me."

"Wait a minute," Sparks said. "I think I want that drink now."

Dave signaled a waitress with his head. While they waited, Sparks got up and went over to his two cohorts. After a minute of earnest discussion, they got up, although they seemed reluctant to leave. Sparks was insistent, and they left the lounge. When his scotch arrived, Sparks took a substantial hit and then indicated for Stafford to continue. His expression grew angrier when Stafford told him about the bunker, and then the lie-detector test. He drained his drink when Stafford finished.

"This is fucking outrageous," Sparks declared. "Just fucking outrageous. The Army has no damned jurisdiction."

"That's not what's important here, Ray," Stafford said. "Yeah, what they did is outrageous. But they wouldn't have done it unless they were panicsville. They've lost a weapon. But they're stuck—they can't tell anyone."

"But why the hell did they just let you go, then? You obviously know about it. 'Have you seen it?' and 'Do you have it?' Unless you think you beat the flutter?"

"I doubt it. The flutter tech was a Bureau man. They don't hire amateurs."

"A Bureau man?" Sparks looked around the lounge carefully. It wasn't crowded, given it was a Sunday night. "You're telling me the Army and the Bureau are working together? That is seriously disturbing news. And it might explain why I'm getting sudden heat from DCIS Washington to get your ass back on the reservation."

"The whole fucking thing is disturbing, Ray. Especially if whoever has the weapon is trying to sell it. Think about one of the wacko militia groups armed with a cylinder of blood boiler."

"*Blood boiler?* Jesus H. Christ. Where'd you pick up a term like that?"

"During my little séance with the high pooh-bah in the bunker, whoever he was. I'm telling you, Ray, this thing is real. And I don't know who the hell to tell. Especially if the Army won't even admit it's missing."

"What were you planning to do?"

"First tell me where we stand, Ray. You and me. Where'd your two buddies go?"

Ray nodded and rattled the ice in his drink. He put down his glass. "We came down here to take you back to Smyrna. I have orders from Colonel Parson's boss, Mr. Whittaker, to get you under government control, as he put it. But that's before I'd heard this Army shit."

"Whittaker? He replaced Bernstein, right? SES-Two type?"

"That's right. Senior Executive Service. Political appointee. Came over from the Justice Department. Still wired directly into the Justice Department. Connected. Seriously connected. He's starting to talk bent-cop talk. I don't bring you in, I've gotta explain why, and not necessarily to my friends."

"Where's the colonel on this one?"

"In the dark, like the rest of us."

Stafford nodded. "Okay, I can see that. Let me propose something: You tell them I never came back to the hotel. You don't know where the hell I am. Then request the electronic net be activated—you know,

I use my government gas credit card or my government phone, Visa card, whatever, the system alerts. I'll use those cards so you can quote/unquote track me. You give me one day. I've got to go to Graniteville, warn those people there's a shit storm brewing. They trusted me, and now I can't protect them."

"Why can't you just call them?"

"Because I want to see that girl again. I want to question her myself. I've got to know if this is real or if it's bullshit. The first time, Gwen Warren wouldn't let me. This time, she might, after I tell her what might be coming down."

"And then?"

"And then I come back to Atlanta. This is Sunday night. I go up there tomorrow. I come back into town—what, Tuesday? Or wherever you want me to go."

Sparks gave him an appraising look. Stafford leaned forward. "Ray, think about it. I haven't done anything wrong. I've stumbled into something that could be fucking huge. A missing chemical weapon. It's probably right here in Atlanta, Georgia. The Army is breaking all the rules, detaining some of their own people illegally, sending CW emergency teams into the city at night, detaining federal agents. I don't care if the whole government gets into the cover-up—this *is* going to come out. You want to be on the side of the angels when it does, Ray."

"There's nobody up in D.C. who'd consider you to be one of the angels, Dave."

"If I'm trying to find this thing while everybody else is trying to cover up the fact that it's even missing, anybody who's my ally is going to dodge a bullet. You don't have to get out front, Ray. Let me do that—I'm already expendable. You be my agent in place, within the system. I think it's this Carson guy who has it, or knows where it is. Give me a day to warn the people up in Graniteville, then let me come back here and work this bitch."

Sparks ran his fingers through his hair while he thought about it. "What I still can't figure," he said, "is why the Army let you go."

"Maybe it's because someone *wants* me to find the fucking thing. If they can't admit that it's lost, then they can't really mount much more of an operation to recover it than they have. That would explain the session in the bunker. Why treat me to a scary-monster Kabuki drama if they just wanted to put me in a box? Plus, they don't know what I know about Carson."

"From a psychic."

Stafford hesitated. "Yes, that's true. But Ray, that thing I saw on the monitor was identical to the kid's drawing. How else can you explain such a thing?"

"I do not fucking know," Sparks said. "I do *not* fucking know. And I don't like all these wheels within wheels here."

"You mean you know your government too damned well. Will those two guys keep their mouths shut about tonight? The fact that you and I had a meet?"

"Yeah. They will, unless it means their jobs. You're asking a hell of a lot, Dave."

"But you know I'm right, Ray. Give me thirty-six hours. Then I'll come back to town, and we can meet off-line somewhere and work the Carson angle. All I need is thirty-six hours. I may be a loose cannon, but I'm not a bent cop. Besides, what the hell can happen in thirty-six hours?"

Sparks snorted. "With you in the game? Shit!" He looked across the table at Stafford for a long moment. Then he sighed. "Fuck me," he said. "If this isn't a Dave Stafford special, I don't know what it is."

Dave got up. "I'm going upstairs, and I'm going to try to get some sleep. Look at it this way, Ray: If this is all bullshit, you can cut me loose. It's not like anyone in DCIS would blame you."

Sparks shook his head and signaled the waiter for another one as Stafford left the lounge.

10

Dave Stafford drove into Graniteville a little after eleven on Monday morning, suppressing the umpteenth yawn. He had not slept well at all. He had vague memories of disturbing dreams, courtesy, no doubt, of his late-evening excursion to the field of tombs at the Anniston Depot.

In contrast, this Monday was bright and sunny, and the north Georgia mountains had greened out into their early-summer colors. He wasn't looking forward to his upcoming talk with Gwen Warren. She would be horrified to hear that they had been swept up into something that was probably going to get worse before it got better. He had left a message on the office answering machine to say he was driving up to Willow Grove, calling early enough to be pretty sure he would get the machine and not Gwen Warren.

He drove down toward the square, where the streets were busy with Monday-morning traffic. A noisy line of gravel trucks from the quarry passed him going the other way, leaving clouds of black diesel smoke and white dust in their wakes. There was no sign of the sheriff as he drove around the courthouse square, but he was grateful to be in a nondescript rental car this time. He decided to proceed to the Waffle House for a late breakfast of "strangled and smothered," or whatever they called it, and then call Gwen. Throughout the morning drive he had resisted the temptation to call Ray Sparks to make sure he still had an ally; now that it was Monday morning, things might have changed. He had duly used the government gas card to fill up the rental halfway up to Graniteville.

There were clearly some things going on behind the scenes in Washington that were being aimed right at him. Ray had revealed that Bernstein's replacement was going around making not so subtle hints that Stafford might be a bent cop. And the Bureau had been present for the

189

polygraph in Anniston. If Washington pressed Ray Sparks hard enough, he might not have thirty-six hours, so this had to go right, or else he might have to execute his one remaining option.

He drove into the diner's potholed parking lot and parked among the usual collection of dusty pickup trucks. His rental was the only sedan there. He took a corner booth away from the door and ordered a breakfast platter. While he was waiting for his breakfast, he got up and placed a call to Willow Grove, holding the phone pinched between his chin and his shoulder while he dialed. He again reached the answering machine. He left a message that he was at the Waffle House in town and needed to speak to Gwen, that it was urgent, and that he would call back in an hour.

He was just finishing breakfast when the sheriff pushed through the glass door, spoke briefly to the cashier, looked around, and came over to his table. Stafford indicated that he should sit down, and the big man obliged.

"Morning, Sheriff," Stafford said.

"Mr. Stafford. Gwen called me, said you called her and that it was urgent. She asked me to come down here, see what this was all about."

The waitress brought Stafford some more coffee, along with a cup for the sheriff. Stafford wasn't quite sure how to handle this. He really wanted to talk to Gwen Warren, not to the sheriff, but it seemed that Gwen had made the sheriff her gatekeeper for the moment. Besides, it might be a good idea to tell his story to the sheriff before the Army told theirs.

"I need to meet with her," Stafford began.

The sheriff gave him a long look over his coffee cup. "So she said."

"I'd be happy to do that with you present," Stafford continued. "But there's a chance she may not want you there once I tell her what this is about."

The sheriff smiled, but there was little humor in it. The crow's-feet around his eyes were pronounced. "This is a very small town, Mr. Stafford. For that matter, it's not a very big county, either. There aren't any real secrets among folks up here. This still have to do with Jessamine?"

Damn, Stafford thought. Had she told him? His surprise must have registered, because the sheriff was nodding understandingly.

"Mr. Stafford, lemme ask you something. You're a federal agent. And yet here you are, all by yourself. I've never in all my years in law enforcement seen a fed operating alone, lessen he was undercover. Any

190

chance you're flying solo on this? See, you were driving a government car the last time. White Crown Vic, Army plates, as I recall. Now I see a piece-a-shit Atlanta rental in the parking lot. Surely your office gave you a cell phone, but the cashier told me you called Gwen on the pay phone here. See what I'm sayin' here, Mr. Stafford?"

Local he was, dumb he was not, Stafford acknowledged with a mental smile. "You don't miss much, do you, Sheriff," he said.

"They pay me not to," the sheriff said patiently.

Stafford nodded. "This is complicated, and possibly very dangerous. And I am absolutely flying solo. Let me ask you to trust my judgment, at least temporarily. This does involve Jessamine, and it also involves Gwen Warren, as well as the U.S. Army, my service—the DCIS—and probably the FBI before we're all done. The problem isn't here, but it has the potential to bring federal trouble down on Gwen and the girl, and my ability to prevent any or all of that is diminishing with time. So I really need to talk to Gwen, and now I think I really *want* you there."

The sheriff's face had tightened when Stafford mentioned federal trouble. "This something you did, Mr. Stafford?" he asked in a tone of voice that made it clear Stafford had better say no.

"No, no," Stafford replied. "This is something I stumbled onto, just like Gwen and the girl did. But I believe it's real trouble, and I believe it may come up here."

"What the hell's this all about, then?" the sheriff asked, his voice rising. His tone of voice and expression caused the two men in the next booth to finish their breakfast prematurely and get out of there.

"Time is of the essence, Sheriff," Stafford said. "Right now we're wasting it."

The sheriff stood up slowly and looked down at Stafford in the manner of a hawk calculating the range to a rabbit with its foot caught under a rock. A cone of silence began to spread through the diner.

"Okay, mister," the sheriff said, "let's get to it."

Stafford wasn't quite sure if that was an invitation to a gunfight or to the sheriff's car; judging from the stares around the room, it could have been either. He fished out a ten-dollar bill and left it on the table. Then he followed the big man out of the diner with as much dignity as he could muster, which was not a lot.

He followed the sheriff's car to Willow Grove. Gwen was waiting for them on the front porch. She was wearing a simple skirt and blouse, with a light sweater thrown causally over her shoulders. Dave felt the familiar surge of interest when he saw her as they got out of the sheriff's car and walked up to the porch, but she was somewhat distant in her greetings to both of them. "The children are in class," she announced. "There's some coffee out on the porch."

When they were settled on Gwen's porch, Stafford thanked her for seeing him again and then launched into a recap of the whole story, beginning with the incident at the airport. He couldn't be sure how much of this the sheriff already knew, but John Lee Warren was paying very close attention. Stafford told them everything, excluding only the political background on why he had been sent down to Atlanta.

"My conclusion is that by some incredible incompetence or bad luck, or both, the Army has managed to lose a chemical weapon. I think that's the object the girl 'saw' after encountering Carson in the airport. I think Carson has or knows about the weapon, and that he's trying either to steal it or sell it, or both. I suspect it's hidden away somewhere at that DRMO, which, by the way, is an exceptionally good place to hide something."

"And what exactly is this weapon?" the sheriff asked.

"I don't know its name. Some kind of chemical weapon."

"We talking poison gas of some kind?"

Stafford described some of the things the tall man in the chem suit had told him in the bunker.

"Dear God!" Gwen exclaimed when he finished. "Americans built these things?"

"Following the lead of our European ancestors. The way I understand it, our possession of chemical weapons has been the only real reason no one has used them against us since World War One."

"But what's going on, Mr. Stafford?" Gwen asked. "You're a federal agent, and you've reported the possibility of a serious crime. Why aren't the federal police forces investigating your allegations?"

Stafford got up and began to pace around the porch. "Because I think there's a humongous cover-up being laid down on this problem, probably orchestrated in my very own hometown. I suspect the Army can *never* admit they've lost a weapon, which makes any allegations, especially ones based on the input of a psychic child, somewhat moot. Meanwhile, they'll be quietly tearing up the countryside looking for it, and anyone who happens to stumble into that little effort will be snatched up and held incommunicado, like those soldiers at Fort McClellan, until they either find it or decide they've successfully buried the whole issue."

"Anyone?" Gwen asked. She had a strange expression on her face; Stafford couldn't tell if it was one of fear or anger.

"Yes," Stafford said, looking right at her. "Anyone. That's why I'm here. To warn you." Stafford hesitated. This was going to be the hard part. "My boss knows about Jess. I'm pretty sure Carson knows I came to Graniteville that last time. Right now, he probably thinks that I found out about the weapon based on something this guy Dillard said."

"So why would Carson come here?" the sheriff asked.

Stafford kept looking at Gwen. "Because, Sheriff, he was the guy who fainted at the airport during a one-on-one with Jessamine."

An anguished look passed over Gwen's face, prompting the sheriff to take her hand. "Gwen?" he said. "What is it?"

"He's right, John Lee. It is Jess. When she . . . intrudes into another mind, the person passes out."

"Great God Almighty," the sheriff said softly. "I forgot that."

Gwen leaned forward in her chair. "Does Carson know about Jess?"

"You tell me, Gwen," Stafford said. "Is it likely he would remember what happened to him at the airport?"

"I don't know," she said with a sigh. "There's very little that we know about her . . . abilities."

"And he knows you came up to Graniteville," the sheriff said. "That's just damn wonderful."

Gwen put her hand on his. "*I* called Mr. Stafford, John Lee, remember? At the time, there was no way he could have known why."

Stafford sat back down. "The cylinder in her drawing meant nothing to me until that response team showed up at the DRMO," he explained. "And I saw that same cylinder on the PC monitor in one of their trailers."

The sheriff leaned back in his chair, rubbing that big mustache with his fingers. The bucolic tranquillity of the yard outside was in stark contrast to the tension on the porch. Stafford massaged his aching right arm; he had not done his exercises for a couple of days. "What happens next," he said, "will depend on what some badly frightened people in Washington set in motion."

The sheriff absorbed that thought for a moment. "Well, maybe I'm just a dumb-ass country sheriff," he said, "but I guess I don't understand why everybody who knows about this isn't jumping out of his hide trying to find the weapon, instead of all this cover-up stuff."

"Cover-up is the hallmark of effective government these days, Sheriff," Stafford replied. "You need to know something else. I've already told Gwen this, but let me tell you the real reason I was sent down here in the first place."

"Where the hell did this come from?" General Carrothers asked, waving a piece of paper in the air. Major Mason's face was grim.

"From Army Criminal Investigation Command, General. I just called them to verify it. They got it from the FBI intelligence division."

Carrothers examined the spot report again. The first paragraph contained the usual warnings and caveats about protecting sensitive intelligence methods and sources. It was the second paragraph that had his attention, the one reporting that word was circulating among the clandestine international arms network that an individual by the name of Stafford had put feelers out into the market regarding the possible sale of stolen chemical ordnance, for which he was reportedly asking a million dollars. No further identifying data on subject Stafford. The FBI was investigating, and requesting any available corroborating information about missing chemical ordnance from the Army.

Son of a bitch! He thought.

"I assume the implied question there is whether or not we've had any weapons stolen," Mason said.

Carrothers nodded slowly. "Not so implied, is it, Major? And the technically correct answer is no, we have no reports of *stolen* chemical weapons. Tell them that at once. Then hopefully they won't come asking if we've *lost* any CW ordnance. Jesus H. Christ, Mason, if this is true . . ."

"Yes, sir. Understood, sir. That name, Stafford—"

"No shit. How many Staffords have we encountered recently? And there's the matter of his evasions on that lie-detector examination. Damn it. Maybe I fucked up. We should have held him."

A front-office clerk stuck his head into the general's office. "A Colonel Fuller is here, General? Shall I have him wait?"

"No, send him in."

Colonel Fuller came into the office and shut the door behind him.

"Morning, General, Major Mason," he said. Then he saw their faces. "We're reconstituting the Security Working Group? Has something happened?"

"After a fashion, Colonel," Carrothers said.

Fuller looked from Carrothers to Mason and back. "Does General Waddell know about this?"

Carrothers said nothing, and Fuller nodded slowly. "All right," he said. "Let me guess: You don't think that thing went into that demil machine, do you?"

"Colonel Fuller, I have a question for you," Carrothers said. "Why did General Waddell pull you into this thing?"

"Well, Myer Waddell and I go way back," Fuller began, but Carrothers raised his hand.

"No, I mean why *you*, a BW expert?"

Colonel Fuller sat down in a chair and pulled at his shirt collar. He glanced over at Major Mason, but Carrothers indicated that Mason was staying.

Fuller nodded. "Right. The problem is I have specific orders from General Waddell not to discuss this with anyone, including you, sir."

Carrothers turned on the frost. "Care for a little temporary duty out on Kwajalein Island, Colonel? I can have you on a plane this afternoon."

Fuller smiled, then put up his hands in mock surrender. "The Wet Eye weapon is a hybrid, General. It contains a biologic component. An unstable biologic component, if my information is correct."

"Jesus H. Christ," Carrothers muttered.

"Unstable how, Colonel?" Mason asked, making notes.

"Unstable in that the biologic component may mutate in the absence of the environmental controls provided by its coffin."

"In other words," Carrothers said, "we don't know what the hell might be going on in that cylinder?"

"That's correct." Fuller paused, as if he was about to amplify that, but then went on. "Let me give you some history, General."

Fuller described how the United States had come into possession of the weapon, and what the biological weapons program had decided about Wet Eye all those years ago.

"So this wasn't even one of ours?"

"No, sir. And this is all archive information on the offensive BW program. That's all gone now. All we do out at Dietrick now in BW is on the defense side. We develop vaccines to inoculate our troops against the BW programs of the Saddam Husseins of the world, you know, all those upstanding countries who won't sign the treaties banning this stuff."

Carrothers got up and started pacing behind his desk. "Major," he said, "tell Colonel Fuller about that FBI intel report."

Fuller listened carefully and then shook his head. "Not likely, General," he said. "The group's information was that Stafford got there *after* the containers had come in from Tooele and been destroyed. We checked with DCIS when he popped up at the first response-team insertion."

"What did they tell you about him?"

"That he blew the whistle on an SES-Two, which, of course, did not endear him to senior officials in DCIS. They hinted pretty strongly that the guy had been shit-canned. But they did say he was a first-class investigator. Just has no political sense."

"In other words, not the kind of guy who's likely to steal and then try to sell stolen chemical weapons to, say, the Iranians."

"No, sir. He's an ex-cop and now a GS-Fifteen federal agent. That's too much of a reach."

Carrothers pointed to the intelligence report. "Then what the hell's this all about? Where's it coming from? And if this guy Stafford knows something, why in the hell hasn't he come in to talk about it?"

Mason cleared his throat. "He did, General. In a manner of speaking, that is." This comment earned him a quick glare from Carrothers. Mason squirmed uncomfortably.

"If we refuse to admit we've lost a weapon, where else could the guy go?" Fuller asked.

"To his boss, goddamn it!" Carrothers said. "Major, get that guy I talked to the other night—I think his name was Sparks—on the horn. He's down in Smyrna."

Mason got up and left the office. Fuller was shaking his head. "And tell him what, General? We've lost a chemical weapon and we really need to talk to Stafford?"

"Of course not. I'll tell him we've received this report and we wanted to know if it's credible."

"By definition, it's not credible. We aren't missing a weapon. As long as we can't admit this, it seems to me we shouldn't go talking to *anybody*."

Carrothers started to reply but then sat back down at his desk. Fuller was right. What he really wanted to do was talk to Stafford, this time without the atmospherics of the tombs at Anniston. But he was not so sure he wanted to tell this slippery colonel what he was really thinking. Fuller was still Waddell's man, and Carrothers knew he was on thin ice with what he was doing vis-à-vis Waddell's orders.

"What you say is true, Colonel. But I think we have a responsibility to make damn sure this weapon isn't still out there somewhere, especially if there's an unknown biological capability hatching out in that cylinder. I think Mr. Stafford knows more than he's letting on."

"Based on what, General?"

Carrothers started to tell him, but then he thought better of it. Waddell did not know about his little excursion to Anniston. Fuller is Waddell's man, he reminded himself again.

"I just do," he said. "A hunch, I guess."

Mason came back into the office. "DCIS regional office, Symrna. Mr. Ray Sparks, regional supervisor. I have the number here."

"Get him on secure."

As Mason left the room, Fuller asked Carrothers if he'd like to see a video on Wet Eye he just happened to have.

■ MONDAY, FORT GILLEM DRMO, ATLANTA, NOON

Carson's secretary came in with a yellow message slip. "Another losing bidder, wants to complain," she said, handing him the slip. He nodded and went back to the paper he was working on until she left the office. He glanced at the 800 number. Tangent. Good.

He waited fifteen minutes and then told her was going to lunch. Ten minutes later he was standing in a phone booth out on State Road 42. He had to close the door because of all the truck noise. The booth immediately began to cook in the bright Georgia sun. He'd been doing a lot of thinking about how to make the transfer.

"Carson," he said when the phone was picked up.

"Right. We've dropped a little nugget into the FBI's intelligence system. Stafford should now be in deep *kimshii.*"

"How in the hell did you manage that?"

"The FBI pays confidential informants to report interesting rumors in the international arms markets. A lot of it's total bullshit, but sometimes they get lucky. We're one of the informants."

"Jesus, that's playing with fire, isn't it?"

"Not really. You want to hide from the FBI, do business with them right out in the open. They tend to make everything they do really hard."

"Won't DCIS find out about it?"

"Very probably, but we didn't identify Stafford as a government guy. Just used his name. But because we said chemical weapon, the Army will probably get a call from the Bureau, and they'll know *exactly* which Stafford. That way we get one government agency leaning on another one. They'll get all wrapped around the axle over jurisdiction, and we, in the meantime, will get a window to do this thing. You ready?"

"Yeah, but all this other shit's been distracting the hell out of me. But I've decided one thing: I want the money in cash. Greenback dollars. Hundreds."

"You do know you're talking ten thousand hundred-dollar bills, right? That's a stack of hundreds about ten feet high."

"That's a footlockerful. And that's how I want it. I don't know anything about diamonds or any of the rest of that stuff. And I really think we ought to do it here, at the DRMO. Now that the Army's looking, I don't want to move that thing."

Tangent was silent for a moment. "Okay," he said. "I suppose we can do it there. My client is nervous about our going onto a federal facility for this kind of transaction, that's all. Some gate guard searches the vehicle, finds the money, it'd be tough to explain."

"There aren't any gate guards here at Fort Gillem. It's an open post."

"Okay. How's about the 'when' question?"

Carson was ready. "This is Monday. How soon can you have your people here in Atlanta? With the cash?"

"Hell, logistically, we're ready now. To get down there, get set up, eight, twelve hours."

"Okay, here's how I want to do it. I'll assume your people can be ready by midnight tonight. That's twelve hours from now. Sometime in the next twenty-four hours after that, I'll call them at a number that you designate and tell them to come to Fort Gillem. They get here, there will be instructions on what to do and where to go next."

"Don't make this too complicated, Carson."

"I'm trying to make it safe. For me. A million in cash is a tempting amount of money."

"How do we know *you* won't stiff *us*?"

"What else am I going to do with this thing except sell it, huh?" Carson asked. "It's not like I want to own it." Especially, he thought, after I found out it might be cooking.

"Okay, that works for us. I'll call one more time to confirm all this. In about two hours."

"I'll be waiting."

■ MONDAY, THE PENTAGON, WASHINGTON, D.C., 12:20 P.M.

"I've got Mr. Sparks's office on secure, General," Major Mason said from the doorway. General Carrothers picked up his handset.

"This is Brigadier General Lee Carrothers, deputy commander of the Army Chemical Corps," he announced.

"This is Leslie Smith, General. I'm the regional DCIS office manager in Smyrna. As I just explained to the major, Mr. Sparks is not available to speak to you, sir."

"He's not there? When will he be available?"

"He's not available to speak to you, General," she repeated patiently. "I can't say when he will be available, sir."

Carrothers frowned. "You telling me he *won't* talk to me, Ms. Smith?"

"I'm just telling you what Mr. Sparks told me to tell you, sir."

Carrothers held his temper. She wasn't being disrespectful; she was merely doing what her boss had told her: that he wouldn't take this call.

"Okay, Ms. Smith, I understand. Do you have a secure fax number? I need to send something down there that might make Mr. Sparks change his mind."

She gave him the secure fax number. He thanked her and hung up.

"I'll be damned," he said. "This guy Sparks won't take my call."

Colonel Fuller gave the general a bemused look. "You practically arrested one of his people," he said. "Held him for a day on a closed post, made him take a lie-detector test, and then turned him loose without so much as a by-your-leave, and his boss won't talk to you? Unusual boss, this day and age."

"Maybe. Although I don't think Stafford knew who I was."

"He knew it was Army Chemical Corps hassling him, General."

"Yeah, well. Mason, send a copy of this spot report to this number," he ordered, handing Mason the paper. "Addressed to Mr. Sparks. Make sure my name and secure drop are on the cover sheet."

"Yes, sir. Right away." Mason left the office.

"And Colonel Fuller, when he's done, I want you and Major Mason to sit down and design a special response team that would be capable of recovering and decontaminating, if necessary, a Wet Eye exposure incident. From both the CW and the BW perspectives."

Fuller nodded slowly but then frowned. "I can do half of that, General. The CW side should be pretty straightforward. The chem team and their transport vehicles MOPPed up to the max. Standard decontamination procedures. Current MOPP gear will protect the troops against the chemical agent. But as I told you, we can't know what the bugs are doing in there. Or what kind of toxins they might be generating. What granularity, for instance vis-à-vis the respirator filters."

Carrothers considered that. "What's the only absolutely, positively surefire method of eliminating biologic toxins, Colonel?"

"You just said it, General. Fire. Serious fire. As in napalm, thermite, carbon-arc fire, atomic weapons fire."

"So if I thought a cylinder of Wet Eye was hidden in a building?"

"I'd incinerate that building. I'd bring up a flame-throwing tank and burn the bastard into lampblack. Think Waco, Texas. Burn it to a smear."

"That's a bit extreme, Colonel."

"So's a Wet Eye exposure event, General."

Colonel Fuller left the office, closing the door behind him. He looked around for Major Mason. The clerk told him the major was down the hall using the secure fax station. Fuller stood there thinking for a moment. He asked the clerk where General Waddell was.

"He's on the West Coast, Sir."

"Do you have a phone number for him?"

"We can reach the general, sir," the clerk replied warily.

"General Carrothers has asked Major Mason and me to reconstitute the Security Working Group. We'll need that secure conference room again. And I need you to get a discreet message to General Waddell to call me immediately. And I mean *me*, not anyone else. Understand, Sergeant?" He looked meaningfully at General Carrothers's closed door. "General Waddell and I are longtime personal friends, and I need to talk to him very privately and very soon. You can word that anyway you want to, as long as it goes out in the next five minutes or so."

The clerk was writing this all down. "Got it, Colonel. I'll let you know as soon as I reach the general, sir."

▬ MONDAY, GRANITEVILLE, GEORGIA, 1:00 P.M.

Stafford asked to use the phone in Gwen's office, where he called Ray Sparks. Ray's secretary put him on hold for a minute and then came back on the line.

"Mr. Sparks wants to know if you have your portable with you," she said.

"Yes. It's out in the car."

"He said to get it and then call back in secure. Quickly."

Stafford hung up and went out to get his computer. The sheriff asked him what was going on. "Gotta make a secure call to the local DCIS office, Sheriff."

"That looks like a portable."

200

"It is; there's a secure telecomm function built in." The sheriff followed him back into Gwen's office but withdrew when Stafford gave him an "excuse me" look. As he dialed the Smyrna secure number, he saw the sheriff and Gwen exchange a few words on the porch, and then the sheriff was picking up his hat. Gwen came over and stood in the doorway. He decided to let her stay and listen. The secure link came up with the Smyrna office. Sparks came right on, and Stafford put him on the portable's speaker.

"Dave. There's something you need to know about. It was faxed down here from the Pentagon by a brigadier general in the Army Chemical Corps. It's an intel spot report, according to which, a subject named Stafford has gone into the arms business."

"Ducky. What is this Stafford Communist supposed to be selling?"

"A chemical weapon. He's asking for a million bucks. This general wanted to talk to me this morning, but I stiffed him."

"And who originated that report?"

"Three guesses."

Stafford thought about that for a minute. "It was a Bureau guy who fluttered me at Anniston."

"Bingo. So we definitely have the Army and Bureau working a problem together."

"Right. All over a weapon that isn't missing. You feeling a little better about this, Ray? Like maybe I'm not totally crazy?"

"Let's not leap to assumptions, Dave," Sparks said with a nervous laugh. Stafford felt a surge of relief to have Ray back in his corner, but it was short-lived.

"Dave, you do know I've got to forward this to DCIS Washington, although, now that I think about it, they may already have it. And I'm going to have to tell Colonel Parsons what the hell this is all about."

"Damn, I wish there was a way around that," Stafford said, very much aware of Gwen in the doorway. "At least the part about the people here in Graniteville."

"I can try. Give them the old confidential informant bit. But it's all going to come apart anyway when the colonel closes the loop with the Green Machine, and they hunker back down and say, 'What missing weapon?' The thing I can't figure out is where the hell this intel report came from. I mean, I know the FBI intel division is the source, but who's feeding them this shit?"

"Somebody who wants to put the heat on me and take the heat off of him."

"You mean Carson?"

"He said he had friends in D.C., and he's the guy who knows where this thing is."

"You suspect."

"I know."

"No, you don't, Dave. You don't know. You suspect. You *know* when you can present evidence. Proof. Witnesses. Documents. The little girl with the crystal ball doesn't count."

"For Chrissakes, Ray, she doesn't have a goddamn crystal ball," Stafford said, louder than he had intended. He was now painfully aware of Gwen standing in the doorway, and she was giving him a peculiar look. There was an awkward silence on the line.

"Who exactly sent this fax to you?" Stafford asked.

"It came from the office of a Brigadier General Lee Carrothers, the Pentagon."

"And you refused to talk to him?"

"Hell yes. This is interdepartmental. If anyone's going to start talking to the Army headquarters, it's got to be DCIS headquarters. As in Colonel Parsons or higher. This general undoubtedly anticipated that. He wants me to pass it up the line."

Sparks the ever-obedient bureaucrat. "How about giving me that general's phone number?" Stafford said.

"Negative, Dave. Let Parsons or Whittaker handle this. You've warned those people up there in Hicksville, or wherever you are? Then you're done up there. Come back to Atlanta. I want you here in Smyrna when Washington starts sending cruise missiles down to Georgia. You know DCIS is going to go snakeshit."

Stafford thought fast. He had promised to go back. But he suddenly did not want to do that. "Okay. I'll wrap it up here and get back," he said.

"Good, you do that," Sparks said.

Stafford hung up before Sparks could say anything more. He didn't want to tell Ray any more lies than were absolutely necessary. Gwen looked as if she wanted to say something, but Stafford held her off by raising his hand. Then he typed in another number on the secure autodialer.

"Pentagon secure operator."

"I need the secure drop for a Brigadier General Lee Carrothers, U.S. Army. He's in the building. And request a patch, please, operator."

"Stand by." Dave motioned for Gwen to sit down. The sheriff was nowhere in sight.

"General Waddell's office, Sergeant Clifford speaking, sir."

"Sergeant, this is David Stafford, DCIS, calling for Brigadier Car-rothers."

"Stand by one, sir. I'll see if the general is available."

Stafford put his thumb over the microphone spot on the portable. "I'm going out of channels, Gwen. I'm going to try to point these people at Carson and still keep you and the girl out of it. Can't promise—"

"This is General Carrothers."

Stafford thought he recognized the voice behind the mask at Anniston. "Hello again, General."

There was brief hesitation. "Hello again, Mr. Stafford. I was actually hoping you might call."

"Do we have something specific to talk about yet, General? Or are we going to dance some more?"

"You tripped on two questions in your test, Mr. Stafford. You remember which ones they were?"

"Yup. And the true answers are yes, I've seen it, and no, I don't have it, no matter what the Feebies are telling you. But I think I know who does have it. You need to get your hands on the manager of the DRMO, one Wendell Carson. And you probably ought to do that sooner rather than later, General."

"Very interesting, Mr. Stafford. Will you tell me where you saw it?"

"On a PC monitor in one of your response team's trucks, General, the first time you had them go to the DRMO. A cylinder. Three feet long or so. About three, four inches in diameter. It looked like a CAD-CAM view, revolving slowly on the screen in three-D. Or am I mistaken here? Maybe that was just a screen saver?"

The general never missed a beat. "That's exactly what you were looking at, Mr. Stafford. A screen saver. I guess I'm disappointed. I thought you might have something substantial for me. Something real."

"And I thought you guys were missing a chemical weapon, General. Something substantial, something real."

That brought a moment of silence. Then the general asked another question. "Why were you there at that DRMO, Mr. Stafford?"

"I was sent there, General. That's usually how it works in DCIS. I was there to investigate a possible fraud case. DCIS had uncovered a pattern of evidence that someone was rigging the auctions of surplus military material. We actually picked the Atlanta DRMO at random to test the pattern theory. We don't really have a case on any person or persons yet."

"Well, then, Mr. Stafford, I guess we're still dancing. I think you're not telling me something. I need more than your say-so to go after this Mr. Carson."

"I'm protecting a confidential informant," Stafford said, looking over at Gwen, "who, interestingly enough, saw the same thing I saw. All I can tell you is that somebody really, really needs to go back to that DRMO and get his hands on Carson. Maybe do to him what you did to me. Before this thing that isn't missing gets any more missing."

"Where are you now, Mr. Stafford?"

"In Atlanta, General," Stafford lied. "I'm calling you on a secure comms PC."

"If I need to talk to you again, where do I call?"

"The DCIS office in Smyrna, General. Leave the message with Mr. Sparks." He gave Carrothers the number.

"Mr. Sparks wouldn't talk to me this morning. He hurt my feelings."

"Mr. Sparks has a good nose for trouble, General. It's nothing personal, you understand."

Stafford thought he heard a small chuckle. "Good-bye, Mr. Stafford."

He secured the computer. Gwen was watching him carefully when he turned around. "Now what?" she asked.

"I don't know. I promised Ray I'd go back to Atlanta. But I don't really want to go back there."

She looked momentarily relieved. "Why?" she asked. "Will something happen?"

"It shouldn't. That fax was just an intelligence spot report—one grade better than rumor. Not even the Bureau arrests people on rumors, or they didn't used to, anyway. Either way, that spot report's going to stir up a fire at the DCIS headquarters as soon as the Army talks to them. There are people there willing to believe anything about me."

"And what would they do?"

"Recall me to Washington, which might be why that spot report was generated. My guess is that Carson has the thing they're looking for. He may be in the process of selling it to someone, and that someone has connections good enough to start this crap."

Gwen looked down at the floor. "You work in a strange world, Mr. Stafford. Are you telling me that the only way you could convince your bosses, or that general, is to have Jess corroborate your story?"

Stafford shook his head. "I actually don't think that would do any good. And it would definitely turn into a circus, as I think you already know. No. I've made the best use of her . . . faculties that I can. The Army has to be desperate to find that thing. I've given them a new target. My guess is they'll take a shot at it, one way or another."

She persisted. "But didn't you say Carson knows that you know? Does he know *how* you found out?"

"Initially he's going to think it was one of his own people. But if he goes back and thinks about everything that's happened since I entered the picture, he might guess. We were all there in the airport, Gwen. You, Jess, Carson, and me. Carson's a run-of-the-mill civil servant who's probably operating way out of his depth right at the moment. But he's not stupid. I guess it depends on what he saw or experienced when Jessamine saw what she saw."

"In the two prior cases, they appear to remember nothing."

"Well, then, that might work in our favor."

"Do they know where we are? All these people—the Army, the DCIS, the FBI, or even this Carson?"

Stafford stopped to think. Sparks knew that he had come to Graniteville. The Pentagon could probably trace back the secure phone call he had just made. The FBI probably did not know, but they also weren't looking yet. And Carson? Did Carson know about Graniteville? Had he mentioned Graniteville to Carson in the car that day?

"The government agencies can find out," he said finally. "I don't know about Carson. But if someone in Washington is helping him, someone with connections, then, yes, he might be able to find out."

"Then we should tell John Lee about your call this morning, don't you think?"

"Yes. But unless the Army goes after Carson, he probably won't do anything. Unless—"

"Unless what?" Her hands were folded in her lap, but he could see the tension in her fingers.

"Unless Carson does recall what happened at the airport. Then he might consider the girl a witness. A stolen chemical weapon would be worth a ton of money in certain quarters, but not if there's a witness."

"So now Jess is a witness." She sighed. "And from what you say, only the bad guy will believe her. That's rich." She looked across the room at him, her eyes pleading. "I really wish you could stay here. Until we know."

He smiled. "I'm definitely thinking about it. My bosses probably won't see it that way, of course. It's going to depend upon what the Army does with my phone call." He rubbed his temples. "I'm getting the mother of all headaches. I need to take a walk or something."

"Let me make a quick check on how the afternoon's going. Then I'll join you."

■■■ MONDAY, FORT GILLEM DRMO, 2:30 P.M.

Carson began his preparations after lunch. First he made a walking tour of the entire DRMO to see that everything was operating normally. He walked through all of the warehouses, the tarmac area, the receiving building, and even the demil assembly and product lines. He did not detect any unusual vibes from the employees; even Corey Dillard gave him a cautious nod of recognition. He looked for any signs that the Army teams had left behind some covert surveillance equipment but found nothing.

He had the man in the security control room walk him through the closed-circuit television surveillance systems that covered the high-value military equipment warehouses, the tarmac, and the entrance to the demil complex. He paid attention to the camera-viewing angles and got a feel for what the displays showed and did not show. This office was manned up during normal working hours, but all the budget cutting had forced them to go to intrusion alarm–activated tape after hours. His plan for the transfer included use of the television cameras, so he made sure he had the current cipher-lock code for the control room.

He ended his tour in the demil assembly building, where Boss Hisley and his crew were building up the feed run for the Monster. Hisley gave him his usual blank face and kept the crew going despite Carson's presence. Carson walked around the assembly area, looking at everything, trying to figure out where and how to set the thing up. The key was going to be the closed-circuit TV system. He did not bother going into the demil building. If this worked, nothing was going to happen there, except for the small matter of a trunk with a million bucks in it. He walked casually back to his office across the tarmac, trying hard not to look at his watch. He wondered if Tangent's team was in Atlanta yet. He'd told Tangent they could get the go order anytime after midnight tonight. He planned to make the call at twelve-fifteen. In the meantime, he had some more preparations to make.

The clerk knocked once on the door of the conference room and stuck his head in. "Colonel Fuller, sir, there's a call for you from your office."

"So patch it in."

"Uh, sir, I can't patch that particular line." Fuller turned around in exasperation and then saw the look on the clerk's face. "Oh, okay. I'll be right out."

"Trouble?" Mason asked, his desk cluttered with old microfilm prints on the Wet Eye weapon.

"Something from USAMRIID," Fuller muttered. "You know, budget time." He went out to the clerk's desk. The clerk pointed him over to the couch on the other side of the office, where a secure phone extension was blinking. He picked it up.

"Colonel Fuller," he said.

"Ambrose?"

"Yes, sir. We have a problem." In a low voice, and with one eye on General Carrothers's closed office door, he brought General Waddell up to speed on what Carrothers had reported. The general swore and then asked Fuller what might be happening in the cylinder.

"That's the bad news, General," Fuller said. "My people have finished the simulation run. Based on that, they're predicting an exothermic reaction in the cylinder, capable of blowing the end caps off in thirty-six hours, plus or minus four hours."

"Damn. Which would release what, exactly?"

"That's just it, General, we don't know. The heat might kill the bugs, or they might mutate to something truly virulent. Either way, the underlying chemical agent would still be present. That thing lets go in the right place, we could have us a real situation."

There was long silence, which Fuller knew better than to interrupt. Finally, Waddell spoke. "Okay," he said. "Thirty-six hours. We keep coming back to that DRMO in Atlanta. I take it there's no point in searching the damn thing again."

"No, sir. A DRMO is basically a warehouse complex. Thousands of things on shelves. You'd have to—"

"Yes, yes, I understand all that. Carrothers is having you plan another sweep with the Anniston team?"

"I believe so, sir."

"Forget that. This problem has reached zero-option status. I'm going to call General Roman, and then I'm going to task a Special Forces team from Fort McPherson, which is right there in Georgia. I'll have them at Fort Gillem by 2400. Get the Anniston team there by 0100, reinforced, just like the last time."

"Hell, Myer, there's no point in—"

"I know that, Ambrose. But we're not going to search that place again. You had the right idea. The snake-eaters will have a Humvee full of thermite bombs. I want that DRMO incinerated. The whole fucking ball of wax, right to the ground. I want the Anniston team there to secure the perimeter, test the smoke, probe the ashes."

Fuller was aghast. "But, sir, if the cylinder *is* there, that smoke might— I mean, Jesus, we're talking metro Atlanta here. We have no idea—"

"It's a stainless-steel cylinder, Ambrose. Any external fire hot enough to rupture it is hot enough to burn anything that comes out of it. Especially any living organisms. And with Wet Eye, shouldn't we have a fluorine organophosphate residual after combustion?"

Fuller thought for a moment, trying to recall the baseline modulus on Wet Eye. "Yes, sir, I think we would. It would be molecular concentrations, though. Pretty damn faint signature."

"Our new mark-seven gear can detect at that concentration. Now, patch me back to my clerk. I believe it's time to share my thinking with General Carrothers. And Ambrose?"

"Yes, sir?"

"Close-hold on the mutation problem. That's between you and me until I tell you differently."

"Even General Carrothers?"

"Especially General Carrothers."

"Understood, sir," Fuller said, hitting the patch button. Share my thinking, he thought, his throat suddenly dry. He swallowed. Suddenly, he was glad the general hadn't asked him about whether or not the Army's chem suits could hold off a mutated agent.

■ MONDAY, WILLOW GROVE HOME, GRANITEVILLE, GEORGIA, 5:30 P.M.

They hiked only as far as the first waterfall this time, mindful of the setting sun. Along the way, Gwen made her case for Stafford's not going back to Atlanta. Her biggest fear was for the little kids, coming as they

often did from horrific circumstances. The prospect of government in-
terrogation teams, or, worse, the media, might set them back for years.
Jessamine, she said, was particularly vulnerable. She was a teenager, with
all the emotional baggage that that entailed, who had witnessed a terrifying event as a very small child.

He remembered her saying that before. "Can you tell me what happened?"

Gwen hesitated, then answered, "I'd rather not, actually. It involved
an incident with her mother."

Stafford nodded, then asked about Jess's speech disability.

"She has been mute from childhood. I know she seems pretty competent now—goes to school, rides her horse, picks up after herself. But
underneath, there's a lot of cracked emotional glass. I just can't have
her exposed to some media feeding frenzy, which is the main reason
I'm asking you to stay for a while."

Stafford didn't really have to be convinced to stay, but he would
have liked to hear some evidence that she wanted him there for a reason
besides protecting the kids. He asked her if the sheriff couldn't protect
them from undue public scrutiny.

"John Lee would just get himself in trouble, I'm afraid. He's an old-
school Georgia county sheriff. It wouldn't occur to him that someone
might disagree with what he ordered, much less try to run over the top
of him."

"If the FBI comes, they will absolutely run right over the top of him
and everybody else," he said. "They'll go through the motions, but they'll
do it their way. And the Army? God only knows what those guys will do."

"John Lee would probably get the deputies out and start shooting
or something. He's a tough old bear."

They started back toward the house. "You sound like you're still fond
of him, at least a little," he said.

She turned and smiled. "In a way, I am. Is that such a bad thing?
Give me your hand. No, your right hand." He did, and she took it gently,
returning to the path. "John Lee had an affair. He was so sorry for what
he did, but once I found out, well . . ."

"I know that feeling," he said. "It's a kick in the teeth, no matter
how it's presented."

"My very words. I could no longer be married to him, so the only
option was divorce. Everyone in Graniteville was pretty upset. At him
for doing what he did, and at me, for not forgiving him. 'Good ole boys
make mistakes, Mizz Warren; ain't nobody perfect.' "

"Nobody ever promises to be perfect. Just to love, honor, and cherish."

She squeezed his hand. "So now he comes around," she said. "Looks after us, does things for the school and the kids, smoothes the way with the state when we need it. He helps. He hopes, I think."

As she held his right hand in her left, he did not feel like a cripple for the first time in months. "And so he never remarried?" he asked.

"No, he did not. Neither did I. How about you, David Stafford? Will you remarry?"

Her question startled him. "Never again," he said too quickly, but then he wondered if he really meant that. "I mean, hell, I don't know that. Just about every aspect of my life has come apart lately—my career, my marriage, this useless damn arm."

"Not so useless a damn arm right now, is it?"

He grinned. "No, now that you mention it. I rather like holding hands with you, Gwen Warren."

She stopped, released his hand, and looked over at him. Her face was partially in shadow, and he couldn't read her expression. "Then please," she said softly. "Please stay here with us. I'm afraid of your world and what might happen it if it comes here."

He remembered Ray's warning. "If I do that, Gwen, I might be an unemployed ex-cop."

"Would that be so bad? Is your career going all that well right now?"

He looked down at the ground. The lady had a point there. "You know, as unbelievable as this might sound, I've never considered leaving the business. Even after all that's happened. Maybe I should."

He looked around at the forest. They had walked almost to the edge of the willow grove. The sounds of the little kids at the barn were filtering through the mass of greenery. "It's just that I feel I didn't do anything wrong. Politically dumb, maybe, but not wrong. Not up there, nor down here with this Carson thing. I've tried to do the right thing."

"And do your superiors value that ethic?"

"I thought they did, but now I wonder. I guess I've never thought that through. Been too busy being sorry for myself."

"Think about it now, Dave."

One of the kids saw them through the willows and began to call her name. He wanted to continue their little talk, to explain how he felt about her, but the moment had passed, and she was already moving, calling back to them. He still wasn't sure: Did she feel something for him? Or was it more a case of her needing him to help them with what might be coming toward their little world? He followed after her, exploring in his mind for the first time the prospect of not being a cop, of doing something entirely different with his life.

He had dinner that evening with Gwen, Jessamine, the little kids, and Mrs. Benning in the communal dining room. They had spent the rest of the afternoon watching the afternoon activities at the barn. Later they had another chance to talk, he of his life and experiences in law enforcement, she of her many years of building up Willow Grove while pursuing knowledge about the way cast-off children communicate with a world that has rejected them. He gained the sense that while she was smart enough to fill her days with commitments, at heart she was a lonely person, a woman who had never quite gotten over the hurt of her husband's betrayal. He followed her lead in the conversation and did not try to steer it toward how he felt about her. Either she had not noticed or there was nothing there but his wishful thinking.

At dinner the kids were cute, but hardly angels, and the supervising adults had their hands full. He watched Jessamine covertly during dinner, wondering if she could really read minds, if she was reading his mind now. But then he remembered that the person being probed supposedly had to be extremely agitated. He still found it tough to believe. And yet the police literature was full of documented cases where so-called psychics and profilers had led an investigation right to the perpetrator's front door, and usually after the cops had run into what seemed like a stone wall. This girl looked like every fourteen-year-old girl he had ever seen—a bit awkward, insecure, feigning utter indifference to what was going on around her while simultaneously being keenly interested in how she was being perceived. He wondered what it might be like to peer into someone else's thoughts, emotions, or memories, and he decided that it might not be so terrific. Such an ability would be the ultimate infraction of the old Washington rule: Don't formally ask a question if you can't stand *all* the possible answers.

After dinner, he found himself alone at the table with Jess while the two women took the little kids upstairs for the nightly battle of getting them to bed. He was finishing a cup of coffee and wondering when Sparks would call. She made a pretense of reading a book, but she was watching him when she thought he wasn't looking. On an impulse, he asked her how she liked school, forgetting for a moment that she did not speak. She signed briefly, then pulled over a pad of paper and a pen and began writing. "Boring," she wrote. "They think I'm stupid."

"The kids, or the teachers?" he asked.

"Some of both," she wrote. "I'm not dumb."

He almost asked her why she did not speak, but then he remembered what Gwen had said about her background. It occurred to him that here was his chance to ask her something he really did want to know.

"Jess," he said, "do you remember the man at the airport?"

She frowned and did not immediately respond. But then she nodded.

"Gwen told me you sensed that he was a bad man. That he frightened you."

She was watching him very carefully now. Another slow nod.

"Can you write down for me why you think he was a bad man? Did he *do* something bad?"

She began signing to him, then stopped when she remembered he could not understand. She picked up the pen, put it down, and then picked it up again. The sounds from upstairs were diminishing. Dave wondered what Gwen would do or say if she knew this conversation was going on.

"Killed someone," she wrote. Then she shivered.

Lambry? He wondered. "Is that the only thing he did?"

She shook her head, and started to write a reply, then stopped. She took out another sheet of paper, scrunched up her face in concentration, and then began to draw instead. From across the table, he was able to recognize the cylinder immediately. She drew confidently, quickly, almost expertly. It was as if the image on the monitor in the Army trailer was reappearing right here on the dining room table. She pushed the drawing across to him, then signed again.

He took the piece of paper and looked at it. This drawing was a hell of a lot better than the one Gwen had shown him. She tapped the pen on the table, and he pushed the paper back across to her. "Very bad thing," she wrote, and then underlined that several times.

"Yes, you're absolutely right, Jess," he said. "It's a weapon. An Army weapon. I think that man stole it. I'm trying to get it back." This drawing is almost perfect, he thought. So where the hell had that crude drawing come from? Jess was already scribbling another question.

"Is something coming?" she wrote.

He felt a chill when he read that question, but he was saved by the sounds of Gwen coming back down the stairs. The girl put a finger to her lips, grabbed the piece of paper, and hid it in her book. She had turned around in her chair by the time Gwen came back into the room.

Stafford finished his coffee while trying to clamp down on a feeling of apprehension. He didn't know which bothered him more: her question—"Is something coming?"—or the fact that she had asked it. Damn!

■ MONDAY, FORT GILLEM DRMO, 10:00 P.M.

Carson sat at the control booth in the security control room. He was wearing slacks, a business shirt without a tie, tennis shoes, and a light windbreaker. He hadn't been able to wait any longer, and he had gone ahead and made the call. The man at the other end of the line had obviously been waiting. Carson had given Tangent's man directions to the DRMO, then told him to park out front and look for an envelope on the front door of the admin building. He warned the man about watching for patrolling MP cars. He suggested they come just after midnight.

Now he had to wait. He reviewed the rest of the plan in his mind: The envelope on the door would direct them to drive back through the truck alley, where he had unlocked and opened the main gates into the area of the receiving bay. They were to drive out into the middle of the tarmac and look for a pallet of airplane propellers, which should be distinctive enough. There would be a second envelope there, which would direct them to warehouse four, where they would find a third envelope, taped to the side of the building. This one would instruct them to go to the feed-assembly building. To get each envelope, they would have to stand in a cone of light, at which he had aimed one of the surveillance cameras. He wanted to get a good look at these people before proceeding.

The final envelope instructed them to take the money into that building and wait for instructions, which would come by phone. He felt reasonably confident that he would be able to watch their every move. If one or two of Tangent's people drifted away into the darkness, possibly to set up on Carson when he tried to leave, he wanted to be able to see that. All these envelopes and the resulting scavenger hunt would probably piss them off, but for a million in cash, too bad. Carson was a party of one; Tangent could send as many people as he wanted. Should have specified something about that, he thought.

Once Tangent's people were in the feed-assembly building, he would remotely disable the front door's cipher lock from the security control room, which would effectively lock them in. Inside the assembly area, they would find the conveyor belt running. He would call them on the building phone and instruct them to put the money into some demil containers and send them into the demil building, where he had repositioned the surveillance camera there to focus directly down onto the belt. Once he was confident they had put money in the containers, and not newspaper or bricks, he would kill all power to the demil assembly building. This would leave them in the dark, except for the battery-operated fire lights. He would call them again and tell them that he was going to retrieve the money, and that he would call one last time to tell them where he was leaving the cylinder, which he had already hidden in the outside toolbox on one of the semis parked down in the truck lane. He would then let himself into the demil building, verify that the money was real, pack it into two prepositioned duffel bags, then go out the back fire door of the demil building, across the alley to the fence, and get to his truck.

He had parked his pickup truck in an old fire lane that ran parallel to the DRMO perimeter fence a hundred yards away. Between the fire lane and the fence was a dense stand of brush, small trees, and high weeds. He had cut a man-sized slit in the chain-link fence at the end of the truck and trailer parking lane. His plan was to drive off the post, and when he was at least a mile away, call the DRMO automatic exchange from his car phone, dial the extension for the feed-assembly building, and tell them how to bypass the cipher lock to get out and where to find the cylinder. By then he would have disappeared into the streets of southeast Atlanta, with a million bucks in cash, and with that damned cylinder off his hands once and for all.

After that, well, he was making no plans. Tangent's team, of course, wouldn't know any of this until they arrived and began the process of envelope hunting. They might be annoyed at being locked up in the feed-assembly building, but, again, that was tough. He had warned them he would be taking precautions.

He had also made provisions for the two most serious problems he could think of. The first would be if they brought counterfeit money. This certainly was a possibility, since it all was going to be in brand-new hundreds. He had obtained four new one-hundred-dollar bills from a bank so he would have something to compare the prize money with. About the only test he had been able to devise was to cart a desktop copier machine into the demil building. If the bills were real, they would not copy properly; he'd tried it with the real ones and certain elements of the engraving had not come through. If Tangent's bills did make an exact reproduction, then they were probably fakes.

He wasn't sure what he was going to do if that happened. Probably the safest thing to do would be to go retrieve the cylinder and put it with the fake money back on the conveyor belt, fire up the Monster, and destroy it. If he couldn't sell this damn thing to Tangent, then he probably couldn't sell it to anyone, and the game would be over. Let the demil system shred the fake money and the cylinder, and at least there would be no evidence left behind. And if by chance a whiff or two of whatever was in the cylinder made it back into the feed-assembly building—if he cut all the power again just as the Monster was starting to chew things up, for example—well, that would be justice, wouldn't it?

The second problem would be if Tangent and his crew brought real money but then tried to get it back once the transfer had been made. He assumed that if this was their plan, they probably wouldn't want to make their move until they knew where the cylinder was, which was why he had set up the transfer in pieces: Unless they brought a whole lot of help, it would be next to impossible for them to set up some kind of an ambush. But what if they did bring lots of help? Assuming he would be able to detect this fact through all the surveillance cameras, he'd go to plan B, which was to go get the money but not try to leave the DRMO. Instead he would lock himself in the demil building, call them as planned, tell them how to disable the cipher lock, and give them a false location for the cylinder. When they left the feed-assembly building, he'd go through the interbuilding aperture into the feed-assembly room, and from there he'd make his way back through the connecting warehouses to the other end of the DRMO while they scrambled around outside looking for him. There were many places he could hide in the warehouses until morning, by which time they would have to leave when the employees came back to work. Those semis in the truck park weren't scheduled to go anywhere for a week, so he could retrieve the cylinder, toss it into the demil run for that day, and leave with the money whenever he wanted to. And just to be sure, he had positioned forklifts across all the entrance doors in the rest of the high-security warehouses, and more forklifts next to each connecting doorway.

But he knew that, in a sense, plan B was all wishful thinking. This thing had better go right, or life was going to get really complicated. He looked at his watch: 10:10 P.M. Two more hours. He scanned the bank of televisions screens, but all the gray-and-black images shimmering silently on the monitors were lifeless. There was one other nagging thought hanging just out of reach in his mind, something about the cylinder itself, but he could not summon it. He waited.

■ MONDAY, WILLOW GROVE HOME, GRANITEVILLE, GEORGIA, 10:00 P.M.

Stafford took his coffee mug and walked with Gwen through her parlor and out to the side porch facing the pecan grove. There was just the bloom of the moon showing above the peak behind the house, and the tree frogs were out in full strength when she sat down beside him on the porch swing. He noticed that she had fixed her hair and put on a touch of perfume. He put the coffee mug down on a table, unsure of his left hand's trustworthiness not to spill on a moving swing.

"I'm a little surprised Ray Sparks hasn't called," he said.

"Oh, he did," she replied. "Just before dinner."

"Really."

"Yes. He wanted to know if you had left. I told him not yet, that I had invited you to stay for dinner with the kids. I asked if there was any message, but he said no, thanked me, and hung up. I hope you won't be mad at me for not telling you."

"So he didn't want to talk to me?"

"Apparently not."

Stafford didn't say anything at first, and then he said, "That's a good sign. I think."

"You're sure you're not angry? It had been such a pleasant afternoon. I didn't want to spoil it."

"No, not at all. I've been thinking about what you said up there on the trail. You pointed out something that I should have seen. I could walk away from the DCIS tomorrow morning, and nobody would care. In fact, news of my resignation would probably brighten several peoples' day."

"How about your pension, things like that?"

"I've got a 401-K," he replied. He turned to look at her. "I haven't the foggiest idea of what I'd do next, but whatever it might be, it'd be better than what I'm doing right now."

"It's something to think about, then, isn't it?" she said. "In the meantime, you could stay here for a while. My father's old room upstairs is our official guest room, and there is something you could contribute here, something that I can't do. These kids have either never had a father or have had a monster masquerading as a father. You said you've worked with kids in the Boys Clubs. You could do that here."

She really is quite beautiful, he thought. He resisted an impulse to reach out and touch her hair. "If I did stay," he said, "it wouldn't be just because of this Carson mess."

She looked away, and he wondered if he had made a mistake. He felt himself blushing a little, and he was glad that it was dark on the porch.

"I think you would be very good for the kids," she said, still avoiding eye contact. "Beyond that, I think it might do you good to get away from your world for a while. It doesn't seem to be doing you much good these days."

"That's for damn sure," he replied, following her lead, grateful to talk about something else, but also a bit disappointed.

They talked for another half hour about the school and the kids. When he sensed the evening was running down, he got up to go. She walked him to the front porch. He had told her he would go to the motel for the night and then return in the morning. He added that he would have to call Sparks in the morning. She nodded, then seemed poised to say something else. He waited.

"Everything's not as it seems up here, Dave," she said finally. "There's . . . history. Family history. I sense that you are interested in me—as a woman. You need to think about *your* future, and not about me." She gave him a sad smile, squeezed his hand, and went back into the house. He stood there for a moment, feeling like a disappointed teenager, and then went down the steps to his car.

Well, he thought to himself as he drove down the drive, there's your answer. Why in the hell should he have assumed she saw anything desirable in him, a one-armed civil servant whose career was on the rocks, along with his marriage, not to mention this little imbroglio with Carson and company? He turned on the car radio and brought up a country station, where a singer was wailing on about love and tears. Perfect, he thought. Just fucking perfect.

11

Brigadier General Carrothers rendezvoused with the Anniston team at a large Trans-America truck stop near the intersection of the Atlanta Perimeter and Interstate 20. The Anniston task unit consisted of four Army semis and six large Army MP Suburbans bristling with whip antennas and police lights.

Carrothers had been waiting at the truck stop for half an hour, sitting in the parking lot in a black government sedan requisitioned from Dobbins Air Force Base in northwest Atlanta. His driver, an Air Force sergeant, was a smoker. He was standing outside the car, puffing away anxiously among all the diesel fumes. Carrothers had come down on an Army Learjet by himself. The only other officers in the task unit would be the Anniston Depot operations officer and two Chemical Corps captains to supervise the decon sweep teams. Major Mason and Colonel Fuller had remained behind in the Pentagon to man up the CW operations room. Carrothers had not wanted Fuller there, but it had become obvious that Fuller had had a talk with his old friend the CG.

General Waddell's sudden return to the Pentagon had been unpleasant, to put it mildly. The commanding general had also been very busy on the flight back from the West Coast. Waddell did not care for surprises, and Fuller's back-channel revelations had come as a very unpleasant surprise. Ominously, Waddell had not indulged in any sort of shouting match. Instead, he had summoned Carrothers into his office and had him stand at attention in front of his desk.

"General," he said, his face grim, "I thought we had a mutually agreed 'right answer' to this little problem, but evidently I was mistaken. And now we have some outsiders in the game. Is it your position that this missing cylinder might in fact be hidden somewhere in the Fort Gillem DRMO? That it did not end up in the demil machine?"

"Yes, sir, that might be the case, General. But—"

"Don't want to hear any damn *mights* or *buts*. The only *butts* I have a long-term interest in have two *t*'s in their spelling and they are destined for some chain-saw surgery for disobeying my orders. That's a problem we will discuss at some length later, as well as your future in this organization. Right now, however, I propose to take some direct action, and you are going to feature prominently as a co-conspirator in the effort to put this incubus back in its box, assuming you want to keep that star."

"General Waddell—" Carrothers began.

"Be quiet, General," Waddell interrupted. "As far as I'm concerned, we had this mess contained, and you have managed to uncontain it. Now, I have spoken to General Roman, and he agrees with my assessment that we are at the zero-option point. He has authorized me to proceed with some fairly drastic action. For the good of the Army and for the larger purpose of ensuring the national security, you are going to incinerate that DRMO."

His instructions had been very specific: "You will go to Georgia and run this thing personally. You will destroy the Fort Gillem DRMO by fire. General Roman has made available a team of Special Forces people, who will go to Fort Gillem. You will establish two perimeters: Anniston MPs on the outside, the Anniston CERT on the inside. The Fort Gillem MPs will be engaged in investigating a faked break-in at the Army–Air Force Exchange Service warehouse on the other end of the base when the action goes down, courtesy of the Special Forces team. The snake-eaters will arrive early and will hide out at the abandoned airfield. While they're waiting, they will disable the fire-fighting water supply to the DRMO complex and sabotage the fire alarm systems. When they get the go order, they will go through that DRMO with thermite bombs. I want them in and out of there in fifteen minutes."

The Gillem military police would be lured away to the other end of the base by the break-in alarm. Once someone noticed the conflagration at the DRMO, the Fort Gillem fire engines would respond, but by then, all the buildings would be fully involved. The firefighters would be delayed at the scene when none of the hydrants worked. Then someone would tell them there might be explosives in the warehouses. The Fort Gillem post commander, who would be cut in on the plan, would make the decision to hold back the Gillem firefighters, on the premise of not risking lives trying to save obsolete military equipment.

When Waddell had finished, Carrothers tried to object again. "Do not argue with me," Waddell interrupted. "It's not like we're destroying valuable government property. Those warehouses are fifty years old. All of that stuff is there because it's obsolete or otherwise surplus. The dollars we lose in not selling it are far outweighed by the possibility—a possibility regenerated by you, as far as I'm concerned—that some lunatic fringe might get their hands on a can of Wet Eye. You know about the biologic component."

"Yes, sir, I do. Now."

"So give this plan the *Washington Post* test: If it ever does come out that the Army torched five or six warehouses full of surplus junk in order to make damned sure that some *germ*-warfare stuff didn't get loose into the renegade international arms market, who's going to fault us?"

Carrothers could not deny that. The DRMO was on a remote part of a partially shut-down post, out at the end of a disused runway, surrounded by concrete aprons, and at least a mile away from the civilian population in all directions. Even with a fire that size erupting in the middle of the night, the worst that might happen off the base would be a grass fire. The post-fire investigations would be done by the Army CIC, whose report would be carefully managed by Army headquarters. A Pentagon public-relations team was probably already being positioned to brief the press. No one at Fort Gillem below the level of the post commander would know the real genesis of the fire.

"You started this shit with this DCIS guy," Waddell concluded. "Now you go put an end to it. General Roman has already conferenced with the head of DCIS, and he confirms this guy Stafford is a squirrel. They've ordered the regional supervisor to reel him in and get him back to D.C. General Roman has assured them that Stafford's allegations against the DRMO manager are total bullshit."

"But what if they're not? What if this Carson actually does have it?"

"That's the final part of your mission: When the DRMO goes up, the Fort Gillem duty officer will notify Carson. When he shows up, take him into custody. Bring him back to Washington. We'll let another government agency take him out to a safe house in the Virginia woods to see what he knows or doesn't know. Now, one further thing."

Waddel had stood up behind his desk. Carrothers remembered the look on the older man's face only too well. "The Army chief of staff has been fully briefed on this problem. He is in full concurrence with our taking such drastic action. I can't emphasize this enough: The Army did *not* lose a weapon. Is that clear, General? We did *not* lose a chemical weapon. The Army Chemical Corps is in the fight of its budgetary life with this damned quadrennial review, and the Chemical Corps cannot *begin* to stand a hit like this. Is that understood?"

"Yes, sir, it is."

"Good. So you go down there, and you *incinerate* that place. Burn it to a fucking shadow, along with any trace of that damned Wet Eye. And while you're at it, give some consideration to where you're going to retire. You had your chance, General Carrothers. As best I can tell, you've blown it. That's all."

Carrothers had spent the rest of the day coordinating the planning for the operation from the Army Operations Center in the Pentagon's basement. Now he stood by the lead Suburban under the white sodium glare of the truck stop's light towers and rubbed his face. He was tired, disappointed, and very apprehensive. He could well understand the three-stars' fear of the missing Wet Eye becoming public knowledge, and burning the DRMO would yield an almost 95 percent probability of destroying the cylinder, assuming it was still there. But what if it wasn't? What if Carson did have it but had stashed it somewhere else? And how in the hell had this Stafford found out about it? Or that Carson had it? There were too many loose ends here, and, given that, he hated executing this operation, especially when he knew the whole thing was inspired by panic at the higher echelons of the Army. He knew that somehow he had become a pawn in the Army's cover-up, and that bothered him most of all. The scenes from Fuller's video kept coming back to him. And then, of course, there was Waddell's parting shot: the fact that Carrothers should start planning his retirement. Well, the more he thought about that, the less that prospect bothered him, unlike what they were about to do tonight.

▮▮ TUESDAY, FORT GILLEM DRMO, 12:20 A.M.

Carson watched Tangent's crew arrive on a television monitor in the security control room. They were driving a large, dark four-door sedan. For another five minutes nothing happened. Then there was the glow of the interior light in the car, which quickly went out as the headlights of the Gillem MP patrol flared briefly in the roadway. Three more minutes after that, they tried again. Four men got out, their faces indistinct in the black-and-white image. One went to the back of the car, opened the trunk, and pulled out what looked like a Navy seabag. The car's trunk shut soundlessly, and two of the men carried the duffel bag between them as they approached the front door of the admin building. Carson lost sight of them as they neared the front door.

Okay, he thought. Four of them. One guy in charge, three helpers. Not too bad. He waited, visualizing the seconds passing as they read the envelope. They'd be pissed off to have to lug that bag back to the car and then drive around, but that wasn't his problem. He needed to get them off the road and back into the tarmac area, away from patrolling MPs. One of the men went back to get the car; ninety seconds later, he saw it emerge from the darkened space between the warehouse buildings where he had left the gate open. The car came out onto the tarmac with its lights off. Good, he thought. There's plenty of lighting there. They found the pallet of propellers and stopped. This time, only one man got out, and he picked up the envelope. He read it, then walked across to the warehouse with the large numeral 4 painted on the end.

I should have made a provision here to close that truck gate, Carson thought. If they have unseen helpers, they'll have a free shot to the tarmac. He scanned the outside perimeter monitors, some of which he had repositioned, but there was nothing going on. He looked back at the car, which was just sitting there on the tarmac. Then the driver was walking back to the car. He opened the door and leaned in. They all got out again, looked around, extracted the bag, and this time dragged it over toward the feed-assembly building.

Carson studied them in the patch of light at the entrance to the assembly building, keeping his finger on the cipher lock's release button until he had them all in the light. Four white men, thirties, forties, in decent shape, all wearing slacks and unzipped windbreakers. The windbreakers meant they were carrying, he thought. Fair enough. So was he.

He hit the button, and four heads in the monitor turned to the door in a blur of white faces. One man pushed it open, two others dragged the bag through the door, while the fourth watched their backs on the tarmac. Carson turned toward the monitor that showed the inside of the feed-assembly area as all four came through the door. He could see the conveyor belt off to the right of the image as it proceeded slowly into the screened hole in the far wall. He picked up the handset and made the call. One of the men walked out of camera range, and a moment later the phone was picked up.

"Put the money into those open boxes by the belt. When you've got it all boxed, step back to the front door," Carson ordered.

The man did not reply, simply hung up. Carson watched as they dragged the bag over to the belt line and began unloading it. Unwittingly, or perhaps on purpose, they positioned themselves between the camera and what they were doing at the belt, three working, the fourth watching the rest of the room, his hand inside his jacket. Carson could see that they were dumping something into the carrier boxes, but the belt was too far away from the camera for him to tell it if was money. They seemed to take a long time, until he realized they probably had to pack the money into the boxes to make it all fit. Then they were done, and they stepped back from the belt, looking around.

Okay, he thought. He called the number again. The same man walked over to the phone and picked it up.

"Put the boxes on the belt. When it's in the next building, I'm going to stop the belt. When I'm satisfied that the money is real, I'll call you back and tell you where I've put the item. Until then, I'm disabling the cipher locks. Don't try to leave."

"How long?" the man asked. It sounded like Tangent; Carson was pretty sure he recognized the voice. He could not, however, see the man's face on the monitor. "Fifteen minutes," he replied, hitting the button to disable the lock. "The item is prepositioned."

"How do we know you won't just take off?"

Yes, that was Tangent. "We've been through this. The item is worth nothing to me. It's of use only to you and your ultimate customers. Believe me, it's not something I want to keep." He hung up then, not wanting to waste any more time talking.

He watched them upload the boxes onto the belt. They stood together in a group, watching the belt slowly carry the boxes through the interbuilding aperture. He switched monitors, focusing on the boxes as they came into view in the demil room, into the lighted area between the aperture and the intake of the Monster. When all four boxes were visible, he walked over to the emergency fire-fighting control panel and remotely opened the circuit breakers for the conveyor belt. He could reset them if he needed to once he got to the demil room itself. Then he studied the image of the demil room on the monitor. The security cameras inside the building could not zoom down, as they were only there for intruder detection and filming, but it looked like money: stacks of bills crammed into the boxes, each stack bound in a narrow paper wrapper.

Show time, he thought. Time to go see if it's real or if it's Memorex.

Before he got up, he took one last scan of the entire monitor bank: the tarmac area, the individual warehouse surveillance cameras, the feed-assembly room. The men were still all there, sitting now on upturned boxes, almost invisible in the dim lights of the battery-operated fire lights. One of them was smoking a cigarette, the glowing tip unnaturally bright in the grayish low-contrast display. The demil room, with the boxes in clear focus under the ceiling light. The admin building, with its empty corridor. The admin parking lot—empty.

Not empty.

He froze halfway out of the chair, staring at the image. All the way at the back of the parking lot, deep in the shadow of a line of parked boxcars, he could see the grille of a car. A big car. That's all he could see. Nothing of the interior, just the grille. The rest of the car was in deep shadow.

So where in the hell did that come from? Has it been there all along?

"I don't think so," he intoned to himself. He scanned the other monitors again, looking hard for any other changes, especially in the cameras pointed out onto the tarmac area and the truck lane.

The truck lane. There were four trailers parked in a row on their jack stands. Next to them were two tractor trucks, in one of which he'd planted the cylinder. He looked hard. Something wrong with the image of the trailers. There. The last trailer on the line was sporting some extra tires, smaller tires, about halfway back along the frame on the far side.

A car there. Or was it *two* cars? Son of a *bitch*! Tangent had brought help. Lots of help, from the look of it. In the time it had taken to get them into the feed-assembly building, at least three vehicles had moved into position. Waiting for what, a signal of some kind? There was no camera looking into the approach to the truck lane, but he was willing to bet there was another car there, too. Damn, damn, *damn*!

So move your ass. Time for plan B.

He smacked the switch to turn out the lights, grabbed the empty briefcase, and slipped out of the control room. He walked quickly to the back door of the flea-market warehouse and looked through the window out onto the tarmac. His original plan had him walking across the tarmac to the demil building. He thought about those three cars. The one out front of the admin building could not see into the tarmac area. The one hidden behind the trailers also had its view blocked, although there might be watchers positioned behind those big truck tires. But if there was another car in the approach to the alley, they would have an unobstructed view of the tarmac, at least once he stepped out into the open area between the last lane of pallets and the demil building.

He took a deep breath. Tangent and his crew had seemed relaxed in the feed-assembly building. I'd be relaxed, too, if I had eight, ten more people outside, he thought. They probably weren't planning to do anything until they had the cylinder and he had the money. Which meant that his walk to the demil building would be the get-ready signal to them, but they'd have nothing to gain by moving on him yet. By carrying a briefcase, he hoped they'd think he had the cylinder with him. Since they didn't know what the cylinder looked like, they could not know it wouldn't fit in a briefcase. He was counting on that.

He wiped the sweat off his forehead, took another deep breath, and put his hand on the door release. Okay, then, let's do it.

He stepped through the door and walked directly out across the tarmac. The night air was colder than he had expected, and his footsteps on the tarmac echoed off the sheer metal walls of the warehouses. He resisted an almost overwhelming urge to look left, down into that truck alley. If they saw him looking, the whole thing might kick off prematurely. They obviously planned to make the swap and then get their money back. Well, he had provided for that little contingency.

He walked down the nearest lane of pallets to the one containing the propeller blades, then past Tangent's car, and across the seemingly endless open space between the car and the demil building. The skin on his face felt unusually warm in the night air, and he briefly imagined night scopes tracking him from unseen watchers at either end of the tarmac. He felt like the original sitting duck out here.

Twenty feet.

Ten feet.

Could they hear him next door, in the feed-assembly building? Almost there. Stay cool.

He reached the demil building, punched in the code, and let himself into the anteroom. He dumped the briefcase and walked quickly into the control room, which housed the Monster's control console. He'd earlier placed the console in standby mode, so all the buttons were lighted. He found the button that placed the demil building's access devices in local-operator control and shut down the cipher lock on the front door. It was a heavy steel door, so it wasn't like someone could just kick it in.

He walked over to the conveyor belt and examined the boxes. It looked like real money. Tightly wadded packages of hundred-dollar bills were crammed into the boxes. He pulled the first of two duffel bags he'd positioned near the conveyor belt and began unloading the money. It was packed very tightly, right up to the top of each box, so he had to pry at the edges of the top layer to get to the rest of the money. The second layer down looked and felt just like the first layer. All right! He pocketed several of the banded packages from the top layer in case something went wrong. If they had put counterfeit in, it would be deeper in the box; the top layers were probably real money.

Next he had planned to test it. He wished he could get one more look at the monitor bank to see if anyone was in motion out there. But he had the sense that he was running out of time. So far, they had followed his orders. But for how long would they be so cooperative? Tangent was obviously preparing to double-cross him. Okay, then; they simply wouldn't get the cylinder.

You're out of time. Move it. Make the call.

He shoveled the rest of the money into the duffel bags and zipped them up. Then he picked up the extension phone on the control console and called next door. One ring. Two rings.

"Yes." Yes, that was definitely Tangent.

"The item is in my office," Carson lied. "On top of the bookshelf. You go across the tarmac, into the warehouse one, and go through that building to the admin building. The doors are unlocked. Turn left, down the hall, last office on the left."

"How do we get out of here?"

"You'll find a sledgehammer next to the door you came in. It's in an empty cardboard box right by the door. Knock the hinge pins off and then you can push the door straight out."

"Okay." There was a pause. "Carson."

"What?"

"Our association doesn't have to end here, you know."

"Yes, it does. You brought too many friends with you tonight. Otherwise, it was nice doing business with you."

I probably shouldn't have said that, he thought as he hung up the phone, grabbed the two duffel bags, and walked over to the conveyor belt. Now they'd know he was onto them. He got up on the motionless belt and scuttled into the safety cage, dragging the two bags, until he reached the steel bat-wing doors of the interbuilding aperture. He listened, and sure enough, he could hear shouts and the banging of the sledge on the front door in the feed-assembly building. He also thought he heard a car engine somewhere outside. He waited impatiently, and then suddenly there was a banging and hammering noise coming through from the demil building's front door. They're hee-e-e-re, he

226

thought irreverently. Then, to his surprise, someone started hammering away on the connecting door between demil and the feed-assembly room. Unlike the front door, the connecting door was aluminum. That damn thing wasn't going to hold very long.

Shit! Now what? He began to panic, especially when he became aware of someone on the other side of the aperture doors. He backed away from them as they were pushed in toward him, held only by the belt cogs. He could see through the side of the cage that whoever was using the sledgehammer on the connecting door had battered the middle of the door into an ominous bulge and was now going after the hinges. The guy in front of him was pushing and shoving, and, slowly but surely, the crack between the aperture doors was widening. He was trapped.

At that moment, he caught a glimpse through the crack of a single baleful eye in a straining red face. Almost instinctively, Carson kicked out at the doors, catching the man on the other side full in the face with the edge of the door. There was a grunt and the pushing and straining stopped.

Carson had forgotten about the belt cogs and their locking effect on the aperture doors. He had to start the conveyor belt again in order to escape. He scrambled back out of the cage and ran for the console, very conscious of what was happening to the connecting door, and of the sounds of vehicles and shouting from out in front of the demil building. He smashed down on the button to start conveyor belt, but nothing happened. Then he remembered he had opened the breakers. Panicking now, he ran across the room to the wall that had all the breaker panels. Frantically, he searched for the right breaker, straining to read the labels. Then he kicked himself mentally: Look for an open breaker! He finally found it in the fourth panel, reset it, and bolted back over to the main control panel. He hit the button again and the belt cranked into motion. Then he realized that they would hear the belt, which might bring the rest of the crew back into the assembly building to aid the man on the belt, whose inert form was even now pushing through the aperture doors.

Got a cure for that, he thought, hitting the main power switch for the Monster, which came to life with a reassuring roar of pumps, motors, blowers, and steel teeth. Keeping an eye on the disintegrating connecting door, he ran to the belt and hauled the two bags of money off. He waited a couple of seconds for the man's unconscious body to come past the edge of the safety cage. Whoever he was, he was middle-aged, still red in the face, especially with that nasty gash across his forehead where the door had taken him out. He was also wearing some kind of shoulder rig.

Carson was about to haul the man's body off the belt when the top hinge of the connecting door came flying off in a loud crash, pinging down onto the concrete floor between his feet. Carson didn't hesitate. He jumped onto the moving belt and crawled against the direction of the belt's travel and through the now-unlocked aperture doors. He stopped just inside the cage on the other side, marking time on his hands and knees against the movement of the belt, until he saw another man thirty feet away complete the destruction of the connecting door and step through. The instant the man was out of sight, Carson scrambled out of the safety cage with his bags, jumped off the belt, and ran for the back of the feed-assembly room. Over the noise of the Monster, he heard one prolonged scream and then the sounds of more vehicles roaring down the tarmac with what sounded like several sets of brakes screeching to a halt. He had just about reached the very back of the feed-assembly room when someone yelled from the front doorway for him to halt.

Halt, my ass, he thought as he rounded the partition of the coffee area at the back and went through the steel fire door into warehouse four, encouraged by the sound of a bullet ricocheting off the door frame. He dropped the bags, slammed the door shut, and then rolled the fork-lift he had prepositioned against the fire door, snubbing the back right wheel tightly against the door's bottom. He grabbed up his bags and walked quickly, not running now. That forklift was going to buy him all the time he needed. He trotted down the first row of multitiered shelves stacked up to the ceiling. Behind him someone was banging on the fire door.

By the time he reached the door into warehouse three, he knew he was going to pull this off. All the doors were blocked from the inside. He could get out of any building he wanted to get into, but *they* would need some heavy equipment to get in. Even with that crowd out there. One more warehouse and he could duck out into the fire lane, and from there into the woods outside the fence. He had decided to cut the fence in two places, one down near the demil building, the other at the opposite end of the warehouse line. He was still furious about Tangent's betrayal, but what the hell—he had the money, and Tangent wasn't going to get his precious cylinder. He'd have to figure out how to dispose of that thing later. He was sorry about the guy on the belt, although the other guy should have reached him in time. That scream, however, didn't augur well.

He hurried through the door into warehouse three and was in the act of rolling the next forklift into position when he heard the unmistakable earsplitting roar of a chain saw starting up down at the far end of the warehouse, followed by a terrible screeching noise as someone obviously started to cut through the far metal wall of the warehouse. He couldn't see through the forest of steel shelving towers, but he could sure as hell hear it. What the hell was this?! Had he miscalculated? They had *chain saws*?

He grabbed the bags and zigged to the right, instinctively heading toward the fire doors on the rear wall of the warehouse. These rear doors all led into the back alley, his escape route to his truck. As suddenly as it started, the chain saw went silent. He stopped ten feet from the fire door and crouched down behind a shelf tower. He peeked between two shelves in time to see a large man wearing a helmet and oversized goggles about two hundred feet away down the aisle, trotting toward him between the shelving tiers, casually throwing things into the lanes as he came. And then the shadows behind the man erupted into dazzling sun-bright light, accompanied by a *whoomping* sound and then the roar of fire. Stunned, Carson saw other blooms of incredible fiery radiance exploding in the warehouse to the right and left of the lane where the helmeted man was still coming, each succeeding blast of the incendiaries throwing every detail of the high metal roof beams and trusses into stark relief, even as clouds of bright white smoke billowed above the shelving tiers.

Carson finally moved when the helmeted man was only sixty feet away. Scrambling on his hands and knees, he pulled the bags with him, desperate now to reach the end of the shelf tier and the fire door before the helmeted man got there and threw one of those things at him. Keeping low, he pushed backward to open the fire door with his feet, even as one of the incendiaries clattered up against the back wall in the next lane down to his right and then exploded in a blinding wash of incredible light, producing a wave of heat that singed his cheek as he rolled through the fire door into the alley behind the building. He kicked the door shut just in time. As he got to his feet, there was that terrifying *whoomp* behind the door and then the cracks around the door turned arc-light white, and the door vibrated as if the Devil himself was behind it and badly wanted out.

He dragged himself and the bags across the alley to the fence, staying low, skinning his knees on the concrete; then he got up and started trotting down the alley toward the nearest cut in the fence, which was behind the demil building. As he ran, he felt, rather than saw, that each of the warehouses was being racked by internal explosions, the gable vent screens of each building now etched in bright white light as the old steel shook and rumbled from the sudden release of energy inside. Glowing white clouds of smoke were starting to pump out of ridgeline ventilator cowlings.

When he got to the cut in the fence, he dropped the two bags and then began to pull apart the chain link. But then he stopped. He was right behind the demil building, which apparently had not been fired yet. There were clear sounds of shouting and vehicles on the other side of the demil building, but no one had come around back. He could just see the snout of the semi where he'd hidden the cylinder, maybe forty feet away. There was a loud roar as warehouse three's roof lifted off, releasing a huge bolus of yellow-and-red flame into the night sky. Christ, he thought. I was just in there.

He made his decision. Leaving the bags, he sprinted down the back wall of the demil building, reaching the truck in a few seconds. He climbed up two steps to reach the outside toolbox and cracked it open. There was pandemonium going on around the corner out on the tarmac, a cacophony of shouting men, vehicle engines, and the rising rumble of a major fire. Incendiaries exploded inside the demil building, sending a sheet of flame into the alley as the rear fire door opened momentarily.

The cylinder was right where he had left it. He grabbed it and ran back to the fence, barely avoiding the sheets of white flame howling out around the deformed fire door, only to find that the two sides of the cut fencing had sprung back together again. He pushed the cylinder through the cut in the fence, then started to struggle with the obstinate fencing.

"You!" thundered a voice from behind him "Halt! Freeze!"

He looked over his shoulder and was stunned to see two uniformed men pointing shotguns at him from the corner of the demil building. Soldiers! As he stared in shock, the demil building's back wall began to shake like a single sheet of steel, and then the back edge of the roof opened like a loose sail and belched out a sheet of flame from one end of the building to the other. Some of the roof truss ends were snapped off and there was a sudden rain of hot steel and rivets clanging all along the alley. The two men jumped back around the corner of the building to avoid the hail of hot shrapnel, at which point Carson threw his whole

230

body through the opening and then turned to grab the bags, but the damned fence wire had sprung back again. He grabbed the cylinder, but the bags jammed in the wire when he tried to pull them through. A great sucking sound from the demil building just then caused him to look up, and he saw that the whole back wall was bulging toward him, about to come crashing down into the alley. Out of the corner of his eye, he thought he saw the two soldiers again, still pointing their guns at him, but he wasn't waiting for them anymore.

He turned to jump down into the bushes, even as the demil building collapsed along its full length in a horrific crash. Something lashed the skin of his back as he bolted through the high weeds, which he realized were now on fire behind him. He raced along the path to the truck, pursued by the crackling and snapping sounds of a brush fire. He got to the truck, opened the door, threw in the cylinder, and climbed in. He was barely able to get it started and get out of there before the roaring brush fire was up on him. Yelling in fear, he flattened the accelerator and drove blind, careening through the smoke and flames until he shot out onto the gravel road that ran along the back perimeter fence of Fort Gillem. Behind him, the whole world appeared to be on fire.

Carrothers had staged the Anniston team out on the abandoned runway about five hundred yards from the darkened shapes of the DRMO. The trucks were parked in military order, in line abreast. The Suburbans were parked in front of the trucks. A six-man perimeter of Anniston military police was stationed out in the darkness along the edges of the runway. Carrothers stood by the right-front fender of one of the Suburbans. It was a clear, dark night, with little wind, which was fortunate. The lights of Atlanta to the northeast suffused the night sky with a faintly orange glow.

He had ordered everyone into MOPP gear, including himself, but he'd relaxed head hoods until the operation got under way. The protection suit wasn't heavy, but it wasn't comfortable, either, and he was already itching. He didn't really believe there was any risk from the cylinder, but he wanted his people to remember why they were there and why they were going to destroy a government facility in the middle of the night. When the Special Forces team radioed in the code word indicating they were in position along the side walls of the first two buildings and that the DRMO appeared to be clear of personnel, he had given the go order himself. The lead Suburban had moved out quietly to the airfield end of the DRMO complex to the team-extraction position.

Nothing happened for a minute, and then the sound of chain saws erupted at the far end of the DRMO, sending their characteristic buzzing howl into the quiet night air for about twenty seconds before going quiet. Another sixty seconds of silence, and then he thought he heard the first incendiaries igniting in a series of dull thumps. The first signs of fire became visible a minute or so after that, starting at the far end and working toward his trucks. He gave the order to complete dressing out, pulled on the rest of his hood assembly, and then got into his Suburban. The fires were going pretty well by now, with one building really burning and a lot of multicolored white smoke climbing into the sky. He nodded at the driver and they pulled out, heading down the runway toward the DRMO complex. As they arrived, he could see several figures converging on the extraction vehicle, getting in, and then that Suburban was accelerating off to his right, away from the DRMO.

Good, the team's out. He looked behind him as the rest of the Suburbans fanned out along the DRMO fence on the airfield side to set up the exclusion perimeter. The big semis were still back where he'd parked them. The sweep teams wouldn't come in until the buildings had all gone down. He wondered what the troops were thinking. He had given everyone a quick brief as to why the Army was having to do this, that foreign terrorists might have hidden a chemical weapon in the complex and could be planning to move it to their target area tonight. The DRMO was too hard to search; therefore, the decision to destroy it had been made. He'd put as much drama into it as he could, knowing that everyone would have to be debriefed back at the depot to ensure security. One of the warehouse roofs fell in, masking the words as his radio spat something at him.

"Say again?" he said.

"Vehicles sighted in the tarmac area," reported the excited voice. It sounded like one of the captains, but the hoods made it hard to tell. "There are civilians running around out on the tarmac."

"*Civilians?* Oh shit, he thought. "How many?"

"Maybe a dozen, sir. Looks like they were trying to get into the big building at the end. But that fire's gonna get 'em pretty quick. There're four cars out there on the tarmac, and their tires are smoking. Whoever they are, they're going apeshit out there."

Son of a *bitch*! Four cars? What the hell was this? Had the Fort

Gillem security people screwed up? He gave the signal to his driver to move forward, right up to the fence.

"Can you drive through that fence?" he shouted to the driver. The noise of the fires was much louder than he had expected, even in the hoods. The snake-eaters had done their job very damn well.

The driver's hood nodded and he headed the big vehicle toward a center section of the chain-link fence, accelerating. Carrothers almost got his seat belt on over the MOPP gear before the big vehicle left the edge of the runway with a bang, fishtailed a couple of times on dirt and gravel, and then hit the fence at about forty-five miles an hour. The fence didn't give; instead, it slid up over the hood and then the windshield as the Suburban plunged ahead, audibly ripping off wipers, police lights, and antennas on the way. Carrothers could hear the stuff snapping off as the fence clattered overhead, and then they were through. The driver brought the vehicle to a screeching halt at the edge of the tarmac, unable to get it over some concrete barriers lining the edge of the open area.

Carrothers piled out into a scene from a war zone. All of the DRMO buildings except the demil building were fully engulfed in fire, and it was starting to bulge ominously. The heat and the noise were nearly overpowering. He was grateful he was in a chem suit, because those poor bastards out on the tarmac were probably starting to barbecue. There were four sedans out there, now clustered in a circle among the pallets. There appeared to be about ten men out there, hunkering down behind their cars and under some of the larger pieces of palletized equipment to escape the rain of flaming debris and sparks. He yelled to his driver to summon the other vehicles, and then he ran toward the men on the tarmac, stumbling awkwardly in the chem suit as he tried to get through the lines of pallets while avoiding small fires on the ground. The heat was very much stronger than he had expected, and he had to duck his Plexiglas mask away when the near end of the admin building bulged out and then collapsed in a wall of flame. Behind him, the back wall of the demil building came crashing down, sending a wave of flame across the tarmac. He could see that the fields behind the fence were also on fire.

One of the men crouching behind a pallet of propellers saw him when he was about fifty feet away and stood up. Carrothers waved at him to come ahead, waited to make sure the guy understood and was going to get the rest of them, and then began to back out of the tarmac area, very conscious of the thumps and crashes of objects coming down out of the burning sky. The Plexiglas of his mask was beginning to singe his cheeks in the intense heat, and he could see that the running men were having trouble breathing as all the oxygen at ground level was sucked into the conflagration surrounding them.

There were two more Suburbans nosed in at the uprooted fence by the time the running men converged on Carrothers. The MPs had piled out of the vehicles to let the unprotected men climb in. A minute and a half later, they were all back out on the runway, where even at five hundred yards there were bits of flaming debris raining down out of the spark-filled smoke cloud boiling overhead. Carrothers could hear the faint sound of distant sirens as he pulled his hood off. He yelled at one of the captains to execute the chemical perimeter operation, then walked over to the first of the other Suburbans, where some of the civilians were opening doors and looking cautiously out. Their faces were smudged with soot, and they all seemed to be having trouble getting their breath back. Out on the tarmac, the first of the cars' gas tanks let go in an orange blast, followed immediately by another one.

Carrothers signaled two large MPs to come with him. They wordlessly assumed covering positions with twelve-gauge military riot guns held at port arms across their chem suits. A couple of the civilians froze when they saw the shotguns. As Carrothers walked up, a fiftyish man looked around. He was bent over, coughing his lungs out, while trying to wipe his glasses with a handkerchief. Behind him the DRMO roared into fiery extinction.

"I'm Brigadier General Carrothers, U.S. Army Chemical Corps," Carrothers announced over the noise of the fire. "Who are you people and what in the hell were you doing in there?"

The man tried to speak but then erupted into another fit of coughing that bent him almost in half. When he had control of himself, he pulled out a leather credential case. "Special Agent Frank Tangent, FBI," he wheezed, showing Carrothers his credentials. "Did you say Army Chemical Corps?"

"Yes, I did."

The agent wiped his forehead and looked back over at the destruction going on behind them. "Well, sir," he said, coughing again, "I guess you and I need to talk."

Carson pulled off the interstate into a rest area at a little after 3:00 A.M. He was about fifty miles out of Atlanta on Interstate 85, which ran northeast toward Greensboro and the Carolinas. He had been having trouble keeping his eyes open as the adrenaline finally wore off. He parked the pickup at the far end of the parking area, backing it in to conceal the government license plate, and shut it down. He leaned back in the seat and immediately sat straight back up. He put his right hand between the windbreaker and the back of his shirt and felt the large wet stain across his back. Jesus, he thought. This is all I need. The damned fence wire must have gotten me. He carefully peeled the windbreaker off to see if it was stained through, and it was, but only on the inside lining. He felt his back again, and this time his hand came away with blood on it. Shit, he thought. Then he noticed the hole in the side of the windbreaker. He grabbed it, stared at it, and then turned the jacket over and found another hole on the other side. It hadn't been the fence. Those two bastards had shot him.

He opened the truck door and got out gingerly, because now his entire back was really hurting. He slipped the jacket back on, then reached into the backseat of the truck for his trip kit, a small bag containing toiletry articles and a hand towel to use at rest stops. He locked the truck up and walked over to the facilities, which at this hour of the morning were empty. He went into a stall and took his jacket and shirt off and then his undershirt. The undershirt was soaked with blood, and the shirt was only in marginally better condition. He went back out to the sink, turned around, looked at himself in the mirror. There was a long red furrow cutting across the top of his back at a slight diagonal. It did not appear to be very deep, but it was red and angry-looking. Even as he watched, a thin trickle of blood seeped out on the left-hand side.

He got out the towel and tried for some hot water, but only the cold faucets worked. He wet the towel, considered putting some soap on it, decided against that, and then folded the towel into a long bandage and draped it over the cut. The stinging was intense, but then it subsided. The towel didn't reach around to his chest, so he put the shirt back on, trying to hold the towel in place with the shirt. He put the bloody undershirt in the trash can. He thought about that for a moment, fished it back out, and flushed it down a toilet. It took two tries before it disappeared. If they were hunting him, there was no sense in making it easy. He put the jacket back on, adjusted the towel under it all, and went back outside.

A large van had pulled in next to his truck, backing in just like Carson had done. The driver, who appeared to be a fat man with a huge mountain-man beard, was already asleep in his seat, his mouth partially open and his snores audible outside the van. Magnetic stick-on signs on the van announced an Atlanta-based heating, plumbing, and air-conditioning company.

Carson got back into his truck and tried lying sideways on the front seat. His eyelids felt like lead, but sleep would not come. He kept seeing the holocaust at the DRMO. He imagined he could still feel the intense heat of the flame wall in the brush as he escaped. But he had escaped, at least for now. There had been MPs at the front gate when he drove out, but they were on the incoming side and had waved his government truck right through. The cylinder was now stashed out in a toolbox in the back of the pickup. The bags of money were undoubtedly long since toast.

So Tangent had been planning to double-cross him all along. A million bucks. He should have known. They'd probably planned to take him to some dark alley in south Atlanta and donate him to the city's nightly body count. The real question was, Where in the hell had those other guys come from, the guys in helmets and goggles, throwing incendiaries into all the warehouses? Certainly that hadn't been Tangent.

Despite his fatigue, his eyes opened as the answer came to him. Those had been Army guys. Soldiers. The Army had sent a team in to destroy the DRMO!

Fucking Stafford *had* talked.

He put his head back down on the seat and closed his eyes again. The packs of hundreds he'd put into his pants pockets dug into his thighs, but he was too tired to care. The rumble of idling diesels came through the partially opened window as he tried to figure out what had happened tonight. The Army had gone there twice to search the place. But there was no way in hell you could search a DRMO, not in under a year's time. So someone very important had elected to burn the whole damn thing down and, hopefully, the missing cylinder with it. That fire would have done the job, too. He was amazed at the scope of the Army's reaction. They must be some desperate sumbitches indeed, he thought.

He tried to think clearly, to overcome the drugged feeling that was seeping into his brain. A dull, throbbing pain was pulsing in his upper back. He would have to get that cut cleaned up and disinfected pretty soon. He wondered what had happened to Tangent and his little crew. Had the Army sent some kind of Special Forces team, or had there been lots of Army hidden out there in the dark on that airfield? If so, had they captured Tangent? That would be interesting. He wondered how a Washington arms dealer was going to explain what the hell he and a dozen accomplices were doing there in east bumfuck Atlanta, Georgia, in the middle of the night. Even the Army would *have* to make a connection between Tangent and the missing weapon.

He shuddered. If the Army was sufficiently upset about the cylinder to burn down a government installation, they probably wouldn't have a whole lot of trouble getting information out of a bunch of civilians. And if Tangent was singing, then the Army had to know by now that he, Carson, had the cylinder. None of them would know, of course, that he'd lost the money, although those two soldiers might have seen the bags, and seen the back wall collapse on top of them. But probably not. They'd fired at him all right, but then they would have been shagging ass.

The big question was, What would the Army *do* about this new situation? If they were ready to admit the cylinder was missing, then he was screwed. Every law-enforcement agency in the country would be looking for him. But if they weren't, well . . . He still might have a chance to get away. He knew he must have a couple thousand dollars in cash in his pockets. And a government-issue pickup truck.

That woke him up. Here he was, sitting in a public rest stop in an Army-green government pickup truck, complete with a government license plate and a bunch of U.S. Army serial numbers stenciled on the doors. Need to do something about that. He heaved himself up, looked out the window, and saw the magnetic signs on the van next door. Those signs would cover up the stencils on his doors. Steal his license plate, too. Hell, put the government plate on the van, throw some shit in the game.

Fully awake now, he grabbed a screwdriver out of the glove compartment and slipped out of the pickup truck. His back let him know it wasn't pleased with that maneuver. He went around to the back and stopped to look and listen. Behind the parking area was a dense stand of loblolly pines. He could hear occasional traffic beyond that, out on the interstate. The rest stop was well lighted, but he was in shadow behind the truck and the van. The nearest vehicle was parked on the other side of the parking area. He listened. The man in the van was still snoring away. He bent down and removed his plate and switched it with the van's plate. Then he stood up, looked around again to make sure no one was walking to or from the rest rooms, slipped between the van and his truck, and lifted off the magnetic sign, which he transferred to the door of his pickup truck. He went around to the other side and took that one, too, which he slapped on the driver's side of his truck.

He got back into his truck, careful not to lean back, and started the engine, watching the snoring man through the window on the passenger side. The big man never even twitched. Carson drove out of the rest stop in his newly commercialized pickup truck, which in Georgia made him practically invisible. He got back on the interstate and drove for twenty minutes before realizing that he was poking along at fifty-five in a seventy-mile an hour zone. This won't hack it, he thought, with a mighty yawn. I've got to get some rest.

Ten minutes later, he rolled up to a budget motel and rang the bell for the night attendant. An aroma of curry accompanied the sleepy young Pakistani man who took his money through a sliding glass door and handed him back a key. He drove around to the back wing of the motel and parked. He got out and looked around. Almost all the parking spaces in the lot were filled, with every vehicle's windows made opaque by a heavy dew. There was a low drone coming from several climate-control units. He debated with himself about what to do with the cylinder. Take it in or leave it in the truck? He decided to leave it.

He went into the room and sat down on the edge of the bed, exhausted and depressed by the night's events and his escape from Atlanta. Everything he had worked for was gone now. The DRMO was gone, the money was gone, he was wounded, and his fancy Washington fence was probably singing to the military police, which meant that the government would be looking for Wendell Carson gangbusters in very short order. That fucking Tangent.

Okay, so he still had the cylinder, but what the hell could he do with it? Tangent's arms-sales channel had been his best and probably only bet for making something of the cylinder, but now . . . tired. Too damn tired to think. Get some sleep. Figure out what to do in the morning. What to do and where to go. Maybe he could approach the Army somehow, sell *them* back their precious little horror. His last thoughts were of Stafford, that interfering son of a bitch who was behind all this somehow. However this all came out, he knew he had a score and a half to settle with Special Investigator David Stafford.

He lay back on the bed, cried out, and rolled quickly over to his side. He'd forgotten about the wound. You need to clean it, he thought. You need to go take a hot shower, get some soap on that. I will, he thought. In just a minute. And then he was asleep.

▉ TUESDAY, FORT GILLEM DRMO, 4:00 A.M.

Carrothers sat slumped in his chair inside the traveling command center, waiting for the conference call from Washington. He was still wearing the body part of his chem suit, minus the gloves, hood, and mask. The back doors of the trailer were thrown open to let in some cool air, but everything in the area of the operations trailer still stank of smoke. Except for the communications console, manned by a Spec-4 in full chem gear, the rest of the consoles and monitors were unattended. He could hear the murmur of radio conversation outside on the airfield concrete as the monitoring team made final reports from the fire perimeter. He could not see the remains of the DRMO because the trailer doors were pointed away from the wreckage, but the destruction had been complete.

Carrothers was trying to keep his emotions in neutral. He was tired and barely able to think. No eating or drinking had been permitted because of the possibility of chemical contamination in the air, which meant he had had no coffee. He was waiting for General Waddell to come up on a secure satellite conference net.

The Fort Gillem firefighters had been allowed into the fire perimeter after two hours, giving the chem sweep team time enough to test the atmosphere surrounding the fire site. The DRMO was gone. The only vestige of the installation left standing was the chain-link fence. All the brush and trees over on the back side had gone up, giving them all some anxious moments as it spread toward the main fence of the base, but a quick-thinking fireman had taken a truck outside the fence and started a backfire. Of the buildings, there was nothing but rectangular piles of red-hot ashes. The partially melted remains of the demil machine crouched in the ashes like some blackened fossil.

A helicopter, presumably from one of the local television stations, had buzzed overhead toward the end of the conflagration, but the Fort Gillem post commander had a professional briefing team set up to handle those people. Carrothers could visualize it: Yes, big fire, lost all the buildings, but there was no danger to the surrounding community. Army fire-investigation team en route. Several weeks before any findings. No, not valuable property. Just warehouses storing surplus and obsolete military material. No injuries. Employees being told to take two days off, with pay, of course, while post officials sort things out. Blah, blah, blah. He wished the upcoming call would be that innocuous. They had found not one trace of the weapon.

"General, we have a circuit," the comms specialist announced through his mask.

"Put us on the speaker, soldier, and then you may stand down."

"Yes, sir. Patching."

There was a hiss of static, a tone burst of the security systems synching into the trailer's satellite dish, and then silence.

"This is the Army Command Center, calling for Brigadier Carrothers," the speaker announced. The comms operator got up and left.

"General Carrothers present. This node is secure."

"Stand by one, sir."

"This is Major General Waddell. General Carrothers, you there?"

"Yes, sir, General." He noted the formal address.

"Very well. What is the status of the DRMO?"

"The DRMO is destroyed. The perimeter has been maintained. The sweep is concluding now. Unfortunately, we have no detections."

"Nothing? Not even a trace?"

"No, sir. Nothing. It was a hell of fire, General. A zero trace detection was always one of the possible outcomes of the fire. As is another possible outcome, which is worrying me even more."

"Meaning the cylinder got away, I presume. Is there press interest yet?"

"Absolutely. Our press team is preparing to do a tape for the local morning news segments, but General, there is something else. We weren't the only government agency down here at the DRMO tonight."

There was a pause on the net. "I don't think I want to hear this," Waddell said.

"You'll be seriously pissed when you do, General. In the process of destroying the DRMO, we've captured ten FBI agents."

"*What?* What did you say?"

Carrothers sighed. "It seems," he said, "that the Federal Bureau of Investigation has had a sting operation running, for several years, actually. The guy in charge of the FBI team that was here tonight is one Special Agent Frank Tangent. He's been running a back-room cell in Washington that has been paying inside thieves at various DRMOs around the country for military components, mostly military electronics and software. Then they've been turning that stuff around, after the FBI lab altered it a little bit, so it doesn't work quite like it's supposed to, and selling it to some major-league foreign arms dealers in Washington and New York."

"The *FBI's* been doing this?"

"Yes, sir. They're apparently big into sting operations these days. Their objective was to build an intelligence database on the international arms market, and thereby see if they could catch some big-time bad guys, but they had to have real stuff from the DRMOs to make it look like they themselves were real."

"All right. But why Atlanta?"

"Because one of their pet thieves was here, one Wendell Carson, the manager of this DRMO. It seems that Mr. Carson called awhile back and offered to sell them what he believed to be a chemical weapon."

"Great God! And they didn't inform us?"

"No, sir, they did not. At first Tangent said they didn't really believe the guy. Now, General, it's been a long night, and an unpleasant couple of days, so when I corralled Tangent and his crew down here, I started speculating to the air about having a six-pack of MPs throw his ass back into the coals, and then he told me the real reason."

"Which was?"

"Which was that he personally was trying for a 'coup,' as he called it. He was gonna come down here, buy back the cylinder with a hundred thousand of real money laid on top of about million bucks in counterfeit, and then grab up Carson. Then the plan was to stage a press deal to show how fucking good the FBI is. It seems that Bureau management has been putting a lot of heat on the worker bees to generate some good news about the FBI, instead of all the flak they've been taking recently."

Waddell groaned out loud. "Not to mention making the Army look like king-sized assholes for losing the cylinder in the first place."

"Well, General, if the shoes fits . . . Anyway, that didn't seem to matter very much to Tangent and company, although I got the impression his supervisors may not have known about this particular operation."

"Judas Priest," Waddell said. "And where was that DCIS guy in all of this?"

"In the cold. Somehow he stumbled onto what Carson was doing. Tangent panicked, figuring Stafford was going to blow away his cover, so it was Tangent who generated that intel spot report we saw. He was trying to discredit Stafford and get Washington to pull him back. Of course neither the Bureau nor DCIS had any idea we were going to come down here and burn this place down. And, oh, by the way, they lost an agent in there tonight."

"How?"

"Seems he got caught up on some kind of conveyor belt just as they were about to arrest Carson. The belt took him into the demil machine—literally. We've got some pretty shocky agents out there on the tarmac right now. They got to watch."

"My God," Waddell said again, as if he couldn't think of anything else to say.

"Yes, sir. It's a full-blown cluster fuck. The really bad news is that we think Carson got away with the cylinder. Two of the perimeter MPs tried to stop a guy going through the back fence just as the last building went up. One of them took a shot at him, but apparently he missed. The guy got away."

"Did he have the cylinder? Was it Carson?"

"Unknown to both questions, sir. But Tangent said he and Carson had already traded the money, and they were about to the trade the cylinder when the first Ranger started throwing thermite. After that, it was pandemonium. It's so totally fucked up, I don't know whether to laugh or cry, except that we may now have some desperate sumbitch on the run with a can of Wet Eye under his arm."

"Great God," Waddell said. Carrothers had never heard Myer Waddell at a complete loss for words; it was a bad sign.

"Where's this Tangent guy now?" Waddell asked finally.

"He's right here at Fort Gillem, along with his crew. I gave him a satellite-link call to his headquarters in Washington. If they truly didn't know about this, that will be an interesting phone call. Either way, General, I think it's time for the elephants to get into this one. If we're going contain this thing now, it's gonna take more stars than I've got."

"Yes, you're absolutely correct. And cover it we will. I'll call General Roman right away, and get a line of communications opened to the Bureau. The only thing we have going for us is that both agencies will have every reason to cooperate in smothering this little PR disaster in its crib. And find Carson. You wrap things up there at Fort Gillem, and keep the command trailer set up. We'll be back to you. My God, Lee, this is about the worst screwup I've seen in thirty-five years in the Army."

"Roger that, General. Carrothers off net."

Stafford was awakened by the shrill ring of the motel telephone. He sat up in the bed, momentarily disoriented, squinting at his watch.

"Yeah?" he mumbled. What had he been dreaming about? Something about a waterfall. And Gwen Warren. You're pathetic, he thought to himself as he rubbed his eyes.

"This is John Lee Warren, Mr. Stafford. You seen the news yet this mornin'?"

"No, Sheriff. I just woke up."

"You ought to have a look. The NBC channel from Atlanta is on 41. Then I think you'n me ought to meet for some breakfast. Say eight-fifteen?"

Dave looked at his watch again. Seven-fifteen. "Yeah, fine, Sheriff. Let me get my heart started here, okay?"

"Watch the news. That'll do it."

Stafford hung up and sat up straighter, looking for the TV remote. He found it after some searching and flipped on Channel 41. The helicopter shots of the Fort Gillem DRMO came up on the screen. He unmuted and then listened with fascination as the newscaster described a disastrous fire at Fort Gillem, just southeast of Atlanta, Georgia, with the complete destruction of the Atlanta DRMO. "Complete destruction" about describes it, he thought, looking down at the rectangular outlines of blackened ashes. And then the scene shifted to a makeshift press conference set up at what looked like the main gate of Fort Gillem, which he noticed was now crawling with MPs. A tall hawk-faced brigadier general decked out in Desert Storm–style cammies stood in front of a makeshift podium. The man, identified on the screen as Brig. Gen. Lee Carrothers from Army headquarters in Washington, was reassuring the whole world that there had been no personnel casualties and that the damage had been restricted to some warehouses full of obsoleted and surplus military gear, a lot of which had been already slated for destruction.

Yeah, right, Stafford thought. And I wonder if you've told the reporters you're Army Chemical Corps there, General.

The general stated that initial theories included a malfunction in the demil complex, where the possible explosion of combustible waste products might have started the fire. He said it would be several weeks before the cause could be pinpointed with any accuracy, given the extent of the destruction. And then came the kicker: The FBI had been called in to locate the manager of the DRMO, one Wendell Carson, who was missing. Carson was wanted for questioning in connection with reports of safety violations at the DRMO, and about problems that had surfaced recently in a Defense Criminal Investigative Service inquiry about the auctioning of defense materials.

Stafford sat up straighter when he heard that little announcement, but there was no further explanation given. A snappy-looking colonel followed the general to entertain questions, but no one pursued the matter of the DRMO manager.

He switched the TV off and went in to shower and shave. Standing in the shower, he speculated about the fire and its origins. It had happened sometime the previous night, and yet there was already an Army brigadier down there. The same brigadier he'd spoken to in Washington as late as yesterday afternoon. The same brigadier, he was pretty sure, who'd shanghaied one David Stafford to Anniston, Alabama, and subjected him to a lie-detector test about what might or might not be lurking at that DRMO. He began to wonder if maybe the Army itself had burned the damned place down. That would sure be one way of eliminating the DRMO as a hiding place. And now they were searching for Carson, based in part on a DCIS investigation? How very interesting. And then it hit him: This was the one contingency that threatened Gwen and Jessamine: Carson, on the run.

■ TUESDAY, QUALITY FIRST MOTEL, I-85, 8:30 A.M.

Carson jumped in his sleep and then opened his eyes. He was lying on his side on the bed, still fully dressed. He felt a surge of cold panic. Something had awakened him, something bad or threatening. His breathing was rapid and his heart was beating like a jackhammer in his chest. He rolled his feet over the edge of the bed and tried to sit up, gasping as a sheet of pain ripped across his upper back, taking his breath away. There was bright sunlight streaming through the crack in the curtains, and he could hear the sounds of the maids' carts outside. He looked at his watch and saw that it was almost eight-thirty. His back was really hurting now.

It took him several painful minutes to peel his shirt off, and he knew he had torn parts of a clot when he did it. He got the rest of his clothes off and got into the shower, starting it on warm and increasing the heat as much as he could stand. He gingerly washed the wound first with his hands and some soap and then with a washcloth. He did it all by feel, watching the runoff turn pink at the bottom of the tub. Then he turned off the hot water, running only cold, in hopes of reducing any swelling and to accelerate clotting. When he got out, the wound looked redder in the mirror, with a pink discoloration blooming in the skin all along the length of it.

Gotta roll, he thought, although then he realized he had no idea of where he was going to run to. Or, for that matter, if anyone was even looking for him yet. He held one of the bath towels across the wound as he searched for the television remote. Finding it, he switched on the television, punching through several stations, looking for anything about the fire. He finally found a report running on one of the Atlanta stations. He watched the overhead shots taken from a helicopter, amazed at the level of destruction, and then a press conference where some Army general was putting out a line of bullshit about the cause of the fire. And then came that one-liner about himself. And the FBI. And the DCIS.

He sat back down on the bed as a wave of fear washed over him. The FBI. And it wouldn't just be the FBI; it would be every law-enforcement agency in the state. The country, maybe. Safety violations and problems with the public auctions? DCIS inquiry? Bullshit! They *knew*. Whatever Tangent had told the Army and the FBI, that fucking Stafford must have corroborated. He could understand Tangent squealing to save his ass, but that fucking Stafford had put the nails in his coffin.

The urge to bolt was very strong, but he forced himself to slow down and think. There was no point in getting out on the highways, even in a disguised pickup, until he had somewhere to go and a reason for going there.

Keeping the damp towel over his shoulders, he went back into the bathroom and shaved, which helped him to wake up. The guy in the rest stop might or might not have noticed by now that his signs were gone and that his plate had been switched, but eventually he would, which would give the authorities an indication that Carson had been out on the northbound side of I-85. Okay, so now he needed to get it off the interstate. He counted the packs of money and found that he had a little over six thousand in cash that he'd taken from the bags before losing them in his escape. Assuming the hundreds weren't counterfeit, he had enough money to go to ground somewhere, maybe in one of those cabins up in the north Georgia mountains.

First he needed to get some meds for this wound, and then he needed to think. Right now, the only thing that counted was that he had the cylinder. They couldn't be absolutely, positively sure he had the cylinder, but they would be acting on that assumption. Which meant that the cylinder was a powerful bargaining chip: The Army desperately wanted it back, and just as desperately, wanted to keep the whole deal secret. Good news and bad news there, he thought as he put his clothes back on. They might be willing to bargain with him, or they might just put out orders to kill him, justifying such an order on the basis of how dangerous the cylinder was. So, first, meds. Then he needed to hide.

He got dressed again, stuffing the bloody bath towel inside the shirt to act as a temporary bandage. He put on his windbreaker and, leaving the key on the bed, went out to his truck and got in, resisting the urge to check the toolbox to see if the thing was still there. He drove out of the motel lot and onto an access road that led back to the interstate interchange, passing a Waffle House diner on the right. He was hungry, but he was too near the interstate. It'd be just his luck to stop for breakfast and have the Highway Patrol pull in for coffee. That reminded him: He needed to get rid of those magnetic signs. Maybe he'd stop in a Kmart somewhere and get some green spray paint to take care of those serial numbers on the door. And one of those Styrofoam coolers and some ice—the cylinder was definitely cooking, and that was really beginning to worry him.

The interchange consisted of an overpass for a state highway that ran north-south. He paused for a moment at the stop sign. South would take him back down toward I-20 and the approaches to Atlanta. Lots of places to hide, lot of people. Also lots of cops. North would take him into the Georgia and Tennessee mountains. Fewer people, fewer cops, but the more remote his surroundings became, the more he and the truck would stick out. He made his decision: Go north, get a cabin, hide the damned truck, and regroup. He turned left to go over the interstate, then headed north toward the mountains, visible as blue-green lumps on the distant horizon. As he cleared the interchange, a sign announced the miles to three towns, Dorey, Blairsville, and Graniteville.

Graniteville. Why did he remember that name? But then he was coming into the outskirts of Dorey, where he saw a Kmart in a shopping plaza. Good enough for government work, he thought. Get some real bandages, an ointment of some kind, and some Advil. And green spray paint. Don't forget the paint. And some ice for Baby back there.

■ TUESDAY, THE WAFFLE HOUSE, GRANITEVILLE, GEORGIA, 8:30 A.M.

Stafford found the sheriff ensconced at his usual table. "Guess there's no way around it," Stafford said, sliding into the booth and putting his computer down on the floor. "I'd better call Atlanta."

The sheriff was inhaling his usual cholesterol extravaganza. He nodded but kept eating. "Use my office, you want to," he said finally. He kept eyeing Stafford, as if waiting for something.

"Okay," Stafford said. "That fire has to be connected to this business. My guess is, the Army torched the place." He explained why.

"No shit?" the sheriff said. "Burned down a government installation? Just like that?"

"You never burn a problem out up here in the hills, Sheriff? I'll bet you have."

The Sheriff gave him a speculative look. "Mebbe," he said.

"Well, think of it as a matter of scale. Yeah, it's drastic, but it's in their power to cover it up. Remember, that's an operational consideration these days in government. My question is, Where's Carson? They said at that press conference that they're looking for him."

The sheriff nodded again. "I can tell you the whole damn state is looking for him," he said. "We've had ten telexes on him this morning. He's supposedly driving a green pickup truck, government plates. Suppose Carson took that thing, whatever it is. Where would he go? What would he do with it?"

"Don't know," Stafford replied. "That's why I feel obliged to call in. Otherwise, I'd sit back and await developments. One of the leads the Army will want to pursue now is how *I* knew about the weapon."

The sheriff finished his breakfast. "The Army knows about Gwen and the school?" he asked. "About Jess?"

"No, but my boss does. I suspect the Army has told the FBI some kind of story about Carson. They can't tell the truth, so they'll say he's a foreign agent or some shit like that. The FBI is, if nothing else, thorough. They're going to go to Ray Sparks probably sooner than later. Probably right about now."

The sheriff gave Stafford a long, searching look. Then they walked out of the diner together.

The sheriff's office was in the county courthouse. It was not a large affair: a reception desk, a bull pen for admin and communications, a hallway that led back to the holding cells, and an office for the sheriff himself. Inside Warren's office, Stafford plugged the phone line into his portable.

"I'm going to put this on speaker," Stafford said. "We'll be secure, but I think you should hear this."

The sheriff nodded once, acknowledging the professional courtesy being extended, and went to his desk.

"Defense Criminal Investigative Service. We are secure. May I help you?"

"Ms. Smith, this is David Stafford. Is—"

"Oh! Yes. Just a minute, Mr. Stafford."

"Think they want to talk to you?" the sheriff asked innocently.

Stafford grinned. "Bet they're running a trace while we wait."

The speaker erupted with the voice of Ray Sparks. "Goddamn it, Dave, why aren't you here? Where the hell are you?"

"And good morning to you, too, Ray. I'm on speaker here in the sheriff's office in Graniteville. Sheriff's name is John Lee Warren, and he's in the room. Heard you had a fire last night down there in Atlanta?"

"Wait a minute. Don't go anywhere, you hear me?"

"Waiting right here, Ray."

The sheriff leaned back in his chair and sipped some coffee. "Boy sounds put out," he said.

Sparks came back on the line. "Dave, you there?"

"Right here, Ray." Sparks sounded slightly less agitated. "Had to close my door. Christ, it's been a bitch of a night. I've had the Army and the FBI and the Atlanta cops and our own Washington headquarters down my neck since zero dark thirty this morning. I take it you heard about the DRMO?"

"Yes, I saw it on the news. What the hell happened down there?"

"It's a stone-cold mystery is what it is. The Army's got the scene clamped down like a bell jar and nobody's talking a whole lot. I thought you were coming back here yesterday. You weren't involved in that fire, were you?"

"Nope. Been right here in Graniteville. Scout's honor. And Ray? I've decided to stay here. To protect my confidential informant."

"Headquarters thinks otherwise, Dave. Headquarters—"

"Ray?" Stafford interrupted.

"Don't interrupt me, Dave, because—"

"Ray. Put a sock in for a moment. I've decided to resign. As of right now. You're technically my immediate supervisor, so you have been duly informed."

There was a moment of stunned silence on the line. "Well, shit" was all Sparks could manage.

"One of the reasons I'm doing that is so I can stay up here in Graniteville. So I can protect my erstwhile confidential informant. You know who I'm talking about, Ray?"

Sparks had to think about that for a moment. "Oh. Right. Her. Well, look, the Army's got a brigadier general down here, and there's a senior FBI guy from the Atlanta office riding shotgun with him, although there's something odd about that arrangement. They really, really want to talk to you. It seems that Carson guy has disappeared, and they think you might know something."

"Not about Carson, I don't. But I'll bet I know why they're still agitated. And I've met the general before. In Anniston."

"*He*'s the guy?"

"I think so. The voice is the same."

"You talked to him? The guy that called me?"

"Yeah, Ray, I did. Somebody had to point them at Carson before it was too late. You wouldn't do it, remember? Especially after somebody planted that IR on me? I'm guessing they moved on Carson but that he got away. Now he's on the run, with the weapon, the one that isn't missing."

Sparks's voice became quieter, as if he was trying not to be overheard. "Okay, that computes. You think he has it with him?"

"Yes, I do. That weapon is the biggest, most valuable thing he's ever stolen. If they'd found it the ashes, they wouldn't be coming to see you."

"Well, look," Sparks said, "it's like I said: Nobody's telling me shit about that fire. So far, everything I know about this, I'm finding out from you, which is probably why they're really serious about talking to you. I guess that means you can either come back here or I have to tell them where you are. In Graniteville."

"Ray, what have you told them about my source?" Stafford asked.

"Nothing—yet. Just that you had a CI and that's how you backed into this situation, whatever the hell it is. Now listen, Dave, the colonel has ordered me to put you together with these people. You want to protect someone in Graniteville, wouldn't it be better if you did it here?"

"I don't work for him anymore, Ray, remember? Besides, if I return to Atlanta, can you guarantee that I'll be free to walk out of there when we're done?" Sparks did not reply. Stafford looked across the desk at the sheriff, whose expression said, You have your answer.

"Look, Ray," Stafford said, "I'm more worried about what Carson's going to do than what the good guys are going to do."

"Why? You mean he'll go there? To Graniteville? Why would he do that?"

"Because as long as the Army won't admit there's a weapon missing, he's got some maneuvering room. Unless somebody else knows about it, that is. And somebody else does."

"Oh, you mean her. But how would he know to go to Graniteville?"

"Because I think I told him that's where the woman and the girl were from, back on day one. Back before I knew any better. Now he might not make the connection. But if he does, I want to be here and not in some sweat room at FBI headquarters."

Sparks was silent for a moment. "Well, I don't know what the hell to do," he said with a sigh. "All I do know is that the Army and the FBI are waiting outside my office right now. And they really want to talk to you."

Stafford did not reply to that.

"Dave?"

"Yeah, Ray?"

"You're not giving me much of a choice here. I'm getting a ton of heat on this. You don't come in, I'm going to have to tell them what I know. If they have to go up there, they'll take a crowd and they'll probably act like some serious assholes."

The sheriff leaned forward in his chair. "Mr. Sparks? This is John Lee Warren. Sheriff of Longstreet County. We don't take kindly to serious assholes up here in the hill country, Mr. Sparks. Don't much care who they are."

"Well, Sheriff, on behalf of the government, let me apologize all to hell in advance. But these aren't my people, and I think they're used to going wherever the hell they want to. They want to go up to Graniteville, they'll just do it."

"I'm not doubtin' they can come to Graniteville, Mr. Sparks. It's just the leavin' in one piece than can get tough."

"I'm not sure they're gonna worry too much about that, Sheriff. This general who's out in my anteroom right now? He looks like a real go-ahead kind of guy, you know what I mean? And he'll have the Bureau with him. You don't want to play hardball with the Bureau. They want to come to that school and see some people, they'll probably just do it, Sheriff."

This brought the sheriff straight up in his chair, glaring down at the portable as if he was about to mash it. "Mr. Sparks," he said slowly and distinctly, "been lots of nosy folks come up here to these hills over the years, some of 'em federal. You tell your federal friends there, they come ugly, pokin' their nose where they don't *even* belong, harassing people, frightening people, they gonna get run over by a gravel truck, after which we'll chop their arrogant heads off and throw 'em in a wolf pit up on the Carolina border, you hear me, mister? You can tell 'em I said that."

Stafford leaned forward to break the connection. "I'll guess I'll have to get back to you, Ray. Tell those guys to concentrate on finding Carson. He's got what they want, not me. I have no idea where Carson is or what he's going to do, and I am now formally out of the game." Stafford broke the connection before Sparks could reply.

" 'Wolf pit'?" he said, eyeing the sheriff.

The sheriff shrugged, the barest hint of a smile on his face. "Gives the tourists something to talk about when they get home. They need to hear bullshit like that; otherwise, all they remember is the poverty and the unemployment. Think of it as mountain lore."

Stafford grinned. "Wolf pit. I love it. And I'll bet everyone they bring with them will have heard about it before they get here." Then he grew serious. "But they will come. You know that, don't you? We've got to screen Gwen and the kids somehow. If the Army's got the FBI with them, they'll come on like gangbusters."

The sheriff stretched and cracked his knuckles loudly enough to make Stafford wince. His hands looked as if they were made of hickory, smooth, white, and hard.

"Will this Sparks fella tell 'em about Jessamine?" he asked.

"You heard him. Ray Sparks is a good guy, but he's not gonna buck the system if his ass and his pension are on the line, which I suppose they now are."

The sheriff nodded. "Then we've got to warn Gwen," he said. He stood up. "And now you're gonna learn the advantages of living on the edge of a federal wilderness area."

■ TUESDAY, DCISREGIONAL OFFICE, SMYRNA, GEORGIA 9:45 A.M.

The office manager showed Carrothers, accompanied by Senior Special Agent Hermann Kiesling, into Sparks's office. Sparks offered coffee, which both men accepted.

Having been up all night, Carrothers was running on a caffeine sine wave, with episodes of mental clarity following each succeeding cup of coffee, after which the only thing that kept him awake were some truly vivid stomach cramps. Agent Kiesling had been detailed to the Georgia damage-control effort from the Atlanta FBI office at 0630 that morning by the deputy director of the FBI. He was a tall, heavily built, red-haired man with an intense, florid face. Carrothers was willing to bet they called him Hermann the German—behind his back, that is. Way behind his back.

"So what do you have for us, Mr. Sparks?" Carrothers asked wearily.

"I've just talked to Stafford," Sparks said. "He just called in. I—"

"Where is he?" Kiesling interrupted. After learning about the agent going into the demil machine, Kiesling was a man with a mission.

"He's in a small town in north Georgia called Graniteville. He called me from the sheriff's office. He got a telecomm PC, so he could go secure, but the sheriff was in the room and Dave was on the speaker."

"So he's getting help from the local law?" Kiesling made it sound as if Stafford was the fugitive, not Carson.

"He actually hasn't done anything wrong, to my knowledge," Sparks replied, giving Kiesling a steady look. "It's our policy to coordinate with local law."

"And we expect cooperation from other federal law," Kiesling snapped. "Like coming in when we ask them to."

"Little problem with that, Mr. Kiesling," Sparks said. "Seems that Mr. Stafford has resigned."

This announcement didn't phase the FBI man. "Okay, so tell that sheriff to arrest his ass and hold him, now that he's just another civilian."

"Arrest him for what, exactly?" Sparks said. "And under which warrant?"

"Gentlemen, gentlemen," Carrothers interrupted. "Let's stay on point here. We're here to find Carson. He's the objective, remember? Does Mr. Stafford have any idea of where Carson is or might be?"

"No, sir, he does not."

"Then why won't he come here? Why all this arm's length stuff?"

"Before I answer that, General, let me ask you one. You are missing a weapon, right? Some kind of chemical weapon?"

The room went very quiet. Carrothers glanced sideways at Kiesling, then looked across the desk at the DCIS supervisor. He had to decide how much to tell Sparks, and his brain simply wasn't working that well. General Waddell had met with the Deputy Director of the Bureau in Washington to coordinate political damage control, following which the Attorney General and the Secretary of Defense had been briefed by their respective staffs. DOD and the Justice Department had agreed on an official cover story for local law-enforcement consumption, which was that Carson was wanted on an intelligence beef. Carson was a foreign agent who had been diverting defense material to certain Middle Eastern governments via an arms-merchant conduit in Washington. The fact that an agent had been killed provided more than enough impetus for the search, which conveniently made the cover story less important. Kiesling, a protégé of the current FBI Director, was the only one on the local FBI team who knew the real reason why they were searching for Carson.

Carrothers also knew that a joint task force was being convened in Washington at that very hour at the Justice Department to decide if Carson should be declared armed and dangerous, which would then authorize the use of deadly force in apprehension. General Waddell had continued to remind him that keeping the fact of the weapon's loss secret was just about as important as getting it back. After what had happened at Fort Gillem, there were some officials at both DOD and Justice who were fervently hoping Mr. Carson would resist arrest when the time came, albeit for different reasons. Carrothers had made the point that first they ought to get their hands on the weapon; if they killed Carson before that, the weapon might stay lost. And get found again later. So what should he tell Sparks?

Carrothers leaned forward in his chair. "If I answer that, Mr. Sparks," he said, "you will become one of the government officials who will have had prior knowledge of what can only be described as colossal government screwup. Do you really want to join that select group? Or would you rather cooperate with military and FBI authorities, on a strictly need-to-know basis, so that afterward you can truthfully say you had no idea of just how big a mess this was? Because I do believe there will be one or two searching questions asked about this when it's all over."

Carrothers watched as Sparks thought that one over. Now we'll see just how savvy a bureaucrat this guy is, he thought, but Sparks wasn't going to give up so easily.

"How about us chickens indulge in a some hypothetical discussions, then, General?" Sparks replied. "For instance, what are some of the possible consequences if an individual were, hypothetically now, to get loose with a chemical weapon?"

Carrothers sat back in his chair. This was a game he knew how to play. "Hypothetically, Mr. Sparks? Well, hypothetically, it would depend on this individual's state of mind. If he'd stolen such a weapon with the notion that he was going to make a fortune selling it on the international arms market, and something upset his big deal, then right now he might be seriously pissed off. No telling what he might do then. He could, for instance, take such a weapon into Atlanta. Or even out here to beautiful downtown Smyrna, Georgia. He could get on one of your commuter trains, maybe open a couple of windows, and then break a seal or two on the weapon, hang it out the window, and then get off at the next stop. You know, let the train take the weapon for a little ride. And sometime after that, you'd have a few hundred thousand screaming people stumbling out of their homes and cars and all those pretty office buildings you've got here with what looks like red jellyfish hanging out of their eye sockets." He paused for a moment, watching Sparks's face go pale as he absorbed that image.

"Their optic nerves would be eaten away back into their brains, Mr. Sparks, and when they tried to put what was left of their eyeballs back in their heads, they'd feel the tissue squirming in their hands. I say 'feel,' of course, because they would no longer be able to see, would they? Now some of them, the lucky ones, would just up and die from the pure shock of it. But a lot of them wouldn't. Probably most of them wouldn't. They'd be the ones who'd be hiring legions and legions of lawyers to come after *all* the government people who had known about this *hypothetical* problem in advance, *and who wasted fucking time talking about it!*"

Now that he had Sparks's attention, Carrothers bored in. Kiesling watched with an approving look on his face. "Mr. Sparks, this man Stafford has been cropping up in this *hypothetical* problem since I first got into it. Now we've had a major disaster down at Fort Gillem, and a

254

federal agent has been fed into a machine that turned him into Jell-O feedstock. Now Stafford didn't do that, but Stafford knows more about all this than is healthy for him. Or for you. So I want you to start at the beginning and tell me everything he's told you. Don't leave anything out. Don't ask any more *stupid fucking* questions, or try to play any more *stupid fucking* games with me. And do it now. Right now, if you please."

■ TUESDAY, VERNON CREEK CABINS, HIGHWAY 213, NORTH GEORGIA, 10:30 A.M.

Carson sat in the cabin and studied the cylinder, which was sitting partially on ice in the white plastic cooler in the middle of the room. It was going on midday, and the sunlight filtering through the trees along the creek was getting stronger. He had a mild headache, which he thought might be attributable to a low-grade fever. His upper back had settled into a throbbing pelt of low-level pain, but as long as he didn't lean back on it, he was reasonably okay. He was counting on an antibiotic cream to knock down any infection.

After leaving the shopping center, he had traveled north on the state road, climbing into the Georgia foothills. He'd passed several places with vacation cabins, all filled, until he found one near the bottom of a long canyon that wasn't very big, or very nice-looking, for that matter. This one had only ten potty-looking cabins, all ranging along a crooked small creek that came tumbling down a rocky, tree-covered hillside. The complete absence of beautiful mountain views meant the place had several vacancies.

The owner-manager probably had something to do with the vacancies: He was a scraggly-faced old man with tobacco-stained teeth and a disposition to match, who kept complaining about Floridiots, apparently in reference to the many Florida license plates in the area. Carson had asked for the last cabin on the row in order to put himself as far back from the road as possible. He had flashed his cash roll when he went in to register in order to make sure the manager had something to look at besides his face and truck. Only one of the other cabins appeared to be occupied.

There were no phones or televisions in the cabins, and the nearest grocery store was in Graniteville, about eight miles farther up into the mountains. The cabin had cooking facilities, a single bedroom, a living room and eating area, and a tiny porch overlooking the ravine where the creek ran. Carson had paid in advance for three nights. Now he sat in the bare cabin, his shirt off, with the motel towel still pressed over the salve-covered wound. His revolver lay out on the table as he watched the sunlight reflect off the smooth sides of the cylinder. The top of the stainless-steel cylinder still felt warm to the touch, but the ice was helping.

He'd been doing a lot of thinking since he'd holed up in the cabin. The Army had to know by now that Wendell Carson had been trying to shop a stolen chemical weapon. He didn't know if that guy from Tangent's team had been consumed by the Monster, but that wasn't his problem. The authorities wouldn't care: just one less bad guy to prosecute. The big thing was that there had to be a massive manhunt in progress by now. They could not know where he might run, because he himself did not know. He had simply bolted out of Atlanta and gone to ground like a harried fox at the first available hole. He also had to assume that the bearded man in the van would report his signs and plate missing, and that the cops would eventually make the connection with the rest area. That discovery would narrow the search down to the I-85 corridor northeast of Atlanta. They might assume he would keep going north on the interstate into North Carolina, but they would surely sweep both sides of it, using the Highway Patrol and the network of local county sheriffs.

Face it, he told himself: This is only a matter of time. Hours, maybe. Even up here in the mountains, some deputy sheriff will eventually come nosing into the driveway up there by the state road. And it wasn't like he could slap on a backpack and take off up the Appalachian Trail. He had never been much of a Boy Scout. And he couldn't go back to normal operations, because every aspect of his former life would be crawling with feds right about now. The FBI would have the damned IRS seizing his bank accounts, and there were probably federal marshals camped out at his house by now. He face twisted in a smile at the thought of Maude dealing with federal marshals, and federal marshals having to deal with Maude.

Face it, man: It's over. It's all over. Your only buyer is in custody, and probably singing his lungs out. All that money went up in smoke, and the whole world is now searching for Wendell Carson and the Army's precious damned cylinder.

He thought about Stafford, coming on the scene just as Wendell Carson's main chance was dropping into his hands. He went back through the familiar mental litany: How had goddamn Stafford found out? He stared down at the gleaming steel cylinder. Stafford had even been able to describe it. How the hell could he have known that? And then a new possibility came to him: Tangent had said that Stafford had been shit-canned from his Washington assignment over some unspecified problems up there. Could he be a dirty cop? Could Tangent have paid Stafford off to verify that Carson really had the weapon, and maybe to scope out the DRMO, before Tangent came down there with a million in cash? They were both from Washington, and everybody paid off everyone in Washington. But then he reconsidered: That didn't work, because he was pretty sure he had never told Tangent exactly what the thing looked like, only that he had the guts of a chemical weapon.

No, Stafford had been freelancing. He'd stumbled onto knowledge of the weapon somehow and then told the *Army*, not Tangent. That's right, because Tangent had almost backed out of the deal when he heard the Army was coming to have a look. But this still took him back to Stafford: How had Stafford *known* Carson had the weapon, as well as what it looked like?

More to the point, he told himself, what options do I have now? He couldn't bring himself just to ditch the thing. He did not know precisely what was in it, but he sensed that it was beyond dangerous. But therein might lie his one chance to help himself. The cylinder was his only leverage with the authorities. Maybe he should call them on the cell phone. Offer to give it up in return for what, a reduced sentence? No. Hide the damn thing, get a deal in writing, signed by a judge, and *then* tell them where it was. But if he called them, especially on a cell phone, wouldn't they just come pounce on his ass?

It was getting warm in the cabin. He got up, wincing at the sharp pain from his upper back, and went over to open the porch door. It isn't as if I've gotten away with their money, he thought bitterly, although they might not know that. He was actually more scared of the Army than of the FBI. If the Army caught up with him before the FBI or the local authorities did, they might just flatten him like they'd flattened the DRMO last night. He could not erase the image of that helmeted, faceless man walking purposefully down the aisles, almost casually dispensing his firebombs. That whole scene had shocked him to the core. Being manager of the DRMO had meant something to him. Even though he'd been stealing from it for years, he'd taken a sort of perverse pride in running it well, despite the scam, but they'd burned the damn thing down without a moment's hesitation, on just the *chance* that the cylinder was in there. What would they do to him if they caught him alone out here in this cabin? Ruby Ridge part two, that's what. Six monsters with green paint on their faces and branches and leaves in their hair would come diving through the window, screaming "Hoo-aah," and cut Wendell Carson's head off, that's what.

The sunlight outside was definitely getting brighter, which was not helping his headache. Somewhere out there on the highways and byways there were hundreds of cops of all kinds looking for him. They'd have his picture by now from DLA security. They'd be stopping by convenience stores, Waffle Houses, Huddle Houses, McDonald's, Burger Kings, rest areas, motels and minimarts, and at every gas station. "You seen this man? You seen this Army-green pickup truck?" Eventually, there'd be that deputy's cruiser quietly pulling in at the front entrance of this little dump. Maybe not this morning, but certainly in the next twenty-four hours. And then what? He could visualize one of those standoff scenes he'd seen a hundred times on television, with a hundred cop cars flashing blue strobes all over the woods while a SWAT team aimed carefully at the cabin, and for a chemical weapon, they very well might just kill him first and ask questions later. Especially out here in these remote mountains.

If he had salvaged the money, there might be a reason for going on with this thing, but now . . . now he knew he'd better make a deal while he still held some cards. But just once, just for a minute maybe, he'd like to have that fucking Stafford at the end of a gun barrel. Even if Tangent had been planning to double-cross him all long, Wendell Carson might have pulled it off if Stafford hadn't tipped off the Army.

And then it came to him: Maybe there was a way to get back at Stafford, like contact the feds and tell them he'd give the cylinder back in return for consideration in court, but he would give it only to Stafford. And then when he had Stafford, do what? Shoot him? That might feel good, but it wouldn't help his own situation. Suppose, just suppose, he could *implicate* Stafford? Tell the FBI, for instance, that Stafford had found out about the cylinder and then tried to horn in on the deal: He'd keep quiet about the weapon in return for a share of the money, which was why Stafford had been there when the Army team first showed up: He'd been protecting his interests. That's how he had known what the cylinder looked like: He'd forced Carson to tell him. Stafford the dirty cop. From what Tangent had said, Stafford already had problems within DCIS. If he already had enemies, Stafford could be well and truly fucked up.

258

He paced the room, thinking hard, sensing a weakness in his plan. Calling the cops—would that work? No. The moment he called, they'd trace the call and come gunning. They were focused on the cylinder; Wendell Carson was a secondary target.

Then he had an even better idea: Contact Stafford, not the feds. Tell *him* he'd turn over the cylinder in return for some consideration. And once everyone was focused on Stafford, then implicate his interfering ass. Tell the feds *Stafford* had the money. It almost didn't matter what he told them, because they were probably pissed off at Stafford anyway.

Yes, by God, that would work. Wendell Carson was going down the tubes anyway, but this way, he could take that bastard with him. For free. Forget Tangent: He was already in the shitter. But what sweet revenge it would be to tar Stafford. The government would hound Stafford for the rest of his life, looking for that money, with IRS audits every year, twice a year, while Wendell Carson raked leaves at Club Fed. Yes!

But first, he had to find Stafford. He went out to the truck, retrieved his briefcase, and extracted his phone list. Yes, there it was: the number for the DCIS office in Smyrna. There was no phone in the cabin, and he didn't want to use the cell phone yet, or the cabin manager's office phone, not with that long-eared creep standing there. The manager had said the nearest town was Graniteville. He'd have to risk using the truck; the spray-paint job had been pretty effective on the serial numbers, but it wouldn't fool an alerted cop. He could go to Graniteville, find a pay phone at a minimart, invent some telephone identity, maybe pose as someone from Washington, and call the Smyrna office. Then what?

He sat down. Damn it. His headache was getting worse, not better, and all this plotting and scheming wasn't helping. Where would Stafford be after that fire? He should be at the DCIS regional office down there in Smyrna. There'd be a big-deal investigation in progress, and probably some degree of chaos at the DCIS office. So do what? Get him up here into the mountains? Make him come where, to the cabin? To the nearest town, Graniteville? He knew nothing about Graniteville, other than that name was still tickling some memory. And would Stafford come alone? Or would he say anything Carson wanted to hear, and then bring the whole world with him? Including those terrifying Army people?

He went over to the bathroom and washed his face with ice-cold water, trying to wake up, trying to bring some clarity to his thinking. The bandage across his shoulders felt tight and just a little bit hot. Time was running out. If Wendell Carson was going to pull this off, he'd better get on with it, because if they found him before he made his move, he would have zero options left. He dried his face, pushed the cylinder down into the slush in the cooler, and went out to his truck.

■ TUESDAY, DCIS REGIONAL OFFICE, SMYRNA, GEORGIA, 11:30 A.M.

Carrothers sat there in open disbelief when Sparks had finished explaining everything he knew. "A psychic?" he said. "You're asking me to believe that a psychic told Stafford about this thing? A teenage girl? Who cannot speak? Jesus Christ, Sparks."

Ray Sparks threw up his hands. "You did ask, General. I'm only telling you what he told me. You figure out some other way that Stafford could know about your so-called hypothetical weapon, and I, for one, am more than ready to sign on. But that's what he told me. That's why he's in Graniteville. That's why he isn't here to talk to you."

"And there's a woman involved in this?" asked Agent Kiesling.

"The woman who runs this orphanage, school, whatever it is. I don't know how much she knows about this problem you're chasing here, but he did tell me she interprets for the girl."

"Where are they, exactly?"

"At a place called the Willow Grove Home. It's a combined group home and special school. An orphanage, basically."

"Are the woman and Stafford involved with each other?" Kiesling asked.

"Don't know. His wife left him last year. They might be involved with each other, or he may just be trying to protect her. She's apparently scared to death of a government witch-hunt and the media exposure that would follow, especially on the psychic angle. Stafford's afraid Carson might come after them, because he told Carson about Graniteville, that day after the airport deal."

Carrothers thought about that. "Psychics. Next you're going to tell me she's on contract to the CIA."

"Yeah, right, remember that goat rope?" Kiesling said with some relish. "Where the Agency spent a gazillion bucks trying to get psychics to read spies' minds. Then got their asses handed to 'em when the media and Congress found out. Embarrassed the shit out of them."

"They should have been embarrassed," Carrothers said, getting up to refill his coffee cup. "Psychics, mind probes; the Shadow knows . . . what utter bullshit."

Kiesling began to pace around the room. "I know I'm the newbie to this case, General, but I'll tell you what I'm beginning to think. I think this Mr. Stafford may have had an ulterior motive going here. You said Tangent put a million in cash on the table?"

"Now wait a fucking minute," Sparks spluttered.

"Hold on, Mr. Sparks," Carrothers said, sensing where the FBI agent was going to go with this. "So?"

"I made some calls while we were waiting. My sources tell me this guy's down here in Atlanta because he's on his own agency's shit list—no offense, Mr. Sparks. His wife had just dumped him, his career's down the tubes, and he's lost the use of one arm. Every time he looks up, he sees the rim of the toilet bowl swirling past his face. And all of a sudden he knows an awful lot about *your* hypothetical problem, General. One of the ways that could happen is if he and this Carson guy made some kind of deal."

"No way," Sparks said immediately. "Dave Stafford is a maverick, but he's no bent cop. Look, if he was involved in this, why in the hell would he have told me jack shit? Huh? You explain that, Kiesling!"

"In case it went wrong, Sparks. He was covering his ass. He was a civil servant, just like the rest of us. Gimme a fuckin' break here: Which one of us ever does anything without first covering our asses?"

Sparks just glared at him.

"Besides," Kiesling said, "look how he probably worked it. Suppose he found out about the weapon deal and horned in. Forced Carson to split the money. If the deal went right, he stood to collect five hundred large. If it went south, he could always say he warned you, his boss, about it, but he couched it in such terms that you wouldn't have believed it in a hundred years. A teenage psychic, for Chrissakes? And now he's resigned? How fucking convenient."

"But most of the money was counterfeit!" Sparks said. "You said—"

"Fuck that!" Kiesling shouted as he bent over Sparks's desk. "Neither of *them* knew that. Either way, I don't give a shit. I've got an agent dead. He was married. Had kids. I don't even have a body for them. You listening to me? We had to go get a funeral home to give us an urn so we could sweep up some ashes from what was left of that fucking DRMO!"

Sparks started to reply, but Carrothers raised his hand to stop it. He thought about what the FBI man was insinuating. In a way, Kiesling's theory made some sense, more sense than Sparks's story about some psychic kid. On the other hand, Stafford had not impressed him as being that kind of guy, and his own long and successful Army career had taught Carrothers to trust his own judgment about people.

"Okay, people," Carrothers said. "Let's cool it for a moment. Put that theory on hold. Let's get back to our primary objective: finding Carson and the weapon. Mr. Kiesling, could you please go check on what the sweep has produced?"

Kiesling took a deep breath to compose himself, glared at the red-faced Ray Sparks, and left the office. Carrothers closed the door behind him for a moment and turned to Sparks. "I'm not sure I subscribe to Mr. Kiesling's theory, Mr. Sparks," he said. "That doesn't strike me as being Stafford's style, having met the man."

Sparks threw a pen across the room. "I was about to suggest there was another way Stafford could have found out," he said. "And that was if *Tangent* had told him."

Carrothers shook his head. "We're wasting time and energy with all this 'Who shot John?' stuff. Of course, the Bureau and the Justice Department are probably very anxious to divert attention away from their man Tangent's little stunt, especially after it got one of their own people killed last night."

"Cover-up," Sparks said in disgust. "That's becoming the Bureau's hallmark these days. I remember when they were the best of the best. Look, General, Dave Stafford's a pain in the ass, and, yes, he put some senior people in the shitter, but they were bent and he is not. This is partly my fault, because I reacted the same way you did to the psychic business. But what if the damned girl *is* a psychic? I mean, I wasn't going to bring this up in front of Godzilla out there, but the police have been using psychics and profilers for years. Hell, it was a *Bureau* guy who wrote the book on profiling. Now, hypothetically and all that shit, I don't know just how desperate you guys are, but if it was my ass, I'd be asking the girl some questions and hoping like hell she *was* a fucking psychic!"

Carrothers nodded but did not reply. He had had exactly the same thought. Kiesling had been cut in on the real problem here, but he was obviously letting himself be swept up in the cop-killer frenzy that was developing. With Sparks following, he went to the DCIS conference room, where Kiesling's FBI team had set up a temporary command post.

The lead agent reported on the statewide search for Carson and his government pickup truck, an effort that included state and local law-enforcement agencies. There had been no contact reports on Carson, but there had been a report of a stolen license plate and magnetic door signs at a rest area out on I-85 northeast of Atlanta. The man making the report remembered parking next to a green pickup truck, although there had been no one in it when he went to sleep. The time frame fit for someone trying to get out of Atlanta after the Fort Gillem fire.

Carrothers went to a map of Georgia and was shown the location of the rest area. The agent reported that there were vehicle checkpoints established on all the interstates in Georgia, with a double barrier on the Carolina and Tennessee borders. Local law in three states had been alerted, and the fact that an agent had been killed would keep them focused. Carrothers studied the map. Georgia was a much bigger state than he had realized. He looked at the single red pin sticking into the rest area on I-85. All that geography, and all they had was that one pin. Then he spotted the name Graniteville, next to a tiny dot up along the Carolina border, about two inches above the red line of the interstate highway. Wasn't that where Stafford was?

"Graniteville," he muttered to himself. He looked over at Sparks, who was talking with the DCIS office manager, who had come in with a stack of phone messages for him from Washington. Sparks only frowned and stuffed them in his pocket. The office manager began to tell him something else, but he waved her off. Carrothers looked back at the map.

Stafford is supposedly in Graniteville, he thought. If Carson had heisted those plates and the signs to cover up the government serial numbers on his truck, then he could be in or near the Graniteville area. More importantly, so could the Wet Eye cylinder. He felt a growing urge to do something besides sit around and wait. Perhaps he should go to Graniteville and talk to Stafford directly, or, hell, even the girl, but he did not trust the FBI just now. They were too fired up about getting Carson, and their bosses were under enormous pressure to find a way to shovel this tar baby into someone else's yard. In fact, they had every incentive just to shoot Carson on sight, which would not necessarily solve the Army's problem.

He glanced over his shoulder at Kiesling, who was talking to his agents. From their expressions alone, he confirmed his sense of it: If they did find Carson, he was going to die resisting arrest.

"Mr. Kiesling," he said. "I'm going to go back to Fort Gillem, where my mobile command center is. I need to check on the progress of the DRMO fire investigation and dampen down any residual press interest. Why don't you stay here with your team until we get some locating information on Carson? You can call my mobile command center as soon as you have something."

"Yes, sir," Kiesling said. "Although I still think we ought to be having some face time with Mr. Stafford."

"Well, we know where he is. If nothing turns up on Carson in the next six to eight hours, maybe we'll go check out your theory. But please let's remember the objective here: Carson."

After Carrothers had left, Sparks headed back to his office. The office manager intercepted him again. "I was trying to tell you earlier," she said. "There was one message in that stack for Mr. Stafford, from his ex-wife's lawyer. He said they were reopening the court case and that they needed some more discovery papers. I told him Mr. Stafford was on assignment in Graniteville, at that Willow Grove Home, and gave him the number. I hope that was all right."

Sparks gave a hollow laugh. "That's just what Dave needs at this juncture: a call from his ex-wife's damned lawyer. He'll hate you for that one, Leslie." He shook his head and went back into his office, closing the door behind him.

■■■ TUESDAY, WILLOW GROVE HOME, GRANITEVILLE, GEORGIA, 12:30 P.M.

Stafford was waiting in Gwen's office while John Lee was having a long talk with her out on the porch. It had turned into a warm day for the mountains, and the house had not been shut up for air conditioning yet. The sheriff wanted Gwen and Jessamine to leave Willow Grove until Carson was caught and the matter of the weapon resolved. What Stafford had not yet picked up was where she was supposed to go. Besides that, Gwen was visibly unhappy with the idea of leaving the little kids behind. They had moved out to the porch to continue their discussion, and Stafford had tactfully withdrawn from what might become an argument. He thought there might be more to their conversation than just Gwen's leaving.

He thought about what he had done that morning, and he was surprised to feel no regrets. He knew there'd be fallout over the mess at the DRMO, and that he wasn't going escape all of it, but he was hoping

264

his resignation would take him out of the direct line of fire once the big guns at DCIS headquarters got embroiled in the Army's problem. He had been ready to accept Gwen's invitation to stay at the house, except that now John Lee's insistence on her going into hiding somewhere might have upset that plan. He wondered again if John Lee's motive was to get Gwen out of harm's way, with *harm* having multiple definitions.

He got up and moved around her small office, looking at the certificates and the family pictures. That one must be her father, he thought. Same strong face and eyes. Strangely, there were no pictures of any women who looked like Gwen. There was one somewhat faded local newspaper picture of Gwen getting her degree down at the university, with her father standing proudly beside her. He peered closer to read the caption identifying them, and he saw the last name: Hand. Dr. Winfield Hand and his daughter, Gwinette Hand.

He looked around at Gwen's desk, saw the nameplate: Gwen H. Warren. And where was Gwen's mother? Gwen had said her mother had died, but nothing about a divorce. He remembered her saying that her father had helped to found the orphanage. He heard sounds of Gwen returning, and he went into the kitchen to meet her. The kids had just finished lunch and were being shepherded upstairs by Mrs. Benning while the cook cleaned up. Gwen led him out the back door and onto the lawn behind the house. The sheriff, apparently, had left. He asked her what was going on.

"John Lee wants me to disappear for a little while, with Jess," she said. "Part of me says that's a good idea; the other part is worried about the little ones. I don't like leaving them alone with all this trouble brewing."

"John Lee might be right, Gwen. It's not the little kids who would be the focus of the government's attention, assuming it's coming this way, I mean."

They reached the barnyard gate and turned around to go back toward the house. The sun burned through the high mountain air with a vengeance. "I know that," she said. Then she stopped. "I think John Lee might have another reason than just getting us clear of trouble."

He nodded and kicked a pebble off the path. "Yes, I understand. I've been thinking about what you said last night. And you are right: I'm quite attracted to you. But John Lee's also right: You and Jess ought to bail out. The best thing I can do is to stay here, hold down the fort, until we see what happens."

She nodded. "Those feelings are not necessarily just one way, Dave. I like you very much. But there's too much you don't know about me, and with all this other—"

"I could just go," he said. "Get out of here, get out of your hair entirely."

"I'd feel a lot better if you stayed, especially since you're one of them—the government, I mean." She faced him then, and there was some pain in her expression. "John Lee has been making the same assumptions that you have," she said. "I like you very much, but a lot of that is sympathy for your situation—what you've been through this past year, with your job, your wife, your injury. I guess what I'm saying is that I'm simply not 'available,' not the way you imagined. I—we—do need your help. But not—"

"I understand," he replied, suddenly anxious to shut this off. The message was clear, and he was beginning to feel acutely embarrassed. "I helped bring this thing into your world, so the least I can do is to see it through. If the FBI or the Army comes here, I do know the beast when I see him, and I can talk the talk. Will you stay with relatives?"

She nodded absently but did not really answer his question. He did not pursue it. If he didn't know where she was, no one could make him tell. He took a deep breath and asked her about the pictures. Once again, she didn't look at him, turning instead to look back at Howell Mountain.

"Jessamine Hand is my half sister," she said finally. She gave him a moment to absorb that news before continuing. "By marriage. It's a bit complicated. As I told you, my mother passed away in 1974. My father remarried two years later, to a woman named Hope, who was much younger than he was. In the course of time, three children came along. Jess is Hope's youngest child."

Stafford kept quiet. Maybe this would explain why she did not want to enter into a relationship. A breeze stirred the willows; Gwen turned and began walking toward them, and he followed.

"Hope had an older sister, Charity, who drowned in a quarry when she was sixteen. Officially, it was ruled an accident, but most folks who knew about it said she jumped. Charity was quite beautiful, and apparently, also quite mad. So, unfortunately, was Hope. The difference was that it took a lot longer to manifest in Hope. She was twenty-eight when she married my father. He was fifty-two. The marriage was fine for a while, until the kids came along."

"What was her illness?"

"You're in the north Georgia mountains, Dave," she said with a bitter smile. "Specifics of that nature are rarely discussed in these parts. Suffice it to say, Hope's descent into madness was not graceful. By the time Jess was born, she was in full cry. My father was a doctor, so he knew. In retrospect, we all knew, but this is a small southern mountain town, and decent people averted their eyes."

"What finally happened? Was she committed somewhere?"

"No." There was another pause, and Stafford could see that she was dredging up some painful memories. "No, it ended one terrible winter night in 1986 when my father was not here. She apparently had one of her visions, as she called them, killed two of her children, and then turned the gun on herself, although she failed to kill herself. Jess was the only survivor."

"Good Lord. And how did Jess survive?"

Gwen paused again before answering. "No one knows, or no one was willing to say at the time. I was married by then and living with John Lee."

"But you have an opinion?"

"Jess was not quite three," she said softly, staring out at the willows. "I think perhaps her mother just could not bring herself to shoot her baby. But there's another possibility. Knowing what I know now, I think perhaps her mother, crazy as she was, recognized something in Jess. I think it's entirely possible that Hope's insanity was somehow caused by or reinforced by unformed mental acuity of her own. As I mentioned, she claimed to see visions, hear voices."

"She was schizophrenic."

"Yes, that was the official diagnosis. But no one really knows what's going on in a schizophrenic's mind; we have only their word for it, you see. She's down in Milledgeville now, at Central State. Quite hopeless now." She smiled a sad smile at the unintended play on words, then turned back toward the house.

"So Jess has been at the Willow Grove Home from the start," she continued. "She was withdrawn as a child, but no one told her until she was seven what really happened that night."

"And when did she stop talking?"

"She never spoke after that night. I had hopes that she was going to be able to grow away from all that, until the manifestations of her . . . ability began. Now I just don't know."

"So you kept her here first because she was family, and second, because you're not sure of what's going on in her mind."

"That's correct. Consider her antecedents: Hope and Charity, both violently, self-destructively insane; her own two sisters cut down before we could know anything about their mental development. And now Jess is manifesting mental—what, irregularities? I didn't know what else to do."

Stafford let out a slow breath as he thought about this history and the fact that everything he had been assuming up to this point had been wrong.

"Well," he said. "I apologize again for bringing this other mess into your lives, and of course I'll stay here while you and Jess get clear of it for a while. There's a huge hunt on for Carson. He's not a professional bad guy, so I suspect this will be resolved before too long."

They heard the phone begin to ring up at the house. As they turned toward the back door, she took his hand.

"Dave, I'm sorry. About the other, I mean. And the offer still stands. For you to stay here and get your life reassembled. But—"

"I understand," he said. "And I'll think about it. But in the meantime, we need to get you and Jess to safety."

■ TUESDAY, FORT GILLEM DMRO, ATLANTA, 1:30 P.M.

Carrothers sat at the communications command post, waiting for the secure patch to General Waddell at the Pentagon. He had taken a nap in the car on the way back from Smyrna, and he felt marginally better, but only marginally. The cylinder was still lost. The individual most likely to have it was on the run somewhere in Georgia. Now he had to report to Waddell, and through him, to the Army chief of staff. He had a sinking feeling that they wouldn't be able to keep a lid on this thing much longer. For the moment, the Pentagon and Justice were in this mess together, but the instant the Justice Department saw a way to shift all the blame to the Army, they'd seize it. What had his wife said? To trust *all* his instincts. His instinct was to talk to Stafford, without the FBI. He had done what he had been ordered to do and had discovered an even bigger mess than before. It was time to start doing the right thing.

While he still couldn't feature Stafford for a crooked cop, the facts of the problem certainly raised reasonable doubt on that score. For one thing, Stafford sure as hell didn't act like the typical federal agent. He must understand the degree of concern this mess was generating at the national level, and yet here he was, handing in his resignation and holing up in some godforsaken mountain village. Maybe Kiesling was right. On the other hand, maybe Stafford knew something that the Army, in its determination to bury this fiasco, didn't know or didn't want to know. Either way, doing something would be better than just sitting here waiting for something to happen.

"This is the Army Command Center with a secure satellite call for General Carrothers," the headset announced.

"Carrothers here, secure."

"Stand by one."

A moment of silence, punctuated by a tone burst. "Lee?"

Well, now, he thought, we're back to Lee? "Yes, sir, General. We still haven't found him. They've got the whole damn state looking for him, though."

"All right. Justice has him listed as armed and dangerous. They've told the Georgia law-enforcement agencies to capture him alive if at all possible, but the Bureau people are saying that might be tough in Georgia. The lawmen down there purportedly do not screw around, especially with a cop killer. I wish we could we confirm he has the weapon."

"So do I, General. There were no traces of the Wet Eye in the products of combustion during the fire, or in the ash piles and debris afterward, but as I reported, two of our people saw him getting away with an object."

"But basically, we still don't *know* shit."

"That's correct, General. Everyone's operating on assumptions here. That's why *we* should want him alive. There is one other development." He described Sparks's strange story about a psychic child and the FBI's speculation about Stafford, and that Stafford had resigned from the DCIS and was holed up in Graniteville. These revelations produced a hiss of silence on the net.

"A psychic?" Waddell said finally. "What kind of shit is that?"

"Beats me, General. I guess anything's possible at this juncture."

"The FBI really serious about suspecting Stafford?"

"I think they're mostly circling the wagons. They're desperate to broaden the target. I assume senior management in the Bureau is appropriately galvanized?"

"Oh, yeah, you might say that. That guy Tangent is in so much trouble, they don't have a name for it at the Bureau, not only because he didn't tell them what he was doing but also for losing one of his agents. But the Attorney General apparently reminded SecDef that none of this could have happened if we hadn't let one get away."

"Tough to argue that one, sir. I'm thinking of going to find this DCIS guy, Stafford, see what else he knows. Without the FBI people."

"Has he been cooperating?"

"In a manner of speaking, General, although by resigning, he's kind of out of it now. He did warn us that Carson had the item, and that was *before* the balloon went up. Anyway, here's what I'm thinking: I want to go up in the mountains to talk to Stafford. And this psychic girl, if I can. If she detected the cylinder, maybe she can tell us where it is now."

"For Chrissakes, Lee—"

"I know, General. But we've got the whole state of Georgia turned upside down looking for this guy, and sooner or later, some inquiring minds are going to want to know why. I have nothing better to do. If I get the sense that Stafford is bent, I'll turn him over to our own Special Forces for some counseling."

"I'd do that right now, if it were me, and the Bureau's gonna howl when they find out they're being cut out."

"Their job is to find Carson, and right now, anyway, their guy here is fairly passionate about doing that. I can always tell them later I was consulting the psychic. Gun-shy as they are right now, they won't want any part of that. Remember the Agency's Stargate flap?"

"I do indeed. Okay, but remember, nobody here gives a shit about Carson, as long as we get the weapon back. He's responsible for the death of an agent, so in a way, he's a traveling free-fire zone. On the other hand, if he calls in, wants to make a deal, for instance, we tell him anything he wants to hear, understood?"

"Absolutely, General."

"And as far as I'm concerned, that DCIS guy is expendable, too, especially now that he's quit. If he was involved in this little caper, go ahead and put his ass in the crosshairs with Carson. Nobody on either side of the river up here will object."

"I don't think he was on the take, General, but there's something strange about the way he's acting, which is why I want to go up there."

"Well, nothing beats personal reconnaissance, Lee. Keep your comms suite with you, and keep us informed."

"Yes, sir, General. Carrothers off net."

He pulled the headset off and rubbed his perspiring ears. He thought about what the general had just said. Jesus, Stafford, he thought, you've really made some friends in high places, haven't you?

He stepped out of the trailer and told the regular team to return to their positions. Then he summoned one of the MP captains, who came trotting over, pulling out his notebook.

"I want to requisition two of those Suburbans," Carrothers ordered. "Lose the police lights. I want the two biggest MPs you've got, a medic, and a two-man CW monitor team, fully equipped. I want you, the medic, an MP driver, and me in one vehicle, the other three and the gear in the other. I want side arms for everyone, a night scope, a SATCOM terminal, and GPS tracker in my vehicle. Then get directions to a north Georgia burg called Graniteville, and once there, to something called the Willow Grove Home. And, finally, I want a total blackout on my movements, especially with reference to the FBI. Anyone asks, I've been summoned to Anniston to await developments."

"Got it, General."

"Good. A departure anytime in the next twenty minutes will do just fine."

■ TUESDAY, THE LAUREL MOUNTAIN MINIMART, GRANITE-VILLE, GEORGIA, 2:30 P.M.

Carson sat in the pickup truck, trying to eat a seriously awful microwaved hamburger while he watched the state road leading up into Graniteville. Even though he had the windows open, it was hot inside the truck. Or his temperature was elevated. Probably both. He was perspiring freely, and the huge cup of Coke wasn't helping very much. The wound on his back was actually feeling better, although the stiffness was increasing. He reminded himself to change that bandage when he got back to the cabin.

He had pulled into the minimart twenty minutes ago, parking behind the store and near the pair of phone booths at the edge of the parking area. He'd gone in and bought food, hiding most of his face behind a pair of opaque sunglasses and a ball cap. It was the middle of the afternoon, and fortunately there wasn't much going on in and around the gas station. In the whole time he had been there, he hadn't seen a single cop car come down the road, which hopefully meant the manhunt hadn't reached the mountain towns yet. He needed just a few more hours.

He looked down at the piece of paper with the number of the Willow Grove Home on it. He'd been amazed that the woman down in Smyrna had just told him where Stafford was. Graniteville. Willow Grove, a school of some sort. "Yes, I can give you the number. He doesn't really work here, you know," she'd said. He had thought about calling the place, getting directions, and driving out there, maybe surprising Inspector Stafford, but it was a school. He didn't like the idea of starting something in a schoolyard, not unless he could pin that on Stafford, too. Besides, he reminded himself, he was going to let the government do in Mr. Smart-Ass Stafford.

He looked at his watch, crumpled the remains of the hamburger into a greasy ball, got out of the car, and went to the phone booth, where he placed the second call. A woman's voice answered. "Willow Grove Home and School. This is Mrs. Benning."

"I'm calling for a Mr. David Stafford," he replied. "My name is Carson."

"Just a moment, sir." The woman put her hand over the mouthpiece and said something to someone else in the room. Then she was back, her tone breathless. "Just a minute, Mr. Carson. We're getting him."

He waited impatiently, very conscious of just how visible he was in the glass booth. But the road remained comfortingly empty, the old concrete shimmering in the midafternoon sun.

Stafford hurried through the hallway to Gwen's office, John Lee Warren right behind him. Gwen was standing by her desk, looking anxiously across the room at them as they came in. She held her palm tight across the mouthpiece.

"Can you trace this call?" Stafford asked the sheriff quietly as he reached for the phone.

John Lee shook his head. "Not without prior arrangements. The nearest manned central office is over in Reidsville."

Stafford mouthed a silent curse and took the phone from Gwen. "This is Stafford," he said. The handset was slippery. It was warm and humid in the house.

"I want to make a deal," Carson said without preliminaries. "I'll hand over the weapon in return for a maximum five-year sentence at Club Fed."

"Why the hell you calling me, Carson? I'm not a judge. How did you get this number?"

"Your office in Smyrna told me where you were, Stafford. I figure I don't have much time. I'll turn over the weapon to you and only to you. Up there in Graniteville. You arrange the deal with whoever's on my trail. I'll call you back in an hour."

"Wait!" Stafford said. "Why call me? Why not call the Army?"

"Did you see what they did to my DRMO? That was no accidental fire. Those bastards are crazy. Besides, I want to see you one more time. For old times' sake."

"Sure you do. And what if I don't want to play?"

"I can always find a suitable home for it, Stafford. I don't know what's in that thing, but I'll bet it's a little bitch with its top off. What do you think?"

Stafford relented. "Right. Okay, deal. I'll make some calls. Where are you?"

There was no reply. Stupid question, Stafford thought. "Right," he said again. "Scratch that. You call me back here in an hour."

There was a click on the line and Carson was gone.

"What did he want?" the sheriff asked. "What's this 'deal' all about?"

"He's figured out that he's dead meat and that the weapon is his only leverage. He wants to trade the weapon for a reduced sentence."

The sheriff mopped his brow. Gwen was shaking her head. "This is the man in the airport, isn't it? He wants to bring that *thing* here?"

Dave sat down at her desk. "He says he wants to turn the weapon in. Getting that weapon back under government control is more important than hanging the guy who stole it. I'm sure everyone involved is going to think that way. It sounds like he's ready to come in after that, preferably before some Army sniper team finds him. I've got to call Atlanta."

"Why doesn't he take his damn deal to Atlanta?" the sheriff growled. "We don't need any chemical weapons here."

"He insists on dealing through me. Look, I'm just going to tell them what he told me. Let them make the decisions. He's afraid of the FBI and the Army, as well he should be."

"I wonder where the hell he is," the sheriff said.

"This is the age of cell phones, Sheriff. He could be anywhere. He could be here already. Now let me get on this." He called Ray Sparks.

Afternoon shadows were gathering along the creek when Carson made his second call to Willow Grove. He decided it was okay to use his government-issue cell phone this time, figuring there was no longer any need to hide the transmission. This time, Stafford picked up, ready to offer what he'd discussed with Sparks.

"Where do we stand?" Carson asked.

"I've talked to Atlanta. I've got the deal. Club Fed. Five years. There's an FBI team coming up with the papers. I expect them by eight o'clock tonight."

"That's over four hours from now. Why so long?"

"They have to get a federal prosecutor and a judge to sign off on the deal. Then it takes two, three of hours to get here. The guy heading up the FBI team is named Kiesling."

"Why don't they fly up? Use a helo?"

"Probably don't want to do that in the mountains at night. I don't know. The FBI isn't into explaining."

"Okay. We meet where?"

"The sheriff's office, at the county courthouse in Graniteville. His name is John Lee Warren. You come into town, you'll run right into the courthouse square."

Carson thought about that. "All right," he said. "I assume the whole world is looking for me right now. If I come driving into Graniteville, I expect this to be civilized, right? I'm not looking to be put on my face in the street by a bunch of Georgia no-necks with sticks and dogs."

"You're turning yourself in as part of a federal plea-bargain arrangement. You come in alone, and you come in unarmed, and everything will be businesslike. You do understand that the government is more interested in retrieving that weapon than in busting you, don't you?"

"I do. I also understand my government might be very interested in silencing me. Permanently. So *you* understand that I won't have it with me, right? That I'll want to see civilians in coats and ties, not soldiers in chem suits when I get there?"

"Yes."

"Because if I see any sign of the Army, the deal's off. Those fucking Army guys are acting like a bunch of psychos."

"Maybe that's because they're scared of what's in that cylinder, Carson."

"Then everybody better play by my rules," Carson said. "Here's the rest of it. I want an attorney. Any Shylock will do. Waiting on the courthouse steps. He will go with me into the sheriff's office, where he will swear in writing that the FBI's paper is legitimate." He had to pause to get his breath. "Then I want that attorney to go with me to wherever they take me in Atlanta. To witness the fact that I was alive in federal custody when I left Graniteville, and still alive when I got to Atlanta. After that, I'll take my chances, and I'll tell you where the weapon is."

"They'll probably go along with most of that," Stafford said. "Except for two things. Make that three things. First, I don't think you're going to leave here until they have that weapon in federal custody. I understand you won't bring it with you, but they'll want to see it as soon as you sign the paperwork."

Carson thought about that. It was hard to think; his head was really pounding now, and that greaseburger was not going to remain down for much longer. Getting the deal was important. But what else? "Okay," he replied.

"And the second is that the attorney cannot know what this is about. You tell him, or anyone else, and your deal goes south."

"I can live with that," Carson said. "What's the third?"

"I'm not going to be there. You'll have to deal with the FBI. I've set the deal up, but then I'm out of it."

Carson frowned, trying to concentrate. Then he remembered what he was going to do to Stafford once he was in custody. "Why?"

"My agency doesn't love me anymore, so I've resigned," Stafford said. "They've told the FBI that, so they don't want me involved. So you deal with them."

"That's not what I wanted."

"Way I see it, it's them or the Army."

Carson thought about that. He really didn't have any other options, and then he realized he could still implicate Stafford. "Okay," he said. "We have a deal. I'll be at the Graniteville courthouse at eight P.M. And remember, no fucking Army."

It was cool, almost cold up at the top of the notch; Stafford wished now that he had followed Gwen's advice about a jacket. With no moon yet, there was no view, only the dark mass of the mountains on either side of them, and the deeper darkness below, where the gray path dropped down into the wilderness area. After being briefed about the agreement between Stafford and Carson, the sheriff had recommended that Gwen and Jessamine should get away from the home. Gwen and John Lee Warren were talking quietly over by the drop-off. Stafford stood there with Jessamine, who was wearing a jacket and a backpack.

"Are you frightened?" he asked her.

She turned her hands up and down and shrugged.

"Have you been out there before?" he asked, pointing with his chin toward the wilderness area. A steady cool breeze spilled into the gap from that vast expanse of wilderness north of the notch. It carried the scent of pines and ancient stone.

She nodded emphatically. She pointed to Gwen, then herself, and then made some signing motions Stafford did not understand. Gwen joined them.

"She's telling you that we have friends out there. People who will keep us safe. I'm more worried about you than us."

He smiled at her. Her eyes were almost invisible in the darkness. "I think we'll be okay. Carson's not coming here. We'll have John Lee's people and the FBI in town when he shows up. Besides, he's only one guy."

"With a lethal cargo."

"Yes, and no. It's not like he can use it without killing himself. The only thing that worries me is that he didn't sound right. I wonder if he was injured in that mess at the DRMO. Burned maybe. He sounded a bit feverish."

"Well, good," she said. "That should make him less of a threat."

Stafford glanced over at the sheriff, who was visible only as a small red dot from the cigarette he was smoking. The pungent smell of tobacco infiltrated the forest air. "So you really do have people back there? People who will give you a place to stay?"

She nodded in the darkness. He could just see her face now that his eyes were fully night adapted. "Yes," she said. "We really do."

"What's the connection?"

"It's the school, you see. Most of them back out there will never leave. But once in a great while, there's a child . . ."

"How can we contact you if we have to?"

"There's a cell phone at a ranger cabin." She looked out behind him into the darkness. "Ah," she said. "They're coming."

He went with her to the back edge of the notch and peered down into the darkness. The path was barely visible as a serpentine, gray stripe down the back side of the mountain, ending in the deeper darkness of the forest. "Look down there," she said softly.

He looked, and saw flames. Small flames, just at the edge of the forest below them. No, not flames. Lanterns.

"That's them?"

"Yes. We should go now. We'll . . . visit out there for a day or so, and then send for word to see what has happened."

"What if—" he began, but then he stopped. He had just told her this thing was going to go all right. He plunged ahead. "What if there's trouble? What if it's necessary for you to stay hidden for a while?"

"If there's trouble, we'll hear about it." She smiled, a flash of white against the gray oval of her face in the darkness. "Jungle drums and all that. You'd be amazed at how well they keep in touch."

Dave nodded. There was so much he didn't know about how things were up in these remote hills, and since he was an outsider, he would probably never know. Just like he had known nothing about Gwen's family, or how Jess had come to live at Willow Grove. There was an arcing shower of red sparks in the direction where John Lee had been standing.

"Time to go," she said. She stepped forward suddenly and hugged him. "Be careful," she whispered. Then she took Jessamine's arm and together they walked off into the darkness.

The sheriff approached, his boots crunching in the gravel and shale that littered the floor of the notch. "They'll be fine," he said. "We'd best get back to the house. It's slower going downhill."

As they walked down, Stafford asked the sheriff about the people waiting for Gwen and Jessamine.

"Mountain folk" was all he said.

They reached the house about forty minutes later, emerging from the willows by the pond to a pool of porch light. The upstairs lights were on in the bedrooms. Gwen had shown him her father's room upstairs, but he planned to wait for the children to go to bed before going up there. He presumed the kids and Mrs. Benning were probably in the room where the tinted white shadows of a television flickered on the part of the ceiling visible through the curtains. Stafford was almost anxious to get inside; the night air had begun to chill him in earnest halfway down the trail. They let themselves in through the kitchen door, which the sheriff then locked behind them.

"Haven't had to do that in a long damn while," he muttered, putting the ancient brass key on the kitchen table. They could hear the sounds of a television laugh track coming from upstairs and the occasional patter of small feet overhead. Stafford looked around for a coffee pot while the sheriff shucked his hat and coat and extracted the big revolver from his holster.

"Looking for coffee makings?" the sheriff asked. "Perk pot's in there. Coffee's in the fridge."

"You must spend some time here," Stafford said as he went to prepare a pot of coffee. Then he thought about the question his comment implied. The sheriff was giving him an amused look when he finally had the percolator set up and bubbling. Stafford was once again struck by the sheriff's appearance: the tall, rangy body of a lumberjack, with that young-old face, the grayish white hair contrasting with the heavy black eyebrows, and that Wyatt Earp mustache. He wondered how old the sheriff really was.

"We were married when she came back from the university," the sheriff said, easing his tall frame into a kitchen chair. "I think that was one of the things that screwed it all up in the end. She got out of Graniteville, got an education. I never did."

"But she came back."

"Hill country does that to young folk," the sheriff said. "Either they fly out of the mountains and never come back or they can't leave for very long. We'd been dating in high school. I was something of a football star, and Gwen, well . . . even now she'll turn your damn head straight around, you just walkin' by."

Stafford nodded but was careful to say nothing, realizing that the sheriff had decided to get something into the open.

"I went to work for the county force soon's I graduated and Gwen left for college. By the time she came home to teach, I was senior deputy. A year later, old man Slater—he was the sheriff then—he up and died at his desk, and I took over. Ran for the election the next year, never looked back."

The percolator stopped making its noises. Stafford found two mugs in the pantry and filled them. He gave one to the sheriff and sat back down to listen.

"We got married the year I was elected. She was living here at the time, but it was a mite awkward, with the doc's new wife and all."

"That was Hope?"

The sheriff eyed him across his coffee mug. "She tell you about all that?"

"Yes."

"She tell you her momma died? That the old doc remarried a couple years later?"

"Yes, that's right."

The sheriff nodded and blew on his coffee. "Not quite how it happened," he said. Her momma went crazy. It took a while, but by the time she took bad, everyone knew it. Especially old Doc Hand. He had to take her down to Milledgeville in 1974. She died there from some stupid little infection that they never caught. Some flu that got away from 'em."

"And then Hope ends up the same way?"

"Yup. After blowing away two of her kids with Doc's twelve-gauge, and then tearing off her own arm trying to kill herself. Which lovely scene I got to investigate."

Stafford shook his head in wonder. "Come visit the nice peaceful north Georgia mountains," he said. "Relax, take your pack off, listen to the gunfire."

The sheriff nodded absently but did not reply.

"You lived here?"

"No, sir," the sheriff said with a touch of pride. "Don't much hold with the idea of a man not providing a house and home for his own family. No, we lived across town, near the quarry. She came out here every day, and I usually came here for lunch. Other than what family did to family, it's not like we had or have a big crime problem up here."

Stafford nodded. So what led to the affair? he wanted to ask, but he knew better than to do that. The sheriff was staring down into his coffee cup as if looking for the answer to the riddle of the universe. "See, like I said, I never left Graniteville," he said again. "I was a local success story. Everybody knew me from high school days. My classmates in high school, the ones who stayed, were now the citizens. I was the

279

youngest sheriff in the state. Big man on campus, 'cept'n this wasn't no campus." He looked up at Stafford and there was a blaze of pain in his eyes.

"You had an affair," Stafford said.

The sheriff nodded slowly, the expression on his face a mask of regret. "Yes, I did. It didn't start out to be one, mind you. But Gwen and I were having some problems—over whether or not to have our own kids—and I began to spend time with another woman, a woman I had dated back while Gwen was away at college. For six months or so, it was just that: spending time, getting sympathy. Then one afternoon it became something else, and I became the biggest damn fool on the face of the planet."

"She found out."

"She found out. Like I said, we'd been having a touch of trouble anyway: I wanted kids. She, for reasons I didn't understand at the time, said she wanted to wait. It wasn't what I'd call serious trouble, mind you, but sufficient for me to justify seeking a sympathetic shoulder, or so I thought, anyways. But, yes, she found out."

"Someone tell her? Small-town grapevine?"

"I don't think so. Gwen just had a habit of knowing things. Still does."

Stafford nodded. He didn't know what to say, so he asked a question about Gwen's reluctance to have kids.

"We'd been married seven years when the trouble with Hope came to a head. Hope didn't just rise up and do that: For the two, three years before that, Gwen had kinda become mother to Hope's kids, especially when Hope wandered off the planet. It was real tough on the Doc, tough on everybody. And after that night, Jess, who was the baby, came to live with us."

"So suddenly, you did have a child."

"That's it. Course, I didn't see it that way. Bein' not too damn bright, it took me many years to figure out the real reason."

"Which was?"

"Old Doc Hand marrying up his new, young, and, eventually, insane wife, Hope."

"I don't understand."

"Hope was related to Carrie, Gwen's mother."

At first Stafford didn't see it. And then he did. "Ah," he said.

"Yeah. Gwen's own mother, then Hope. And, of course, before that,

Hope's older sister, Charity, the one who went flying with her unseen companions at the flooded quarry."

Stafford sipped his coffee for a few minutes. "And now there's Jess."

"That's right. Now there's Jess. Who we hope like hell really is a psychic, and not—"

Stafford nodded again. There was no future in it, Gwen had said. Because of the madness. Her own mother, her mother's relatives, and now possibly her half sister. Gwinette Hand Warren had decided never, ever to have children, and when she had decided that a long time ago, her husband had sought the comfort of another woman. No future in that, either. Damn.

"That explains a lot," Stafford said. "I guess what I find curious is your relationship now. You're obviously friends; you obviously still care very much for her. See, my wife divorced me this past year. Ran off with some Air Force guy. I could never see myself in the same room with her ever again."

The sheriff nodded. "Gwen told me something about that." He looked up at Stafford, who was surprised to hear this. "Oh, yes, she did. I think I'm more like her big brother now than her ex-husband. We've known each other since we were kids, and then almost eight years as man and wife, and for ten years since." He sighed. "The plain fact is that I was the one who screwed that one up. She could forgive me for it, but she couldn't be my wife anymore. So what we've got now is the best I can make of a poor-ass situation. That I created. I take what I can get."

"You never remarried."

"Nope. After Gwen found out, she went to see the other woman. Told her she was going to leave me. That if we wanted to get married after that, it would be all right with her. Was as nice and sweet as she could be."

"Ouch."

"Yeah, buddy. When I went to see her after that little session, she told me she couldn't marry me, because if I couldn't be faithful to such a good woman as Gwen, I'd never be faithful to her. Always some truth to that notion, I reckon. So that was that. I figured life didn't have to go hittin' me between the eyes with an ax handle more'n once to teach me a lesson."

Stafford smiled ruefully across the table at this complex man. He wondered if he would ever get the chance to reach such an equilibrium in his own tattered personal life. He had hoped, assumed, really, that there was something developing between himself and Gwen Warren, but now he knew better. Gwen was being kind and sympathetic, but that was all. He was the one who was infatuated with her, but after hearing the full story of her life, he could well imagine that she, like John Lee, had decided not to let life swing any more ax handles at her, either. The sheriff had sensed what was developing, and he had decided to let him down easy.

He concentrated on his coffee. There were sounds of a juvenile altercation upstairs, which ended with a single sharp word from Mrs. Benning. He looked at his watch. Just about an hour to go.

▬ TUESDAY, VERNON CREEK CABINS, 6:15 P.M.

Carson was sitting outside, which seemed to help his headache, when he decided he needed something to eat. Stafford had promised that the cops would leave him alone. Maybe there was one of those fancy mountain-lodge restaurants nearby. For a moment he pictured a large wood-paneled dining room with white tablecloths, quiet, polite waiters, and a good wine list. He even went in and checked his cash and saw that he had plenty of money. Then he saw his reflection in the bathroom mirror through the open doorway. His face looked puffy, and there were pronounced pouches under his eyes. His hair was damp and matted. Yeah, right, let's go to a fancy restaurant. His stomach brought him further back to reality with another wave of nausea.

Getting a little spaced-out here, he thought. You don't need to eat. You need a drink. That's it. A brandy. A slug of whiskey. Something to keep me going, stiffen my spine. That hillbilly cabin manager, he'll have some whiskey. All these mountain guys are serious boozers. He'll have a jug up in that office. Just have to go up there. He looked out the window at the sloping gravel driveway, which seemed to tilt a little as he stared at it. Don't remember it being that steep. Just have to walk up there. Yeah, right.

He sat down heavily on the edge of the bed, wanting desperately to lie down and sleep for a while. No way, he thought immediately. You lie down now and you won't get up. He forced himself to get back off the bed, carefully, doing it in stages so as not to provoke the pain monster sitting on his back. He had tried to change the bandage, but by then it had been stuck in place, and he was afraid of opening up a

282

scab and starting more damned bleeding. There were shooting pains in his upper arms now, and he was suddenly very thirsty. He remembered that the manager had bottled water for sale to the hikers. That's what you need. Not whiskey. You need water.

He went out to the truck and looked up the hill. It hurt to crane his neck even a little. Damn driveway definitely looks steeper than it did before. Loose gravel, too. Can't afford to fall. So take the truck, dumb shit. He pulled himself into the truck, closed the door, started it, and drove it up to the office cabin, the engine complaining in first gear. Just to be safe, he parked it below the crest of the driveway entrance, just out of sight of the road. He was opening the truck door and turning carefully in his seat to get out when he heard a powerful vehicle coming up the mountain road to his left. He stopped to listen. Make that a couple of vehicles, he thought.

Some instinct made him hesitate. He pulled his door closed to extinguish the cabin light, then pulled the ball cap down over his face a little. He leaned sideways in the driver's seat, not wanting to touch the seat with his back. Then he waited, fighting his hot lungs a little bit for breath. A minute later he saw two large green Suburbans come whipping by the driveway.

Green. He recognized that color, even in the twilight. That was Army fucking green. His heart started to beat faster. Unmistakable. Army fucking green. Just like his pickup truck, complete with white serial numbers and two whip antennas on the back. Front vehicle with three, maybe four people in it; the back vehicle had more riders and a bunch of gear. The Suburbans roared past the driveway and disappeared around a curve up the road. Toward Graniteville.

Carson exhaled and pushed the cap back on his head. That *fucking* Stafford! 'I've got the deal. There's an FBI team coming up with the paper. I expect them by eight o'clock.' Lies. All lies. He called the damned Army instead, just like he did before.

Those were Special Forces on their way to set something nasty up in that courthouse square. Gun him down the moment he stepped out of his truck, with the connivance of some damned ruthless Georgia sheriff. He swore even harder when he realized he was trembling. Then he realized he was wrong: They wouldn't just shoot him down. They had to have the cylinder first, so they'd capture him and take him out into the woods and rip his fingernails out or something until he told them where it was. Right. That had to be the game.

He looked at his watch. He squinted in the low light until he remembered there was a light button on it. It was almost six-thirty. By the so-called plan, he had less than two hours, during which time the cops supposedly had been told not to mess with him. Time enough to do something, but what? He closed his eyes, trying hard to make his brain work. His overheated, feverish brain. Can't think, that's my problem. This is bad shit here, but I have to *do* something. Can't just let them take me down like a dog. And I want that bastard Stafford.

He reached into the glove compartment and found the bottle of Advil. He swallowed three of the sugar-coated pills, then really wanted that bottled water. Stafford, he thought feverishly. Lying through his teeth. Graniteville is a trap.

Graniteville. Graniteville. Why did he remember that name? He squeezed his eyes shut and thought hard. Fragmentary images swam across his brain.

Graniteville.

Why was Stafford in Graniteville?

And then it hit him. The black-haired woman at the airport. That child with those borescope eyes. His fainting in the baggage-claim area. A real chill swept over him, because he knew what was coming next. "No, no," he murmured as he tried to open his eyes, but it was as if they were glued shut, and he was back in the dream, in that vast river. With all those people. All those lost souls. Sweeping down toward the falls. *That's* how Stafford had known. Somehow the *girl* had seen it. Those piercing eyes, the dream, his passing out in the airport. It was the *girl*. She'd told her mother or whoever that woman was, and the woman had told Stafford. That's why Stafford had gone to Graniteville, and that's why he was in Graniteville now instead of in Atlanta: Stafford was just the messenger. The *girl* was the witness!

If that was true, then his plan to implicate Stafford wouldn't work, not as long as she was alive. Well, hell, he thought, she's just down the damned road. That Willow Grove Home. How hard could this be? But first he had to get a drink of water. Any damned water. Then he needed a map. There had to be more than one road into Graniteville besides this one.

Stafford put a jacket on this time when he went out with the sheriff to check the grounds. The skies had cleared somewhat and there was more starlight, which ended abruptly where the mountains created their own high horizon. They made one circuit of the yard, the pond, both groves, and the barn area. They walked quietly, the sheriff smoking another cigarette, and Stafford thinking about what the sheriff had told him. They were headed back toward the side of the house from the barns when the sheriff stopped and put his hand up in the air, signaling for silence.

"Listen," he said.

Stafford listened, and he heard it immediately—the sound of a large vehicle climbing the mountain road that ran in front of the house. No, not one, but two vehicles. Powerful engines, but not trucks. He thought he recognized the sound. "Those sound like Army vehicles," he said softly. "What the hell are they doing here? I thought it was just to be the FBI."

"It was," the sheriff declared, dropping and mashing out his cigarette. Together they walked around the pond side of the house as the Suburbans slowed down out on the road and then turned into the driveway, their headlights on bright, momentarily blinding both men. The vehicles came up the driveway and then turned into the circle, parking in an echelon next to the sheriff's car before shutting down. Stafford recognized the shape of the tall man getting out of the lead vehicle.

"Mr. Stafford," the general said. "We meet again."

"General Carrothers, I presume," Stafford replied. "This is John Lee Warren, the sheriff of Longstreet County."

Carrothers approached, his combat boots crunching on the pea gravel of the driveway, and shook the sheriff's hand. He was about an inch taller than the sheriff, and the two big men sized each other up for a second as they shook hands. Stafford explained who Carrothers was.

"We weren't expecting the Army," Stafford said. "You're not really part of the deal. In fact, if Carson—"

"Deal?" interrupted Carrothers. "What deal?"

"Ray Sparks didn't tell you? Carson called me. He's agreed to turn himself in. As soon as he's convinced he's physically safe, he'll turn over the cylinder. Or tell the FBI where it is."

The general exhaled softly. "Son of a bitch. No, I was not told."

"Well, your being here is a complication. Carson's scared shitless you guys are out to kill him. He sees these vehicles, he says the deal is off. He's supposed to come in at eight. That's about thirty minutes from right now."

"He's coming *here*?"

"No. Into Graniteville. At eight."

The phone in the sheriff's car began to chirp. The sheriff went across, opened the driver's door, and picked it up. He listened, spoke for a minute, and then hung it up. "The FBI's here, General. I told them you were here. Some guy named Kiesling wants you to call him. He sounded some agitated."

"I don't care to talk to him just now, Sheriff," Carrothers said.

"Well, then, what do you say we stash you and your vehicles up at the quarry above town. You'll be close by but out of sight. You got radios in those things?"

"Yes, of course."

"Then I suggest you hurry," Stafford said. "I'm going to stay right here while the deal goes down."

"Why?" Carrothers asked. "If he called you, I'd think he'd want you there."

"He did. But I don't trust him or the FBI. I believe I know more about this little mess than is healthy for me."

"You're a very perceptive man, Mr. Stafford," Carrothers said. "I came here to talk to you, but I guess we'd better get going. Later, perhaps."

Stafford nodded. The sheriff and Carrothers got back into their respective vehicles and they all drove off. The sudden silence was almost deafening. Stafford sat down on the front steps of the big house and listened to the assorted vehicles go humming down the road back toward town. If the plan works, he thought, this whole mess ought to be over in about forty minutes.

He looked up at the bright stars twinkling along the ridgeline of the mountain across the road. Now that the vehicles were gone, he could hear the night sounds from the willow grove, dominated by a chorus of peepers serenading the pond. There was quite a bit of starlight in the clear mountain air, and he could see surprisingly well. It was a very romantic setting, leading him to wonder where Gwen was. Safe, from all appearances, among her people, who could never be his people. A large mosquito banked noisily past his right ear, and he slapped the air. So much for the romance, he decided, and got up to go back into the house.

Wendell Carson watched from the edge of the pecan grove as the Army vehicles and the sheriff's car left Willow Grove. He was crouched down behind a tumbling-down stone wall, about fifty feet in from the pavement. His truck was parked a quarter mile back up the road, hidden in some trees on the opposite side of the highway.

It was exactly as he had thought. No FBI. Just those damned Army goons, being helped by the sheriff. He hadn't been able to see too clearly in the darkness, but the third man standing by the cars had to have been Stafford. Everything Stafford had told him about the FBI and their deal had been a lie. He nodded to himself in satisfaction. Thought they'd put one over on old Wendell Carson, but he'd figured it out. The question now was what to do about it. He shifted his position behind the wall to try to ease the pain. The muscles in his upper back now felt like football pads, swollen, hard and tender all at the same time. He'd taken more Advil to keep the feverish headache at bay, and he'd used up all but one of the six-pack of bottled water he'd swiped from the cabin office before he left. And still he was thirsty.

It was so hard to think. Every time he tried to arrange his mind, the pain in his back and his head intruded. He was perspiring, even though the surrounding night air was almost cold. His clothes stank and he stank. He'd tried a shower in the cabin and had ended up nearly falling out of the tub. He tried to resurrect the plan. Turn himself in. Verify the government's deal. Tell them where the cylinder was, which right now was in the back of the truck in its cooler. Implicate Stafford in the theft of the cylinder.

But Stafford had lied. There was no deal waiting for him down there in Graniteville. Just the Army, waiting in ambush for him to show his face, which they would then proceed to blow off. They wanted the cylinder, and they wanted it in secret. He exhaled a long, hot breath. He was sick, his body probably infected by the untreated bullet wound. He did not want to die out here in the woods like some gut-shot deer for this damned thing, but that's what was going to happen unless he did something. The Army was waiting for him in town. Once they figured out he wasn't coming, what would they do?

He closed and opened his eyes. He had no idea of what they would do. He had no idea of what the hell *he* should do. He looked over at the house. It was a school and an orphanage. There were lights on upstairs, which meant there were kids in there. Stafford had stayed behind. Suppose he went in there, got the drop on Stafford, took the place hostage. Threatened to open the cylinder. Then called—who? The sheriff? No, he was in league with the Army. Better: Threaten to call the media, some Atlanta television station, unless the Army backed out and the FBI came back into the picture to make the deal Stafford had promised him. Yes, that was right, that was his leverage: The Army couldn't stand any publicity. Take some hostages, threaten to tell the media, and if they tried some shit, threaten to shoot a kid or open the cylinder. Get a hundred cops and three TV trucks up here, and then let them find out the bad guy inside had a nerve-gas bomb.

The question was, Could he *do* any of those things? Shoot a kid? Open the cylinder? He didn't think he could, but then again, they couldn't know that, and they'd have to assume he could and would. What he did know was that he didn't have much time.

He looked back over the wall at the big house. The front porch lights were on, and there appeared to be lights on in the back, maybe in a kitchen area. There didn't appear to be any dogs. Stafford was in there, and some kids upstairs. Maybe a nurse or someone to take care of the kids. How many kids? Doesn't matter. Stafford matters. Going in circles here. So go get the cylinder. Then creep over there, find Stafford, and go surprise his ass. He straightened up and his back shot lines of fire up and down his spine. Go fast, he thought, staggering a little. James Bond you are not. Go fast while you still can.

The phone in the kitchen rang at quarter to nine. It was the sheriff. "He's a definite no-show," Warren announced.

"Damn," Stafford replied. "The Bureau people were there on time?"

"Oh yeah. Three cars' worth. Coats and ties, real stern faces, the whole bit. They're not happy. The boss man thinks you are not Mr. Clean."

"Yeah, well, Ray warned me about that. They being civil?"

"In a manner of speakin'. They say 'sir' a lot."

Stafford laughed. "Well," he said. "I don't know what to do but wait. I think he meant it—about coming in. He knows that cylinder is all he's got to trade."

"Okay. They're all set up outside. He shows, they'll take him, and from the way they're actin', he better not twitch a whole lot. We'll wait some more, but these feds want to start the statewide search up again."

"I can understand that," Stafford said. "They know the Army's there?"

"Yeah. I told them. The Army's been waiting up at the rock quarry. They've been calling, too. The general's on his way down here now."

"Okay," Stafford said. "Carson contacts me here, I'll let you know immediately."

"Everything okay there?" the sheriff asked casually.

"You mean is Carson here with a gun at my head? No such luck. No, all's quiet here."

They hung up and Stafford went to make some more coffee. That dumb bastard was going to screw this thing up. He wondered again about the weakness in Carson's voice, and whether or not he'd been injured. He also did not like the sounds of the FBI thinking he was part of this, especially now that Carson was a no-show.

■■■ TUESDAY, THE SHERIFF'S OFFICE, GRANITEVILLE, GEORGIA, 9:00 P.M.

Carrothers walked into the sheriff's office just as Warren was hanging up the phone. The senior FBI man, Kiesling, came in right behind him. He still looked unhappy.

"So where the hell is he?" Carrothers asked.

"Anybody's guess," Kiesling said disgustedly. "I thought the deal was that you were going to stay at Fort Gillem, General."

"I received new orders," Carrothers said. "The Pentagon wanted me to talk to Stafford."

"You could have told me. I still think our boy Stafford is fucking with us."

"To what end?" Carrothers interrupted. "If he were part of this, he'd be long gone with Carson and your money, not sitting up here talking to us on the phone."

Kiesling frowned, then went back out the door to check on his people in the square. The sheriff explained that there were three cars out there, each with two agents, positioned to close in on Carson as soon as he showed up. Carrothers noticed that the sheriff was standing at his desk, looking distractedly at the phone.

"What?" Carrothers asked.

"Something Stafford just said. I asked him if everything was okay out there at Willow Grove. And he said, 'You mean is Carson here with a gun at my head? No such luck.' "

"Maybe he was just being funny. He's out there by himself, right?"

"Effectively. One of the night nurses is there, plus the kids, of course."

"Is there any reason Carson would go there?"

The sheriff gave him a studied look from underneath those huge black brows. Carrothers though the sheriff appeared to be about the same age as he was, but with a much better poker face. "Not that I can think of," the sheriff replied finally. "You want some coffee, General?"

"Yes, please," Carrothers said almost automatically. He was living on caffeine these days. They walked out into the hall, where the coffeepot was. The offices along the hallway were darkened except for the deputies' dayroom. "How much have the FBI told you about this business, Sheriff?"

"Not very much a-tall," the sheriff said. "Although that is their style. But basically this Wendell Carson is supposedly a bad guy, armed and dangerous, and he's got something the government wants back, and the government's willing to deal. That about it?"

"Yeah, that's about it," Carrothers said, wanting to tell the sheriff the whole story but remembering his orders. Right now, only Kiesling, Sparks, and Stafford knew what Carson was carrying.

The sheriff was giving him a peculiar look, as if he was trying to decide something. Then he nodded to himself. "That is total bullshit, I do believe," he said matter-of-factly. "I believe the real story is that this Carson's run off with a container of some kind of Army nerve gas, which Mr. Stafford learned about with the help of one of the children out there at Willow Grove—a girl who is a psychic. And the reason Carson might go there instead of here is to silence that little girl, along with Mr. Stafford. Now, is *that* about it, General?"

Carrothers didn't know what to say. He just stared at the sheriff for a moment, looked up and down the empty hallway to make sure no one had been listening, and then nodded. "Almost," he said, and then told him of the FBI's role in Carson's original attempts to sell the cylinder.

The sheriff grinned and shook his head when he heard that story. "Now there's federal screwup of the first water for you," he said. "First y'all misplace this thing, then a government employee steals it and tries

290

to sell it to the FBI, who keeps it a secret from you? Ain't no wonder the bad guys are doing so well these days."

Carrothers could only nod his head.

"And both of you have to get this thing back. You can't admit you lost one, and the FBI can't admit that their guy had a hand in Carson getting loose with it, right?"

"Plus the fact that they lost a guy during the incident at Fort Gillem."

The sheriff stopped grinning. "They did? Tell me, does Stafford know that? Or about the Bureau's role in the original scheme?"

"Not to my knowledge. Stafford tried to warn us that Carson had it. Told his boss first, then even told me. We didn't listen so good. Problem was, nobody could figure out how he could know about it until his boss, Sparks, told us about the girl. That was after Carson got away, of course."

"The girl, yes," the sheriff said softly, sinking back down into his desk chair. "See, we were all sort of worried that this thing might come here to Graniteville. So earlier tonight, we sent the girl off with the lady who runs the school, Gwen Warren. She's my ex-wife, by the way."

"Where did you send her?"

"Somewhere safe, General," the sheriff said, giving him a look that said, That's all I'm going to tell you. "So if Carson is going up to Willow Grove, he's going to be disappointed."

"But he can get to Stafford. And he may very well want to."

The sheriff thought about that for a moment. "Yes," he said. "He could get to Stafford. You know, I don't like the way he talked about having a gun at his head when I talked to him. I think I'm going to take a quiet ride out there. Have me a look-see."

"Nothing beats personal reconnaissance, Sheriff. In the meantime, we wait some more, I suppose." And try to mollify Kiesling and his troops, he thought. Kiesling had undoubtedly already called the Justice Department to report Carrothers's presence in Graniteville. Need to do some damage control there.

"Yes, sir, General, that's what I'd recommend. I was you, I'd keep your people out of sight up at that quarry and let the FBI take him. They want him pretty bad."

Carrothers was getting worried about that. Based on the way Kiesling was acting, the FBI wanted Carson in a body bag. As probably did General Waddell.

Carson did not approach the house directly. He had gone back to the truck, retrieved the cylinder, and put it in a bag. He got his revolver, finished the last of his water, and then made his way along the stone wall that paralleled the state road. He hesitated when he reached the eastern property line, but then he decided to stick to the road, go all the way across the front of the school, and then cut across that low dam into the dense stand of willow trees on the other side of the pond. The willows would give him much better cover to approach the house than the widely spaced pecan trees on the other side. It took him fifteen minutes to cross over in front of the house, get up and across the dam, and make his way through the willows until he was parallel with the back of the house. He could see what looked like kitchen windows, but he needed to get closer to see if Stafford was in there. He also discovered a problem as he pushed through the dense willow branches: He was on the wrong side of the creek that fed the pond. Where he was standing, it was nearly ten feet across, and, although it didn't look deep, the ravine it had cut over the years offered very steep banks. He didn't think he could get down and back up those banks with his back the way it was.

Now what? he thought wearily, trying to focus. I've got to get over this creek to the yard. He wondered if there was a bridge farther upstream, but the thought of pushing through more of the willow branches deterred him: It had been hard, sweaty work getting this far in the dark, and the branches were full of biting insects. He was having trouble enough concentrating as it was. Okay, he thought, so go back to the dam. Come up the main drive, keeping in the shadow of the line of trees that borders the drive. Not as good cover as the willows, but better than this.

He rested for a few minutes, absorbing the night sounds while he got his breath back, and then started back the way he had come, toward the road, pushing the swaying branches out of his face and fending off the squadrons of bugs he was stirring up. He kept losing his way, and twice he had to retrace his steps until he found the pond. Keep the pond on your left, and you'll hit the dam and the road, he told himself. He was sweating profusely now in the clammy air around the pond. He had just about reached the edge of the dam when he stopped to catch his breath. It was then he heard a distinctive noise: a car door being closed, out there on the road.

He froze and listened hard. At first there was nothing but the sound of his own heartbeat in his ears. How had a vehicle come up that road without his hearing it? The willow branches, he realized. All those branches in his face and ears had masked the sound. Especially if someone was trying to be quiet. Then he heard another sound, of someone on the other side of the dam pushing his way through the stand of willows over there. Not in a hurry. Deliberate movements, interspersed with moments of silence.

He's listening before he moves, Carson thought, like I should have been doing. He put the bag carefully down in the grass and pulled out his revolver. There was a mass of greenery right next to the edge of the dam, and he sank down into it, on his knees, trying not to grunt aloud as the shooting pains lit up his back again. Insects whined in his ears, but he ignored them. From his position, he could see clearly across the top of the dam, a space of about twenty feet.

He waited, feeling his back and legs getting stiff. After a few minutes, he heard the unseen intruder pushing through the final willow tree right before the dam, and then he saw a tall gray-haired figure step onto the top of the dam and start across. When the man was halfway across, Carson rose from his hiding place, which was when he saw the star on the other man's chest.

"That's far enough," he announced, and the sheriff froze, his hands at his side.

"And you must be the famous Mr. Carson," the sheriff said. The top of the concrete dam was about a foot and half wide, but the sheriff seemed to have no problem balancing on it. To the sheriff's right was the still black surface of the pond; to his left, a drop of about ten feet down into a pool. The sheriff stood right in front of a shallow channel that had been notched into the middle of the dam to let the overflow drop into the pool below. Carson checked over his left shoulder, but the lights from the house were barely visible through the branches of one large willow tree.

"That's right. Where'd you leave the Army?"

"The Army? They're up at the rock quarry, waiting for the FBI guys to tell them where to find the weapon."

"What FBI guys?"

"The ones you were supposed to turn yourself into, Mr. Carson. They're down at my office in the courthouse."

"I don't believe you. There's just the Army. Stafford was lying. You're all lying."

The sheriff slowly raised his right hand and slapped a mosquito on his cheek, prompting Carson to lift the barrel of his revolver. The gun was beginning to feel very heavy in his hand. The sheriff put his hand back down, and Carson noticed that somehow he had managed to undo the safety strap on his sidearm.

"No, he wasn't," the sheriff said. "I've got a whole passel of feds drinking my coffee and calling you names down there right now. We've got the lawyer laid on and everything. You come in with me, we can get this thing done. Ain't no need for any trouble."

Carson shook his head, wincing. He wasn't going to be fooled again. If everything was the way the sheriff was describing, what was the sheriff doing here? Creeping around in the bushes? He asked the sheriff that question.

"Because I called Mr. Stafford a few minutes ago. Asked him if he'd heard from you, because you hadn't shown up in town. Asked him if everything was okay here. He said something about your holding a gun to his head and then said everything was fine. Didn't sound right, so I came to take a look."

"Alone?"

The sheriff glanced to his left into the dark woods. "Yep. All alone," he said.

Carson moved a little to put a tree trunk between him and any helpers the sheriff might have out there on the road or in the woods. But then he realized the sheriff was bluffing.

"Take your gun out of that holster and drop it in the pond," he ordered.

The sheriff gave him a long, flat look, and Carson raised the barrel of his revolver again. "It's only about fifteen feet," he said. "Even I can hit you at fifteen feet."

The sheriff continued to look at him, his hand now dangling very close to the butt of his sidearm. "Yeah, Mr. Carson, you might get lucky and hit me. But I wonder whether or not you can actually shoot some-one. That's harder than it looks on the TV. Specially when the other fella is bringin' up a forty-five at the same time. Besides, you don't sound so good to me. You're weavin' around a little bit, and your voice sounds a mite strained. I'm thinkin' this might be a pretty even contest. 'Cause I *know* I can hit you at fifteen feet."

"Pull it out with two fingers and drop it in the pond," Carson said, steadying his right hand with his left, the way he'd seen shooters do in magazines. His mouth was dry and the pounding in his head had accelerated dangerously. A small breeze rippled across the pond. Carson cocked his revolver and pointed it right at the sheriff's midsection. "Do it, Sheriff."

The sheriff put two fingers on the butt of the automatic, paused for a long moment, and then lifted it out of the holster. He bent and dropped it onto the concrete, but it did not go over the edge. He looked at it for a second and then continued to bend down slowly.

"Use your foot!" Carson barked, but the sheriff kept reaching down. At the last moment, he nudged the big weapon over the edge with his knuckles, where it went into the pond with scarcely a sound. Carson, who had been holding his breath, started to relax, until he saw the glint of metal in the sheriff's right hand as he brought up the ankle gun. Carson did not hesitate: He pulled the trigger and the .38 bucked in his hand with a flash of red light that momentarily blinded him. He heard the big man grunt and then there was a sliding noise as the sheriff went over the road side of the dam, tumbling down the sloped surface of the concrete and entering the pool with a heavy splash. Carson knelt down at the edge of the dam and scanned the surface of the pool, but there were only small waves and ripples, and then silence in the black water below. He noticed there was a dark smear running vertically down the face of the dam, but the overflow stream was already washing it away.

He stood up, his heart pounding, and backed farther into the bushes to retrieve the bag with the cylinder. The smell of gunpowder was very strong in the close branches of the willow trees. His ears still rang, and he realized he had a death grip on the butt of the .38. He stuffed the gun in his waistband, conscious of the warm barrel against his belly. He couldn't believe what he'd done: He'd killed a policeman. The pain in his back forgotten for the moment, he grabbed the bag and pushed hurriedly across the dam. He broke out of the willows and, gasping for breath, began to run across the lawn toward the side of the house.

Stafford jumped up out of his chair in the kitchen when he heard the gunshot, spilling some coffee onto the table. It had sounded as if it had come from across the pond. He listened for a moment, then reached for the phone. He didn't know the sheriff's office phone number, so he dialed 911. A woman's voice answered, asking in a twangy southern accent what his emergency was.

"Gunshots at the Willow Grove Home," he shouted. "Get Sheriff Warren up here!"

He slammed down the phone and looked hurriedly around the kitchen for a shotgun, or any other kind of weapon. But he knew that if they had anything, it wouldn't be out where he or the kids could ever find it. From upstairs, Mrs. Benning's voice called down to him, asking what that noise was.

"Stay upstairs, Mrs. Benning," he called. "Keep the kids up there with you until I tell you differently. I'm going to see what that was. I've called the sheriff."

He turned out the lights in the kitchen and then those in the front hall. The front door was open, but he couldn't see anything outside because of the front porch lights. He finally found the switch for those, turned them off, and then stood just inside the front door, his face near the screen, listening. All he could hear were the night sounds from the pond and the surrounding trees. A gentle breeze stirred the tops of the pecan trees, then slid across the pond and whispered through the willows. He could hear Mrs. Benning moving around upstairs, a door closing, but it didn't sound as if the children were awake. He looked at his watch. Nine-twenty.

He concentrated on the sounds from outside, trying to detect footfalls or any other human noise. The old house made its own night noises as the day's heat finally gave way to the cooler night air. That had definitely been a gunshot, probably a short-barreled .38, from the sound of it. He felt helpless with only one functioning arm and no weapon, although his ability to shoot left-handed was just about nonexistent.

The problem was that this house had too damned many doors and porches. He stepped back into the hallway, gently shut the front door, and locked it. Then he went through to Gwen's part of the house and shut the open French doors leading out to her side porch. He went through to her bedroom, where there were more French doors, which he also shut. Then through the office, with a quick check into the equipment alcove, but there were no doors there. Finally he went back to the enormous kitchen. He'd forgotten to turn out the porch light by the back steps. By that single white light, he could see that there was no one in the kitchen, although the dining area was in shadow. But because of the light, he could not see out into the immediate yard behind the house, nor, for that matter, onto the porch area by the kitchen door. The sheriff had already locked the kitchen door. He stopped just inside the kitchen and listened again, really wishing he had a weapon. But he didn't, so the best he was going to do was to get the doors locked and wait for the 911 call to have an effect.

He stepped across the kitchen, trying not to make any noise, past the huge old woodstove, past the table with the bag on it, past the—He froze.

"Wondered when you'd see it," Carson said from the darkness in the dining area.

Stafford sighed and turned to look in the direction of Carson's voice. He could see the man's shape, sitting in a chair, but nothing else.

"You lied to me, Stafford. You said we had a deal."

"We did have a deal. There're a half dozen FBI guys waiting for you with the sheriff at his office in Graniteville right now, wondering where the hell you are."

"Another lie, you son of a bitch," Carson said, moving slightly so Stafford could see the glint of the revolver in Carson's lap. "The sheriff and I just met up. He wasn't in town. He was sneaking up on the house."

"What happened?"

"He got shot, that's what happened. He went into the pool beneath the dam. I made him get rid of his gun, but he had another one in his boot. Reached for it. He was going to shoot me. It didn't work out."

Dave thought about his 911 call. The FBI would come even if the locals didn't. Except if Carson was telling the truth, the sheriff had already been on his way. He wished he could see Carson's face; the man didn't sound right. He started to move closer, but the sound of a revolver being cocked stopped him.

"That's close enough. I've already shot one cop tonight. He didn't think I had it in me. Hell, *I* didn't think I had it in me. But in for a penny, in for a pound, you know? A second one wouldn't make that big a difference. Now, there's a cylinder in that bag. Take it and put it in that big icebox."

"In the icebox?"

"Just do it. Something's cooking in that little jewel, and I'm not ready for it to pop open. Not yet, anyway. Then get me a phone."

"A phone?"

"There an echo in here? Yeah, a phone. Put it over here on the table, and then sit down right next to it. I want you to get me the number of the NBC affiliate in Atlanta. Wendell Carson's going into the publicity business."

Stafford opened the bag and extracted the heavy cylinder. It looked just like the drawing and the image on the Army monitor. The metal surface was damp and warm. He shivered involuntarily when he realized what he was holding. He opened the oversized refrigerator's door, slid the cylinder in next to a container of milk, and closed the door. He then walked over to where the phone lay on the kitchen counter. When he picked it up, he realized he'd knocked it off the hook when he slammed it down. He replaced the handset and took it over to the dining table. As he got closer, he could see a little more of Carson's face, but not enough to make out an expression. He could hear the man's labored breathing. As Stafford sat down, the phone rang.

"Go ahead, pick it up."

Stafford did. It was the 911 operator, asking for confirmation of his call. Stafford looked over at Carson. "I called nine one one," he told him, tilting the phone so the operator could hear what he was saying to Carson. "What do you want me to tell them?"

"Tell them the truth. Tell them I'm holding you and everyone in this house hostage. Tell them I have a gun and a cylinder full of nerve gas. Tell them anyone tries to get close to the house, I'll start killing kids. If they try to storm the house, I'll open the cylinder, kill everyone in the fucking county. Tell 'em all that; then hang up. I want to use that phone."

The wait for the Atlanta television people had not gone peacefully. A small army of vehicles had assembled on the state road in front of the house, with county sheriff cars, the FBI and their three vehicles, the Army and its vehicles, lots of state police, and some curious would-be onlookers and citizen volunteers from the town milling around down there.

Carson had set the tone for things early on. He'd been furious when he found out Gwen and Jessamine were gone. He'd made Stafford go in front of him in a room-to-room search before believing it. Then the state police had brought up some portable floods, which they placed in the driveway entrance and behind the house to light up the grounds. Once the lights were on, the phone rang. Carson picked it up and told them to turn the light off. The cops said no, and put a hostage negotiator on the line. Carson responded by forcing Mrs. Benning to bring the little kids downstairs. Herding Mrs. Benning and the kids in front of him, he ordered Stafford to go around the first floor and pull all the curtains and shades closed, plunging the interior into total darkness. Then he assembled the kids and Mrs. Benning into their classroom, made them stand in front of the windows, opened the curtains, and turned on the lights so the cops could see them. He had Stafford crack open the front door and then get down on his knees. Over Stafford's head, he fired two rounds down the driveway in the direction of the floodlights. He didn't hit any of the lights, but they apparently got the message and turned them all off.

After that he turned out the lights in the classroom and had Mrs. Benning pull the curtains shut. He sent them all into the parlor across the hall, where he made them lie down on the floor, with orders to stay there, after which, he locked them in. He took Stafford back into the dark kitchen and made him sit in a chair backlit by the porch light. Carson then retired to the shadows at the back of the dining area to await the media's arrival. When the phone rang again, with an FBI negotiator on the line, Carson told them he'd talk to the Atlanta media, and no one else, and that he was going to wait until they showed up. The cops mulled that one over, then called him back and told him they were not going to let the media in. They had hardwired the phone line to the command center in one of their vans, and would await his call.

Stafford had listened to this discussion, and he could just imagine the twelve-monkeys-trying-to-breed-a-football scene that had to be going on down there on the road among the local law, the FBI, the state cops, and the Army. The Army would be shitting little green apples at the thought of the media getting a look at the cylinder, or, worse, Carson trying to open it in an orphanage.

They'd been waiting in the darkened kitchen for over an hour when Stafford asked Carson if he could make some fresh coffee.

"Yes. But first put a pitcher of ice water and a glass over here on the table. No lights and no tricks."

Stafford got him the water, trying to see Carson's face in his corner of the dining area when he opened the icebox door, but Carson remained hidden in the shadows. Stafford had forgotten that he had put the cylinder in the refrigerator. Its stainless steel sides were sweating visibly when he got the ice tray out, and he realized the refrigerator had been running ever since he'd put the cylinder in there. He wondered about that as he went to make coffee.

He had been trying to think of some way to get an advantage over Carson, but nothing brilliant had come to mind. If that was a six-shooter, then Carson should have three rounds left. Or only two, if he practiced the safety precaution of keeping the hammer chamber empty. But in the whole time Carson had been in the house, Stafford had not actually been able to get a direct look at him. All the interior lights in the house were off, and all the blinds and drapes were drawn, making the darkness just about complete, and while Carson could not see out, no sharp-shooter with a night scope could see in, either. Stafford knew the cops outside would not storm the house with the children inside, so somehow, this thing was going to have to run its course. With only one functional arm and no gun, Stafford wasn't going to be much help in any physical sense. He would have to use his brain instead, and that was small comfort.

Carson remained quiet over there in the darkness, his silhouette barely visible at the end of the table. The standoff was beginning to get to Stafford. He desperately wanted to see the man's face, to see if the face matched up with the intense weariness in Carson's voice. More than anything else, he wanted to *do* something. On the other hand, maybe if they just waited, Carson might collapse on his own. As long as he didn't go after the kids. The cops had last called thirty minutes ago, but Carson just picked up the phone and hung it up. Standoff.

When the coffee was ready, he asked Carson if he wanted some.

"No. You stay over there. Sit down. There, where I can see you."

Stafford did as he was told. After a few minutes, he asked Carson what had happened to Bud Lambry. Carson told him.

"Wow. What'd he do—put the squeeze on you? Wanted more money than he'd been getting?"

At first Carson didn't respond. Finally, he did.

"We had us a sweet deal going at that DRMO," he said. "I guess we all got a little greedy when that thing showed up."

"So what are you going to do now?"

"I'm going to wait for the TV people."

"And then what?"

"And then I'm going to put a bullet through your fat head if you don't shut up."

That's perfectly clear, Stafford thought, so he shut up.

Slumping sideways in his chair in the darkness, Carson allowed his eyes to close for just a moment once Stafford had shut his yap down at the other end of the long table. Drinking his fucking coffee. Waiting him out. Well, he could wait until hell froze over, because Wendell Carson wasn't falling for any more of Stafford's tricks. Wendell Carson was running out of time and patience. Those people should have been here by now.

He opened his eyes and blinked several times, regaining his focus. Stafford was still sitting there, in profile to him in the gloom of the darkened kitchen. The fever was bad, and he knew that Advil and water were not going to hack it anymore. The cops had said they weren't going to let him talk to the media, and the cylinder, for all its deadly contents, was as good as useless sitting in the refrigerator over there. If he opened it, he would be the first to experience whatever horror lay inside. He thought about getting one of those kids in here, getting on the phone, and telling the cops he'd start shooting the kids unless they sent a television crew in.

He sighed, unintentionally loudly. Stafford looked over in his direction but kept his mouth shut, as ordered. I can make that threat, Carson thought, but I couldn't do it. He was amazed at what he had done to the sheriff. Bud Lambry had been as close to a case of self-defense as anything, but not shooting the man on the dam. He could have yelled 'Drop it,' or something. But he hadn't. Wendell Carson had aimed at that bastard's midsection and put one right through his heart, like he was some stone-cold killer. He could still hear that mortal grunt, see the dark smear all the way down the face of the dam into the stillness of the pool. And the hell of it was, he didn't feel an ounce of remorse. He didn't feel anything at all about shooting that guy. Just like he didn't feel anything about Tangent's guy on the conveyor belt.

Goddamn, this thing has gotten way out of hand, thanks mostly to this piece of shit sitting down the table from me. And that damned weird girl. Twenty-four hours ago, I had my hands on a million bucks and a whole new life in front of me. Now? Now I'm fucked. The government is going to win this one. *God,* that pisses me off!

He shifted in his chair, precipitating sharp lances of pain throughout every joint in his body. Time is definitely running out. Can't just let it end with me passing out here in this chair and Stafford calling in the cops. At the very least I'm going to take Stafford with me, and somehow that girl. Suddenly he knew just how to make that happen.

Stafford's stomach was raising hell about all the coffee. The caffeine was keeping him awake, but the acid and stress were churning up his guts. He had been desperately trying to think of something he could do to

301

break the impasse, something that wouldn't get him or the kids killed in the process. He jumped when Carson spoke his name from the darkness.

"All right, Stafford," Carson said, his voice coming out in a hollow croak.

"What?" Stafford said.

Carson slid the phone across the table in Stafford's direction. "Call them. Get whoever's in charge of the Army people on the phone."

"And tell him what?"

"Do it, goddamn it. I'll tell you what to say."

Stafford reached across for the phone and picked it up. A voice answered immediately. "Yes? Wendell?"

"No, it's Stafford. He wants to talk to the Army honcho. That general."

A new voice came on the line. "He can talk to me. No one else."

"Who is this?"

"Kiesling, FBI."

"There are five kids in here, Kiesling. This man isn't up to playing games just now."

"Taking his side, Stafford?"

"I'm the guy with a gun pointed at him. Just get the general, would you, Kiesling? I'm sure he'll let you listen in."

There was silence on the line for a few minutes. "What're they saying?" Carson asked.

"He said you could talk only to him. But I think he's getting the Army guy."

"He'd better."

There was another wait, almost five minutes this time. Then a voice came on the line. "This is General Carrothers."

"Dave Stafford here, General. Stand by one." He looked in Carson's direction. He could make out the white blur of Carson's face, but not his features. "Well?"

"Give me the phone. Carefully. Push it over here."

Stafford leaned forward and pushed the phone across the table as far as he could. Carson told him to sit down in the end chair, away from the phone, and then he got up, very slowly, Stafford noticed, and reached for the phone.

"General? This is Wendell Carson."

Stafford could not longer hear the other side of the conversation, but it wasn't very long.

"Here's the deal, General. You want your little toy back, preferably unopened. I'll give it to you. Then you can disappear into the woods and deny it ever happened. That's what you people want more than anything, right?"

Carson was silent for a moment, and then Stafford saw him nod his head. "Okay, then. But here's the price for that. You bring me the girl—the one that can't speak. You know the one I'm talking about. You bring her with you, and then you'll get your cylinder, the nurse, and the kids. Otherwise, I'm going to open it. Think about how you'll explain that to your superiors, General. And to the public. Call me back when you have the girl."

Stafford heard the phone slam down. "They'll never do that," he said to the figure in the darkness.

"Won't they?" Carson asked. "They get this thing back, and trade two hostages for seven. It's not perfect, but life's not perfect. You watch. This is end game. They'll do it."

"Two hostages?"

"Yeah. I want the girl. I've already got you."

It was Kiesling who briefed Carson's demands to the state and county law-enforcement supervisors in the mobile command center. He didn't specifically mention the cylinder, focusing on the hostages instead. There was a babble of negative reactions around the command van. General Carrothers listened to all the simultaneous opinions, the exclamations of 'No way in hell,' the outraged fulminations of Kiesling's FBI men, and then he quietly excused himself and walked through the cordon of police slouching behind their cars to the other side of the Willow Grove fence. When he had heard that the Atlanta media was inbound, he had ordered his people to break down the stone wall in the adjoining field and drive the military Suburbans up into that field and out of sight behind some trees. Fortunately, the television crews and their antenna-studded trucks were being held back down on the road to Graniteville, about a quarter of a mile from the scene.

Carrothers glanced at his watch. It was now almost three in the morning. With sunrise would come press helicopters, which would spot his vehicles. He wished like hell that sheriff was around, but he had disappeared, and the consensus was that he might have run into Carson. His deputies had been frantically searching the grounds all night, while trying not to be seen from the darkened house.

He reached the Suburbans. The captain came forward in the darkness. The rest of the soldiers were doing what sensible soldiers always do: sleeping in their vehicles. The captain was the only one awake.

"Yes, sir, General," he said, saluting.

"Get the satellite link up, Captain. Get me General Waddell on secure."

Two minutes later, he was patched through to Waddell, and he described the deal that Carson was offering.

"So he definitely has it in the house," Waddell said.

"Sounds like it, sir. He's got Stafford, a night nurse, and five little kids. We give him this girl, we get everybody but Stafford out, and we get the cylinder back. It'll be daylight in three hours or so, and the Atlanta media is already here."

"What have they been told?"

"That there's a wacko holding kids hostage in this orphanage. That we know he has a gun, and that he's claiming to have some nerve gas, which is why the Army is here, although I said we don't really believe he does. Just a precaution."

"What do the civilians on scene say?"

"What you'd expect: No way in hell. The problem is, only the FBI supervisor knows what this thing is *really* all about. The other problem we have is that no one has any idea of where the girl is. She and the woman who runs this place were spirited away by the sheriff, before he disappeared."

"This is the so-called psychic?"

"Yes, sir."

"Has Carson ever seen her?"

"Yes, sir, unfortunately. I had the same idea: Get a female FBI agent in here and send her in. But he knows what she looks like."

At that moment, Agent Kiesling materialized out of the darkness. The captain tried to keep him away from the general, but Carrothers waved him over. "I've got Agent Kiesling here, General. Stand by one, please, sir."

Kiesling stepped close so as not to be overheard. "They've found the sheriff," he said. "He's dead. Heart shot. He was in the creek below the dam."

"Jesus," Carrothers muttered. He had liked the sheriff. "Now what?"

"I've talked to my people in Washington. If we can find that damned girl, they're ready to take his deal. Before daylight and television helicopters, if you take my meaning. But supposedly only the sheriff knows—knew—where they are."

"I think my boss is ready to do the same thing," Carrothers said. "But if Carson killed the sheriff, we'd probably be sending the girl to her death. Not to mention Stafford."

"Why?"

"Because if we retrieve the cylinder and Carson kills them, there's nothing we can do to him. The government can't reveal what this has all been about, and the two witnesses would be dead. So my vote is that we don't do it."

Kiesling glanced over in the direction of the captain to make sure he would not be overheard. "My instructions from the Attorney General's office are to do whatever it takes to get that cylinder back. Whatever it takes. Her understanding is that's the Pentagon's position as well. We get those kids and the cylinder out of there, then we have a new ball game. He shoots his remaining hostages, we'll shoot him down like a dog. But the focus is the cylinder."

Carrothers just looked at him. The FBI man sighed. "Look, Stafford took his chances when he stuck his nose into this thing. I'm sorry about the girl, but she knows something she should not know. Hell, maybe we can give the girl a weapon and she can get it to Stafford."

Carrothers just stared, and Kiesling shrugged. It was weak, and he knew it. Carrothers shook his head and went back on the satellite link to brief General Waddell, who immediately seconded Kiesling's plan. "Find the girl," he ordered. "Take his deal. That cylinder can kill thousands of people, he lets it loose. The SecDef is willing to trade two people—one actually, when you think in terms of innocent civilians— to get that thing back. Do whatever it takes, General. That's why you're there."

"But first we have to find her, General," Carrothers reminded him. If we can't find her, he thought, we can't send her in there. There was a pause on the net.

"I understand, General. But be advised, if you can't find that girl and get her in there before sunrise, we're authorized and prepared to take other measures to neutralize the Wet Eye."

Carrothers felt his heart stop. "Other measures, General? You mean like the DRMO?"

"Precisely, General."

"But there are five—"

"I have those orders from the National Command Authority. This is a weapon of mass destruction. We either get our hands on it or we must ensure its destruction. Do we know that's Carson in there?'

"Yes, sir. They found his truck."

"Then find the girl, General, or get everyone away from that house by sunrise. Waddell off net."

Carrothers looked at the handset in disbelief for a moment before hanging it up. He was sweating despite the cool night air. He told Kiesling what the general had just said. Kiesling looked at his watch and swallowed. "We'd better find that girl," he said.

As they pushed their way back across the wet grass to rejoin the command center, two FBI agents, flashlights swinging, met them at the gap in the stone wall.

"There's a woman down on the Graniteville road," one reported to Kiesling. "Showed up at the police line in some beat-to-shit pickup truck. Says she's the owner of this place. A Mrs. Warren? Wants to talk to whoever's in charge. She has a teenage girl with her."

Kiesling and Carrothers stared at each other and then hurried down to the mobile command center. As they approached the van, they could see Gwen Warren standing by the side doors. The girl was standing a few feet away from her, looking very frightened, her hands jammed into the pockets of her sweater, her eyes enormous. Three Longstreet County deputies were with them, along with two state troopers. The lights from inside the mobile command center spilled out onto the state road, throwing all the faces into garish relief. Under different circumstances, Carrothers thought, the woman would be quite attractive, but now her face is a mask of worry.

"Don't say anything about the sheriff," Carrothers whispered out of the side of his mouth. "He was her ex-husband. According to the deputies, they were still close."

As it turned out, John Lee was Gwen's first question. "Where's John Lee?" she said to Kiesling. "The deputies called. They said there was trouble here. Has something happened to him?"

Kiesling looked at Carrothers, who wasn't sure what to say. Gwen looked from one to the other, and then she saw the expression on the deputies' faces. "Tell me, damn you," she said.

The senior deputy stepped forward and took off his hat. "Sheriff John Lee's dead, Miz Warren. Bastard holed up there in the school shot him, best we can tell. Over by the dam. I'm real sorry, ma'am. We're all *real* damned sorry."

Gwen put a hand to her mouth, her face draining of color as the shock set in. She sat down abruptly on the side step of the van, and Carrothers thought for a moment she was going to be sick. He stepped forward, pushing past Kiesling, and squatted down. "Mrs. Warren? I'm General Carrothers, U.S. Army, ma'am. I'm deeply sorry for your loss. I just met Sheriff Warren. He struck me as a good man."

She nodded but didn't say anything. The girl pushed her way between the men standing around her and sat down next to Gwen, her hands flying in some kind of sign language. Gwen just turned her face, and the girl made a small mewing noise, and then she began to cry. Gwen put an arm around her and held her while she dabbed at her own eyes.

"What is happening here?" she asked finally. Kiesling started to reply, but Carrothers gave him a sign to wait a minute. "Mrs. Warren, may I suggest we take a little walk, ma'am? Bring the girl if you'd like."

Gwen looked up at him, momentarily confused, but then got up and went with Carrothers and Kiesling. They walked through the crowd of policemen standing around parked police cars, going away from the driveway in the direction of the field in which the Army vehicles were parked. The three deputies followed ten feet behind.

When they reached the wall, Gwen sat down again, the girl at her side. Carrothers told her of what had happened that night. He had assumed that since the girl was mute, she was also deaf, but it was obvious as he was talking that she could hear just fine. He was a little nervous when he realized that this must be the psychic. Kiesling said nothing, but he made a show of looking at his watch frequently.

"He's got the kids up there," Carrothers concluded. "And an older woman."

"That would be Mrs. Benning."

"Yes, ma'am," Carrothers said. "And he's got Stafford. He has one gun that we know of, and one other thing." He waited to see if she knew what he was talking about. According to Stafford's boss, she was the one who had brought Stafford into it in the first place.

She looked up at him. She has truly beautiful eyes, he thought. "That thing," she said. "He has that thing with him. The cylinder."

"Yes, ma'am. He does. Mrs. Warren, that 'thing' contains an extremely deadly substance. If that substance gets loose, there is literally no telling how many people in this area might be harmed."

She nodded, as if this wasn't news. "And what does he want?" Her voice sounded dead.

"Something very unreasonable, ma'am," Carrothers said, glancing over at Kiesling. "He's willing to give us the cylinder, the kids, and Mrs. Benning."

"In exchange for?"

"He wants this girl here," Kiesling says. "And he keeps Stafford."

"You've got to be out of your mind," she said, staring rigidly into the darkness.

"Mrs. Warren, we don't—" Kiesling began smoothly, but Carrothers cut him off again.

"I agree with you, Mrs. Warren," he said. "So I'm totally opposed to that course of action. We're trying desperately to think of something else, but we don't have much time, and he's threatening to hurt the kids."

At the mention of the kids, her head snapped up. Kiesling tried to mollify her. "We don't think he'll do that, either, Mrs. Warren. This guy is not a hardened criminal. He's a middle-aged civil servant who got way the hell out of his depth. But we don't think he's the type who could start shooting children."

"Just full-grown sheriffs?" she asked quietly. Kiesling opened his mouth, but then he shut it. She looked back at Carrothers. "What other plan do you people have in mind, General?"

Carrothers hesitated. "We don't, Mrs. Warren. We were hoping you could tell us something about the house, some vulnerability we might exploit. Or maybe I could go in with the girl. I don't know. But we have to do something."

She sighed. "He said he would hurt the kids?"

"Yes, ma'am," Carrothers said, thinking about what he had just offered to do, and wondering where the hell that idea had come from. Kiesling horned in again. "We can also just wait," he said. "We can cut the power to the house, isolate him, make him understand he has zero options here. Wear him down. Talk him down."

"But you can't storm the house, can you?" she said. "Not while he has that *thing* in there."

"There are other measures that could be taken," Carrothers said, looking over her head at Kiesling, and then back at Gwen. "Measures that *will* be taken, if we don't resolve this thing very soon."

"What does that mean?" she said.

Carrothers again did not know how to tell her. He had hoped it wouldn't come to this. "The National Command Authority has authorized the destruction of the house," he said. "My guess is an air strike of some kind at first light. I'm sorry, Mrs. Warren. In its own way, that cylinder is a weapon of mass destruction, not so very different from an atomic weapon. I guess what I'm saying is that the real choice is that the girl goes in, or no one comes out. Again, I volunteer to take her in. Maybe together we—"

"That's no choice at all, General, is it?" she said, standing up, brushing off her clothes. "This is truly wonderful. You people let this monstrosity get loose, John Lee Warren is dead, and now you're willing to snuff out five innocent children and two adults, just like that, to cover your tracks? What's that Army slogan, General? 'Be all you can be'? *Is this all you can be?*"

"Yes, ma'am," Carrothers replied, unable to meet her gaze. Even Kiesling looked embarrassed.

"Well, there is a way to do this. *I'll* take Jessamine in."

"You?" Kiesling said. "But—"

"No, I don't expect you to understand, and according to the general here, we don't have time to discuss it. I will go in with her. You go tell him that. The kids, Mrs. Benning, the cylinder, in exchange for the two of us."

Kiesling looked at Carrothers, shrugged, and headed back toward the command center, calling for his agents to get Carson on the phone again. Carrothers watched him go, then turned back to find both women watching him. Their expressions were disturbingly similar, although the girl looked scared to death, while the woman looked mostly determined. Then he realized what she might have in mind: Take that girl in there, and then the girl was going to do something to Carson. With her mind. He felt a sudden chill of fear, and then a desperate need to know.

"Can she do this?" he asked softly. "It's real?"

There was a flicker of understanding in her eyes, but then she was all business again. "Make your arrangements, General," Gwen said. "Then call us when you're ready. She and I need to talk now. Privately, please."

Carrothers backed away, his throat dry. He tried not to walk any faster than he absolutely had to. He looked at his watch. Not much time. He'd better call the Pentagon, let them know they might again have a deal to get the weapon back. He wondered how he would ever explain all this to Sue. Be all you can be. Jesus H. Christ!

■　　■　　■

Carson hung up the phone and pushed it away. Stafford could hear him do it, but he still could not see much in the darkened room.

"Well, well, well," Carson said. "They're going to do it. They're sending in the girl. With the woman who runs this place, it seems, in place of the general. Suits me. You go get the old woman and those brats into the front hall. Remember: No lights, and don't you try any bullshit. I'll be right behind you and I'll put one through your spine. Then I'll shoot as many kids as I have bullets."

Stafford couldn't believe what he was hearing. It was against all procedures for a hostage situation, which meant they had to be trying something. But why at this hour? Why not wait until daylight? And why Gwen?

"Move it, I said," Carson rasped. He was obviously trying to put some force in his voice, but the weakness was clearly evident. Stafford got up, wondering again why the forces outside didn't simply wait Carson out. Because they don't know something's wrong with him, he realized as he went to the parlor door and called Mrs. Benning. If there was only some way he could communicate with them, but every window in the house was shut up tight. Then he was conscious of Carson standing behind him in the hallway as he waited for Mrs. Benning to get the kids up. Carson told him to unlock the door.

He's got three rounds left, he thought; maybe only two. If I rush him, I might achieve surprise, take him down. He's feverish, and probably weak. I know he is: I can hear it in his voice, see it in the way he's doing everything very slowly. He was standing right next to a chair in the hallway. Maybe wait for the kids to start out, grab the chair and hurl it in Carson's direction, and then charge him. Even if he got shot, Carson might be out of ammo, and the kids could run for it. But would they know to do that? He sighed. And how well could he throw a chair with one arm? Carson was a desperate man, talking about opening that cylinder, shooting the kids. You're the one who ought to be desperate, he thought. Why do you suppose Carson wants you and the girl in here?

He kept trying to think of a plan, any plan. Gwen and the girl were coming in. The kids and Mrs. Benning were being released. That would put three of them in the house with Carson. Three rounds left. But maybe only two. Was there some way to get him to shoot? Get the number of bullets left down to fewer than the people facing him and they could take him. But not without coordinating their action.

Hell, I'm going in circles here, he thought. Just play it as it lies.

"Figured out a move?" Carson asked him in a mocking voice from the end of the dark hallway. "Because I don't think you have one."

The kids came out into hallway, holding hands, their eyes wide. Mrs. Benning came out behind them, encouraging them to move toward the door but to stay together.

"Hold them right there," Carson ordered. They all froze when he spoke. Stafford was standing near the bottom of the steps; he thought he could just make out the kids' faces. Then he heard Carson pick up the hall telephone.

"Okay," he said. "Have the woman and the girl come up the walk to the front door. I want them standing on the porch outside the front door, where I can see them. I want them to ring the doorbell when they're in position." He hung up the phone before the hostage negotiator at the other end could complicate it. "You people stand in front of the door. Stafford, you get down on the floor, facedown. Spread out your arms and legs."

Stafford did as he was ordered, and he thought he felt Carson getting closer, but from his spread-eagled position on the floor, he could not even begin to move without giving Carson plenty of warning. Mrs. Benning herded the kids over in front of the door. Stafford could just see them silhouetted against the glass. Then they waited.

Three minutes later, everyone jumped when the doorbell rang. There was a flare of light out in front of the house, probably from someone pointing a car's headlights up the drive.

"Stafford," Carson said, and Stafford tuned his head to look down the hallway. "Catch this."

Something came sliding across the floor and collided with Stafford's left arm. He reached for it with his left hand. It was Carson's bag.

"Slide it up to the front door. Don't you move; just slide it over there."

Stafford did as he was ordered, sliding the bag like a shuffleboard disk into the small knot of children plastered against the front door. As he did, he realized the bag was too light. Son of a bitch! Was it empty?

"Mrs. Benson, or whatever your name is, pick that up. When I tell you to, step outside and show it to the cops. Then step back in, let the two of them in past you, and then take the kids and the bag and get out of here. Understood?"

"Yes, sir," Mrs. Benning whispered. The kids were dead silent.

"Open the door. Do what I told you to do."

Mrs. Benning tried to open the door, but it was locked. With shaking hands, she unlocked it and opened it. There were two figures silhouetted against the lights coming from the drive. Mrs. Benning stepped out onto the porch and waved the bag around like some kind of signal lamp. Then she stepped back inside.

"You two out there, step in," Carson called out. "Step in and close that door."

Stafford watched helplessly from the floor as Gwen and Jessamine came through the door. He wanted to warn them about the bag, but if he did, Carson might start shooting.

"Now, take those children and the bag and get out of here."

Mrs. Benning did not hesitate, and they were out of the house in a flash.

"Close that door," Carson ordered. Stafford heard the front door close.

"No lights," Carson said. "Stafford, get up. Move back here toward me. All of you. Back toward me, into the kitchen."

Stafford got up slowly off the floor, and then the three of them felt their way along the hallway to the kitchen door. The light was still on out on the back porch, so they could just make out the shapes of the stove and the big refrigerator, the tables and chairs. Carson had backed into his former position at the end of the dining table. He remained in deep shadow.

Stafford could hear the man, but he still couldn't see him, couldn't see his eyes, gauge his readiness. It made it impossible for him to formulate any plan, any course of action. It was maddening. And he had tricked the police outside.

"Sit. All of you."

As they sat down, the phone on the table began to ring. Carson barked out a laugh that ended in a dry, congested cough, but he didn't pick it up. He did something at the end of the table, and then there was a heavy metallic thump. Dave saw the gleam of metal. The cylinder. He'd been right: Carson had kept the damned thing.

"Insurance, that's what this is, so no SWAT team comes lunging through the windows with their stun grenades. Not until I'm done in here."

"You are done in here," Gwen Warren said from her side of the table. Then, to Stafford's amazement, she slid her chair back, reached over her shoulder, and hit the light switch.

"Turn that off!" Carson shrieked, but she ignored him, sitting back down in her chair. When Stafford's eyes adjusted to the sudden brightness and he finally got a look at Carson, he was stunned at what he saw: pale, parchment white face, deep green-black circles under red-rimmed eyes, his hair damp and plastered down on his head like wet weeds, and an angry red swelling like a necklace visible around his neck. The cylinder gleamed malevolently on the table.

Carson stood up in front of his chair, weaving noticeably, and menaced all of them with the gun, a .38 revolver. "I mean it," he yelled. "Turn that fucking light off, or I'll . . . I'll kill all of you! Turn it off!"

"No," Gwen said. "If you're going to kill us anyway, we're going to look you in the eye while you do it."

Carson put his left hand down on the edge of the table to steady himself. Stafford cursed himself mentally for not having made a move earlier: The guy was a wreck, obviously on his last legs. But that gun looked pretty functional. Jessamine sat next to Gwen, staring blankly across the table at the far wall, looking as if she were trying to transport herself somewhere else. Gwen held her hand. Then the phone started ringing again. This time, Carson picked it up.

"What do you *want*?" he screamed into it. He listened for a moment. "Of course I have it." He looked up at Stafford. "My partner changed his mind at the last minute. Said you people would storm the house the moment I sent it out." Another pause. "Stafford. Who else, you fucking idiot? He's been in on this thing from the start. Why the hell do you think he's here? Why the hell do you think he hasn't tried to jump me?" His feverish eyes were gleaming with triumph. "That's right, Mr. FBI Man. All along. See, he was a smart little civil servant. Wanted it both ways, especially when the deal started turning to shit." Another pause. Stafford just stared at him and shook his head. Carson laughed again, a horrible sound. "How else could he have known about the cylinder, Einstein? Don't tell me the FBI believes all that psychic bullshit!" Another silence. "Yes, I have it. What I don't have is my goddamned money. You guys need to ask Stafford about that."

He slammed down the handset, ripped out the wall cord, and pushed the phone onto the floor while he sat down heavily in his chair. He pulled the dripping cylinder over toward himself and rested the barrel of the gun on it.

"I owed you that," he said. "You fucked up the best chance I was ever going to have. You and your little spirit medium there."

When he said the word *spirit*, the girl turned to look at him. Her expression had changed. She no longer looked like some wild animal

313

about to bolt. She shifted her body slightly so that she could look right at him, and Stafford felt a tingle at the base of his spine. Gwen was still holding the girl's hand, and she, too, was staring at Carson. The expression on her face was unfathomable.

Carson leaned forward, his face getting redder and his wild eyes blazing. "Oh, no you don't, little girl. I'm ready for you this time. No more mind-fucks like in the airport. No more bad dreams." He tapped his forehead with the barrel of the gun. "You want to take a look in here, you're going to have a meltdown, because if you do, I'm going to kill you. I'm going to point this gun right into your ugly little face and blow your warped little brains all over the kitchen. You want to take a reading on that, do you? You go right ahead. See what I'm thinking; it'll fry your fucking circuits!"

Carson's face was now purple with rage, and there was a thin line of spittle on the right side of his mouth. He stopped to gather his breath, but his eyes never left the girl's. Stafford could almost feel the desperate hatred emanating from this man. Carson had brought the gun down to the table again, and he was pointing it in the girl's direction. His left hand maintained a white-knuckled death grip on the cylinder.

Stafford looked over at Jessamine. To his amazement, she had closed her eyes. Her hands appeared to be shaking. She again looked like she was about to cry. Damn! Carson had beaten her. He looked back at Carson, and then something happened. Carson's eyes began to lose their focus. His right hand, the one holding the gun, began to tremble, and his face became even more distorted. Stafford thought he saw an opening to make a move, but to his surprise, found himself frozen in his chair. Carson was trying to say something, but all that came out was a series of strangulated grunts. His mouth twisted to one side, and then the gun barrel drooped to the table and began to tap, faster and faster, beating out a frantic cadence like some animal thrashing in its death throes. He looked like a man in the grip of a stroke. Then Carson's whole body relaxed, and he slumped forward with a great sigh, his forehead descending to the table, where it lay against the smooth wet steel of the cylinder.

Stafford finally found his legs and stood up. Gwen had not moved and her eyes remained locked on Carson. He moved carefully around the table to get the gun. Then he stopped short. To his astonishment, he realized Carson was *not* unconscious. His eyes were still open, fixed on a point two feet in front of his face. The expression in them reminded

Stafford of the off-center look a dog gives just before it bites. He was almost afraid to reach for the gun.

"Take the gun," Gwen commanded.

Stafford looked across at her for a second, but she never took her eyes off of Carson. Her face was frightening, radiating with undiluted fury. Stafford reached over and extracted the gun from Carson's rigid fingers. Carson's skin felt hot and feverish, but there was nothing wrong with his grip. Once he had the gun, he reached for the cylinder, but Gwen spoke again. "No! Don't touch it," she ordered. Then she stood up, as did the girl, their chair legs scraping on the linoleum.

"But we can't leave this thing," Stafford protested.

"Yes, we must. Feel it."

Stafford reached out again and touched the cylinder this time. The metal was hot. "Hot," he whispered. "It's hot."

"Yes. It's going to burst. We must leave. Now."

"*Burst?* Jesus Christ, Gwen, we can't let that happen. That stuff can——"

But Gwen was already moving toward the door. "It's going to burst. We must get out of the house and warn the others. Now."

Carson's left hand was gripping the cylinder so hard, his knuckles were white, but he was still staring into space. Stafford thought about grabbing the cylinder, but he realized it would take a lot of strength and both of own his hands to do it, and he didn't have two hands. Besides, did he want to be standing there when that damned thing popped open? He looked down at Carson's hand and saw tiny white blisters starting up where Carson's skin was in contact with the metal. That did it.

He backed away hurriedly and followed Gwen and the girl down the hall. Gwen turned on the porch lights and opened the front door. The headlights were still fixed on the front on the house, and the three of them were somewhat blinded as they came out. He closed the front door behind him and hurried down the steps. There appeared to be a commotion going on behind the headlights.

They trotted quickly down the front drive, Gwen, the girl, and Stafford, in a line. When they reached the first police car, they were surrounded immediately by state police, one of whom asked Stafford for the gun in his hand. Almost indifferently, he handed it over, and then he saw the general approaching, along with a man who looked like FBI. There was a lot of milling about and then people began asking Gwen questions, but she was suddenly surrounded by some Longstreet County deputies.

"Where is it?" Carrothers asked without preamble.

"It's in there," Stafford said. "But—"

"How the hell did you get out?" the FBI man interrupted "Where's Carson?" His tone was not at all solicitous.

Stafford didn't know what to say. "I'm not sure what happened," he replied. "He had some kind of seizure, and we got out of there. But he has the cylinder. And I—we—think it's going to burst. It's hot."

"It's *hot*?" The general exclaimed. "Are you sure?"

"Yes. The house is shut up. All the doors and windows are closed. But I think it's going to do something. He's got it in his hand. He had me put it in the refrigerator earlier, but it's hot." He looked over toward Gwen for corroboration, but she was drawing away into the crowd, still surrounded by the deputies.

"Why the hell didn't you take it away from him?" Carrothers thundered.

"I couldn't," Stafford said. "He's got it in a death grip. It would have taken two hands." He held up his left hand. "I don't have two hands."

The general swore forcefully and turned away, then stopped and turned back. "Mr. Kiesling, I strongly recommend you get all these people the hell out of here. We're about to experience a catastrophic chemical emergency."

"What the hell is that, a chemical emergency?"

"Let me put it this way: If that thing bursts, every living thing within five miles of this house is going to experience a grotesque death. I mean it. I've got to get some help up here. You get these people the hell out of here. *Right fucking now!*"

There was a sudden stunned silence on the road. The state cops and the county deputies had heard all this and were staring at Kiesling as if to say, What part of grotesque death don't you understand? They parted for the general, who began *running* toward his vehicles in the nearby field. The sight of the general running did it: The cops all started to back away from the house.

"Okay," Kiesling said in an unnaturally loud voice. "You heard the man. Let's clear out. You—Stafford!"

Stafford, who had been looking for Gwen, turned to face the FBI man. "What?" He still felt dazed by what had happened inside.

"We want to talk to you. First I need to know what the hell happened in there. Then we want to discuss what you knew about this mess and when you knew it."

Stafford nodded absently. He wasn't thinking very clearly. He couldn't forget the picture of Carson frozen at that table, as if in a state of suspended animation. And of himself, completely unable to act. He wanted very much to talk to Gwen, but she had disappeared in the great rush to get everyone out of there.

"Yeah, fine. Whatever," he said. "Where's Mrs. Warren?"

"I don't know," Kiesling said, looking nervously over at the house, which was becoming visible in the dawn light. His tone became more solicitous. "Why don't you come with us," he said. "I think this is an Army problem from here on out. What the fuck happened in there? How did you guys get out?"

Stafford looked again for Gwen and finally saw her, still surrounded by her phalanx of deputies. There was some kind of altercation going on between the deputies and the state police. Cars were starting to move.

"I'm not sure," Stafford said. "Carson's pretty screwed up. Has a hell of a fever, looks like death warmed over." I know what I saw in there, he thought. But I do not understand it. Yes, you do, a voice in his head told him. Where the hell was Gwen?

Kiesling was trying to hustle him along the line of state police cars, which were all trying to get turned around at the same time in a building circus of revving engines and crunching gravel. Up ahead the mobile command center was being disassembled and made ready for the road. "Well, shit, if he was that fucked up, why couldn't you jump him?" Kiesling asked over his shoulder.

Stafford stopped. "I couldn't see him. Once he had us, he made us close all the curtains and blinds in the house. It was pitch-dark in there. He made sure I never got a look at him. But he's on his last legs." He finally spotted Gwen. "Look, I must talk to Gwen Warren."

Kiesling stopped, and the camaraderie went out of his voice. "Well, I think it would be best if you came with us. There are some things we need to sort out. *After* we get the hell out of here."

"No," Stafford said, turning around and dodging between two state police cars that were making serious tracks out of there. He didn't know why, but he felt compelled to get to Gwen. Kiesling was suddenly stuck on the other side of the stream of fleeing vehicles, yelling after him.

By the time Stafford reached Gwen and the deputies, it was apparent that she was refusing to leave. Jessamine stood behind her, still holding her hand and looking apprehensive. The three large deputies were facing off with two state police officers and one young-looking FBI man. The latter was arguing vigorously with her.

"This is my house," Gwen said as Stafford walked up. "I'm not leaving it."

"But Mrs. Warren, you yourself said that thing's gonna pop. You heard the general: Everybody has to clear out of here."

The largest of the deputies got between Gwen and the FBI man. "Miz Warren don't want to go, she don't have to go," he announced. He was considerably bigger than the FBI agent. The two state troopers looked at each other and made an unspoken decision to back right out of this little federal problem before all their vehicles left.

"Gwen, what's this?" Stafford said. "I think we have to get out of here."

"No, Dave. I think the government is going to do something to my house. That general wasn't running away. He was running to his phone. I simply won't have it."

Kiesling finally reached them and started raising hell about anyone remaining in the area. Stafford put up a hand to silence him, especially after he saw the looks on the deputies' faces. "Look, Kiesling, she wants to stay, that's her choice. I'm staying with her. You go get your people and clear out."

Kiesling's face hardened. "I don't give a shit about her, Stafford. But you are coming with us. Carson directly implicated you in this mess, and I want some questions answered. There was a lot of real money that's gone missing. Now you just—"

The biggest deputy leaned forward and let go a great brown glop of chewing tobacco that landed right between Kiesling's highly polished shoes. The FBI man stopped talking and stared first at his expensive shoes and then at the deputy. Up at the deputy.

"Time for y'all to be down the road and gone," the deputy drawled. "We don't need no G-men tellin' us or our people what to do hereabouts in Longstreet County." The other two deputies stepped forward to reinforce the first one's suggestion. The young FBI agent looked at them and then at Kiesling. "Mr. Kiesling, sir?" he said hopefully. "Remember all that talk about gravel trucks and wolf pits? This sure sounds like a local problem to me, Mr. Kiesling. Mr. Kiesling?"

Kiesling's face was beet red. But Gwen and the girl had already turned around and started walking back toward the driveway of the house. Kiesling finally gave in, especially when he realized that, other than the county cruisers, his car was just about the only one left in front of the house, and it was rolling.

"Just remember, Stafford," he yelled. "When this thing is over, your ass is mine, you understand?"

"Happy to know where your interests lie, Kiesling," Stafford said, as he followed Gwen and the girl. Kiesling started back toward him, but the younger agent grabbed Kiesling's sleeve and hustled him away toward the waiting FBI car.

When everyone had gone, Gwen thanked the deputies. "Now you boys go on and get back to town. Folks are going to be stirred up when that mob gets there."

"Ma'am, we can stay right here, you need some help," the big man said. Stafford could not quite read his name tag in the dawn light, but he would have sworn the tag read HAND.

"Mr. Stafford will stay with us. The Army people are still here. We'll be all right. Y'all get along now."

With a chorus of "Yes, ma'am," the deputies retired to their cars and swung them out onto the state road, headed back toward Graniteville. Stafford thought they weren't entirely reluctant to get out of there, but he appreciated their loyalty. He was about to ask what in the hell had happened back there in the house when they heard the roar of engines from the adjoining field.

As soon as he had reached the Suburbans, Carrothers ordered the men to suit up immediately and get the satellite link up. He began pulling on his own protective suit while waiting for the link. The soldiers had not moved very quickly until he told them over his shoulder that the cylinder of Wet Eye over there in that house was maybe going to burst, after which it was all assholes and elbows as the men dived into their suits.

Carrothers briefed Waddell as soon as the link came up. All the hostages were out of the house, the bad guy was still in there by himself, with the cylinder, and the hostages were reporting that the cylinder was hot. Waddell asked him to repeat that last, and then he asked Carrothers if he had any thermite with him. Carrothers did not. Waddell told him to get all the civilians away from the house, to establish the downwind danger area, and to get everyone out of that sector for five miles.

"We've done that, General. Is there something I should know about that cylinder?"

There was a long hiss of static before Waddell responded. "We weren't going to distract you with this, Lee, but Fuller's people ran a simulation on that thing. It's the biologics. They gave it thirty-six hours before it blew its end caps off."

"Jesus Christ! Starting when?"

"Thirty-six hours ago. That's why the Cobras are coming."

Carrothers thought fast. "We have MOPP gear and weapons. I'd like to take a team into that house, see if we can stop this disaster."

There was a pause on the net while Waddell had him stand by. Then he was back.

"Our information is that our time on target is thirty-five minutes, General. You want to try a run on the house, go to it. But be advised we'll have Cobras on top in . . . lemme see, thirty-four minutes. You need to be out of that house before they get there, because they're gonna shoot it to ribbons, and then there's a flight of Warthogs coming in right behind them with nape."

"We're on our way," Carrothers replied.

"Oh, and Lee? I recommend just shooting that bastard the moment you see him. Save everybody a lot of trouble, if you get my drift."

Carrothers acknowledged and then hung up. He gathered his team around him and explained the situation. The soldiers had all their gear on except their hoods.

"No time for any fancy planning here, guys. We have about thirty minutes before Washington drops an air strike on top of us. Captain, I want you to take your men into that house. Nothing sexy here: We'll complete MOPPing up, then drive the vehicles over there to the front door and go in with guns. He's supposedly somewhere on the ground floor with the cylinder of Wet Eye. Shoot him if he makes a move, then get the cylinder. If it's still intact, put it in the freezer of the icebox. If it's popped, then we bail out and let the games begin." He looked at his watch. "We have about twenty-nine minutes from right now. After that it's Warthogs and napalm. Any questions?"

The young captain looked as if he might have a few, but the general's expression did not encourage a lengthy discussion. The soldiers were reaching for their weapons. One raised his hand.

"What, soldier?"

"This Wet Eye stuff, General? Our MOPP gear good to go for that agent?"

Carrothers had to think fast. Their protective gear would certainly protect them against the chemical constituents of Wet Eye. But the biologics obviously were still alive. If they had mutated . . .

"Yes. This is an old agent. The old-style chem suits would protect you from it. These new suits ought to do just fine. Anything else?"

There were no more questions.

"Okay, hoods on and mount up. Remember: He's just one guy, he's physically ill, and he's a civilian. Take the front door and go in like gangbusters. We're gonna find him, and if he moves a muscle, shoot him, find the cylinder, freeze it, and get the hell out of there, okay? Move out!"

By the time they hit the driveway, all of the other vehicles were gone. Only the portable floodlights, standing by the front wall, gave evidence that the police had been there in force not ten minutes ago. Carrothers drove the lead Suburban so that his driver could join the team going into the house. He turned into the driveway and accelerated toward the house, which was clearly visible now. He drove right up to the front steps, skidded to a stop, and shut off the engine. The other vehicle fishtailed to a stop right next to his in a spray of gravel. Carrothers got out, and the troops piled out behind him. To his surprise, the DCIS man, Mrs. Warren, and the girl were standing by the steps.

"Get out of the way," Carrothers shouted. Stafford pulled the woman and the girl to one side. The captain, Carrothers was pleased to see, didn't hesitate. He charged up the steps, ran right through the front screen door, and then kicked in the front door, their automatic weapons firing directly into the house. The girl made a plaintive noise and covered her ears; the woman's mouth dropped open in surprise. The other soldiers went right in after the captain.

Carrothers pulled an Armalite rifle out of his vehicle and followed them in. There was a haze of smoke in the front hallway. At the end of the front hall, the kitchen door had been reduced to shards of woods hanging in a shattered frame. He realized he could not hear anything inside the house, especially in full chem gear. He looked at his watch. Twenty-four minutes. After first kicking open the doors to the classroom on the left and Gwen's parlor on the right, the team had taken up positions in the hallway. One man was kneeling at the bottom of the stairs, pointing his rifle up the steps. There appeared to be lights on in the kitchen.

Carrothers thought quickly. He did not really want to kill Carson, as Waddell had suggested, not unless he actually did something. But they were rapidly running out of time. The captain looked over at him. Carrothers tried to think of another way to do it, couldn't, and gave the signal. The captain and two men moved forward cautiously, keeping their weapons pointed at the remains of the kitchen door. Carrothers looked at his watch. Twenty-three minutes.

On signal from the captain, all three rushed the door, colliding with one another as they burst through it. Carrothers followed. He had just about reached the kitchen door when there was another blast of gunfire and the sounds of shattered glass falling on the floor. Then silence.

Carrothers approached the door carefully. The light inside the kitchen was hazy from gunsmoke. He poked his rifle barrel around the corner, took a deep breath, and then stepped in. All three soldiers stood in a crouch inside the kitchen, pointing their weapons at the man at the table. All the glass was blown out of the back door, and there was a string of bullet holes marching up into the ceiling above the door. Somebody panicked, Carrothers thought. Then he, too, concentrated on the man at the table.

He saw the cylinder—finally, and intact, thank God.

The man was clutching it in his left hand. His head was tilted forward at an odd angle, as if he was paralyzed. His eyes were open and fixed in a fever-bright stare, but he didn't appear to be focusing on anything at all.

"He won't hurt you." The woman's voice came from behind him, and he whirled and nearly shot her in his surprise. Stafford followed her into the kitchen, with the girl behind him, as Gwen pushed the barrel of Carrother's rifle aside and walked over to Carson. "He won't hurt anybody anymore."

Carrothers stared down at Carson. The man was catatonic. There was no way they could just shoot him, no matter how much the higher-ups at the Pentagon and over at Justice might appreciate that gesture.

Carrothers walked forward and pried the cylinder out of Carson's rigid, scorched fingers. It felt hot even through his heavy gloves. He carried it gingerly across the room to the big refrigerator, swiped everything out of the upper freezer compartment onto the kitchen floor, and put the cylinder gently into the space, where it hissed on the cold metal. Then he closed the door.

"General?" the captain said. "The time, sir?"

Carrothers looked at him blankly for a moment, and then he remembered what was coming. He looked down at his watch. Eighteen minutes. Christ on a busted crutch!

He told the three soldiers to bring Carson with them, then told Gwen and the others to get out of the house immediately. As the soldiers scrambled to get Carson, he tried to decide what to do about the cylinder. Take it with them, or leave it in the house? The freezer would slow whatever the hell was going on inside it, so it was safer to just leave it there. If they didn't manage to call off the air strike in time, it would be destroyed with the house, which was still a safe option. He hesitated. After all this, he didn't want to leave it. He looked at his watch again. Seventeen minutes.

He hurried back out onto the front porch and looked up into the dawn sky. There was now plenty of light, although the surrounding mountains blocked most of the skyline. He realized that, with the cylinder intact, he didn't need this damned mask. He stripped it off and hurried down the steps. The captain, still fully MOPPed up, was already out and had the other Suburban turning around. Carrothers yelled for his driver, who had been the man stationed at the foot of the stairs, to get out here. The man came tumbling out of the house, tripping in his heavy boots over the door coaming.

"Get me the satellite link, on the double!"

He looked at his watch as the man ran to align the antenna and turn on the gear mounted on the front console of the vehicle. Sixteen minutes. The rest of the soldiers came out. Two of them were dragging Carson along. There was no sign of the civilians. At that moment his driver popped back out of the Suburban. "No path right here, General. Mountain's got it blocked. We have to move the vehicle."

Son of a bitch! Carrothers thought. Fifteen minutes. He imagined he could already hear the venomous clatter of approaching attack helicopters. Did he have time to go back in there, warn the woman to get out of there, move the satellite antenna, and still call off the strike? Would she do it, or would she argue? She'd argue. Fuck it.

"Let's go," he yelled. The other soldiers stuffed the catatonic Carson into the second Suburban. "Go! Go! Go!" he yelled. "Air strike inbound! Snakes and Hogs! Chain guns and napalm!"

The soldiers practically levitated into to their vehicle as Carrothers's driver got the lead Suburban turned around. Carrothers jumped in and the driver peeled out, showering the entire front of the house with gravel and fishtailing wildly down the driveway before he got it under control, only to have to slam on the brakes when he got to the road to avoid hitting the stone wall on the other side.

"Which way, sir? Which way?!" the driver yelled.

"For God's *sake*!" Carrothers shouted. "Go left. Go left! Now! Now!

Do it! Back to the fucking field!" Thirteen minutes. He knew the satellite path was clear in the field. He looked back at the house, but there was still no sign of the civilians. He should have gotten them out. *Shit!*

The driver turned left and then hard left through the gap in the stone wall, fishtailed again, and then the rear tires began to howl as they hit a patch of mud. The driver floored it, winding out the engine until Carrothers thought it would come apart, but the vehicle's rear end was settling instead. They were a hundred yards from the place in the field where they had had a clear shot to the satellite before. Would it work from here? Did they have time to get out and try? Twelve minutes.

Then there was thunderous bang from behind, whiplashing both of them as the other vehicle came through the gap in the wall and ran into the back of them. But the crash punched their vehicle out of the hole and they were off again, banging up the hill, bounding over hummocks of grass and rocks. They reached their earlier parking patch and the driver slammed on the brakes, nearly throwing Carrothers through the windshield.

"Go! Go! Go!" Carrothers yelled again, extricating himself from the dashboard. The driver piled out to set up the satellite antenna and try again for a hit on the bird. This time he got a link. The other vehicle arrived behind them, its front grille smashed all to hell. He could see the captain inside, still in the passenger seat, still in his full chem suit. Nine minutes.

"Link's up, General. We got comms."

"Get me General Waddell. Tell the operator this is a flash precedence call."

Eight minutes.

Gwen sat down at the kitchen table and rubbed her face with her hands. Jessamine settled into the same seat Stafford had occupied. There were dried tear tracks on her cheeks and her hands were trembling. She sat there with her eyes closed, completely withdrawn. For want of something to do, Stafford picked up the coffeepot, sniffed it, and decided to pour the contents down the sink.

"Why on earth would they shoot the back door?" Gwen wondered aloud.

"Somebody probably saw their own reflection. Those suits make them look like alien storm troopers, but in reality, those are probably nineteen-year-olds. My guess is that they were pretty scared."

She nodded wordlessly and glanced over at the girl, who appeared to have gone to sleep in the chair. Stafford went down to Gwen's end of the table and slipped into the chair next to her. He spoke quietly. "I don't suppose I'm ever going to know what happened in here, am I?"

"Do you really want to, Dave?" she said, giving him a warm, sad smile.

He looked down at the table. "My investigator's brain wants to know," he said. "The rest of me is yelling to leave it alone. I figured you brought her in to do what she did in the airport. He was certainly in an agitated state. I thought he would pass out again, and then I could get his gun. Something like that." He looked over at her. "But he was ready for that. He *knew* what she'd done in the airport. He wasn't just agitated; he was enraged. Crazy. Out of his damn head. He challenged her. And yet she melted him down." He looked over at the girl. "That's not just a passive capability, Gwen," he said softly. "That's a serious power."

But Gwen was shaking her head. She took his hand. "No, I don't think that's what happened at all, Dave. I think *he* melted down, but not because of some special power on her part. He was running a high fever: All you had to do was look at him. I think he worked himself up into having a stroke. Everything he tried had gone wrong. He was out of his head, just like you said. I predict they'll find a cerebrovascular accident of some kind, assuming he survives the infection. This wasn't Jess. Look at her. She was much too frightened."

He leaned back in his chair, not knowing what to say. As he remembered it, the only one in the room who had been frightened had been him. A sudden yawn ambushed him as the adrenaline began to subside. His yawn set off one from Gwen. "I guess," he said. "Maybe now we'll have some peace. They've got their damned cylinder back."

"Actually, they don't," she said, glancing at the refrigerator and the mess on the floor."

"Oh. Right. They'll be back."

Gwen got up and walked over to the refrigerator. She opened the freezer compartment and ran her hand down the length of the cylinder, which now had a faint covering of frost on it. "So much destruction over just one package."

"Nothing compared to what that package could do."

"Not anymore, I think," she said, closing the freezer door. "Why did they just run out?"

Stafford tried to think of an answer to that, but his mind was still grappling with what had happened to Carson.

"What will happen now?" Gwen asked.

"The Pentagon and the Justice Department will point fingers at each other behind closed doors until it threatens to become public," he said. "Then they'll get scared and bury it. I don't know what they'll do to Carson. How on earth did you know to come back?"

"Word came" was all she said. "What will happen to you? After what Carson said, that FBI man practically accused you of being part of this."

"I think he'll get over it, especially once the big boys stop shouting long enough to think it through. I've already resigned. To link me to it would mean opening the whole thing back up. The only thing I'm very, very sorry about is John Lee."

She nodded. "I know," she said, sighing. "I haven't absorbed that, I'm afraid. . . ."

"You saw that guy. He was a mess. I can't imagine how in the hell he could get the drop on John Lee, shape he was in."

"John Lee probably thought the same thing," she said. "And forgot to pay attention."

Just then there was the roaring, clattering sound of two military helicopters battering the morning air overhead. They both jumped in their chairs, and Jessamine literally jumped out of her chair, her knuckles in her mouth.

"Now what the hell!" Stafford exclaimed, and he ran for the front door. The high whining sound of jet engines keened overhead a moment later, bouncing disturbing echoes off the slopes of the mountain behind the house as he ran out the front door. Two Warthogs and one black helicopter were arcing in formation down the valley toward Graniteville. A second helicopter executed a wide circle over the farm, and then set up for an approach on the field next door, where the Army Suburbans were parked. It flared out over the field, looking like some giant pre-historic insect, with glistening Perspex eyes and claws of armament racks dangling beneath it. Loaded armament racks, he realized. *That's* why the Army guys had bailed out.

Stafford walked over to the field as the Cobra touched down in a cloud of dust and a barrage of rotor noise. The soldiers were still partially dressed out in their MOPP gear, and one of them picked up his Armalite as Stafford approached. Stafford ignored him and headed for General Carrothers. By the time he got near the helicopter, one of the pilots was out on the ground and handing over his flight helmet and harness to the Army captain, who was standing just outside the radius of spinning blades. One of the Suburbans turned around and headed back over toward the house.

Stafford signaled the general that he wanted to talk. Carrothers pointed away from the helo and they walked together down the field until they could hear each other without shouting.

"We all done here?" Stafford asked.

"I think so, Mr. Stafford," Carrothers replied. There was a hint of a frosty smile on his face. "Personally and professionally, in all likelihood."

Stafford smiled back, knowing exactly what Carrothers meant.

"Those soldiers are going in to retrieve the cylinder," Carrothers said. "It's still intact, I take it?"

"Yes, sir. It's in the freezer."

Carrothers nodded. "The captain is going to escort it to Anniston."

"Won't it just heat up again?"

"They're going to fly at max altitude and keep the windows open."

Stafford had visions of the captain flying in the helicopter with the cylinder held out the window. Carrothers must have read his mind, because he just shrugged.

"What will you do with Carson?" Stafford asked. He could just see Carson's slumped silhouette in the backseat of one of the Suburbans, with a soldier standing beside each back window. The medic was sitting in the backseat with him, and he had an IV running.

"For starters, they'll put him in a rubber room up in Washington. St. Elizabeth's probably." Carrothers looked at his watch. "What did you want, Mr. Stafford?"

"I think you and I need to make a deal, General," Stafford said. "Each of us knows something the other would rather keep secret, don't you think?"

Carrothers eyed him and nodded. "What do you propose?"

"You know I had nothing to do with Carson's little scheme, right?"

"That's my take, yes."

"Okay. I may or may not need some support in that area later on. But more importantly, I want nothing to surface about the girl, Jessamine. Best I can tell, Carson suffered a stroke in there, that's all. No psychic probes, no mental telepathy or anything like that. In return for those two concessions, I'll forget everything I know about this incident. And I mean *everything*. Under oath, if necessary."

The general thought about that for a moment and nodded again.

"Deal," he said. Stafford managed to lift his right hand long enough for them to shake on it.

At that moment the other Suburban came back up the field, its smashed-in front bumper dangling dangerously close to the ground. It drew abreast of where they were standing, and a soldier in full MOPP gear got out. He held the cylinder carefully in both hands.

"Sir?" he said.

"That's it, soldier. Give it to the captain. Remind him that it's not binary-safe."

"Yes, sir, General. But sir?"

"What?"

"It isn't hot anymore, General."

Carrothers stepped forward and ran a finger along the frosty metal. He looked over at the house for a moment and nodded. "I'll be damned. Okay, take it to the captain. Tell him they can button up the helo as long as this thing remains cool to the touch."

"Sir, yes, sir!" The soldier got back into the Suburban and the vehicle went on up the hill, where the captain walked down to meet it.

The general frowned as he watched them go.

"Well, it was in the freezer," Stafford said.

"Did you see the burns on Carson's hands? It wasn't in the freezer *that* long, Mr. Stafford. Yet it has frost on it now. Well, I've got a helo to catch."

He nodded once, turned away, but then he stopped and turned around. "Mr. Stafford," he said.

"Yes, General?"

"That girl. Jessamine, is it? She was terrified back there. When they went into the house to face Carson? That girl was white-faced, her knees were shaking, and she looked like she was about to throw up." He paused and looked over at the house again. "If somebody did burn out Carson's circuits, Mr. Stafford, I don't believe it was that girl." Then he turned away toward the waiting vehicles.

Stafford stared after him. The helicopter, with the captain and his cargo now strapped into the copilot's seat, lifted off in a clatter of rotors, tilted forward, and then buzzed over the field, straining for altitude across the face of Howell Mountain. In a minute it was gone, and the silence in the field was profound.

Stafford looked over at the house, where Gwen Warren and Jessamine were waiting for him on the front steps. Even from this distance, he could make out those lustrous green eyes.

F
DEU

Deutermann, P. T.

Zero option

$25.95

DATE			

DISCARD

BAKER & TAYLOR